UNSTAINED HANDS

"Lady Darby is in there!"

I stiffened as a gasp ran through the crowd behind the hedge. It appeared my efforts to go unnoticed had failed.

"Did they finally catch her in the act?" the woman asked.

"The butcher's wife," another one muttered.

I tightened my arms around my body, swallowing the fear and anger that gathered at the back of my throat at hearing the old refrain.

"You know that is absolute nonsense!" my sister exclaimed, joining the group behind the hedgerow.

"Not this time," Lady Westlock declared with decided relish. "She's been caught red-handed. First one at the scene, wasn't she?"

"That is enough!" My sister, Alana, burst through the men blocking her access to the alcove. She marched to my side and wrapped her arm around my shoulders. "I will not listen to any more of this ridiculousness."

"You cannot protect her forever," Mrs. Smythe snapped as we passed. "She must answer for her actions."

Angry that once again I was to be subjected to more gossip, ridicule, and vicious name-calling, I lifted my hands and blinked innocently. "Look, my lady. No red."

She spluttered, and several of the other ladies gasped in indignation, fanning their faces as if they might swoon. A few of the men chuckled nervously.

My sister pulled me harder through the crowd, wrenching my shoulder in her rush to distance us from the mob while they were all distracted. She shook her head. "You just couldn't resist, could you?"

"Sorry," I murmured, even though we both knew that I wasn't.

THE
ANATOMIST'S WIFE

A Lady Darby Novel

ANNA LEE HUBER

BERKLEY PRIME CRIME, NEW YORK

THE BERKLEY PUBLISHING GROUP
Published by the Penguin Group
Penguin Group (USA) Inc.
375 Hudson Street, New York, New York 10014, USA

Penguin Group (Canada), 90 Eglinton Avenue East, Suite 700, Toronto, Ontario M4P 2Y3, Canada
(a division of Pearson Penguin Canada Inc.) • Penguin Books Ltd., 80 Strand, London WC2R 0RL,
England • Penguin Group Ireland, 25 St. Stephen's Green, Dublin 2, Ireland (a division of Penguin
Books Ltd.) • Penguin Group (Australia), 250 Camberwell Road, Camberwell, Victoria 3124, Australia
(a division of Pearson Australia Group Pty. Ltd.) • Penguin Books India Pvt. Ltd., 11 Community
Centre, Panchsheel Park, New Delhi—110 017, India • Penguin Group (NZ), 67 Apollo Drive,
Rosedale, Auckland 0632, New Zealand (a division of Pearson New Zealand Ltd.) • Penguin Books
(South Africa) (Pty.) Ltd., 24 Sturdee Avenue, Rosebank, Johannesburg 2196, South Africa

Penguin Books Ltd., Registered Offices: 80 Strand, London WC2R 0RL, England

This book is an original publication of The Berkley Publishing Group.

PUBLISHING HISTORY
Berkley Prime Crime trade paperback edition / November 2012

Library of Congress Cataloging-in-Publication Data

Huber, Anna Lee.
The anatomist's wife : a Lady Darby novel / Anna Lee Huber.—Berkley trade paperback ed.
    p.   cm.
ISBN 978-0-425-25328-1 (alk. paper)
1. Widows—Fiction.   2. Anatomists—Fiction.   3. Murder—Fiction.
4. Scotland—History—19th century—Fiction.   I. Title.
PS3608.U238A85   2012
813'.6—dc23
2012026983

PRINTED IN THE UNITED STATES OF AMERICA

10   9   8   7   6   5   4   3   2   1

ALWAYS LEARNING   PEARSON

For my husband, Shanon.
With love, always and forever.

ACKNOWLEDGMENTS

There are so many people I wish to thank for making this book possible. A multitude of thanks go to . . .

My agent, Kevan Lyon, and editor, Michelle Vega, for your enthusiasm and confidence in me as a writer, and for your tireless efforts to make this book even better.

The staff at Berkley Publishing for all of your expertise and care in the creation of this book.

My cousin Jackie Musser, and my friend Stacie Roth Miller—writing-group partners, beta readers, and cheerleaders extraordinaire. I owe so much of this book's creation to your care and guidance, and your never-ending belief in me as a writer. You shared my triumphs and my tears, rejoicing with me or bolstering me when I needed it.

My parents, Rich and Judy Huber, for your steadfast love and guidance. Without the confidence you instilled in me, I would never have found the courage to spread my wings and fly.

My siblings—Adam, Christopher, Jeffery, Matthew, and Elizabeth—for helping to foster my imagination from the earliest days of childhood. I couldn't have wished for better playmates.

All my friends and family for all of your support and enthusiasm.

My husband, and my brother Adam, both gifted artists, for answering the many and varied questions I put to you about oil painting. Any errors in this book are wholly my own.

The Surgeons' Hall Museum at the Royal College of Surgeons at Edinburgh, for their fascinating displays, including those on Burke and Hare, and the people of the UK, for welcoming my husband and me with open arms as I did my research.

The staff at my local Starbucks for your support and well wishes, and for keeping me well supplied with chai tea lattes on those days when I simply could not concentrate at home.

My troublemaking tabby cat, Pita, for keeping me company through the long days and nights of writing and editing. And for forcing me to take a break to pet you just when you knew I needed it most.

And, finally, to my husband, Shanon, for everything. For loving me and supporting me. For giving me the strength and courage when I had no more left. For kissing away the tears of my disappointments and twirling me around in your arms when I succeeded. For never giving up on me. And for showing me what true love is.

CHAPTER ONE

Be sure to live your life, because you are a long time dead.

—SCOTTISH PROVERB

AUGUST 1830
SCOTLAND

The scream froze me in my tracks, but the shout that followed propelled me out of my indecision and around the hedge line of the maze. Lady Lydia Perkins continued to shriek at ear-piercing levels while her escort, Mr. Tuthill, stared wide-eyed at the alcove across the path. Alarmed by the pallor of his face and the hysterical edge to Lady Lydia's cries, I wondered if perhaps I should have turned back to search for help instead of rushing blindly toward them. I shuffled closer to see what had so disturbed them, and what I saw there sucked the breath from my lungs.

Lady Godwin lay draped across a stone bench set into the alcove. Her eyes stared sightlessly into the night sky, and her mouth seemed frozen open on a scream. Blood coated her neck and lower face and spread down across her chest, obscuring her delicate skin and soaking the golden bodice of her gown.

I stumbled back a step and clasped a hand over my mouth. Death was not unfamiliar to me. I had seen more than my fair share of corpses in my lifetime, and I had been quite happy to escape them for the last sixteen months. So I hardly relished the appearance of yet another one, and in my sister's garden, no less. I shivered, feeling the fear and shadows stir inside me I had worked so hard to lay to rest since my husband's death.

Lady Lydia's screams, which had transformed into a buzzing in my head, ended abruptly as she collapsed into Mr. Tuthill's embrace. I tore my gaze away from the corpse to watch him struggle with the girl's unconscious form. Lady Lydia was not exactly a small girl, but he managed to heft the earl's sister into his arms nonetheless. Juggling her bulk, he cast a rather desperate look my way, and I wondered whether it was a plea for help or if he was worried I might also faint.

Before I could reassure him of my fortitude, reinforcements arrived. Footsteps pounded over the earth, accompanied by several curses, as they struggled to locate the correct path through the maze. Lord Stratford was the first of my sister's guests to appear around the bend in the hedges, followed closely by Mr. Fitzpatrick and Sir David. They skidded to a halt before us and exchanged glances before edging closer to peer into the leafy recess where I pointed. Sir David sucked in a breath so harshly I worried he might have swallowed his tongue.

My eyes dropped from their horrified faces, unable to deal with the sight of their emotions when mine were still so raw. I studied the misaligned buttons of Lord Stratford's coat and the mud splattered across Mr. Fitzpatrick's trousers—anything to keep my gaze from meeting theirs.

More and more people rounded the hedge of the maze, demanding to know what the clamor was all about. They pushed closer, horrified fascination glittering in their eyes as they jostled each other for a better view. Several ladies shrieked in alarm as word of Lady Godwin's murder traveled back through the crowd, and I heard the resulting tumult from at least one gentlewoman passing out.

I shrank back into the hedges, wishing there was someplace I could hide from their prying eyes. If only the leafy walls would open and allow me inside. My heart raced in panic, as it had so many times during that last month I spent in London.

"Here, now. Let's all remain calm."

A sigh of relief trembled through me at the sound of my brother-in-law's voice. Philip, the Earl of Cromarty, pushed his way to the front of the mob and ordered several of the men to move everyone back, ignoring all of the protests. He spotted me, and his handsome face creased in worry.

"Are you all right, Kiera?" he murmured, placing a hand on my shoulder.

I nodded hesitantly, wanting to convince him I was well and yet knowing it would do no good to force a brave face. Philip would realize how far away I wished myself. No one had forgotten my past—not him, not the other guests, and especially not me.

He bowed his head in acknowledgment before turning to the sight in the alcove. I listened absently to his hushed conversation with the other men, wondering when I could leave and whether anyone would say anything if I slipped past Mr. Tuthill deeper into the maze. I wrapped my arms around myself and studied my route of escape out of the corner of my eye. Perhaps if I were cautious, no one would notice.

"Let me pass," a pretentious voice in the crowd demanded. I pondered which obnoxious male thought he deserved access to the scene, and had just decided it must be Lord Marsdale, the Duke of Norwich's heir, when Mr. Gage slid into view.

Of course. The *estimable* Mr. Sebastian Gage, son of the newly minted Captain Lord Gage, war hero and London's gentleman inquiry agent.

I scowled. What made this golden lothario think he should be there? His father was the one with the investigation skills and reputation to back them up. As far as I could tell, Mr. Gage's only talents seemed to be charming his way into house-party invitations and underneath ladies' skirts.

He tugged his black silk waistcoat into place and brushed his tousled blond hair back from his forehead. I narrowed my eyes, wondering just what he had been doing when Lady Lydia started screaming, and with whom. I vaguely recalled him flirting with Mrs. Cline at dinner.

Before I had long to contemplate the matter, a strident voice called out from the crowd.

"Lady Darby is in there!"

I stiffened as a gasp ran through the crowd behind the hedge. It appeared my efforts to go unnoticed had failed.

"Did they finally catch her in the act?" the woman asked.

"The butcher's wife," another one muttered.

I tightened my arms around my body, swallowing the fear and anger that gathered at the back of my throat at hearing the old refrain.

"You know that is absolute nonsense!" my sister exclaimed, joining the group behind the hedgerow.

"Not this time," Lady Westlock declared with decided relish. "She's been caught red-handed. First one at the scene, wasn't she?"

I glanced sideways at Mr. Gage, who was now watching me with solemn interest.

"Actually," Mr. Tuthill spoke up meekly, still cradling the earl's daughter. He looked like he was struggling to keep her aloft. "Lady Lydia and I came upon Lady Godwin first."

That silenced Lady Westlock, but only for a moment. "That still doesn't make Lady Darby innocent."

"That is enough!" My sister, Alana, burst through the men blocking her access to the alcove. She marched to my side and wrapped her arm around my shoulders. "I will not listen to any more of this ridiculousness. I suggest that any-one who is not assisting Lord Cromarty return to the castle."

She gestured for Sir David to assist Mr. Tuthill with Lady Lydia before tugging me toward the exit, leaving the matter of Lady Godwin's body to Philip.

"You cannot protect her forever," Mrs. Smythe snapped as we passed. "She must answer for her actions."

"When they are *her* actions to answer for," Alana replied without breaking her stride. She had always been a force to be reckoned with when she chose to be, and I was once again reminded how grateful I was she was my older sister.

The guests slowly began to trickle back through the maze as Alana shooed them along ahead of us. Lady Westlock glared at me and huffed, jiggling her double chin.

Angry that once again I was to be subjected to more gossip, ridicule, and vicious name-calling, I lifted my hands and blinked innocently. "Look, my lady. No red."

She spluttered, and several of the other ladies gasped in indignation, fanning their faces as if they might swoon. A few of the men chuckled nervously.

My sister pulled me harder through the crowd, wrenching my shoulder in her rush to distance us from the mob while they were all distracted. She shook her head. "You just couldn't resist, could you?"

"Sorry," I murmured, even though we both knew that I wasn't.

Alana sighed.

CHAPTER TWO

The remainder of the evening was subdued, as was to be expected. Most of the guests chose to assemble in one of my sister's two parlors to rehash the details of what happened in the garden and share their "expert" knowledge. Lady Lydia recovered quickly upon returning to the castle and was even now holding court in the front parlor, describing her ordeal in excruciating detail.

I decided to make myself scarce, checking on my nieces and nephew in the nursery before slipping into the library to sit silently in my favorite spot. It was there that Alana found me just before midnight.

"I am getting too old to keep climbing these stairs," she declared, dropping her skirts into place as she reached the top step. "Why can't you hide in normal places? Like your bedchamber or your art studio?"

I smiled tightly. "Because then people would find me."

Alana sighed and sank into the sofa next to me. "Did you not wish for me to find you, dear?"

I leaned my head on her shoulder. "No. You're fine."

She rested her head on top of mine.

We sat that way for several minutes, staring past the wooden banister, out at the ceiling of the library. A large mural depicting the life of Saint Andrew, patron saint of Scotland, covered the entire space from one wall to another.

Though it was certainly not the work of Michelangelo, it had a charming rustic quality I found soothing. None of the colors were deep or the lines sharp, but the muted shades and blurred lines were somehow appropriate to its location in the far north of the Highlands.

Alana had asked me once why I liked the library loft so much, but I hadn't been able to explain it to her. Perhaps there was some sense of peace being so high above it all, with the saint on the ceiling my closest neighbor. All I knew was that I always felt better, that my thoughts were always clearer, when I was curled up in the little space below the eaves.

"Philip sent me to find you," Alana said. "He wishes to speak to all of the guests in the front parlor." She paused, and I knew her thoughts had returned to the scene in the garden. "I'm sorry you had to hear those accusations again. I would send Lady Westlock and Mrs. Smythe away except for the lateness of the hour and our distance from any decent lodging."

I nodded and reached back to squeeze her hand where it lay over my shoulder. Alana knew I had come here to hide from just such a thing, but I did not blame her for this evening's outburst.

Alana and Philip had not invited guests to Gairloch Castle since my arrival nearly sixteen months ago. When they asked my permission to throw this house party, I felt like the veriest ogre that they felt the need to do so. After all, they were the ones who sheltered me, supported me, and though they never complained, I knew the burden I brought with me. The sales of my artwork, done under an assumed name, of course, provided me with some funds, but Philip refused to take even a penny of it. He encouraged me to save it, to invest it, and he was more than happy to assist me in that regard. However, he would not take payment for my food and lodging.

"I suppose Philip has sent for the local coroner," I said,

fidgeting with the lace trim of my gown. "And they will want to question me."

"Yes and no."

Hearing the hesitation in Alana's voice, I looked up. Her deep blue eyes, so like my own, were clouded with worry.

"I think we'd better hear what Philip has to say. Come on." She groaned like a woman closer to sixty than thirty as she pushed up from the sofa.

I allowed her to take my hand and lead me down the steep spiral staircase, as if we were still young children. Sometimes I still felt like one—hiding away in my older sister's castle, following her instructions, as I'd done most of my life. When living with Alana, I learned long ago it was much easier to simply comply with her wishes than to argue over every last detail. Especially when the outcome of the dispute hardly mattered to me. For almost the entire past year I had obeyed her requests without question, not caring what clothes I wore or food I ate. The only part of my life in which my sister had no say was my artwork, and she knew better than to offer her opinion on that.

The front parlor was located off the great hall near the main entrance to the castle, overlooking the circular drive and the loch beyond. It was monstrous in proportion. Philip's grandmother had decided the former drawing room was too small, so she had removed the wall between it and the parlor to create one cavernous chamber. The shades of Cromarty livery, scarlet and ebony, adorned the room, intermixed with neutrals and a liberal sprinkling of gilding and mirrors. It was the showpiece of Gairloch Castle, and, having been redecorated during the time of Georgian overindulgence, hideous. I always felt that I had wandered into some monstrosity of French rococo excess. Alana agreed but had yet to work up the nerve to tackle the daunting space.

The buzz of agitated voices increased as we stepped through the door. I had done my best to stand in Alana's shadow, hovering behind her as she stepped to the side just within the doorway, but apparently my efforts to go unnoticed had been in vain. Some of the guests' eyes narrowed into suspicious glares as they leaned toward one another, whispering about me. Though I could not hear their words, the skin at the back of my neck prickled, for I knew the accusations being bandied about me. I crossed my arms over my chest and tried to ignore the sick feeling in my stomach.

Most of the guests seemed to be present, but not all. I noticed Lady Stratford was missing, though her wayward husband, the Earl of Stratford, stood near the sideboard with several other gentlemen, including the Marquess of Marsdale, drinking my brother-in-law's fine whiskey. Philip's cousin, Caroline, was also absent, as well as many of the other young, unwed females.

Lord Westlock and the other gentlemen Philip had invited specifically to discuss business matters were gathered near the hearth, while their wives sat on the arrangement of furniture before them, gossiping and sending me spiteful glances.

I shifted uncomfortably, wondering how long we would have to wait for Philip to address us. I considered going to search for him, but then he entered the room through the second doorway. He glanced briefly around the room at those assembled, before nodding to Alana and me.

As he moved forward to address the group, I noticed for the first time the man lurking behind him, though why I should be surprised I didn't know. Of course, Mr. Gage would be eager to hover about Philip. He wasn't one to miss being at the center of attention.

I felt a pulse of annoyance, of dislike for the popular rogue, and wondered what he and Philip had been discussing that had so delayed them. Was Philip allowing Mr. Gage to conduct an investigation? I hoped Philip realized that just because Mr. Gage's father was skilled in such matters, it did not mean his son knew how to conduct a proper inquiry.

"If I could have your attention, please." Philip raised his voice to be heard over the rumble of voices. "This has been a long and unpleasant evening, and I'm sure you would all like to retire to your chambers, so I will make this as brief as possible."

Their attention caught, the room fell silent.

"First of all, I know you are all concerned with the tragedy that befell Lady Godwin this evening, and I want to assure you that everything possible is being done to apprehend the culprit." Philip's gaze swept calmly over everyone as he spoke, as reassuring as any of his words. "Lady Godwin's body has been secured, and a pair of riders has been dispatched to collect the appropriate authorities from Inverness."

"Inverness?" Lord Westlock snapped, clearly voicing what was on the minds of everyone else as they turned to whisper to one another in horror. Even I was taken aback by the news. "But that's at least two days' hard ride to the southeast," the silver-haired baron protested.

Philip lifted his hands to calm the excited murmurs. "I'm well aware. But, unfortunately, we have no other choice. The closest procurator fiscals are located in Fort William and Inverness, and both are several days' journey from here."

"But aren't you the local magistrate? Can't you adjudicate?"

"I'm afraid not," Philip replied with a sad shake of his head. "The crime happened on my property. If it were theft, or even the demise of a servant, perhaps I could handle matters. But with Lady Godwin being a viscountess and her husband in India, I cannot adjudicate over this unfortunate event. My only recourse was to send for the procurator fiscal at Inverness."

"But that means . . ." Mr. Fitzpatrick's eyes darted nervously between Philip and the other guests. "He won't arrive for another four days."

Philip seemed reluctant to admit this, but he really had no choice. "Yes."

The other guests all began talking at once, arguing with one another about the absurdity of living so far from civilization. The pitch of their voices increased with their panic.

"But, see here," one gentleman demanded. "This has no effect on us. My wife and I are leaving at first light."

Several others chimed in with their agreement.

"I'm afraid that's impossible," Philip interrupted.

"What do you mean?" someone asked.

I watched as Philip visibly steeled himself. "Until the procurator fiscal arrives, and is able to investigate the murder and interview any potential witnesses, none of you will be allowed to leave."

"But why?" Lady Darlington asked. "I haven't witnessed anything."

Philip turned to look at her. "You may not realize you have until you are questioned."

"But how could we?" Lord Marsdale argued with a flippant smirk. "Surely the murderer isn't one of us."

The guests turned to stare at one another, wide-eyed, as if realizing for the first time the other unspoken reason that Philip could not let any of them leave. Alana reached over to grip my hand.

"This is ridiculous," another gentleman declared. "I'm no murderer. And I won't be treated like one."

And that statement set everyone off arguing again.

"Please." Philip's countenance was growing more and more haggard with each pronouncement. "Everyone, let's remain calm. No one is accusing anyone of any crime yet. But I must take steps to secure the witnesses, and yes, possible suspects, until the authorities reach us." He looked directly at the ladies. "Now, I realize that you are understandably apprehensive. That is why I ask that you do not go off alone. Keep in pairs, though groups of three or four would be best. And instruct your servants to do the same."

I shivered, thinking of the number of times I had taken

to the countryside alone, especially in the last few days since the house-party guests had arrived.

"In the meantime . . ." He glanced back at Mr. Gage, and I felt something inside of me clench with dread. "I've asked Mr. Gage to conduct an inquiry of his own into the matter. So I must ask all of you to cooperate with him fully."

"I can tell you right now who's responsible, no need for an inquiry," Lady Westlock muttered under her breath, loud enough for most to hear. Her spiteful gaze bored into me.

Alana stiffened beside me. "Come," she told me with a nudge toward the door. "It's time for us to leave. We'll wait for Philip in his study."

Feeling his eyes on me, I glanced up to find Mr. Gage watching me intently as we exited the room. I wanted to snap back, to defend myself, but I knew now was not the time, and that few, if any, of them, would listen to me. So I followed my sister sullenly from the room, angry to find myself once again in such a defensive position.

Philip's study was in a room nestled between the library and the family parlor at the back of the castle. It was not particularly large, especially when compared to the chambers adjoining it, but it was cozy and comfortable. I had spent more than one cold winter night curled up with a book in one of the two red wingback chairs while my sister claimed the other and Philip worked at his desk. The large stone fireplace and low plastered ceilings enabled the room to hold much more heat than any of the places we normally spent our evenings.

Alana sank into one of the chairs while I slowly paced the perimeter of the room. I was too rattled to relax while waiting for Philip to appear. Would the guests' accusations make my brother-in-law begin to doubt my innocence? Would he finally tire of sheltering me? I knew he was a good man—and did not believe me mad so much as eccentric—but he and his family had suffered a great deal of ridicule on my behalf. I would not blame him if he suddenly decided I was too much trouble.

I sighed, looking up at the walls to study the tapestries woven with ancient Highland battle scenes in rich greens, browns, and reds. The cloth was mottled and faded with the dust and the patina of time, but it still spoke of the weaver's talent. When I first came here, still raw from the inquiries after my husband's death, I tried painting a landscape to match. Philip hung it over the fireplace, delighted with the depiction of his Highland home, even though I knew it wasn't representative of my best work. The portrait of Alana hanging in the front parlor and the wedding portrait in their bedchamber were far more skillfully wrought. People captured my eye, my brush—not forests or rivers or castles. And if the person somehow managed to touch my heart, it was all the better—like my sister's portrait, or the study I made of our nursery maid, Betsy, or the sketch of Frederick Oliver.

I shook my head, not wanting to the think about the man. Not after what happened tonight.

I was grateful when I heard Philip approach, interrupting my morose musings, but not so much so when I turned around.

"Well, the guests certainly did not all take our news well," Philip declared, reaching down to lift Alana's hand and kiss it. "I thought we might never escape the parlor."

Mr. Gage appeared just behind my brother-in-law's shoulder, and his gaze immediately searched out mine. I resisted the urge to scowl at him, knowing my displeasure would only fuel his obvious suspicion.

"Kiera, why dinna you take a seat," Philip suggested, pulling my eyes away from Mr. Gage's pale blue ones. Philip's brogue had deepened, as I'd noticed it often did when he was tired. Like most aristocratic Scots, his accent had been educated out of him, until he sounded like any upperclass Englishman. But on nights like the one when Alana had nursed their son, Malcolm, through a dangerous fever while Philip and I sat up waiting for news, by morning his accent was as thick as any Highlander's.

I thought about arguing, but seeing my brother-in-law's obvious fatigue and the warm regard with which he looked upon me, I decided to obey. Things could not be so bad if he still viewed me in such a manner. Philip might have a seat in the House of Lords, but he could never be duplicitous. Unlike Mr. Gage. From all I'd witnessed, deceit and charm seemed the hallmarks of his trade.

"In any case, whether they like it or not, I've delivered my instructions." Philip propped one leg up on the corner of his desk and scraped a hand down his face, bristling over the stubble beginning to show there. "Now let's hope they can remain calm and keep their heads about them until the procurator fiscal from Inverness arrives." He sounded doubtful that was possible.

"Speaking of which, do you know where Lady Godwin's family lives?" he asked his wife. "I dinna think I've ever heard the lady speak of her kin. I sent a letter to be posted to Lord Godwin with the servants riding for Inverness, but who knows how long it'll take to reach him in India."

She tilted her head in thought. "She asked me to send a footman to meet the mail coach in Drumchork this morning with a letter for her sister."

I glanced at Alana in curious surprise. Lady Godwin must have been quite eager for that letter to reach her sister if she'd asked Alana to send a footman especially to meet the mail coach.

"I believe the girl lives in . . . Shropshire?" She shook her head in frustration. "Perhaps the footman will remember the letter's exact direction."

"'Tis no matter." Philip shrugged. "I'm sure one of the other guests will know if the footman can't recall. Mr. Gage can ask them about it."

"Ah, yes, I heard you say you've asked Mr. Gage to begin

an inquiry of his own into the matter." Alana examined the man before us with the same curiosity I felt. "Have you conducted many inquiries, Mr. Gage?" Her tone was laced with light curiosity, but I knew my sister nursed the same skepticism I did.

I pressed my hands against my thighs, rumpling the fine Parisian-blue muslin between my fingers, grateful she had voiced the same question I had been struggling not to ask.

Mr. Gage, meanwhile, appeared perfectly at ease in his dark evening clothes, leaning against the wall near the window, his arms crossed over his chest. "I have assisted my father many times."

Alana glanced at me. We both knew what that meant.

Mr. Gage's face twisted subtly in irritation before smoothing out. "I assure you, I am more than capable of handling this investigation. You ladies have nothing to worry about."

I was not fast enough to suppress my snort and was forced to raise my hand to my mouth and cough to try to cover it. Mr. Gage was not fooled, for his brow darkened.

"Are you all right?" Philip asked, raising a single eyebrow in chastisement.

"Of course," I replied, glancing at Alana, who was studying the red and white floral pattern on her goldenrod skirts intensely. I suspected she was trying not to laugh.

"Good. Because I have a favor to ask of you."

My eyes jumped back to my brother-in-law. My back stiffened when I saw his troubled frown. Whatever the favor was, Philip did not like asking it.

I swallowed carefully before nodding for him to continue.

"I've asked Mr. Gage to conduct the investigation, but I would like you to assist him."

My eyes widened.

"What?" Mr. Gage exclaimed, straightening from his practiced slouch.

Alana reacted no better. "Are you daft?"

"Now wait." Philip raised his hands. "Hear me out."

I kept my lips firmly shut, trying to suppress the quaking I felt in my stomach as I waited for his next expected words. Alana's mouth was also taut, but more from anger than fear.

Philip sighed. "No matter how tragic the circumstances, Kiera does have experience with this sort of thing."

"Philip!" Alana scolded.

"I'm not forcing her to do it, Alana. I'm simply askin'," he argued. "The local surgeon passed less than a month ago, and they've yet to replace him. Otherwise, I would've sent word for him to come. While Gage has often assisted his father, he has little experience with murder." He gestured absently toward the man, who scowled. "If we're gonna be trapped here for four days or more with all o' these guests, and likely our murderer, I'd like to make every effort to catch him in case there's a chance he intends to strike again."

I suppressed a shiver, straining to keep my reaction from the others' notice. Would the killer attack someone else? I blinked slowly, remembering the gruesome sight of Lady Godwin's body. What kind of madman did we have on our hands?

Alana pressed her palms to her stomach and shook her head in bewilderment. "I . . . I hadn't thought of that. I heard you say as much to the others, but . . ." Her troubled gaze lifted to her husband. "Are the children safe?" She suddenly looked frantic. Nothing could disturb my sister so except concern for her children.

"Darlin', they're fine," he said, bending closer to look into my sister's face. "I promise you they're safe, Alana. I placed two footmen outside the nursery door and instructed them and the nursemaids that no one outside of our family is allowed near them without my express permission."

Alana nodded, still looking shaken.

I reached over to take her hand. "I saw them just a little

over two hours ago," I tried to reassure her. "They were being put to bed, and they all appeared to be fine."

"I . . . I should have checked on them," she stammered. "I was just so overwhelmed by the guests . . . and their questions." She shook her head. "I should have looked in on them."

"Stop that!" Philip took her face between his hands and stroked her cheekbones with his thumbs. "Our guests drove me to distraction just in the space o' the ten minutes it took to deliver my instructions. You've been dealin' with them for over three hours. O' course, you were overwhelmed."

"Yes, but Kiera thought to check on the children," she said.

I squeezed her hand and smiled sadly. "Because I was hiding." Alana knew I would never willingly associate with the guests, especially after the accusations flung at me in the garden and again in the parlor, so I didn't bother to apologize for not assisting her. Perhaps I failed her in that regard, but my sister knew my shortcomings, and understood them.

She squeezed my hand in return before taking a deep breath.

"All right?" Philip asked, staring lovingly into Alana's eyes. She nodded, and he leaned forward to drop a kiss on the top of her head.

I glanced up at Mr. Gage. He was leaning against the wall once again, albeit less casually than before. His jaw was dusted with stubble, but the hairs were so light I could barely see them. I imagined they were as blond as the hairs on his head. He was an attractive man—my artist's eye had to give him that—but the way he presented himself, his smug certainty that he was the most handsome man in the room, rankled me more than I wanted to admit. I had met good-looking men before, and most of them had been as aware of it as Mr. Gage, but they had always amused me more than irritated me.

"Now," Philip said, bringing us back to the matter at

hand. "Kiera, I was askin' if you would assist Mr. Gage." I watched his Adam's apple bob, and I knew he was forcing out the next words. "Particularly with examining the body."

I stared at him silently, uncertain how I was going to, or whether I even should, honor his request. I had been finished with dissections and corpses the moment Sir Anthony died, and been grateful for it.

"Forgive me," Mr. Gage interjected with polite severity. "But I fail to comprehend this request." He gestured to me. "Why on earth would you want your sister-in-law to help me with such a matter?"

I studied him warily. Did he truly not know?

Philip seemed just as taken aback, for it took him a moment to reply. "Gage, what do you know about Lady Darby?"

Mr. Gage glanced at me, almost in puzzlement. "Not much. I inferred there was some sort of scandal following her husband's death. Some of the guests seem quite mistrustful of her. I gather many of them actually believe she should be our prime suspect."

His gaze bored into mine, but I refused to be intimidated. He had told me nothing I didn't already know, didn't already suspect. I stared back at him and gave him nothing. Not anger or shock or fear. I understood inquiry agents and their games, and I was not interested in playing.

Philip cleared his throat, and I finally broke eye contact to look at him. He was asking my permission to speak. I shrugged. Gage could hear the facts, but I doubted he would decide to believe me innocent unless it served him.

"Lady Darby is the wife of the late Sir Anthony Darby, a great anatomist and surgeon in his day. He even attended to the health of the royal family."

Mr. Gage took in this information with a nod.

"At the time of Sir Anthony's death, he was working on a human anatomy textbook, a sort of . . . definitive reference for fellow surgeons and medical students. When he embarked upon the project some three years earlier, he realized he would need an illustrator, an artist to depict the images." Philip glanced up at me nervously, but I did not move my eyes from the stone in the hearth I was staring at. "Sir Anthony was rather frugal with his money."

"He was a miser," Alana stated angrily.

"Yes, well, he decided he would rather not pay an illustrator for his work if he did not have to. So he married one."

I did not look up to see how Mr. Gage had taken this bit of information.

"My sister and our father were not made aware of his plans prior to the wedding," Alana told him. "I think if Papa had known what Sir Anthony was about, he would have shot him in a rather crucial part of *his* anatomy."

Philip coughed. "When Sir Anthony died, and one of his colleagues uncovered the finished pages of the book, the man raised an outcry against it. Apparently, many of Sir Anthony's fellow surgeons and physicians knew he rather famously couldn't sketch, especially not with the amount of skill the anatomical drawings showed. It didn't take long for them to figure out who actually created them. Lady Darby is quite well-known for her portraits."

I could feel all of their eyes on me, and it took everything in me not to clutch my stomach where it roiled. I would never forget the looks of disgust on Sir Anthony's friends' and colleagues' faces as they accused me of unnatural tendencies and dragged me before a magistrate. Or the horrible names and epithets hurled at me in public and in the papers. The butcher's wife. The sawbones' siren. The people were still frantic over the recent trial of Burke and Hare in Edinburgh, and terrified that grave robbers turned murderers were also working in London, smothering their prey and delivering them to local surgeons for dissection. I was all too easy a target for their pent-up fears. High society had been particularly vicious, revealing their own fright over the resurrectionists, as well as their horror at discovering a gentlewoman involved in such grisly work as dissections. No one had understood. No one had even tried. Without Philip's and my own brother's intervention, I was certain I would be locked away in Bethlem Royal Hospital or worse.

"I assure you, the magistrate cleared Kiera of all wrongdoing," Philip told Mr. Gage.

The room fell silent as Mr. Gage digested this information. I was simply thankful for another moment to collect myself. It did not matter that it happened over a year ago, it still rattled me to recall any of it. Alana reached out to take my hand, and I squeezed hers in return, to reassure her, but I still did not move otherwise.

"So Lady Darby witnessed numerous dissections years ago," Mr. Gage remarked as if he were restating someone's testimony. "And sketched them. How do you know that she even understands them? Perhaps she was just drawing what she saw. How do you know she can even contribute anything to an autopsy?"

I laughed inside, bitterly. As if I could ever forget.

I looked straight into Mr. Gage's eyes. "I have never held a knife, but I can tell you where to make the cuts, how the intestines turn, what color the liver should be—in my sleep."

Mr. Gage did not flinch from the rawness of my words, but held my gaze steadily. He blinked only once and seemed to come to some understanding, for he nodded slowly, just a single bob of his head. I felt some of the tension drain out of me.

"Will you do it?" Philip asked.

I looked at my sister. Alana was always so strong, so competent, so sure of herself. And she protected me like a fierce warrior maiden. Like one of her children.

She tried to look strong now, but I could see the fear in her eyes. I knew she would never ask this of me, would never expect it of me, but I had to do it. For her. For Malcolm, and Philipa, and little baby Greer. A murderer had invaded my sister's home, and I wasn't about to let him harm my sister's family any more than he already had.

"I'll do it," I said softly.

My sister squeezed my hand again where she held it. A silent tear slid down her cheek, and I knew I had said the right thing.

I glanced past Alana to the man standing beyond her. I knew Mr. Gage had witnessed our silent exchange, but I didn't care. I loved my sister. If that made me seem weak to this man, so be it. And so help me God, if he tried to use that against me, I would hurt him far worse than this murderer ever could. Just because I had never held a knife did not mean I didn't know how to use one.

If only I had known then how greatly such an assertion would be tested.

CHAPTER THREE

The chapel where Lady Godwin's body had been stored was located on the far western end of Gairloch Castle. It often bore the brunt of the ferocious winds coming off Loch Ewe in winter, blocking the rest of the castle from a direct blow. Being the coldest part of the estate, the western block was rarely used anymore, and at an hour past midnight, the rooms and hallways that were shrouded and dusty from disuse felt eerily vacant.

I shivered as we marched down the corridor, grateful I had thrown a shawl over my shoulders before we set out. The lantern Mr. Gage carried barely peeled back the darkness around us, and certainly did nothing to heat the drafty hallway. Much as I had decided to dislike him, I found myself shifting ever closer to his body, trying to stay as close to the center of the circle of light as possible.

I realized we could have waited until dawn to examine Lady Godwin's body. She would stay fresh enough in the chapel cellar. But I had decided it would be better to have the task over and done with. Procrastinating was not going to make it any easier, and I knew I would never get any sleep that night regardless. Mr. Gage had readily agreed, and I wondered if perhaps he felt the same way.

The clatter of our footfalls echoed off the old stone, the only sound other than the creak of the swinging lantern.

The silence unsettled me, but I somehow felt speaking would only make it worse. As if making conversation somehow demeaned the seriousness of our undertaking. Besides, what would we talk about? The weather? The party? It all just seemed foolish.

I wrapped my shawl tighter around me. I didn't even really know Lady Godwin. In the week she spent at Gairloch, I had discovered she was a flirt and many of the men seemed to fancy her. After all, she was beautiful, but in the superficial way that wealthy ladies often are. I believe I'd only spoken two words to her during her stay, an "excuse me" as she nearly bumped into me in the hall one evening. And now I was about to view more of her than any of her gentlemen admirers had ever seen.

The wooden chapel door appeared out of the darkness at the end of the hall, just steps before we would have crashed into it. Mr. Gage lifted the latch and pushed it open with a mighty shove. It groaned in protest, sending a shiver down my spine.

I stepped past him, just to the edge of the light, and studied the shadowy interior of the church. Moonlight poured through the tall, arched windows, casting a hallowed glow across the pews. Two candelabras flanked the altar where a single golden cross stood in the center next to a stand propping up the Bible. The air smelled of damp and beeswax and the musty scent of a chamber that has been too long sealed. Philip and Alana attended Sunday services in the village, so the castle chapel was rarely used. I imagined the housekeeper, Mrs. MacLean, found it pointless to clean it weekly when it was used but once a year at Christmastime.

Mr. Gage shut the door and dropped the wooden crossbar into place, locking us inside. He caught me watching him and shrugged. "Just taking precautions."

My veins ran icy at the thought of someone with nefarious purposes following us here. Our desire for secrecy and privacy had been another advantage to conducting our examination of the body at night. But if the killer had been watching us, waiting to see what we would do . . .

Something of the fear I felt must have shown on my face, for Mr. Gage lifted aside his coat to reveal a pistol tucked into the waistband of his trousers. It did not make me relax, but it did take away some of the breath-stealing panic. Perhaps I had underestimated Mr. Gage. If he had contemplated the danger we might be in and thought to bring a gun, maybe he wasn't so inexperienced.

I followed him down the side of the chapel and into a small room to the right of the altar. Stacks of hymnals and extra candles covered a table, and a wardrobe, containing vestments, no doubt, stood in the corner. He passed these items without a glance and walked straight to a door in the back left corner. I watched over his shoulder as he jiggled the key, which Philip had given us, inside the lock. The door opened to reveal a stairway along the back wall of the chapel, leading downward. Rather than stumble along with the light at my back, I gestured for Mr. Gage to precede me. He took the stairs slowly, allowing me to easily keep up.

I nearly turned around and fled back up the stairs when the stench of dried blood and perforated bowel rose up to fill my nostrils. As it was, I had to grip the banister tightly to keep from pitching forward. I had left the door open behind me, and I was acutely grateful for it. This place needed some fresh air; the impulse to retch was so strong. I wondered how Mr. Gage was holding up and wished I had thought to bring a cloth of some kind to wrap around my nose.

The wooden stairs creaked loudly as we reached the bottom. I hoped they had been inspected recently. The thought of being trapped down here with Lady Godwin's corpse made me unsteady. I reached out blindly and clung to the support of the bottom post.

Mr. Gage moved toward a table positioned near the center of the cellar, where the body was laid. A sheet had been thrown over the corpse, but the blood had soaked through.

There had simply been too much of it. He set the bucket he was carrying in his other hand down on the packed earth floor, sloshing the water inside it. The glow of the lantern he still held cast his shadow across the floor and up the dirt wall behind him. Dislike or not, I was glad he was there with me.

He turned back to look at me. "Are you all right?"

How many times had someone asked me that this evening? I swallowed the bile I tasted at the back of my throat and released my grip on the stair post. "Of course," I replied. However, my voice lacked the certainty I had been aiming for.

I crossed the room to set my bag down on another table, which was scattered with miscellaneous earthenware objects. The black portmanteau looked almost like a surgeon's satchel, but it carried far cruder instruments than the fine sterling-silver implements my husband had used. Two kitchen knives, a pair of pincers, several small vials for collecting any samples, towels, an apron, and an old pair of my kid-leather gloves, which would most certainly be ruined after this.

I tossed my shawl aside, despite the fact that I was still shivering from the cold, and quickly tied the apron around my body. Fortunately, the sleeves of my Parisian-blue gown were already short, so I would not have to wrestle with them. As I pulled the worn gloves onto my fingers and fastened them, I focused on my breath. It was sawing in and out of me at a rapid pace, and I knew I had to slow it, and my racing heart, if I was going to make it through this without completely panicking or, worse, passing out. I had never fainted in my life, and the indignity of the idea of doing it in front of Mr. Gage did much to snap me out of my stupor.

I stepped up to the table and stared down at the bloody sheet, trying to imagine I was back in my husband's private examining room. Sir Anthony had enjoyed the rush of performing his dissections as if he still stood in a crowded medical theater. He had rarely allowed an audience of any kind in those days while I stood behind him making sketches and taking notes. Later I understood why. But there had always been a showmanship to his movements, a pomposity to his voice, as if he were lecturing to an audience of hundreds. I had ignored the pretense and focused on the body before me, losing myself in capturing the beauty of the form, the harmony of the lines, the intricacies of its hidden mysteries. It was the only way I made it through those first few times. Looking down at Lady Godwin, I worried that none of the beauty that had so often called to me could be found on this table.

I glanced up at Mr. Gage. He was studying the sheet in much the same way I was, with a mixture of curiosity and dread.

"Are you ready?" I asked, pleased to hear how detached I sounded.

He met my eyes, letting me know I was not alone in this, and nodded.

Taking one last deep breath through my mouth, I steeled my nerves and reached out to slowly peel back the make-shift shroud.

The first thing I noticed was the paleness of Lady Godwin's face. Her skin had already taken on the opaqueness of death, except for a dull red bruise that had blossomed from her left eyebrow down to her cheekbone. Someone had closed her eyes and mouth, which allowed her expression to appear more composed, but I still couldn't help but remember the mask of terror I had seen stamped there a few hours earlier. I quivered, feeling my impassiveness already begin to waver.

My gaze slid down to where blood splattered her chin and lower face, to the ugly gash stretched across her neck. "He slit her throat," I murmured, stating the obvious.

I was inexperienced with such a sight. Sir Anthony had

opened several cadavers' necks for me to record the intricate workings inside—the bones, muscles, and nerves; the esophagus, windpipe, and vocal cords—but we had never viewed a corpse subjected to such a gruesome injury. The only observation I could contribute was that from the appearance of the cut, the killer had only needed to make one slice with his knife. I knew from watching Sir Anthony make his dissections that it would have taken a significant amount of force to make such a clean, precise cut.

I suppressed a shudder and reached out to smooth back a strand of hair that had matted to the blood on her neck. "Wet rag," I said, holding out my hand. I waited for Mr. Gage to dunk one of the cloths I had brought in the bucket and give it to me.

I carefully dabbed at the wound to wash away some of the tacky blood hiding it, feeling oddly detached from myself. I had never touched a corpse before, and Lady Godwin's body seemed so fragile beneath my fingers. The water ran in pink streams down her neck to the table below. The depth of the gash and the manner in which the skin peeled back from the wound made me flinch.

"What?" Mr. Gage asked. "What is it?"

I shook my head and swallowed, struggling to regain my composure. "Ah, it's just an ugly wound. This one slash alone killed her. Any other wounds she may have suffered are just superfluous."

His eyes slid back up to examine the bruise on her face, and then lifted to meet mine over Lady Godwin's head.

"I can't tell whether she was struck before or after her neck was slit," I told him. "But I imagine there would be some sign of struggle if she had been hit before."

I reached for her right hand and turned it over to look for any cuts, lacerations, or chipped nails. The left hand was more difficult to manage, for I had to reach across her blood-soaked bodice. The body had already begun to stiffen, and the elbow would not bend easily.

Our eyes met once again across the corpse, and I could see the same confusion I felt reflected in Mr. Gage's eyes. It did not appear that Lady Godwin fought her murderer, which meant she probably knew the person. And even more disturbing, the attacker may have struck her after killing her. The bruise was too new for the blow to have been delivered earlier than that day. I didn't recall seeing a contusion there at dinner.

My stomach slowly roiled, and I was forced to step back from the body for a moment. "Did . . . did the body get dropped while it was being transported from the garden?" I asked, hoping maybe one of the men had lost his grip.

Mr. Gage shook his head. His brow was furrowed in concern. "Clearly, someone harbored a great deal of hatred toward the viscountess."

I felt that was somewhat of an understatement. Why would someone murder Lady Godwin and then strike her, as if killing her was not enough? It was appalling. And I was having a very difficult time dealing with it all.

I looked up at Gage, blinking back the wetness in my eyes that I knew had as much to do with my overloaded emotions as the stink of blood and death.

He had the courtesy, or perhaps the intelligence, not to ask me about it. "I never realized a neck wound could bleed so much," he stated, waving his hand over her bloody torso.

I took in the state of Lady Godwin's bodice, my eyes sliding downward to her skirts, and frowned. Neck wounds certainly bled a great deal, but there was no way that this quantity of blood would have trickled down to her abdomen. I thought back to the sight of Lady Godwin laid across the garden bench and the pools of blood collecting in the flounces of her skirt.

"There's something else."

He leaned in again as I smoothed my hands down her torso, smearing more blood across the gold fabric. The seam joining her bodice to her skirt had been carefully ripped open and then rearranged and tied back in place with the sash. I remembered the stench of perforated bowel I had smelled upon entering the cellar and quickly reached out to undo the sash.

Knowing what I would find, I didn't even flinch when I peered through the gap in the gown. Lady Godwin had been sliced open with two incisions forming a *T* over her lower abdomen.

"My God," Gage cried, raising his arm to bury his nose in his sleeve.

"I don't think He had anything to do with this," I murmured, moving closer to peer at something that had caught my eye.

"You're certainly right about that. But I don't understand why the killer made these two cuts?" he puzzled, looking over my shoulder at what I was doing. "As you said, the neck wound alone would have killed her. Was this just another way of taking out his anger? Did he want to disfigure her womanhood in some way?"

I slammed a hand down on the table beside the corpse to steady myself as my churning stomach lurched violently. I could feel Gage's eyes on my face as my cheeks drained of their last vestiges of color.

"I . . . I think she was with child."

CHAPTER FOUR

Somehow I managed to spin away from Lady Godwin's corpse before I emptied the contents of my stomach all over the cellar floor. With my hands held out in front of me still coated in her blood, I retched. I couldn't stop imagining that poor baby's fate—her life so viciously ended. The viscountess could not have been more than five months along. The still-small swell of her belly had been easily kept hidden by the flounces of her gown. I now understood her strange deviation from the fashions with fitted waists and belts the other lady guests wore.

Gage knelt down to support me, lacing his arm underneath mine to cup my shoulder. I panted, still shaking from the force of my stomach contractions. A handkerchief came around from behind me, and I allowed him to wipe my mouth and chin. It didn't even occur to me to feel embarrassed, for I was too overwhelmed by Lady Godwin's wounds.

"Blow," he ordered, refolding the cloth and pressing it to my nose.

I did as I was told, leaning back into the warmth his body radiated behind me. I closed my eyes as he removed the handkerchief. Taking deep breaths through my mouth, I remained in Gage's loose embrace until I felt my muscles steadying. He cupped my elbow to help me rise, and I immediately felt the loss of his comforting hold and heat.

The cellar seemed much cooler than when we arrived, and my knees were quivering from kneeling over. I realized I was not as in control of myself as I thought. There was nothing more I could do here tonight. I needed to clean up and get out while I could still walk on my own two feet.

I swallowed the acid coating my mouth and throat, and stepped back toward Lady Godwin's corpse. "I think that's all we're going to discover tonight," I told Gage. My voice was rough and gravelly from my illness.

"Of course," he replied, helping me place the sheet back over the body. "Wash the blood off your hands. The rest can be cleaned up later."

I didn't argue. The quicker I was away from Lady Godwin's corpse, the better. Besides, I doubted the addition of vomit to the other stomach-churning stenches in the room would make much of a difference.

Yanking the ruined gloves off my fingers, I plunged my arms into the bucket of cold water and scrubbed frantically at the red that had seeped through the worn fabric. Gage handed me a towel to dry my hands while he tugged at the ties of my apron. He clearly understood my hurry. Tossing the apron over my implement bag, I picked up my shawl and headed toward the stairs.

The chapel above felt like London in July compared to the icy cold of the cellar. I made it midway through the sanctuary before collapsing onto the solid wood of a pew. Gage joined me a moment later.

We sat quietly, listening to the winds off the bay rattle the windows, the only other sound besides my frantic breaths. I closed my eyes, feeling the rise and fall of my chest slow as I allowed the peace of the chapel to settle into my bones. Scotsmen had come here for centuries—desperate, remorseful, and grieving—in search of solitude, and comfort from their maker. I felt their ghosts filling the benches around me, offering up their silent prayers. It made my fear and distress somehow easier to manage, knowing I was in their company.

That and the pressure of Gage's sleeve against my own. It appeared I had greatly misjudged him. So far he had been steadier than I, and the fact that he had not lorded it over me or belittled my effort earned my respect and tentative trust. It was tempting to lean into his solid presence, a reaction I couldn't remember ever happening with a man outside of my family. I had never felt so comfortable with Sir Anthony, not even in the early days of our short courtship and marriage. It was puzzling and slightly unnerving.

I sighed, catching a small whiff of his spicy cologne. It helped to clear the lingering stench of the cellar from my nose.

"I should thank you," Gage said softly. His tone sounded almost reluctant. I glanced up at him, but his gaze remained focused on the altar in front of us.

"I never would have uncovered the fact that Lady Godwin was expecting." His eyes finally met mine, but it was too dark to truly see into them. The lantern on the floor at his feet gilded his golden hair but shadowed the features of his face.

I turned away, uncertain how to respond.

"Could you tell how far along she was?" he asked, saving me from coming up with a reply.

"No more than five months. The skin of her stomach was not overly stretched. I never noticed she was showing," I said, recalling the way she had flitted about the parlor only the night before.

Gage nodded, clearly having thought of the same thing. "Are you *certain* she was with child?" he queried. "Could the killer simply have been . . . disfiguring her?"

I blinked slowly, remembering the coil of the severed umbilical cord. "She was enceinte," I stated decisively.

He nodded again, accepting my word without further

argument. "So there is a missing baby somewhere." He sighed. "Was there anything else you noticed? Anything that might help us?"

In my mind, I cautiously returned to the scene downstairs and tried to think like Sir Anthony, like one of his students. But I didn't think like a surgeon. I thought like an artist. I saw everything as it was—the contours, the colors, the rhythm—not how it should be. My mind did not try to correct an image but capture it.

I wrapped my shawl tighter around me and ignored my frustration over what I didn't have the education for, and instead focused on what I did. "Beyond the inflicted wounds, I noticed no particular signs of deterioration or illness. Her bowel would have been fine except . . ." I paused, realizing something. "The cut at her neck was made precisely and, I would venture to add, with some skill. But the incisions on her abdomen were jagged, awkward. I suppose that could be attributed to a certain amount of struggling from Lady Godwin, but I dare say she died, or at least passed out, before her murderer sliced into her abdomen." I glanced at Gage, who had begun to run his index finger over his lips as he thought.

"Maybe our murderer has no experience cutting body parts other than the neck."

"Or they were emotionally distraught," I added.

"Or . . ." He looked up at me. "We're dealing with more than one person. Perhaps our murderer had an accomplice."

I nodded. I had been thinking of one man as well, but we could be dealing with multiple villains. And though I suspected the person who sliced Lady Godwin's neck was a man, the accomplice could be a man or a woman. "Whoever it was, they likely got blood on themselves. Blood sprays when the jugular vein is cut in the neck. I highly doubt they escaped without becoming soiled by it, as well as the mess they made of her abdomen."

"I had thought of that. Your brother-in-law's staff has

been instructed to inform me if they discover blood anywhere on the estate, be it clothing, linens, or the floor." He leaned forward in the pew, propping his elbows on his knees. "Lady Godwin must have been murdered right there in the garden, sometime after dinner."

I nodded. There had been too much blood on and around the stone bench for it to make any sense otherwise. I needed to examine the scene. Perhaps there was some clue as to the location of the baby or the manner of the initial assault. I also wanted to compare the imprint of Lady Godwin's body with the wounds I found. I was about to tell Gage so when he made an urgent gesture with his hands.

"The killer *must* have been aware of Lady Godwin's delicate condition," he declared. "Otherwise, why would he have sliced her open?"

I gnawed my lip, agreeing with him.

Gage sat up slowly. "Didn't Lord Cromarty say that Lord Godwin is in India?"

"He did." I realized what he was getting at. "Do you know how long he's been there?"

"No. But it would be very interesting to find out."

"Did Lady Godwin have a lover?"

He nodded. "Most recently, Mr. Fitzpatrick."

I remembered the man's arrival at the scene in the garden maze shortly after mine, and the mud stains on the back of his trousers, but I couldn't see how that would have any connection to the murder.

"But I do not know how long they have been intimately connected," Gage admitted. "I have not made it a habit to keep track of Lady Godwin's peccadilloes."

No, only Mrs. Cline's.

"Well, then, I suppose we should find someone who does," I replied a bit more testily than I intended. "For if Mr. Fitzpatrick was not bedding her five months ago, he's certainly not the father."

His eyes seemed to laugh at me. "I see that you under-stand how the anatomy of that process works."

My cheeks heated. I may have been forced to watch my late husband dissect bodies, but this was swiftly becoming the most intimate conversation I had ever conducted with a man. And I didn't like how easily Gage unnerved me. "Yes," I retorted. "Should I pretend otherwise?"

"No."

I could definitely hear the grin in his voice now and was not about to stick around to hear what else he had to say. Gage was gentlemanly enough to stand and step into the aisle to allow me to pass. However, he was not gentlemanly enough to keep his mouth shut as I slid by.

"Coward," he whispered.

I did not dignify that with a response, but instead raised my chin and marched down the aisle toward the door.

Somehow having to stand and wait for him to remove the crossbar stole a bit of the thunder from my actions. Gage winked, obviously finding my indignation amusing. I arched an imperious eyebrow but managed to hold my tongue. Even when he swept open the door and bowed like a ridiculous courtier.

I rolled my eyes and strode through the doorway, only to have my dramatic exit ruined yet again. This time by a hard object crashing down on my head.

CHAPTER FIVE

Fortunately, the blow was not hard enough to knock me unconscious. It was, however, hard enough to knock me to the floor and blur my vision. I pressed my hand to the back of my head and tried to rise to my feet, but the pounding in my skull made it difficult to push myself upright. I could hear Gage skirmishing with the culprit, and I worried he might need my help. Someone yelped and howled. I looked up and tried to focus on the man cowering away from Gage as he dragged him back down the hall toward me and shoved him against the wall.

Gage pulled the pistol from the waistband of his trousers and pointed it at the man. Then he slowly backed toward me, kicking what looked to be a pewter candlestick with his heel. It clattered and rolled across the stone floor. All the while, his eyes remained trained on the perpetrator. "Lady Darby? Can you hear me?"

"Yes," I moaned. I pushed against the floor again, trying to sit up.

Gage moved closer and knelt on one knee to assist me. "Perhaps you should lie down," he suggested.

I started to shake my head and then realized what a terrible idea that would be. "No, I'm fine," I protested. "I'm not bleeding." At least, I didn't think I was. "I just need to sit against this wall for a moment."

Even through the haze of my injury, I sensed the worry and disapproval vibrating through his frame, but he couldn't afford to take his attention off the man in the shadows across the hall long enough to express it. Once I was seated upright, blinking as I cradled my spinning head, Gage retrieved the lantern from where he had set it just inside the chapel door. The culprit recoiled from the light but did not try to move.

"Lord Westlock?" I gasped in confusion. The silver-haired gentleman was normally so gentle and congenial; I couldn't believe he'd just attacked me. His wife was the harridan.

"Would you care to explain your presence here, and why you just assaulted Lady Darby?" Gage asked the baron in a firm voice. He set the lantern on the floor and kept his pistol trained on the gentleman.

Lord Westlock instantly appeared contrite. Whether that was in truth or only a pretense, I could not tell. Not with my head still reeling from the blow, as well as the revelation of my attacker.

"Lady Darby, I'm sorry for that. It's just that . . . my wife and her friends were so certain you murdered Lady Godwin." He glanced down at his lap, where he was cradling his arm. "I watched you descend the stairs and turn down the corridor toward the chapel where Lord Cromarty said they laid out her body, and I . . ." He swallowed. "Well, I worried my wife might be right. So I followed the light of your lantern." He glanced at Gage sheepishly. "I didn't know Mr. Gage was with you."

I felt a flush burn my cheeks.

"And what did you expect to find, my lord?" Gage asked. Lord Westlock shifted uncomfortably. "Lady Darby further molesting the body?"

"Well, I thought if I caught her at it . . . I mean, after the inquiries a year ago," he stammered. He pressed his lips together and leaned toward Mr. Gage with a look of pleading. "She's not natural," he whispered.

I'd heard the accusation so many times during the inquiries following Sir Anthony's death, and again during the past few days of the house party, that perhaps I should have become inured to the insult, but I wasn't. And I suspected I never would be. It pinched in my chest like a splinter.

"Sir Anthony and I were close acquaintances," Lord Westlock told Gage, something I did not know. "We were members of the same club, enjoyed the same port," he explained, as if that was all it took for two men to be considered friends. "I happened upon him there one evening a few weeks before his death. He seemed rather smug about something, and when I asked him about it, he told me how pleased he was by how cold and detached his wife was." I stiffened. "Bragged about it, he did."

Gage glanced back at me, but I couldn't tell what he was thinking.

"I asked him why he would be so proud of that fact." The baron's eyes flitted toward me uncomfortably. "Thought maybe he had a lovely bit o' muslin on the side and his wife was indifferent to it. But then he said something about her being a scary good surgeon if only she'd been born a male. Said she had the keenest eye. And that either she had more steel in her spine than the average surgical student or she actually enjoyed the sight of death."

My stomach cramped painfully at the comment. I suspected that if I hadn't already emptied my stomach all over the chapel cellar floor, I would have vomited.

"Are you saying that Sir Anthony actually admitted to you that his wife took part in his dissections?" Gage asked incredulously.

Lord Westlock's gaze darted to mine and then back to Gage. "Well, I didn't take him seriously at the time. He was rather deep in his cups. I thought maybe he was speaking in metaphors."

Gage's hardened gaze searched mine out, and I struggled to meet it. I couldn't believe Sir Anthony had actually bragged about the emotional detachment and stoicism he had forced upon me. Hadn't he seen the torment beneath my feigned reserve? Or had he just not cared? A familiar ache started in my chest upon realizing I already knew it was the latter. He hadn't cared. He had been selfish and cruel, and as long as he got what he wanted from me, that was all that mattered. It was no wonder I'd buried myself in my art. It was all that kept me sane.

I glared at Gage, daring him to believe the damning character reference Lord Westlock had relayed about me. He certainly wouldn't be the first to believe the worst of me, and I was sure he wouldn't be the last.

My head pounded furiously, and I dropped my gaze, too distracted by the pain to continue this ridiculous standoff. If Gage was stupid enough to take my late husband's words as fact, then he was an even bigger fool than I had initially believed.

I heard him shift and sigh in annoyance. "So you're telling me you had nothing to do with Lady Godwin's murder?" he asked, continuing his questioning of Lord Westlock. "You weren't following us to hinder my investigation?"

The baron's eyes widened in horror. "No! I would never . . ." he spluttered. "Why, I was with Lord Darlington in the billiards room after dinner, when the body was found. You can ask him."

Gage slowly lowered his gun. "You can be certain I will."

Lord Westlock huffed in indignation, but his ire was tempered by the wariness in his gaze. He was clearly aware that Gage held all the power in their current situation.

Gage's eyes crinkled in concern as he knelt down beside where I slumped against the wall, but there was also a wintriness that had not been there before we left the chapel. I closed my eyes and allowed him to lightly touch the back of my head, trying not to feel betrayed by the evidence of his renewed suspicion of me.

"Well, you definitely have a sizable lump, but you were

right. I don't think it's bleeding. It appears you have a hard head, Lady Darby. I suppose I shouldn't be surprised by that."

I blinked open my eyes to see his grim smile.

"Do you think you can walk?"

"Yes."

He helped me to my feet and wrapped an arm around my waist for support. I would have pulled away if I thought I could have made it on my own. Then he tucked his pistol back into his waistband and reached for the lantern. "Lord Westlock, if you please." Gage nodded down the hall, indicating that the baron should walk in front of us.

Lord Westlock climbed to his feet, cradling his left arm in front of him. "What were you two doing in the chapel at this hour of night anyway?"

I stiffened, wondering what Gage would tell him.

He narrowed his eyes and his voice turned hard. "Lord Cromarty explained that I would be conducting an inquiry. My methods are my own."

"But surely the other guests would not approve of Lady Darby assisting you."

"Then they don't need to know she's assisting me, do they?" The dangerous look in Gage's eye, though it wasn't focused on me, was enough to make the breath stutter in my chest. It appeared to have the same effect on Lord Westlock, who swallowed and nodded.

"Then, if you would." Gage nodded in front of us once again, urging the baron to move forward.

I leaned against Gage's frame as we slowly made our way back toward the main hall block of the castle. My thoughts were still a bit scattered from the blow, and now they were stunned by Mr. Gage's unexpected defense. I realized his shielding of my involvement probably had far more to do with protecting his investigation than me, but it astounded me nonetheless. It had been so long since anyone but my family had shielded me from even the smallest hurts that

I had learned not to expect it. Maybe Lord Westlock's words had not done as much harm as I'd worried.

Gairloch was silent except for the shuffle of our footfalls and the creak of the lantern. It was our only source of light until we rounded the corner of the central corridor. There, candles had been set into stone recesses spaced evenly down the hall and up the grand staircase. When we reached the stairs, Gage paused so that I could gather up my skirts, an action that seemed to take considerably more effort than usual. Lord Westlock had nearly reached the first landing before he realized we were not behind him. He turned in query.

"Go to bed," Gage told him with the same hard look in his eye. "And keep tonight's events to yourself. Should I hear you've revealed my or Lady Darby's actions, I shall be forced to charge you with impeding my investigation."

Lord Westlock nodded and turned to scurry up the stairs like a rat escaping to his hole.

"Can you really do that?" I questioned Gage.

He supported my arm as we took the first step. "No. But I can ask Lord Cromarty to confine him to his room for the duration of his stay if he continues to get in the way."

I figured that would be a terrible enough threat for a man like Lord Westlock, who greatly enjoyed hunting, shooting, riding, and any number of other outdoor pursuits.

Climbing the stairs turned out to be more difficult than I anticipated. By the time we reached the first landing, I needed to pause to regain control of my faculties. My head was throbbing harder, and I had begun to feel dizzy and, consequently, nauseated. Gage seemed to be aware of this without my having to tell him, for he patiently waited for me to signal that I was ready to continue.

I took a deep breath and swallowed. "All right."

I could feel I was leaning more and more on him with each step, depending on his strength to make it to the top. When we reached the second landing, I sensed he wanted to offer further assistance, but I refused to even contemplate being carried. He had already done more than enough for me that night, including caring for me when I became sick in the cellar and rescuing me from an attacker. My pride would not allow him to carry me as well. Not if there was even a slight chance I could make it on my own. Marshaling my determination, I ascended the third flight and directed him toward my room with only a small wobble in my voice.

We moved slowly, though I felt the need to rush until we reached the family wing. There I could relax, knowing the only people who might catch us in the hallway together at such a late hour were my sister and her husband, and Philip's aunt and cousins. Gage opened the door for me when we reached my room and escorted me inside. I had sent my maid Lucy to bed hours before, but I figured I could manage without her, even with an aching head.

"Thank you," I said, turning to bid him good night. However, he had already followed me inside and closed the door behind him. "What are you doing?" I asked in puzzlement. "You can't be in here."

"Someone needs to examine that wound more closely," he proclaimed, moving toward the fire. "And someone needs to sit with you for a time to ensure your injury is not more serious than it seems." He bent to stoke the flames in the fireplace higher. "As I see it, you have three options. You can ring for your maid and I shall give her instructions on what to look for, you can wake your sister, or you can allow me to assist you."

I scowled, disliking the autocratic tone of his voice almost more than the words coming out of his mouth. I certainly wasn't going to wake Alana. My sister had enough to worry about without my adding to it. If I rang for Lucy, it would only wake Alana's maid as well, and it was only a matter of time before my sister showed up at my door. Not to mention the issue of the entire staff knowing I had been attacked, and that Mr. Gage had been in my room. I sighed, realizing I really only had one option.

"Fine," I huffed, sitting in one of the deep blue chairs positioned before the hearth. I winced, having sat too quickly and jarred my head.

Gage moved to stand behind me, and I felt my scalp prickle as he reached up to touch my head. I breathed in deeply and held myself very still. Something snagged on a tendril of my hair, and I realized he was pulling hairpins from the loose bun fastened at the back of my head just below the bump.

"I can't see the wound properly with all this hair in the way," he complained. "Help me take out these pins."

I could almost imagine him frowning down at the coil of my deep chestnut tresses. I reached back to assist him, bumping his hand. He pulled back, but not before I felt the rough calluses on his palm. I wondered where he'd gotten them. Most gentlemen's hands were smoother than my own, as mine were chapped from the paint, linseed oil, and turpentine I used to create my artwork.

"Talented as I am, it will probably go faster if I just let you do it," he jested in a tight voice, taking a step back from the chair to give me space to work.

My skin flushed at the reminder that what I was doing was normally associated with a far more carnal activity than examining a wound. The only men who had ever seen my hair down were my husband, father, brother, and perhaps Philip. I wasn't certain how I felt adding Mr. Gage to that list.

He, on the other hand, had probably seen more women with their hair cascading to their waists than I would like to count. I wondered if he favored a particular color, or whether blondes, brunettes, and redheads all held equal appeal. Then I wanted to shake my head at the ridiculous thought. What did it matter to me how many women he had seen in their undress or what color their hair was?

I removed the last pin and allowed the rope of my hair to fall, untwisting as it went. Setting the last pin aside, I reached back to spread my hair out so that Gage could part it wherever he wished to see the bump on my scalp. I sat very still, with my hands folded in my lap, waiting for him to begin his examination. When several moments ticked by without him moving forward, I wondered if perhaps he was not paying attention.

"Mr. Gage?"

He shuffled and cleared his throat. *"Mmm . . .* yes." His hands touched my head, and I closed my eyes, feeling oddly giddy from the tingle across my scalp and down my neck. My head still throbbed in time to my heartbeat, but it had dulled since I sat down. His fingers slid through my hair and probed the bump gently. I began to feel rather light-headed, so I blinked open my eyes, thinking it might be better to focus on something other than the glide of his fingers.

My bedchamber was large, but not so large that it was difficult to heat. When I had been given my pick of the vacant chambers upon my arrival at Gairloch Castle, I had chosen this room for two specific reasons. First, for its location at the front of the house facing the steely waters of the loch. It boasted a rather deep window seat where I could read, sketch, or simply sit in quiet contemplation while I enjoyed the view. And secondly, for the rich palette of blues decorating the room. Cobalt linens and canopy swathed the bed. Cerulean drapes flanked the windows. Pale powder blue, periwinkle, and slate blue crisscrossed the rugs, and navy blue upholstered the chairs.

I had always been rather partial to blue. Maybe because it was the color of my mother's eyes, as well as mine, my brother's, and my sister's. My father also boasted blue eyes, but they were more the shade of a stormy loch than the bright lapis lazuli that graced the rest of us. More than one suitor had written poems to Alana's eyes during her two seasons in London, including Philip. I, on the other hand, had declined my father's offer to have a season, content with an arranged marriage of his making so that I might spend the time painting instead. To be completely honest, I had preferred to remain single, but my father would have none of that. Sir Anthony had not been inclined to literary pursuits, and consequently the only words ever written about my eyes had been by a stranger in a scandal rag, calling them "witch bright."

I sighed, wondering why I was thinking about such a thing. Perhaps the blow to my head had addled my wits more than I realized.

"I'm almost finished," Gage said, misinterpreting my sigh. He circled around my chair and leaned down toward me, holding a candle. "Look into my eyes," he instructed, as he moved the candle left and right before my field of vision.

He had blue eyes as well—the pale blue of a winter sky the morning after a snowstorm, almost piercing in their clarity. I would have preferred Mr. Gage's eyes to be brown or green or even hazel.

"I didn't see any abrasions, just a rather unfortunate bump," he informed me, setting the candle back on the mantel above the fireplace. "I would say you were lucky, but sometimes the pressure that builds up inside the head after such a blow can cause serious problems when there is no opening to release it."

I laid my head gingerly back against the cushioned seat. "Was that supposed to be reassuring? Because I found it far from comforting."

"It was the simple truth. You seem the type of person who expects honesty, and you seem hardy enough to take it."

From his tone of voice, I wasn't certain he considered these complimentary traits.

"Besides," he added, settling into the navy-blue chair across from me. "I need you to understand why I will be forcing you to make conversation with me for the next hour." He glanced at the clock on the mantel.

I narrowed my eyes. "Is that really necessary?" All I

wanted was to crawl into bed and go to sleep, preferably sooner rather than later, and without this annoying man watching over me.

"I'm afraid so." He relaxed back into his chair, linked his hands over his stomach, and smiled. It was a rather mischievous grin, which lit his pale eyes too intensely, and I knew I was not going to like whatever he said next. "So tell me about your life, Lady Darby. It seems to have been an interesting one."

CHAPTER SIX

Mr. Gage's smile, and the carefully constructed veneer of indifference he projected, instantly set me on edge, though I knew better than to show it. I was certain Gage thought his intense interest in my answer was well hidden, but the width and whiteness of his smile, rather like a wolf staring at its next meal, coupled with the gleam in his eyes, set the alarm bells ringing in my already pounding skull. Perhaps it was my survival instinct, sharpened and honed from my encounters with inquiry agents and Bow Street Runners a year before, or my natural wariness of the motivation of strangers—all I knew was that I would be foolish to share anything of a sensitive nature with this man.

Struggling to keep the clamor of my nerves from registering on my face, I frowned and lifted my eyes to the ceiling. I hoped he would attribute my expression to the mild twinge of discomfort my head still caused me. "My life is only interesting to those who have not lived it," I replied mildly.

"Come now," he cajoled, still wearing that smile. "You can't tell me you found your existence so dull."

I closed my eyes, deciding it would be easier to hide the irritation and ever-present fear such questioning caused me. "I never said my life had been dull, only uninteresting. They're not the same thing."

"True. But I still find it difficult to believe that spending any amount of time as an anatomist's assistant could be uninteresting. You must have seen some quite appalling things." His voice was pitched low and sympathetic, like a barrister commiserating with a victim on the witness stand. He was not overtly sly, and I realized it might not even be evident to anyone else, but it vibrated through me like a wrong chord struck by a pianist. He was good, very good. I wondered if he used the same tone on the women he wished to coax into his bed.

"Do you know what I find interesting?" I blinked open my eyes, angry he was trying to wheedle me like the witless society ladies. "How all of the ladies find you so charming. I'm afraid I do not see it."

His eyes twinkled with amusement. "You noticed the women find me charming?"

"How could I not?" I scoffed. "They twitter like magpies whenever you so much as bow over their hands. It rather puts me off my appetite."

"So you didn't twitter when I bowed over your hand?" The question was phrased as a jest, but I could see the disbelief in his eyes. The arrogant man simply couldn't believe that a female could be unaffected by him.

I lifted my eyebrows. "You never bowed over my hand, Mr. Gage."

A puzzled look entered his eyes. "Of course I have," he protested, even as doubt softened his voice and insistence.

I started to shake my head, but then remembered my injury. "I'm afraid I've never had the pleasure," I drawled sarcastically. "But I assure you that if I had, I never would have twittered."

My words succeeded in wiping the smile from his face, replacing it with a look of curious contemplation. "I suppose you're *not* the type of female who would twitter."

I smiled tightly, surprised by how it hurt to be reminded yet again of how different I was from others. It was an absurd reaction considering the fact that I had been the one to point out I would never twitter in the first place, nor did I actually want to be like all the vapid ladies populating polite society, but it hollowed me out inside all the same. "No," I finally replied before making an attempt to lighten the conversation. "How exactly *does* one twitter?"

Gage smiled.

"Well?" I asked, reluctantly curious now that I contemplated it. How did other women manage it without sounding deranged to their gentlemen admirers? I had never been very successful at the art of flirtation. I knew my sister was quite capable, having listened to her and Philip verbally banter with one another daily for over a year. My brother Trevor also seemed competent in that arena, if the number of young ladies in London angling for a marriage proposal from him were any indication. I, on the other hand, seemed to be missing that mysterious skill. Sir Anthony had never flirted with me, nor had any of his assistants. Perhaps it was an acquired talent, one that Mr. Gage had practiced dutifully, like learning a musical instrument, until he became a master. It would explain why so many people, men and women alike, seemed to admire him for it.

"Is a twitter simply a nervous laugh? Or does it require some kind of manipulation of the tongue and throat, like a cat's purr?"

Gage's smile widened. "Perhaps you should give it a try?"

I considered his suggestion. "Perhaps. But not now."

He seemed on the verge of laughing. I tilted my head against the cushions in puzzlement, wondering what I had said to amuse him so. He shook his head, refusing to explain, and cleared his throat.

"So," he declared, shifting in his seat. "What's this?" He gestured toward the top of the square mahogany table positioned between our two chairs.

"It's a puzzle."

He leaned forward to pick up one of the unfitted pieces

scattered across the table surface. "A puzzle? I thought they were a child's toy, used to teach them their geography?"

"They are. Philip has a friend in Edinburgh who manufactures them, and he has been trying to market them to adults as well, by using pictures instead of maps and dicing them into a greater number of pieces. They haven't caught on yet, but whenever Philip journeys to Edinburgh, he brings me back some of the prototypes. He has also taken a few substandard paintings to his friend and asked him to cut the images into puzzles especially for me."

"Is *this* one of your paintings?" he asked, gesturing to the image of a castle and surrounding countryside beginning to take shape on the table.

"No. I do have a few puzzles made from the more inferior landscapes I've produced over the years, but most of them are made from pictures Philip finds in Edinburgh."

"No portraits?" he teased.

I met his eyes squarely. "None of my portraits are inferior," I replied, as certain of my talent as Gage was certain of his charm.

He studied me for a moment before nodding. "I've seen the portrait of your sister in the parlor, and a few more of your works. They are exquisite."

"Thank you." I felt a tingle of warmth at the base of my neck, as I always felt when someone praised my work. Since the scandal, I had not received many such compliments.

Gage's eyes dropped back to the table. "So you have an interest in puzzles as well?"

I looked down at the wooden pieces, automatically analyzing the segments for the next section to fit. "They pass the time at night when I can't sleep."

I felt his eyes studying me again. "You have trouble sleeping?" The query was made lightly, but I sensed his interest.

It seemed harmless to assuage his curiosity. "Sometimes."

"Have you tried reading?"

"Yes. But that doesn't make me sleepy. Philip says the puzzles work because they are a mindless activity."

Gage looked confused. "I would think sorting and fitting together a puzzle would be more stimulating. Does it truly put you to sleep?"

"Well, no," I admitted. "But it soothes me." I blushed, feeling somehow I had admitted far more than I wanted to. I breathed deeply, knowing a change of topic was necessary before he pushed me further. "Mr. Gage, I truly would like to go to bed. Do you honestly need to stay here with me for an hour? I assure you my mind is steady." I sighed, sinking deeper into my chair. "I grant you that I may be in danger of passing out, but from fatigue, not physical injury. I promise you I shall wake again in the morning."

He looked me up and down, as if he could see some sort of physical manifestation of the state of my health.

"If necessary, I shall recite all sorts of tedious information to you if that is what it will require to convince you to *leave*," I declared, determined to remove him from my chamber.

His lips quirked at my slip of temper. "I believe you, Lady Darby. You do, indeed, seem sound."

"Then will you please go?"

His hand lifted to cover his heart. "My fair lady, you wound me. Do you not realize what a novel experience this is for me? I have never had a woman request that I leave her bedchamber before. Normally they are begging me to stay."

I rolled my eyes, even as my heart gave a traitorous flip at hearing him call me fair. "My abject apologies," I drawled. "I had no idea your feelings . . ." a soft shush of sound distracted me, drawing my attention toward the door ". . . were so delicate. What was that?" I asked, sitting forward.

"I don't know." He frowned and crossed toward the door. Along the way, he bent to pick up a piece of paper lying on the wooden floor, several inches from the door. "It looks like someone left you a note."

"At this hour?" I reluctantly hoisted myself out of my

chair. "Didn't they see the light under the door? Why didn't they knock?"

A sudden chill raced down my spine. I looked at Gage, seeing the same alertness in his gaze. His eyes slid back toward the door as he handed me the letter.

I recognized the crisp white stationery as being from the generic stock stashed in every guest room in the castle. However, the bold block letters were not familiar and, in fact, seemed printed in such a uniform fashion as to make the sender's handwriting indistinguishable. My hands shook as I read the words.

SHAME ON YOU, LADY DARBY. I KNOW WHAT YOU'VE BEEN DOING.

Gage, who had been reading over my shoulder, threw open the door and darted into the hall, leaving me blinking down at the page. Who would do such a thing? And what did it mean?

Immediately, my mind returned to Lord Westlock and his wife, and all of the other guests who believed me capable of murder. Did they think to frighten me? To intimidate me into doing something stupid, like confessing to a crime I didn't commit? The edges of the paper crinkled beneath my angry fists.

Gage returned to stand in the doorway, clear frustration marring his brow.

"Who would write this?" I demanded of him.

"I don't know," he muttered, closing the door to a gap. "But whoever it was took a pretty big risk by sliding it under your door while there were still candles lit in your room."

"Do you think it was the Westlocks?"

He thought about it for a moment and then shook his head. "No. Westlock was intimidated enough when he scur- ried off to bed. I don't think he or his wife would have screwed up the courage to do something like this so quickly."

"Well, then what of the Smythes? Or the Darlingtons?" I asked, rattling off the families who had been most vindictive toward me.

"I don't know."

"Or Marsdale," I declared with some relish. "This sounds like something he would write, the scoundrel. Although," I added after thinking about it, "I got the impression he didn't care whether my reputation was true or not. Why would he be spiteful?"

"There is another possibility."

The hesitance in Gage's voice made me look up. His posture was rigid, and the wariness in his gaze made me look down at the words again.

"Oh," I wheezed as the realization hit me like a punch in the stomach. I swallowed around the sudden dryness in my throat. "The murderer."

He nodded. "Maybe, like Westlock, they saw us heading to or leaving the chapel."

"Perhaps you'll have a letter slid under your door as well."

"Maybe."

I wondered why he sounded doubtful.

"But either way, whether the killer or a suspicious guest sent that letter, perhaps your continued involvement in the investigation should be minimal."

I frowned, not liking the sound of that. However, I didn't immediately protest. "Maybe," I murmured, deciding it might be best to hedge my bets. "But I would at least like to examine the place where Lady Godwin was found. In daylight. Tomorrow preferably," I specified.

Gage stared back at me with no discernible reaction besides a slight narrowing of his eyes.

"I . . . I need to examine the imprint of her body on the bench, to make sure I haven't missed any injuries." I swallowed and internally shook myself. There was no need to stammer. Gage did not intimidate me. Besides, if he didn't give me permission, I would get it from Philip. "The blood should lie in a predictable pattern if Lady Godwin was in fact cut open in that spot. If there is blood elsewhere, then the body was either moved or I failed to locate an additional wound."

Having given this explanation, I willed myself to be silent and still, waiting for Gage to reply. I did not think I needed to admit how greatly I dreaded having to return to the chapel cellar. If I could confirm my findings in any other manner, then I was determined to do so. And I wasn't going to let a simple letter warn me off this investigation, especially one with only an implied threat.

Gage continued to look at me as he tapped a hand against his thigh, considering the matter. After the struggle Philip encountered in convincing him to allow me to assist, I expected him to make at least a token resistance to my request. So when he nodded his agreement with nary a warning or a bargaining of conditions, I was flabbergasted. I wondered what such a reaction meant. Maybe he was only bluffing about allowing the letter to scare me off the investigation. Or perhaps my competency in examining Lady Godwin's body had persuaded him of my value as an assistant. It was more likely he was doing just as I'd proposed, allowing me to prove my findings on Lady Godwin's wounds without having to make me return to the cellar.

"Lord Cromarty and I will wait for you in the morning," he told me. His pale blue eyes shifted in the dim light. "Until then, good night." He turned back as he was leaving. "Oh, and Lady Darby?"

I nodded.

"Lock your door."

I shivered and moved forward to turn the key. After testing the door was secure, I stepped back to sit on the edge of my bed, trying to decipher the cryptic look I had seen in Gage's eyes at the last.

I had hoped that he was beginning to believe in my innocence, even after the comments relayed by Lord Westlock, but maybe I was wrong. Maybe he believed quite the opposite—after all, I had also discovered Lady Godwin had been expecting—and hoped I would slip up and incriminate myself.

I sighed and pressed my hand to my forehead, too tired to puzzle out such matters at this hour of night. The sun would be rising in less than four hours, and I needed to get some rest before I met Philip and Gage to examine the maze.

Besides, it didn't matter what Gage believed. I knew that I was innocent, and so did my sister and brother-in-law. All I could do was focus on what I had set out to do in the first place—protect my sister and her family by finding the real killer—and in the process, prove my innocence, perhaps once and for all.

CHAPTER SEVEN

I awoke the next morning to find Alana hovering over me, a frown pleating her brow.

"Oh, thank goodness," she exclaimed. "You're awake."

I hadn't been, but I suspected my sister had been standing there for quite some time and very well knew that.

"How are you feeling, dear?" She reached out to place her hand on my forehead, but then hesitated as if the touch might cause me pain. "Does your head ache?"

I scowled, wishing she would go away. It might be difficult for me to fall asleep, but once I did, I slumbered quite soundly. I was also rather cross upon waking, even in the best of circumstances. And especially when someone took it upon herself to wake me.

I swatted away her hands and pushed myself up carefully on the pillows stacked behind me.

"Here, let me help you with that," Alana insisted, fluffing and adjusting the bolsters.

I submitted to her ministrations for about half a minute before protesting. "They're plump enough, Alana."

She clasped her hands over her abdomen, as if she couldn't stop them from fussing over me any other way, and stared down at me in worry.

I sighed, knowing my sister meant well, even if her mothering this early in the morning was more than I could stand. "I'm fine. Just a little tender." I reached back to tentatively probe the lump on the back of my head.

"Mr. Gage said I should check on you," she admitted, sitting cautiously on the edge of the bed.

I closed my eyes and silently cursed the man. I should have known. Who else would have relayed the news about my injury? I highly doubted Lord Westlock had confessed to bashing me over the head to my sister.

"He shouldn't have told you," I snapped, angry that my sister now had something else to fret about.

"Of course he should have," she protested, her own considerable temper sparking. "You should have awakened me last night and sent for the physician. You could have been seriously injured."

"I'm fine," I reiterated sharply. "Waking you would have served no purpose beyond robbing you of sleep. Mr. Gage made certain the wound was not severe. Besides, you know the village physician is useless. He probably would have tried to bleed me."

"You still should have woken me." Alana shifted higher on the bed. Her bright blue eyes had darkened almost to violet against the deep purple of her gown. I suspected she had chosen the gown because it would be fitting for a state of half mourning. Lady Godwin was not a relative or royalty, but given the terrible circumstances of her death, and at my sister's residence of all places, Alana likely felt she should dress in half mourning out of respect for the deceased. I knew I would be expected to follow suit.

Which reminded me how much easier it was to allow my sister to believe she'd gotten her way, whether or not that was true. If I were ever bashed over the head in the middle of the night again, I still didn't plan on waking her, but she didn't need to know that.

I crossed my arms over my chest and glanced at the table next to my bed. "Have you brought me something to eat?" My stomach gurgled and asserted itself, reminding me how

I had cast up my accounts all over the floor of the cellar while Mr. Gage looked on. I felt a blush heat my cheeks at the memory.

Alana picked up the tray and settled it over my lap. I could smell the chocolate even before I lifted the lid of the pot. It was accompanied by toast and a crock of sweet strawberry jam, my normal morning repast. I quickly slathered the bread with jam and took a bite.

My sister watched me with a small smile curling her lips. She waited until I had swallowed several bites before saying anything else. "I'm grateful to Mr. Gage for taking care of you," she said, smoothing out a wrinkle on the skirt of her gown.

I hesitated in taking my next bite, waiting for her to elaborate, for I knew she had more to say.

Her gaze lifted to meet mine. "We've underestimated him, haven't we?"

I studied the deep red of the strawberry preserves. "Perhaps," I replied with a shrug. Popping the last bite of the first piece of toast into my mouth, I poured the warm chocolate into my cup to avoid my sister's eyes. I still held my doubts about Gage's motives, but I didn't feel it necessary to share them with Alana.

"Philip is acquainted with him, you know."

I looked up at her in question.

"Apparently, they attended school together. They were in the same class at Cambridge. Though Philip says for the first year and a half Mr. Gage had special permission to live off university grounds."

I was instantly curious as to why, but I kept my interest to myself. "Is that how he came to be invited to your house party?"

Alana shook her head. "No, Mrs. Cline asked me to include him on the guest list."

I wanted to roll my eyes, and just barely resisted, taking another drink of my rich chocolate. "So Philip didn't ask

Mr. Gage to conduct an investigation just on the basis of his father's reputation. He actually knows Mr. Gage."

"And seems to trust him." She pressed her lips together and watched me take another sip. "Kiera, if Philip trusts him, then I think perhaps we should as well."

I lowered my cup slowly and nodded. It did speak in Gage's favor that my brother-in-law had confidence in him. However, I still reserved my judgment. People changed, often for the worse. Just because Gage had been a good man a decade or more ago, it did not mean he was today. Besides, his belief in my innocence was not necessarily tied to how honorable a person he was. He could easily decide I'd duped my sister and brother-in-law into thinking I wasn't guilty and set out to save them from me. He wouldn't be the first to set upon such a course.

"What time is it?" I asked, glancing toward the clock on the mantel.

"Half past eight."

I pushed the tray forward and tentatively sat up all the way. My head still throbbed dully, but nothing like it had the night before.

"Should you be getting up?" Alana asked uncertainly.

"Why shouldn't I?" I countered. "Ring Lucy and ask her to bring a headache powder. I need to get dressed." I swung my legs over the side of the bed and paused to make sure my skull would not protest if I tried to stand.

My sister touched my arm to stop me. "There's no need to dress. I'm certain no one would mind if you kept to your rooms for the day and rested."

"I told Mr. Gage I would search the gardens with him and Philip. I assume they haven't already done so if Mr. Gage sent you to wake me." I rose to my feet and felt a slight pulse in my head from the change in posture, but otherwise it troubled me no more than it had when I was sitting down.

Alana stood with me. "Mr. Gage didn't send me to wake you," she protested.

I lifted my eyebrows at her. "Why else do you think he sent you to check on me?"

"Because he was worried about your health."

I moved across the room toward my wardrobe. "Maybe. But I have a feeling it was his way of expressing impatience to be at it without being so rude as to order you directly to wake me."

Alana frowned and crossed her arms over her chest. I could tell she wasn't pleased with the idea that Mr. Gage had manipulated her. I turned away to hide my smile and began flipping through my gowns, looking for something suitable for both half mourning and traipsing through the garden. I had left off wearing mourning garments for my husband far earlier than was socially acceptable, but since I lived in the Highlands, where no one saw me, I had been able to get away with it. Fortunately, I had kept a few gowns made up from my half-mourning period. A sturdy gray walking dress with black embroidery on the skirts and collar, and a black belt, seemed appropriate with my kid-leather ankle boots. I pulled the gown from the closet and moved to lay it across the bed.

My sister now stood by the bellpull, and I assumed she had followed my instructions and rang for Lucy. Her brow was furrowed, and I could tell she was puzzling over something. Trusting Alana would speak when she was ready, I poured water from the pitcher into the washbasin and began to scrub my face and neck clean, careful not to move my head too abruptly.

I heard my sister instruct Lucy to bring a headache powder when she appeared, and then Alana closed the door and moved back toward the bed to help me dress. She finally spoke when my back was to her as she loosely laced my corset, knowing how much I hated to be restrained too tightly during the day, especially when I was painting.

"Philip has informed me that I cannot throw Lord and

Lady Westlock out of our home, despite their actions toward you," she stated in a voice tight with anger.

I'd wondered if she knew exactly how I received the bump on my head, and was impressed she waited this long to mention it.

"If I had my way, they would already be banished from the grounds of Gairloch Castle." She tugged too hard on the laces, and I wriggled, letting her know to loosen the last loop. "I know I'm supposed to obey my husband in all things, particularly when I've been give a direct order, but in this I find I cannot."

She tied off my corset and turned me to face her, allowing me to see the rage I had only guessed at until that moment blazing in her jewel-bright eyes. Alana was absolutely furious.

"If you want me to, I will send them away this very minute, regardless of Philip's orders." She nearly spat the word, clearly displeased with her husband's command. "It is an insult to share a roof with them after the way they treated you. For you, I will get rid of them. If you want me to?" She pressed her lips together, likely to stop herself from saying more, and waited for me to reply.

I was touched by my sister's concern and, if truth be told, a little startled by her vehemence. I almost pitied the Westlocks, for Alana was certain to make the remainder of their stay quite uncomfortable. But they did deserve it, after all. Under any other circumstances, such behavior would have seen my brother-in-law flinging them from his home himself. Only the murder investigation saved them from his wrath.

And that being the case, I couldn't ask my sister to do such a thing for me, especially when it would get her in trouble with her husband. Philip possessed just as ferocious a temper as Alana when provoked, and disobeying a direct order would certainly provoke it. I had heard them argue enough times in the last sixteen months to know I did not want to be the cause of such a quarrel. Besides, Philip happened to be right. Lord and Lady Westlock could not leave the castle until after the procurator fiscal arrived to clear them of suspicion.

I lifted my hand and touched my older sister's arm. "It's all right," I assured her. "I know they have to stay."

Her shoulders sagged a bit, and I suspected that despite all her protestations to the contrary, she had not been looking forward to defying her husband in this. Her pride was bruised from being forced to provide accommodations to someone who had so blatantly harmed a member of her family, but I wondered if she was taking out some of her anger at the unnamed murderer on the Westlocks. It disturbed her, and rightfully so, that someone she had trusted enough to invite into her home would commit such a horrific act. It troubled me just to know I had dined with, and likely spoken to, such a person.

The fierce light in her eyes remained even as my sister nodded in acceptance of my decision. "All right, Kiera. They can stay, for now. But should you change your mind . . ."

I squeezed her arm. "I'll let you know."

She studied my face before her gaze rose to my head and the unruly morning waves of my hair. "Are you sure you feel well enough to assist Philip and Mr. Gage?" she asked, as lines of concern wrinkled her brow.

"Yes." I reached for my dress. "Besides, I don't think they know what to look for," I replied vaguely, not comfortable sharing the discovery I'd made about the state of Lady Godwin's health.

Alana did not question my unclear statement, and I supposed it was because she did not want to know. As strong and courageous as my sister was, that strength and courage did not carry over to matters of the internal workings of the human body. She had once asked me about the things I had seen during the years I was forced to assist my husband, and later confessed she had nightmares for a week afterward just from imaging the few things I told her. Telling her to think of the body as a work of art did not seem to console her as it did me.

She helped me guide the gray gown over my head, careful not to touch the sensitive spot on the back of my head. Styling my hair was going to be tricky.

"To be honest, with as much trouble as he gave us yesterday over the matter, I'm surprised to hear Mr. Gage is allowing you to help him today," Alana said as she fastened the buttons up the back of my dress.

"So am I," I admitted.

"You must be pleased that he seems to be taking you seriously?"

Lucy strolled through the door at that moment, brandishing my headache powder and cooing over my injury. I was relieved not to have to answer Alana's question. To me, the real quandary was not whether I was being taken seriously, but whether I was being taken seriously as an assistant, or as a suspect.

CHAPTER EIGHT

I managed to make it down the terrace steps and out of the earshot of anyone listening from the castle before rounding on Mr. Gage.

"What ungodly whim possessed you to tell my sister about my head injury?"

He threw up his hands in defense and paced a step away, his midnight-blue frock coat bunching at the shoulders. "She overheard me telling her husband," he defended, nodding at Philip.

My brother-in-law was frowning at the ground, his shoulders slouched forward, and I wondered again how fierce the argument between he and my sister had been that morning over the issue of the Westlocks.

"Well now, it wasn't very intelligent of you to hold such a conversation where Alana might overhear it," I scolded Gage, irritated that his carelessness had not only caused my sister distress but also stirred up a fight between her and her husband.

"How was I to know Lady Cromarty had permission to enter his lordship's study despite the fact that the door was closed?" he remarked dryly.

I glanced at Philip out of the corner of my eye in time to see the tick on one side of his jaw. So the Westlocks' continued presence at Gairloch was not the only dispute they had quarreled over this morning. Under the circumstances, I was impressed by my brother-in-law's discretion. Had the situation been reversed, I was certain Alana would have embarrassed Philip by retorting that he, in fact, did *not* have permission to enter her study at all times, as I knew she did not have consent to do so in this instance. However, Philip kept his mouth clamped tightly in a line and his gaze on the wet grass at our feet.

At barely nine in the morning, the Highland sun had not yet burned away the dew and lingering dampness of the night. I was grateful for the snug wrapping of my new walking boots. My slippers would have been soaked through a mere ten steps from the stone terrace.

Philip guided me across the stretch of lawn lying between the maze and the gardens proper. It was there that his wolfhounds liked to run and play with him and his seven-year-old son, Malcolm. Alana and I enjoyed watching their antics from the terrace, allowing them to mistakenly believe their laughter and voices did not carry so far. But laughter did not ring here today, only heavy silence. Even the birds seemed to have quieted their songs.

Tension coursed through Philip's body and into the stiff arm pressed against my own. Though I could do nothing about his unease over our current task, I could relieve him on one point. I squeezed his arm with my own. "She won't do anything foolish," I murmured when he glanced down at me.

The tightness around his brown eyes eased a fraction, even if the tautness of his mouth did not. He nodded once, telling me he understood what I was referring to. Alana wouldn't do anything rash. At least for the moment.

The entrance to the maze suddenly loomed before us, sending an unexpected quiver down my spine. I took a steadying breath as Philip addressed the footman he had stationed at the entrance to prevent anyone from entering. I wondered if he and Gage felt the same sick swirling in their stomachs at the prospect of revisiting the site of such a gruesome crime. Gage in particular seemed remarkably calm and unruffled. However, I suspected he was just better at hiding his emotions. Philip pulled my arm in tighter to his side and stepped inside the labyrinth. Gage followed close behind.

The maze was tucked into a corner of the wide cleared lawn on the eastern side of the castle. Forest bordered the maze on two sides, its tall trees stretching their long limbs over the hedges. In spring and summer, when the trees were lush and in bloom, they spread a canopy over the outermost path. I normally found the covering serene and charming, as sunlight filtered through the leaves and dappled the trail in front of me. But today the overhang of vegetation seemed more ominous, more menacing. I somehow doubted I would ever view the leafy bower in such a quaint and harmless manner ever again.

I wrapped my shawl tighter around my shoulders as we made our way deeper into the maze. Most of the path was cast in shadows, as the sun had yet to reach its pinnacle, and the chill of morning still clung to the land. My heart pounded faster with each step we took closer to the alcove where Lady Godwin's body had lain. So much so that by the time we approached the last turn, it was beating so hard I thought for certain Philip and Gage could hear it knocking inside my chest.

Philip paused just before we could see into the alcove and looked down at me. I could see the battle raging behind his eyes. He clearly wanted to protect me from further distress, but he also knew I would never have accompanied them on this errand if I did not think it was important. His faith in my good sense won out. He sighed rather gustily, as if he was giving in against his own better judgment, but he did not try to send me back to the castle. I squeezed his arm in gentle scolding, as well as reassurance.

Gage waited patiently behind us through this exchange. Only the shuffling of his feet told me how anxious he was to continue. Philip grimaced and stepped forward so that we could see into the niche.

As far as I could tell, the scene before me had remained undisturbed since the men removed Lady Godwin's body the night before. The pale cream stone bench was tacky with dried blood softened by the morning dew. The cool, damp air of night had blown away any lingering fumes of death, but I suspected I would still be able to smell the sharp stench of blood once I moved closer. Which, unfortunately, I needed to do to get on with this investigation, no matter how much I would rather keep my feet planted where they were.

Taking a deep breath, I released my grip on Philip's arm and followed Mr. Gage into the alcove. "Did you find anything last night when you moved the body?" I asked them, trying to go about this in as systematic a manner as possible.

"Nothing," Gage replied, kneeling next to the bench on the end where Lady Godwin's head had lain. "Although, we did remove her jewelry before placing her in the chapel cellar. Lord Cromarty has the items locked in his safe."

"What pieces was she wearing?"

Philip's voice softened as if thinking back. "A few rings, one with a rather large diamond, a sapphire-and-diamond necklace, and sapphire earbobs."

My eyes widened. Clearly the motive for her attack had not been theft. "What about a reticule? Was she carrying anything?"

"No. At least none that we found." Gage pointed at the corner of the stone seat. "What do you make of that?"

I knelt down next to him, careful not to touch the bench or the ground. Much of the blood that had covered the earth the night before had soaked into the dirt or been washed away by the dew, but I still felt squeamish about placing my skin against it. I suddenly wished I had worn gloves this morning instead of dismissing them so readily when Lucy offered them to me.

The blood on this end of the stone had left a predictable

pattern. Crimson streaked the limestone where Lady God-win's neck had lain, almost forming a complete stripe of color across the surface. A few droplets decorated the stone in irregular patterns from when she was moved. However, at the corner where Gage pointed there was a short strip of red, as well as a smudge of black. The leg of the bench below was sprayed with blood.

Wrinkling my nose at the blood's faint metallic scent, I leaned in closer to examine the inky black substance. "Have Beowulf and Grendel been kept away from this?" I asked Philip, wondering if perhaps his wolfhounds had found their way inside and disturbed the scene.

"They've been locked up in the stables since the incident," Philip replied, moving to stand behind me and Gage.

I racked my brain for potential substances that could match the stain. It was too dark to be mud or shoe polish. It could be ink, but it looked more like charcoal. I was about to give up and assume the marking had been left there prior to Lady Godwin's murder when I suddenly realized exactly what it was.

"It's kohl," I declared, turning toward Gage. "Lady God-win blackened her lashes and eyebrows. *This* must be how she received that bruise."

Gage rubbed his chin and nodded.

"Her neck must have already been cut," I continued excitedly. "It would explain the spray pattern on the stone here." I pointed at the leg and then rose to my feet. "Which means her throat was likely sliced right around here." I backed up a step, examining the grass and hedges around me for confirmation. "See. Look here." I slid closer to the alcove wall, indicating the crimson droplets scattered across several of the leaves. "When the murderer sliced her across the neck," I mimicked the gesture, "cutting her jugular, blood sprayed across the area. The murderer must have lost his grip on her, either accidentally or on purpose, and she fell forward, striking the corner of the bench."

I looked up to find Gage and Philip watching me with a bit of trepidation, and I realized, with a slight tremor of horror, that my voice had risen in enthusiasm and the corners of my mouth had worked themselves up into a smile. "I'm sorry," I stammered. "I guess I got a little carried away. I just . . ." I glanced back and forth between the men. "It was rather like fitting together a puzzle."

Philip was the first to recover and reached out to touch my arm in reassurance. "It's all right, Kiera."

I nodded and lowered my eyes, feeling hot shame burn my face. This wasn't a game. Lady Godwin had been murdered, and I had just described the killer's methods as if I were playing charades. I could hardly blame Gage for suspecting me of committing the crime after such a display.

I peeked up at him through my lashes to see he had turned away and was frowning at the hedge walls. That was not a good sign. Pressing a hand to my now-cramping stomach, I moved away to study the other end of the bench. The sooner I finished what I came to do, the sooner I could leave this place, and Mr. Gage.

I took a deep breath of the clearer air and allowed my eyes to slide over the stone, and the grass and hedges around it. As far as I could tell, the blood pattern fit what I would have expected, or at least what Sir Anthony had dictated should be expected when I took notes about blood flow during his dissections.

"Have you noticed anything else out of the ordinary?" Gage asked from just over my shoulder.

I nearly jumped. I had been so wrapped up in my thoughts, I hadn't heard him move closer. "No. Everything else appears as it should, considering the injuries that were inflicted."

He nodded, his gaze focused on the bench before us.

"What about you?" I ventured, and he glanced up at me. "Have you noticed anything else out of the ordinary?"

His pale blue eyes bore intensely into me, and I wondered

for a second if I should have kept my mouth shut. Perhaps he thought I was fishing for information. If I were in fact the killer, wouldn't I want to know whether he had uncovered any evidence against me?

I turned away, too tired and disturbed to continue staring him down. I began to move away, back toward the entrance, when he finally replied.

"Nothing," he murmured with a sigh. His pale eyes had lightened, and his lips were pressed together in a gesture of momentary defeat.

I realized then that he had been hoping to find some kind of lead, some clue as to which direction to take the investigation. He was disappointed, and perhaps a bit irritated.

"Something will turn up," I declared, carefully avoiding his eyes. I wasn't certain why I felt the need to offer him such encouragement, but I didn't like seeing him so frustrated.

He shifted his feet but did not reply.

"Are you ready to return to the castle?" Philip asked behind us.

Gage sighed again. "Yes. I don't think there's anything else to find here."

"Then if you have no objection, I'll also have the alcove cleaned and remove my footmen from guarding the entrance to the maze."

Gage nodded and fell into step beside Philip. However, I paused and stared at the turn that would take us farther into the maze. Something had caught my eye, something shiny, but I wasn't certain I had actually seen anything other than the reflection of light off a dewdrop.

"Kiera?"

I glanced distractedly at my brother-in-law. "Did you search deeper into the maze?" I asked, feeling some trepidation about moving in that direction now.

"Yes. Last night." Philip retraced his steps toward me. "What is it?"

I took a deep breath and forced myself to move my feet toward the far hedge wall. Either there was something there or there wasn't. I couldn't leave without investigating. If I asked one of the men to look and it turned out to be nothing more than a bit of water, I would feel ridiculous.

My nerves clanged as I approached, and I realized this definitely wasn't just a drop of dew. Tucked beneath the hedges, so far inside that the leaves almost completely concealed it from our view, lay an object made of some type of metal. It looked as if it had been dipped in red paint. However, I did not need my artist's eye to realize the crimson liquid was nothing so innocuous.

CHAPTER NINE

Gage knelt down beside me as I peered into the hedge trying to figure out exactly what the blood-coated object was. It wasn't a knife or a letter opener, but it definitely had a sharp point—two of them if my eyes did not deceive me.

Gage pulled a handkerchief from his pocket and used it to reach underneath the hedge. He carefully extracted the object and held it up between two fingers for us to examine.

"It's . . . a pair of embroidery scissors," I murmured in shock.

The shears were six to seven inches long and engraved with a finely wrought pattern of vines and flowers. The steel tips were smeared with blood, as well as the round finger holes. It was shocking to see the delicate, woman's instrument splattered with so much gore, and even more shocking to think of it being used for such a brutal purpose. It seemed impossible.

"Well done," Gage told me. He held the object up higher so that Philip could see it over our shoulders.

"Does this mean a woman committed the crime?" Philip seemed aghast. Clearly such a possibility had never crossed his mind.

"Not necessarily." With careful fingers, Gage closed the scissors and wrapped them several times in his handkerchief. "A man could have grabbed them from a sewing basket just as easily as a woman. But it does present some interesting possibilities. I would like to know whose scissors these are, and whether they realize they are missing." A look of grim determination crossed his features. He reached out his free hand to cup my elbow to help me rise.

Philip frowned. "I shall ask my wife for a list of all known scissors on the premises of Gairloch. That will tell us whether these were brought with a guest or taken from somewhere in the castle."

"Gentlemen, these are embroidery scissors," I pointed out. They stared blankly back at me. "That narrows our search considerably, especially when you consider that only a lady would own a pair with such exquisite engraving," I explained. "And I can tell you right now that Alana's embroidery scissors have figural bird handles, and I do not own a pair. So it is likely that this pair belongs to one of the guests. But that is not our only problem."

Gage's brow puckered in confusion. "What do you mean?"

I sighed, knowing he was not going to like the information I had to share. "There is no way that those scissors were used to slice open Lady Godwin's throat. The cut was much too clean. Only a very sharp knife could have managed such a task. The scissors are either a secondary weapon or . . ." I paused. "Or they were placed here for us to find."

Gage and Philip looked at each other.

"You're certain the scissors couldn't have sliced her neck?" Gage asked me. "They look quite sharp to me."

"As positive as I can be, given the circumstances."

"Then we definitely have a problem." He turned away and lifted his free hand to rake it through his golden locks. All the while his eyes stared at the bloody scissors inside his handkerchief.

I looked at Philip to find him studying me. He smiled tightly, and I wondered what he was thinking. Philip had defended me fiercely, alongside my brother, when the accusations of unnatural tendencies and desecrating the dead had been leveled against me in London, but I don't know that he ever actually contemplated what exactly I had endured in my late husband's private examination rooms. Knowing that a person spent time with sliced-open dead bodies is entirely different than being presented with the evidence of such experience.

"Could the scissors have made the incisions in Lady Godwin's abdomen?" Gage asked.

I closed my eyes, thinking back to my examination of the wounds in the cellar last night. "I . . . I believe so. It would have taken considerable effort, but the cuts were ragged, so it seems possible." I looked at Philip, still addressing Gage. "Does he know about . . ."

"The baby?" Philip finished, answering my question. "Yes."

"Does Alana?" I asked him.

His brown eyes were troubled. "No. And I would prefer she not," he added softly.

I nodded.

"What do you suppose the killer did with it?" Gage contemplated, pulling my gaze from Philip. "The baby?" he clarified in response to my confused stare.

I had wondered the very same thing. "Buried it?" I suggested. "Threw it in the loch?" It seemed wrong to discuss the young child's fate so callously, and to call the baby *it*, but we had no way of knowing whether it had been a boy or girl, and somehow I didn't want to. It would make it all that much more personal.

"If the baby was buried, do you think your wolfhounds could find it?"

"Yes," Philip replied. "If a wild animal hasn't already."

I squeezed my eyes shut tight, not wanting to contemplate such a gruesome occurrence.

"I'll take them out to search the grounds immediately," Philip declared. "Perhaps another murder weapon will also turn up, or a jacket or shirt, something that might give us a clue as to the killer's identity."

Gage nodded. "That would be nice. But so far I haven't seen any indication that our murderer is going to make it so easy."

Philip hurried off toward the stables while I struggled to keep up with Gage's long strides as he crossed the lawn toward the castle. His hands tucked into the pockets of his light brown trousers and his head bowed toward the ground, he seemed lost in thought and completely oblivious to my difficulties.

"What are *you* going to do now?" I huffed and lifted my skirts to move faster. I wondered why he wasn't accompanying my brother-in-law.

Gage slowed and allowed me to catch up. "*We* are going to interview Lady Lydia Perkins and Mr. Tuthill." My face must have reflected my extreme surprise, for he laughed. "Come now, Lady Darby. Thus far you've proven yourself to be an invaluable assistant. After all, you discovered not only that Lady Godwin was enceinte but also the manner in which she received the bruise to her face, as well as a potential murder weapon."

"You found the black smudge." I felt it necessary to point out.

"True enough. But you were far quicker than I in connecting it to Lady Godwin's bruise." His voice was tinged with disgruntlement, and I wondered if he begrudged me this achievement as he'd seemed to do when I discovered that Lady Godwin had been expecting.

"What about the letter? Did you tell my sister and brother-in-law about it?" I was reluctant to ask, worried such a reminder would change his mind again about my involvement in the investigation, but I needed to know how much Alana and Philip knew.

"No. I would have told Cromarty, but your sister interrupted us."

I nodded and cleared my throat. "I would prefer it if they both remained ignorant for the time being. There's no need to worry them unnecessarily," I explained, staring down at the hem of my skirts as they sliced through the grass.

Gage glanced sideways at me, studying me for several heartbeats before shrugging. "That's your decision. In any case, neither Lady Lydia nor Mr. Tuthill, nor our murderer, for that matter, will think twice about your presence while I question them, since you arrived on the scene soon after." His head tilted to the side. "How were you able to get there so swiftly, by the way?"

"I was just over the hedge inside the maze," I answered honestly, irritated by his suspicious tone. "I actually didn't realize anyone was so close until Lady Lydia screamed." I peered at Gage out of the corner of my eye and decided turnabout was fair play. "And what about you?" He turned to me curiously. "Why did it take you so *long* to arrive on the scene? You were nearly the last to appear."

He pressed his lips tightly together. "I was otherwise engaged."

"In the gardens?" I queried innocently. "Were you picking flowers or attempting to climb the split-trunked yew tree? Perhaps to impress some fair lady?"

His mouth compressed into such a thin line that his lips almost disappeared. He watched me warily, as if uncertain how to respond to such questioning from a genteel female.

I let him squirm a moment longer before allowing my lips to curl into a satisfied smile, amused by his discomfort. His eyes flared wide in shock before narrowing. I thought he might scold me, but then he surprised me by breaking into a wide, boyish grin. The beauty of that flash of white did more to stifle my mirth than any reprimand ever could have.

"I suppose I deserved that. I must remember that you are not some shy, retiring maiden," he jested right back at me. "But a widow who has seen far more than her fair share of the world, and men's anatomy, than most women of your breeding."

I colored at his crude reference to the lower extremities of my husband's dissection subjects. "I hardly viewed them in such a lewd manner," I replied crossly.

"Then how *did* you view them?" he asked.

His impertinent grin made me want to stick my tongue out at him like a five-year-old. However, the genuine interest that rang in his voice made me consider my next words carefully. He waited patiently as I sorted through my thoughts and impressions of that difficult time.

"I . . . I thought of them as subjects of a portrait."

Gage turned to me with a look I couldn't quite decipher.

"It was easier, you see, to think of them as living—just lying there . . . very, very still . . . or asleep," I tried to explain. "Especially those first few times." I stared down at my feet as we walked. "Under those circumstances, it wasn't difficult to find the beauty in the angle of their cheekbones, or the carmine shade of their hearts, or the intricate stretch of the tendons connecting their muscles. They were just showing me more of themselves than my normal clientele. The light and passion and desires that swim in the eyes of the living were gone, but the rest of them was open to me."

Gage was very quiet, and I wondered if I had inadvertently just proven myself as crazy as most people thought I was by admitting such a thing. I frowned, angry at myself for sharing something so intimate with a virtual stranger— one who was conducting an investigation in which I was quite possibly considered a suspect.

We had nearly reached the terrace before he finally spoke, and when he did, it was to make a rather insightful but unexpected statement. "Is that 'light' you see in others' eyes the reason your portraits are so special?" he murmured softly. It was phrased as a question, but I was rather certain I was not supposed to answer. I'm not sure I could have in any case.

Gage offered me his arm as we approached the terrace steps to the castle, and at first I thought the tingling along my hairline came from his touch. But as a tendril of unease crawled down my spine, I realized that was not the case at all. I hesitantly lifted my eyes to the castle facade, allowing my gaze to sweep over the numerous windows winking in the morning light. A shadow among the drapes on the third floor of the deserted western block made my heart stutter in my chest. My footsteps faltered, and Gage glanced down at me in question.

"Lady Darby?"

I blinked up at him. "Did you see that?" My voice sounded breathless.

"See what?" he asked, following my gaze back up to the window. The shadow was now gone.

I pressed a hand to my forehead, wondering if I was seeing things. I could have sworn someone had been watching us from that window just a moment ago. Did they notice my interest and step back behind the drapes, or was my lack of sleep, and the strange events of the night and morning, simply getting to me?

"Lady Darby?" Gage pressed. Lines of worry radiated from his eyes.

"Oh, nothing," I replied with false confidence. "Just a trick of the light." I offered him a reassuring smile, hoping he wouldn't press further. The last thing I needed to admit to Gage was that I was either imagining things or someone was following our movements. Both would see me removed from this investigation, and I had no intention of stepping aside. Not with so much at stake.

In short order, Mr. Gage, Lady Lydia, Mr. Tuthill, and I were ensconced in a parlor in the family wing sipping tea. It was a small chamber decorated in comfortably worn furniture the shades of new leaves and lemon yellow. On gloomy days, I often read there, for it was bright and cheerful even in the dreariest weather.

Lady Lydia perched at the edge of a green damask settee admiring Gage out of the corner of her eye. She seemed to believe she was doing this surreptitiously, but each time she snuck a glance, she managed to somehow set the caramel-brown curls surrounding her face to bouncing. It was an annoying little gesture that set my teeth on edge. I would have liked nothing more than to inform her of it, but even I knew such a comment would be terribly impolite.

Mr. Tuthill, for his part, was also not oblivious to Lady Lydia's interest in Gage, but he seemed resigned to it. He drank his tea and avoided looking at all of us. I felt a bit sorry for the man. As the second son of a baron, with a moderate income and moderate good looks, he was easy to overlook, and he clearly had developed an interest in the Earl of Yeomouth's youngest sister. One that I thought Lady Lydia returned, even if she *was* currently distracted by a bigger and far more attractive fish. However, Mr. Tuthill seemed sensitive to the fact that Gage would never pursue the girl, and so if he could just tolerate this interview, he would likely never have to endure another one.

"Well," Gage declared, leaning forward to set his teacup and saucer on the table before him. "I'm certain you all understand the reason I have summoned you here."

I wanted to raise my eyebrows at his use of the word "all," but refrained, knowing he expected me to play my part—which included not allowing Lady Lydia and Mr. Tuthill to know I was assisting Gage with his investigation.

He tapped his finger against the wooden arm of his cream-upholstered Hepplewhite chair. "Mr. Tuthill, Lady Lydia," he said, nodding at each of them. "You were the first to . . . stumble across Lady Godwin, correct?"

Lady Lydia nodded, casting her eyes downward demurely and pouting her lips in a manner so pretty I was quite certain she had practiced it to perfection.

"That is correct," Mr. Tuthill replied, setting his own teacup aside. He tugged down on his hunter-green waistcoat nervously and stole a glance at Lady Lydia.

"Can you describe what happened?" Gage prompted, addressing Mr. Tuthill man-to-man.

Mr. Tuthill and Lady Lydia shared a quick look before he formulated a reply. "Well, we were strolling through the maze, trying to find our way to the center. And . . . well . . . we passed the alcove, and there she was."

I wondered whether there was something he was leaving out between the "and" and "well." Something like a kiss. It would explain the man's nerves, as well as the harmless impression I received from them.

"It was horrid!" Lady Lydia cried, really setting her curls to bouncing. "*I've* never *seen* something so ghastly in *all* my life!" Her already wide eyes rounded even more as they turned to me, having realized belatedly the implication that could be made from her statement.

I ignored the girl's distress, knowing it would only make matters worse to address it, and turned to Gage, waiting for him to lead them on with another question. His gaze met mine briefly, and I thought I saw amusement shining in their depths. Whether that humor was at Lady Lydia, me, or the entire situation, I could not be sure.

"Did you see anyone else?" he asked Mr. Tuthill. "Did you notice anyone entering the maze before you?"

"No, sir."

"Did you hear any suspicious noises?"

Mr. Tuthill's eyes lifted toward the ceiling in thought before returning to Gage. "No, sir. I don't believe so."

"What of you, Lady Lydia? Did you hear or see anything?"

She shook her head, and the curls bounced.

Gage frowned, tapping his lip with an index finger. "So when you saw Lady Godwin and the state she was in, you screamed?"

"Yes." She nodded. Bounce. Bounce.

"And I believe I shouted," Mr. Tuthill added.

Gage flicked a glance at him before returning his focus to Lady Lydia. "And you kept screaming?"

Nod. Bounce. Bounce.

"Even after Lady Darby arrived?"

"It was just such a frightening sight," she exclaimed, pressing her hand to her heart. "You're ever so brave for investigating such a gruesome matter," she added breathlessly. Bounce.

"Yes, well." Gage seemed unimpressed by her adoration. "Mr. Tuthill acquitted himself quite admirably, catching you when you swooned and carrying you back to the castle." He nodded at the baron's second son, whose chest seemed to expand with pride.

"Oh, yes," Lady Lydia agreed, turning toward Mr. Tuthill. "He did, indeed."

Gage shared another humored look with me while the two young lovers stared into each other's eyes.

"How long would you say it was until Lady Darby arrived?"

Mr. Tuthill blinked, re-collecting himself. "Only the matter of a few seconds."

Gage's attention swung to me, to play out this last little part of our charade. "Did you see Lady Lydia and Mr. Tuthill enter the maze?"

"No. And I saw no one else enter before or after me."

He nodded. "Do you know the maze well?"

"I do," I replied, feeling the other witnesses' eyes on me. I suddenly had the horrible urge to giggle, and had to fight to suppress it. Gage did not help matters with his eyes twinkling at me. "I can walk straight to the center without a wrong turn. I imagine if Lady Lydia and Mr. Tuthill made enough errors trying to find the correct path . . ." *or stopped to kiss often enough* ". . . I could have easily caught up with them."

Gage and I turned to look at them.

Mr. Tuthill cleared his throat. "We did, indeed, take several wrong turns."

Lady Lydia's cheeks flushed a pretty pink.

"How long did it take until others arrived?" Gage queried.

I glanced at Mr. Tuthill. "But a few minutes?" He nodded in agreement. "We could hear their shouts and curses as they tried to find us in the maze."

Lady Lydia blushed brighter. "I passed out before then."

Gage tapped a finger on the chair arm again as he thought. "Did you notice if anyone acted strangely or suspiciously?"

I furrowed my brow, trying to remember, but all I could recall was that I'd looked away from their faces. I'd been too worried about my own presence being noticed to pay much attention to anyone else. "I don't know," I replied haltingly. "I don't really remember."

Mr. Tuthill shook his head. "My attention was focused on Lady Lydia."

Gage nodded, watching me closely. "Are you aware of anything else I should know?" he continued, focusing on Mr. Tuthill and Lady Lydia again. "Connections Lady Godwin had with the other guests? Disputes she may have had with anyone?"

Mr. Tuthill flushed faintly, and his gaze flicked to Lady Lydia. I suspected he had caught the meaning of "connections" Gage intended. "Er . . . I will think on it and get back to you," he replied. Talk of extramarital affairs was not polite conversation for young, unwed women.

"I know Lord Godwin is out of the country," Lady Lydia chimed in. "And Lady Stratford and she were close friends."

Gage's eyes flared slightly at this tidbit of knowledge. "Then she would be a good person with whom to speak. Thank you, Lady Lydia."

She beamed. And her curls bounced.

"Well," Mr. Tuthill proclaimed, rising to his feet. "If

there is nothing more?" Apparently, he'd taken all the fawning over Gage he could handle.

Gage stood with him. "That's all for now. Should you think of anything else, please let me know."

"We will." Mr. Tuthill shook his hand and then offered Lady Lydia his arm.

She allowed him to escort her from the room, even though she was gazing over her shoulder at Gage until they vanished from sight.

"When would you like to interview Lady Stratford?" I asked, avoiding his gaze while I smoothed down the skirts of my dress as I rose.

"Hold on. Before we come to that." He moved closer and lowered his voice. "Do you truly not remember how the others reacted to Lady Godwin's murder?"

"I . . . I looked away from their faces," I admitted.

He seemed stunned.

"Well, I didn't know I was going to be assisting in an investigation into the matter," I replied crossly. "I was shocked. I . . . I may have seen corpses, but I'd never seen someone who was so obviously *murdered*." I worried my hands together and risked another glance at his face.

"Of course," Gage replied consolingly. He reached out to touch my arm, and I let him, needing the contact of another person.

I swallowed. "So before or after luncheon?" I asked, harking back to my question about Lady Stratford and hoping he wouldn't try to discourage me from joining him.

"After. I have some things I need to do first."

I nodded.

His arm fell to his side as he stepped away, and I felt the loss of his touch more acutely than I expected.

"Until then," he said, a faint frown marring his brow, and then quit the room.

I reached up to cradle the spot where the warmth from his hand still lingered on my gray walking dress. My skin underneath seemed to tingle a bit, and I closed my eyes to better appreciate it.

When I realized what I was doing, I jerked my hand from my arm and opened my eyes. What ridiculousness! I glanced at the settee where Lady Lydia had sat, and shook my head. I was not some silly girl with romantic notions in her head. I didn't want to be.

And with that firm reminder, I escaped to the familiar solitude of my art studio.

CHAPTER TEN

Several hours in my studio did much to soothe my tattered nerves worn raw by the events of the last sixteen hours. The familiar roughness of the charcoal in my hand as I sketched the outline of a new portrait comforted me. Its musk of earth and ashes permeated the air, clearing away the lingering memory of blood and death. I lost myself in the sweep of lines, forgetting place and time.

That is, until Mr. Gage's summons recalled me to it. I sighed at the sight of his message delivered by one of the maids, suddenly reluctant to return to the uncertainty of the investigation. It was easier, safer, to remain immersed in my art. But I had promised Alana I would find answers, and as I returned to reality, my own natural curiosity reasserted itself.

So I consumed several cold bites of the soup of summer squash, which the servants had brought me for luncheon probably hours before, and set out to find Mr. Gage.

I found him pacing before the fireplace in the sunny family parlor where we had interviewed Lady Lydia and Mr. Tuthill. His hands were clasped behind his back and his head bowed as if deep in thought. I hesitated to make myself known, taking a moment to observe his unguarded expression and the deep lines of frustration crisscrossing his brow.

He seemed in that moment like a caged animal circling his enclosure.

He glanced up as he pivoted and, upon catching sight of me, wiped his face clear of all emotion. "Ah! There you are," he declared, moving toward me. He did not sound irritated, but impatient. He was not pleased to have been kept waiting. "Where did you disappear to?"

I was tempted to point out that he had not divulged the destination of *his* urgent business, but I suspected he intended to be vague about his plans earlier and would only smile enigmatically and change subjects. Perversely, it made me want to be just as mysterious. "Does it matter?" I challenged. "I'm here now. Are you ready to interview Lady Stratford?"

He smiled as if amused by my display of defiance. "It doesn't matter. Though why you are so reluctant to admit you were in your art studio baffles me." He reached out to swipe a finger gently across my cheek, bringing it away smudged with charcoal.

Feeling heat steal into my cheeks, I scowled and wiped my palm across my face to remove any lingering traces of the powder.

"Here, allow me." He pulled a handkerchief from his pocket and grasped my jaw between his thumb and forefinger.

I jerked back from his touch. "That's not necessary." I held my hand out for the square white cloth.

His smile widened, but he relinquished his hold on the handkerchief. I fought a blush as I studied my visage in the mirror hanging on the wall behind the door and carefully removed all traces of my art supplies, including a smudge of yellow paint from the side of my left palm. I wasn't certain why I felt so embarrassed by my rumpled appearance. It had never much mattered to me before, but I did know that I did not like the cheeky grin stretching across Gage's face as he stood over my shoulder watching me. I handed the cloth back to him with a curt thank-you, even though I felt more like tossing it in his face. He nodded, folded the square, and tucked it back into his pocket.

"Now," I pronounced, crossing my arms over my chest. "Lady Stratford?"

He cleared his throat. "Yes. We shall be speaking with her in her chambers." I followed him toward the door. "I took the liberty of sending her a note requesting an audience." He chuckled. "The countess is quite a proper bit of muslin. I knew she wouldn't be able to rudely dismiss such a formal request."

I frowned in confusion. "Would she have refused to be interviewed?"

"Only as a matter of principle." His eyes twinkled. "You should know that Lady Stratford does not like me very much."

"Well then, that's something we have in common," I replied tartly.

He did not seem hurt by my comment. "Come now. I know that can't be true. You like me well enough," he said with patronizing certainty.

I arched an eyebrow but decided not to contradict the infuriating man. "Is she waiting for us now?"

He smiled knowingly, which almost convinced me that an argument would not be such a waste of time. "Yes. And I'll be blaming you for making us late."

"That's fine. I doubt she cares much for my company, either. This shall make for an interesting conversation," I remarked dryly. I glanced up at him out of the corner of my eye. "Why *are* you allowing me to accompany you? I half expected you to visit Lady Stratford by yourself and inform me of it later."

"Well," he hedged. "As I said, she is quite staid and proper. I wasn't certain she would see me alone. I thought the company of a female might help smooth things along." He cleared his throat as we turned a corner. "By the way, she's not actually aware that *you* will be the female accompanying me."

I turned to look up at him.

"I may have led her to believe your sister would be the one joining us."

I sighed. It was no wonder Lady Stratford didn't like the man. I wondered if she would turn us away when she discovered he had duped her by bringing me instead.

"Don't worry," he told me confidently. "I have it all figured out."

I doubted that, but I was willing to play along. The nasty comments Lady Stratford was sure to make about me would not be pleasurable, but I thought I might enjoy watching Gage have the door slammed in his face. When she turned us away, I would send Alana to speak with her, armed with all the questions I had for the countess. In the end, I would find a way to get the information I wanted.

Lady Stratford and her husband had been placed in a suite of rooms near the end of the southeast hall block. As we passed by, I realized that Lady Godwin's assigned chamber had only been several doors away. I wondered if my sister had placed them in such proximity because she was aware of their friendship, or if it had been merely a happy coincidence.

The Stratfords' suite was one of the best and largest in the castle. Each room was decorated in sumptuous shades of chocolate and pale sky blue, with gold and buttercup yellow. Most of the furniture was heavily ornamented in a rococo style, although Alana had softened the heavy gilding by simplifying the cloth and wall patterns to solids and wide, uncomplicated prints. The his and hers bedchambers were connected by two dressing rooms and a comfortable parlor.

It was at the door of this parlor that Gage paused and knocked. Lady Stratford's maid showed us in before disappearing through the dressing room to collect her mistress.

When the countess appeared, it was clear that the maid

had already informed her of my presence. Her eyes immediately narrowed on me. The soft gray of her irises had hardened to chips of ice. "Mr. Gage," she bit out in clipped tones. "If I might have a word with you."

I stepped away from the grouping of furnishings at the center of the room and moved to stare out a window on the opposite side of the chamber at the garden below. The wind rippled the leaves on the trees just as the chill in Lady Stratford's voice ruffled my nerves. I hated being confronted with others' disgust and prejudice over something they knew nothing about. It angered me and made me feel small and helpless. I bit my lip to withhold all the words burning inside of me, as I always did, and strained to hear Gage and Lady Stratford's conversation.

"What is she doing here?" Lady Stratford hissed.

"Her sister was detained and asked her to accompany me," Gage replied in conciliatory tones.

"I realize that Lady Cromarty believes her sister innocent as a baby lamb, a testament to her loyalty, I'm sure." The countess didn't sound as though she placed much value in familial devotion. "But the fact remains that most of society believes her unnatural. Is she not your prime suspect?"

"Haven't you ever heard the old adage 'Keep your friends close, but your enemies closer'?" he whispered.

I tensed, wondering just how much of this conversation was truth and how much fiction. Did Gage view me as the enemy?

It irritated me to live with this doubt, especially in the face of the upheaval already caused by Lady Godwin's murder. Did I not already have enough to worry about without suspicion and betrayal being thrown into the mix?

I did not hear Lady Stratford's response, but she must have given her consent, for Gage called me over. He smiled at me as we settled into our seats, but I could not force myself to smile back. Not in the face of his duplicity and Lady Stratford's naked displeasure.

It was remarkable how much a disagreeable expression could sour beauty. Lady Stratford often reminded me of a china shepherdess, with her pale blonde hair, porcelain skin, and slight figure. She was both the picture of hearty country living and fragile womanhood. But a year younger than my sister, Lady Stratford had caused quite a stir the year of her debut. It was rumored that every eligible nobleman had vied for her hand, from dukes to second sons. The ton had delighted in her marriage to the roguish and elusive Earl of Stratford, happy to see a gentleman who had fought the bonds of matrimony for so many years finally caught in its net. She was certainly a diamond of the first water. However, at that moment, with her lips pursed and her eyes hard, she looked anything but lovely and soft.

"How may I help you?" she finally asked Gage, folding her hands over the lavender skirts of her gown. I had not failed to notice she was also wearing half-mourning colors.

"It has come to my attention that you were a good friend of Lady Godwin," he began gently. His gaze dipped to take in her dress, letting me know he had not missed the significance of the color, either. "I wondered if you might answer a few questions for me. To aid in my investigation."

Lady Stratford lowered her eyes for a second. I watched her reaction carefully, perplexed by the nervous fidgeting of her hands. She stilled them when she caught me observing her and turned back to Gage. "I will hear your questions, though I cannot promise I will know the answers," she replied.

He studied her for a moment and then nodded. "Of course." He settled deeper into the chocolate and gold bergère chair. "First, I've been led to believe that Lord ~~Stratford~~ is currently in India?" *Godwin*

She nodded carefully. "That is correct."

"Do you know how long ago he left England?"

She tilted her head in thought. "It was just after the first of the year. I remember I was surprised he would undertake such a journey in the midst of winter. So . . . seven, almost eight months ago now, perhaps."

We were interrupted by the arrival of the tea tray, and Gage shared a glance with me while the maid settled the dishes. If Lord Godwin had departed England almost eight months ago, then Lady Godwin's baby had most certainly not been her husband's.

Lady Stratford poured the tea, politely asking how we liked ours prepared. Then she dispensed hers from a separate, smaller pot included with our tea service that I had been puzzling over. "It's made with red raspberry leaf," she explained when I caught her eye. "For my health." Her eyes cast down again and a pale pink blush suffused her complexion.

"Did Lady Godwin consider accompanying her husband to India?" Gage asked, jumping right back into the conversation where we left off.

"No. At least, I don't believe so. And never did either of them act as if she would. From the very moment Lord Godwin mentioned he would be making such a trip, it was presented as if he would go alone."

"How long did he plan to be gone?"

She took a dainty sip of her tea. "I can't say. Though . . ." She tilted her head to the side in a manner I was coming to realize meant she was thinking. "Helena had mentioned something about his returning before summer's end. But that was months ago. His plans may have changed."

Gage set his cup aside.

"More tea?" she asked.

"Uh, no, thank you."

His brow furrowed, and I realized he was trying to formulate his next question delicately. However, Lady Stratford perhaps did not understand this, and chose to view his expression in a more anxious light. She took another hasty sip of tea and began to fiddle with the gem dangling from her necklace. It sparkled a deep red, almost maroon—probably a garnet.

"My lady, do you know of anyone who might have wished Lady Godwin harm?"

Lady Stratford stiffened. "Wish her harm?" she asked vaguely.

"Yes. Someone she competed against or feuded with? Someone who did not like her?" Gage elaborated.

She set her tea on the table in front of her carefully and cleared her throat. "Clearly, neither of you knew Lady Godwin beyond a passing acquaintance. Because if you did, you would realize she was not the easiest person to get along with." Lady Stratford's eyes flicked to me. "Particularly for other women." She licked her lips and sat back, still rolling the jewel between her fingers. "She was vain and calculating and duplicitous, and prone to make cutting remarks." Her face had hardened in anger as she recited these not-so-positive traits about her companion.

"Pardon me," I said, speaking up for the first time since we entered the room. "But if Lady Godwin was so difficult, then why were you such close friends?"

Lady Stratford smiled wearily, as if I'd just asked a very naive question. "Because it was easier to be her friend than not. Because *she* wanted to be close to *me*."

I studied her features now that the scowl had faded. "Because you're beautiful?"

Her smile turned more genuine, though tinged with a somewhat bitter amusement. "Yes. That was part of it."

From the first, I had seen how someone as concerned with her good looks as Lady Godwin would not want to be outshone by a beauty like Lady Stratford. It was much more pleasant to pretend that you shared the attention and admiration.

"So Lady Godwin had many enemies?" Gage asked.

Lady Stratford nodded hesitantly. "Yes, potentially."

"Any that you believe might commit murder?"

She pressed her hands together palm to palm and stared down at her lap. "I cannot honestly say," she replied in a soft voice. She swallowed. "It seems quite impossible that it actually happened. She may not have been well liked, but I never believed she was so hated as to be murdered." Her arms shook slightly, and I realized she was holding her hands together to try to control her emotions. I wished she would look up so that I might see her eyes.

"I'm sorry. I know this must be difficult," Gage said softly in sympathy.

She nodded.

"If I may, just a few more questions, and I will trouble you no further."

She took a deep breath and finally looked up, giving him permission to continue. Her eyes were shiny and rimmed in red from unshed tears.

Gage shifted uncomfortably in his seat. "It is widely known that Lady Godwin has taken lovers, particularly in the months since her husband left the country."

Lady Stratford did not confirm or deny this.

"Most recently, she has been linked with Mr. Fitzpatrick." He shifted again, and I wondered, with some amusement, whether he was about to tug on his cravat. "Are you aware of any other men with whom she has . . . carried on liaisons?"

Lady Stratford seemed entertained by his discomfort as well. Her pale pink lips tipped up at the corners. "And what makes you think I would share any such information with you?" She raised her eyebrows in scolding.

"Because I think one of Lady Godwin's past lovers may have had something to do with her death."

CHAPTER ELEVEN

I could have smacked Gage for all the subtlety he used in making such a statement. For all my social awkwardness and impatience with the ton, I would never have made such a bald declaration, especially to a woman who was so obviously grieving her friend, even if it was in her own restrained manner.

Being the reserved matron she was, Lady Stratford fortunately did not burst into tears or histrionics. However, a curtain seemed to be pulled over her features, removing all trace of humor, light, and joy, leaving her cast in shadow. Her hands tightened in her lap, and she turned away to stare at the windows looking out on the garden.

I scowled at Gage, not understanding how someone who was so well-known for his charm could be so tactless. He frowned back at me, and then tightly shook his head before focusing his gaze on Lady Stratford once again. Recognizing such a dismissal when I saw one, I bit my tongue. Perhaps he wanted to play this out as if his shocking declaration had been deliberate, but I was not convinced his nerves had not compelled him to be so blunt.

The countess heaved a weary sigh. "I'm sure there are many here in this castle who could, and would love to, comment upon Helena's escapades," she said, her gaze still focused on the window. "After all, she was never very discreet. And she had a rather masculine desire to flaunt her conquests. So I suppose I would not be betraying her by telling you. Perhaps I would even be doing her a favor by relaying the information through friendly lips rather than venomous ones." Her soft gray eyes turned to study each of us in turn as we waited patiently for her to finish. "Other than Mr. Fitzpatrick . . ." She trailed off as if she were still having difficulty answering. She swallowed. "There are only two other men in attendance who have shared her bed. If I tell you those, will that be sufficient?"

"For now," Gage replied gently.

Lady Stratford nodded, understanding the words he left unspoken. Just because a jilted lover was not at Gairloch Castle did not mean he was not a suspect. He could have hired someone to carry out the murder, believing himself safely removed from discovery.

The countess took a deep breath. "Lord Marsdale and Mr. Calvin."

Mr. Calvin came as somewhat of a shock, but I was definitely not surprised to hear that Lord Marsdale was on the list. The Duke of Norwich's son was an ill-mannered swine, by whom I had already had the misfortune of being accosted twice during his stay.

"Do you recall how long ago they were involved?" Gage asked.

Lady Stratford tilted her head. "Marsdale was not long after Lord Godwin left for India, and Mr. Calvin perhaps some time in May or June."

I slid toward the edge of my seat and glanced at Gage, knowing he would realize what that meant. My excitement must have been more evident than I wished, for I turned to find Lady Stratford watching me carefully and guardedly. Something in her demeanor told me it was not fear of me as a suspect but fear of my knowledge.

"One more question," Gage announced, seeming oblivious to our unspoken exchange. "Was Lord Godwin aware of her affairs?"

Lady Stratford's eyebrows lifted. "How could he not be? But since she provided him with two sons, an heir and a spare, he pretty much allowed her to do as she wished."

Gage nodded and rose. "Thank you. We shall not trouble you further."

I followed him to the door, but a question still nagged at me. I paused on the threshold and turned back to the countess still seated on the pale blue settee. "One more thing. Did Lady Godwin confide in you what her plans were after leaving here?"

Lady Stratford met my gaze squarely, and I knew she realized what I was really asking. I half expected her to dismiss me without replying, but she nodded her head once and spoke with quiet dignity. "She planned to stay at an estate owned by my great-aunt, just north of Glasgow. She said she wanted the peace and quiet."

I opened my mouth to thank her when her lady's maid suddenly appeared through the door to the dressing room. "I have your chasteberry tonic, my lady." The servant stumbled to a halt, carefully balancing the small glass full of liquid. "Oh! I beg your pardon." She flushed a bright rose, almost as deep as the tonic. The girl had obviously believed the countess was alone.

"I was just leaving," I said to reassure the maid. With a nod of thanks to Lady Stratford, I closed the door.

"What was that all about?" Gage asked, waiting for me several steps down the corridor.

"She knew she was expecting."

His steps faltered. "What?"

"Lady Stratford knew that Lady Godwin was expecting," I reiterated, continuing down the hall.

Gage's expression was incredulous. "You asked her that straight out?"

"Of course not." I frowned. "Although, if I had, it would have been no worse than your intimating that one of her lovers killed her."

"I wanted to see her reaction." His voice sounded a tad sulky for a grown man. "Besides, it got us the information we needed, didn't it?"

I didn't intend to offer even the smallest amount of praise for his tactics, and I knew agreeing with him was tantamount to doing just that. "Do you really believe one of her lovers murdered her?"

"Why not? It's the best theory we have so far."

"I suppose so," I groused. "But I don't understand the motive for such an attack."

"Jealousy."

"Yes, but . . ." I glanced around to make sure no one was lurking nearby before continuing in a lower voice. "I think it would take an emotion far stronger than jealousy to motivate someone to . . . *violate* a mother and child the way the murderer did."

Gage surveyed our surroundings as I had, and then pulled me into an alcove flanked by two suits of armor. The one on the left gleamed, obviously having seen very little use in battle, while the other was dented and tarnished from blood, sweat, water, and time.

"Maybe her lover was angry. If she'd dismissed him in a cruel manner, or disparaged his manhood in a public way."

I considered his words. "Yes, those emotions make sense for the murder, but the baby . . . ?"

He breathed out impatiently. "Maybe . . ." He exhaled. "Maybe she was blackmailing the baby's father somehow."

I had to admit that was a possibility. Lady Godwin had certainly not been the most principled individual, and it seemed highly plausible that she could have tried extortion. But still, it didn't seem right. There were too many other factors that had not yet come into play, and I could not yet fit them into the picture.

"What of the embroidery scissors?" I asked.

Gage paced the short distance of the alcove and back, stroking his chin. "I don't know. Perhaps this lover had an accomplice."

"Perhaps," I reluctantly conceded.

He sighed. "Regardless, we still need to speak with these men."

"I agree."

He stood with his hands on his hips and stared at the carpet runner down the center of the corridor. "I suppose it makes sense to start with Mr. Fitzpatrick, since he was the most recent man connected with her."

"When do you want to do it?"

"It's too close to dinner to talk with him now. Maybe after, in the library; it's likely to be empty."

This plan sounded as good to me as any. "All right. Shall I meet you there after the ladies and gentlemen separate for after-dinner tea and port?"

Gage looked up at me. "I think it best that you sit this one out."

I lowered my brow in displeasure.

"No matter how indiscreet Lady Godwin was," he continued, "Fitzpatrick is a very courteous and correct gentleman. He would be most uncomfortable discussing a topic such as his relationship with the late viscountess while you are present. In fact, I think it likely he would withhold information to protect your sensibilities."

Gage had a point. Mr. Fitzpatrick was among the more subdued young men I had met, and if most gentlemen would have a problem speaking of such things in front of a gently reared female solely on principle, Mr. Fitzpatrick certainly would. However, I hated to be left out entirely, partly because I wanted to hear his answers, and partly because I wasn't confident that Gage would share every detail of their conversation. Perhaps Philip and Alana trusted Mr. Gage, but I was still reluctant. Especially after the comments he'd made to Lady Stratford.

"I see your point," I admitted. "But I . . ."

"No," he stated determinedly before I could finish my sentence. "You are not taking part in this one."

I frowned. "You haven't even let me . . ."

"I will not hear your objections." He leaned down toward my face, calm but implacable. "Lord Cromarty placed me in charge of this investigation, and I will conduct it as I see fit."

"Mr. Gage . . ."

"No. And if I find you in the library, I shall throw you out."

I gritted my teeth, furious that he wouldn't even allow me to explain. "You . . ."

He turned on his heel and strode away, appearing as unperturbed as ever.

"You buffleheaded fool!" I called out after him.

He didn't even acknowledge the insult I hurled at his back.

I clenched my hands into fists, determined to thwart him in this. Taking a deep, calming breath, I knew what I had to do. And I refused to feel guilty for it. If Gage had only listened, he would not be left in the dark.

CHAPTER TWELVE

In light of recent events, and the unspoken truth that we were all essentially trapped together at Gairloch, I expected the atmosphere in the front parlor to be somewhat sedate and somber when the guests gathered there before dinner. I anticipated hushed conversations and wary glances as they studied one another and wondered who among them had murdered Lady Godwin.

I should have known better.

The upper class's stubborn sense of entitlement could not be curtailed by something so mundane as murder. And as such, they had gathered in their customary, expensive evening attire to gossip and compare and enjoy Philip and Alana's excellent hospitality with all the unconcerned joviality of those who believe tragedy and horror can never touch them. *Lady Godwin's murder was certainly dreadful, but surely she had it coming, what with her immoral behavior and all—* seemed to be the consensus. And by their pointed stares in my direction, most of them still believed I was the culprit who should be brought to justice for the matter.

I entered the parlor quietly, trying to be as unobtrusive as possible, but just as the evening before, the effort was futile. No one had failed to note my appearance. I might as well have worn a scarlet gown rather than a lovely deep plum dress with black trim. They watched me with narrowed, mistrustful eyes and whispered to one another behind their fans. A few brave souls voiced their nasty opinions of me loud enough to be overheard, but most kept quiet—out of deference to their hosts, I had no doubt. Only Lady Westlock insisted upon volleying loud insults about me to her two closest allies, Mrs. Smythe and Lady Darlington, despite Lord Westlock's panicked urgings for her to remain quiet. I gave their circle a wide berth and decided to find a seat on the opposite side of the room before my sister, who was edging ever closer to the Westlocks, tossed them out of the castle with her own two hands.

I settled into a plush beige velvet chair in a quiet corner by the windows and tried to quiet the internal agitation the guests' silent and not-so-silent accusations had caused me. I needed to focus on those assembled around me, to observe their behavior and examine it for any signs of anxiety or guilt. After all, it was the only reason I had agreed to join the others for dinner instead of taking a tray in my room. But I discovered it was more difficult to concentrate than I anticipated, thriving on so little sleep the night before and a dully throbbing skull from the pain Lucy caused me while styling my hair. I wanted nothing more than to abandon the entire enterprise and lay my head down on a soft pillow and close my eyes.

I sighed and focused on Lady Stratford, who held court on a gold brocade settee at the center of the room. She looked cool and composed in a dusky violet gown as she conversed with several other ladies. A group of men, including Lord Marsdale and Mr. Fitzpatrick, congregated on the opposite side of the room, near the grand piano, sipping predinner drinks and laughing heartily at their own jokes. I shook my head at their antics. As far away as the gentlemen were, I should not have been able to hear their crass talk so clearly across the large room if they had been speaking in a normal tone of voice.

Alana stood flanked between the two doorways, looking

lovely in a midnight-blue gown trimmed with mauve ruf-
fles. By all appearances she seemed to be attentively listening to Mrs. Calvin, who was speaking rather animatedly
with her hands. However, I could tell my sister's attention
was far away, and the irritation vibrating through her frame
like a struck bell was likely directed at her husband. Her
gaze darted between him, the Westlocks, and Mrs. Calvin
with such speed I wondered if she wasn't developing a headache. Positioned by the stone hearth, speaking with two
other lords, Philip seemed just as aware of his wife's antago-
nism and returned it full force. I glanced around the room,
curious whether I was the only one who noticed the tension
arcing between the two hosts.

Gage leaned against the sideboard and nursed a glass of
deep amber whiskey. One would have thought he would be
mingling with the guests, trying to gain information for his
investigation or, at the very least, observing them for oddi-
ties in their behavior, as I was. But instead he stood charming a trio of ladies, lapping up their adoration. I frowned at
the two married ladies who touched his arm at every opportunity and giggled at his comments. Their display was nau-
seating, and the very idea that gentlemen actually enjoyed
this behavior baffled me. I watched in puzzlement, trying to
figure out why the appeal of such conduct eluded me.

With the unwed Miss Darlington present, I assumed
their conversation would remain proper, but when Mrs.
Cline pressed her bosom against Gage's elbow and fluttered
her lashes at him like a hummingbird, I wondered if perhaps I might be mistaken. The young Miss Darlington was
not known to be particularly bright, so most innuendos
would likely fly right over her head. One wondered if her
older sister, Lady Lewis, was any quicker. As if on cue she
pressed tightly against Gage's other side and tilted her head
up to speak into his ear, despite the fact that her husband
was standing but a few feet away.

The sight of the two women clinging to him stirred a

strange feeling in my chest. It pinched painfully and made my stomach dip, much like when my father had died, but not nearly so acutely. I frowned and reached up to toy with the amethyst-and-diamond pendant my mother had given me on her deathbed. She claimed the violet stones were for protection, but I had never felt guarded so much as comforted by them.

I lifted my gaze from Gage's arm to find him looking straight at me; a smirk tilted the corners of his lips. The two ladies at his sides followed his gaze and sent me glares filled with spiteful glee. It made me wonder if Gage had told them anything. I scowled, embarrassed to be caught watching, and angry that Gage encouraged the ladies' ill behavior and seemed to enjoy it.

But after all, why shouldn't he be enjoying himself? He wasn't the one being treated to disdainful glances and blatant accusations, or shunned like a weasel in the henhouse. Instead, the men slapped him on the back like a war hero and the women fluttered and flattered like he was the cock of the walk. I looked away, determined to ignore him and cease worrying about what kind of gossip he had shared with the ladies.

When the party finally adjourned to the dining room, I was only too pleased. The dark wood of the long table was polished to a shine, and each place setting gleamed in the light of the many candles. Tapestries spanned the length of one wall, while on the opposite side, tall, pointed Gothic windows provided a magnificent view of the loch. The massive stone fireplace crackled behind Philip's chair at the head of the room.

I discovered I was seated with Lord Stratford on my left and Philip's cousin, Lord Damien, on my right. I knew I could thank Alana for this bit of luck. Lord Stratford was the least querulous of his peers when it came to the matter of my reputation, and Damien was essentially family.

Philip's aunt Jane, Lady Hollingsworth, may have continued to look at me with only a shade less distrust than the other guests did, but her children, Damien and Caroline, had displayed just a slight hesitation that quickly disappeared upon meeting me. Perhaps they were just more tactful than their elders, but I strongly suspected they simply held more faith in the innate goodness of others and the judgment of Philip. Regardless, I was glad the pair had elected to view me with fondness, and even mild interest, rather than distrust, and was happy to be seated next to Damien now.

Given he was the second son of a marquess, and at the relatively young age of twenty-two, it had been a surprise to discover his mother was already pushing him toward marriage as stalwartly as his eighteen-year-old sister. Gentlemen were generally given more time to mature before coaxing them into matrimony. His older brother, the heir, was already wed and expected his first child in early autumn. Since the Hollingsworth title was secured, I did not understand Philip's aunt's rush to see her other children wed, particularly Damien.

"How goes the bridal quest?" I leaned toward him to jest.

He grimaced as he settled his napkin in his lap. "It goes."

I smiled in commiseration. "I take it none of the young ladies here have struck you."

He shook his head.

I sipped my wine. "Your mother won't force you to pick a wife from among the girls present, will she?" Lady Hollingsworth could be quite formidable when she chose to be.

"No. But not out of any deference to me. It's only because she hasn't found a young lady here whom she would like as a daughter-in-law." Damien's tone was light with mockery, and I smiled in appreciation of his forbearance. He picked up his glass, staring at the pale gold chardonnay. "Caroline, unfortunately, has not fared so well in that regard."

"Why? Who has your mother set her cap for?" I was struck by a sudden thought. "Not Marsdale, I hope."

"No, no. She knows what a scoundrel he is."

In my opinion, it spoke well of Philip's aunt that she did not view wealth and title as an excuse to overlook such poor behavior, as so many other matrons did.

"It's Mr. Abingdon."

I glanced down the table at the man in question. "He seems a steady enough fellow," I replied, not knowing much about him other than he was rumored to be an avid horseman. He was taller and broader than most gentlemen, which I imagined accounted for the great black beast of a stallion he rode. More than one of the stable boys had been injured while trying to care for the brute. I wasn't certain if his horse's manners spoke well of him, but I supposed that depended on the behavior of the other creatures in his stables.

Damien shrugged. "My only concern is whether Caroline likes him."

"And does she?"

"I honestly do not know."

My gaze slid down the table to the right of Mr. Abingdon to where Caroline leaned toward Mr. Pullham. From my observations, a quiet, studious gentleman like Mr. Pullham seemed more to Caroline's liking. Mr. Pullham was already wed but perhaps he had a friend or relative of the same disposition to whom he might introduce her.

I skimmed my gaze back down the table and opened my mouth to tell her brother so, when my eyes collided with Mr. Gage's pale blue ones. He studied me openly, not diverting his gaze or pretending disinterest, and I felt my cheeks growing warm in response. Conscious of the prying eyes all around us, I arched an eyebrow in challenge, uncertain of his motivations. His eyes sparked with humor, as if he knew how much his gaze discomforted me.

"So tell us, Gage," a voice boomed from farther down the table, making me stiffen in alarm. Had someone seen our silent exchange? "Have you uncovered who the murderer is yet?"

"Mr. Smythe," his wife hissed, her customary disapproving frown pulling down her face. "This is hardly appropriate dinner conversation."

Mr. Smythe frowned across the floral centerpieces at his wife. "Why not? I daresay we all want to know," he growled belligerently, making me wonder just how many predinner drinks the man had consumed. "So let's save the chap from having to repeat himself twenty times."

Gage smiled disarmingly. "No, I have not uncovered the murderer."

"But you are close? Surely you must have some idea who the culprit is?" Mr. Smythe pressed, leaning forward in his chair.

Gage's grin tightened. "I assure you that when I have news to share, I will share it. However, for the moment, I do not believe it would be appropriate to speculate on such a thing." He glanced up and down the table at all the guests before adding confidently. "We are doing all we can to solve this murder and ensure no harm befalls any of you."

"We? Who's we?" another man asked suddenly.

I tensed, shocked that Gage had said such a thing. Was he talking about me? I cautiously lifted my gaze from my bowl of asparagus soup to see what he would do. He appeared just as stunned, for his eyes flared wide for a split second as the guests leaned toward him in keen interest.

"Why, our host, Lord Cromarty, of course," he replied, recovering himself quickly. He flashed an assertive grin.

Most of the guests settled back in their seats, accepting his assurances of their safety with only a few uncertain glances at one another. It was as if no one wanted to be the first to admit they were even the slightest bit frightened by the idea of a murderer seated among them. I couldn't help but wonder if they wouldn't be better off knowing exactly what kind of monster we were dealing with. Committing murder was one thing, but harming the baby the way they had . . . I shook away the thought. That was another brand of terror altogether.

I sat back as the footmen traded out the first course for the second, and for the first time that evening, I truly felt the fear and uneasiness humming below the surface of those surrounding me. They had done well to hide it earlier, but such a blatant discussion of the incident had stirred up many of the guests' anxiety. I also began to understand why so many of them, both men and women, had nursed glasses of brandy and whiskey in the drawing room, and now downed the wine from my brother-in-law's cellar like it was water. I sipped my own glass a little slower. With so much drinking going on around me, it would be best if I kept my head about me. I knew from personal experience just how hostile some people became from heavy drink, and as the primary suspect for Lady Godwin's murder, I began to anticipate more than one potentially nasty altercation.

I picked at the herb-crusted salmon before me, hoping many of the guests decided to retire early so that I did not risk running into them later. The night before, they had gathered in packs, rehashing the scene in the garden maze, commiserating with one another, and, no doubt, feeling safer collected together in numbers. The fear and shock were more settled now, more tense and wearying, preying on minds and nerves.

I watched as several of the wives darted glances at their husbands, as if seeking comfort and reassurance from the one most directly responsible for their protection. I wondered if the fear generated by Lady Godwin's murder would result in a resurgence of marital cohabitation among the guests. Like fashionable London society, most of our married guests preferred separate bedchambers. Sir Anthony and I had done the same. However, my sister and Philip did not follow the trend, and I sometimes wondered if that was one of the keys to their happy marriage. Even when they were irritated and angry with each other, they still retired to the same room, and often emerged in communion the next day.

I tried to ignore the looks many of the couples shared,

and stubbornly tamped down a sudden longing to have someone gaze back at me with reassurance. A pair of pale blue eyes came to mind, and I shifted in my seat, uncomfortable with the thought. I absolutely forbade myself to sneak a glance to see where he was looking.

Instead, I focused on the meal and the guests seated at my end of the table. It unnerved me to find Lady Stratford staring at her husband in much the same manner as the other ladies looked at theirs. Perhaps it was because the countess always seemed so calm and sophisticated that any sign of an emotion even vaguely resembling pleading or desperation seemed out of place, or the fact that her husband wasn't paying her the least bit of attention. Maybe it was both of those things, or neither of them. All I knew with any certainty was that it was disconcerting to discover the situation was dire enough to rattle even the cool Lady Stratford. And it puzzled me what problems in their marriage would prevent Lord Stratford from granting his wife even the small comfort of his consideration.

I looked away before she caught me watching, but I couldn't erase the impression of hopelessness I sensed in Lady Stratford. It settled like a lump of mealy bread in the pit of my stomach.

"I must say, it is at times like these when I wish my dear Mr. Cline was still with me." Mrs. Cline sighed.

I peered around Damien at the beautiful widow. Apparently, I wasn't the only one to notice the undercurrents passing between the married guests.

"It can be so terrifying without a man to protect you from the small things in life, let alone the monsters," she remarked in her dulcet tones. She brushed her hand across the naked expanse of flesh over her low neckline—I supposed to draw the men's attention there. Or, at least, the attention of one man in particular.

I felt my chest tighten as Gage obliged her by dropping his gaze to her décolletage.

"Have no fear, madam. I'm sure none of the gentlemen here will allow harm to come to you." He smiled coyly as if this were some game they were playing.

"That is reassuring, to be sure, when we are all gathered together. But what about when we are separated?" She pouted her lips and even managed to make them tremble with a fright I wasn't certain she was feeling at the moment. "Who am I to rely on then? I cannot expect the married gentlemen here to abandon their wives for a simple widow like me."

Gage's eyes smiled as if he had anticipated such words from Mrs. Cline and had already formulated his reply. He opened his mouth to deliver it, but unfortunately Lord Damien jumped in to speak first.

"Those of us who are single shall be happy to protect you, Mrs. Cline," he chimed in, clearly not realizing he was interrupting some repartee between the widow and Gage.

Mrs. Cline's eyes rounded in surprise, but she quickly recovered, offering him a syrupy smile. "Why, Lord Damien, I certainly appreciate your concern, but don't you have your mother and sister to care for? Surely you don't need yet another female dependent upon you."

"Not at all," dear, sweet Damien pronounced with chivalrous intensity. "Those of us who might lend our assistance would be remiss not to offer it to you."

The widow's smile faltered as Damien continued his protestations, and she realized she was not going to be able to shake him loose. For Gage's part, he seemed unfazed, even amused by Damien's disruption of his flirtation. And judging from the glares she sent him while pretending to appreciate Damien's courtly overtures, Mrs. Cline was not pleased by that.

I bowed my head over my plate and stifled the urge to laugh. The others already viewed me as a mad murderess, and I doubted erupting into spontaneous hilarity at the dining table would help to convince them otherwise.

"She's not very subtle, is she?" Lord Stratford surprised me by leaning over to remark. He twirled his remaining bite of salmon around in the juices on his plate with his fork. "She never has grasped the concept that gentlemen enjoy the pursuit as much as the conquest. Her dolt of a husband made it too easy for her."

From what I understood, Mr. Cline had been a kindly, handsome country squire who had instantly fallen in love with the beautiful Mrs. Cline and wed her, even though she was only a vicar's daughter. I refrained from saying any of this to Lord Stratford, who likely already knew, and only looked down on Mr. Cline's choice because of his wife's lowly birth. Men like the earl viewed women like Mrs. Cline as good enough to bed, but not wed.

I studied Lord Stratford's countenance as he chewed his fish. I supposed he would be considered by most to be a handsome man. He had rather lovely chocolate-brown eyes and a deep cleft in his chin, which lent a certain ruggedness to his looks, but the rest of him was rather ordinary. He was somewhere between forty and forty-five; his dark hair was dusted with silver, particularly at the temples, and his skin had taken on the saggy dissipation of too much hard living. His body remained mostly lean, but his stomach had begun to develop the paunch that was customary among a large number of wealthy, older gentlemen. In fact, the most remarkable thing about his appearance was the tiny scar that slashed across his forehead and into his right eyebrow, received at some point in his service during the wars with Napoleon. Fortunately for him, most women found such minor disfigurements attractive, reminders of the man's bravery and prowess, rather than off-putting. Even I found the scar intriguing. I wondered what shades of blue and red and brown I would have to blend to get the exact color right.

Clearly accustomed to being regarded by others, he turned to me in the midst of my inspection and grinned. "Considering me for one of your portraits, my lady?"

I offered back a tiny smile. "Perhaps."

He chuckled when he realized no more information would be forthcoming. "Ever the mystery, are we, Lady Darby? See, now that is what I'm talking about. You keep the men guessing. I doubt many become bored with you quickly."

I arched a brow in skepticism. "I highly doubt that many ladies *or* gentlemen consider me a *good* mystery."

"Nonsense," he declared as fragrant plates of braised beef and roasted potatoes with string beans in cream sauce were placed before us. He leaned toward me after the footmen had retreated. "I guarantee that more than one gentleman seated at this table would be very interested to see what you keep hidden beneath that eccentric facade, regardless of your reputation."

My cheeks heated at the implication of his words. He chuckled delightedly and settled back to cut into his beef. I flicked my glance around the table to see if anyone was paying attention to our exchange but only caught Gage watching us with a speculative look. Ignoring him, I tucked into my meal and tried to think of another conversation topic that might interest the earl without causing me further embarrassment. Unfortunately, I was not quick enough.

"I see you don't believe me," Lord Stratford said around a bite of food. "But don't think I didn't notice Mr. Gage watching you just now, or the manner in which Lord Marsdale has been harassing you for several days."

I worked very hard not to visibly flinch at such a pronouncement. Sliding a sideways glance at the earl, I opened my mouth to protest, but once again he spoke first.

"Oh, I realize you haven't encouraged them. I do believe that would be against your nature, Lady Darby. But you're an attractive enough lady. It would take a blind man not to notice the luster of your skin or the way your gowns drape your body. You're an irresistible challenge to rogues like Gage and Marsdale."

I frowned and fought another telling blush, uncomfortable with the way this conversation was going. It put me off my appetite, making me cross that I had yet to manage a bite of the succulent roast as the earl prodded me. He didn't seem to be having any such problem. Forking another bite of beef and potato, he tipped his head toward me yet again.

"You do realize that is the reason many of the women are so openly hostile toward you. Not only do you have a shady past and mysterious manners, but you also intrigue their husbands. They cannot compete with that."

I did not for a moment believe this nonsense and told him so. "Please, Lord Stratford. If you're finished telling me Banbury tales, I would like to ask your opinion on a far more interesting topic. I'm told you are a great patron of the arts. Have you visited the Royal Academy recently?"

He smiled indulgently, as if he were placating a woman denied some bauble. "I have."

I ignored his expression and pushed on. "What was your opinion of Thomas Cole's exhibit? I read that his American landscapes are quite exceptional. That the colors and textures of the untamed Catskills seem almost fantastical."

He appeared to contemplate the matter as he took a drink of his wine. "They are certainly in the class of our John Constable's paintings. And I believe Cole uses light and shadow to even better effect. However, they do have an almost otherworldliness about them. Yes, 'fantastical,' you said? I believe that *would* be the appropriate word."

I nodded, taking a bite of potato. Rarely did I harbor any interest in returning to London, except when news of an extraordinary exhibit reached me. Then the desire to view new art not created by my own hand almost overrode my good sense and self-preservation. I had contemplated journeying to Edinburgh with Philip to scour the few museums and art galleries there, but I already knew they could not compare with the quality and variety of exhibitions in London.

I sighed, pushing the fanciful thought from my head.

"Your own portraits are exceptional," Lord Stratford stated, which made me flush happily from the praise. He turned and lifted his eyebrows at me. "And don't think that you have fooled those of us who know our art that K. A. Elwick is not actually Lady Darby," he murmured in low tones.

I glanced around the table to make certain no one had overheard him. I had not been so naive as to think I could fool everyone, but I never expected to be asked so pointedly about the matter. I didn't know whether to answer the implied question or dance around it. Gratefully, Lord Stratford saved me from my own dilemma.

"*Portrait of a Forgotten Woman* is particularly captivating. I was quite put out when the Duke of Norwich outbid me for it." He frowned.

"Lord Marsdale's father?" I asked in some shock.

A bit of the devilry from our earlier conversation returned to his eyes. "Indeed."

I scowled at my plate, uncertain I liked the idea of Marsdale's father being an admirer of my work. Did Marsdale also know that K. A. Elwick was my alias? Was that the real reason he had been plaguing me since he arrived?

"Where do you paint?" Lord Stratford asked, seemingly oblivious to my distraction. "Do you have a studio here at the castle?"

"Um . . . yes. It's at the corner of the top floor of the east wing, facing both sunrise and the south." He would realize this location provided the best access to the most natural light. The Highlands were not exactly an ideal location for large quantities of unfettered sunshine, particularly in the winter, and one had to make do with what one had.

"Would you be willing to show it to me? And perhaps some of your works in progress?"

I blinked at him. The earl was continually surprising me with what came out of his mouth. And somehow this seemed the most absurd remark of all. I narrowed my eyes in suspicion, and he smiled as if reading my thoughts.

"I promise I have no ulterior motives," he replied, making me blush yet again. "Well, other than maybe to gain an advantage over the competition when your next collection goes up for bidding."

I realized he was trying to flatter me, and because of that, his words failed to please me like spontaneous compliments did. Even though he was an avid art collector, his request to see my studio still seemed off somehow. It would have been much more believable had he asked to view my finished pieces in a comfortable parlor away from the fumes and mess of my studio.

"I will have to think about it," I replied vaguely, not ready to grant the earl permission without considering the matter further.

He smiled as if he understood my hesitation. "Of course. Take your time. After all, none of us are going anywhere for at least another three days, are we?"

Feeling a small shiver run down my spine at the reminder, I returned his smile tightly.

CHAPTER THIRTEEN

Rather than join my sister and the other ladies in the drawing room after dinner, I decided it would be best to slip away. In all honesty, I did not want to sip tea with a bunch of women who politely tried to hold back their animosity toward me anyway. I suspected the fragrant black tea would taste like ash and Alana's mood would only continue to darken in the face of the others' hostility toward me. So it seemed in the best interest of all for me to disappear.

Unfortunately, Lady Westlock was not so willing to allow me to escape unscathed. When I turned right instead of left as I exited the dining room, she grabbed hold of my arm, digging her fingernails into my skin. "I've got my eyes on you," she hissed with enough venom to splatter me with her spit.

I yanked my arm from out of her grasp, feeling the scratches her claws left behind, and reached up to swipe the wetness from my cheek with the back of my hand. "So does your husband," I remarked under my breath dryly.

I hurried away and had almost managed to slip out of sight down the hall, when I heard Philip calling my name. I sighed and reluctantly stuttered to a halt, waiting for him to catch up with me. Whatever he had to say must be important if he was willing to excuse himself from the men drinking port at the dining table.

"Not interested in joining the ladies, eh?" he asked.

I shook my head.

He grimaced in sympathy and glanced back the way he had come before speaking again. "I only wanted to tell you that Beowulf and Grendel did not find anything."

My heart sank, having hoped the two wolfhounds would turn up something—a piece of clothing, the murder weapon, the baby's grave.

"There was a spot just inside the tree line of the forest near the maze that they pawed at quite ferociously, but after a thorough search, nothing was uncovered. I suspect the killer may have laid something there before moving it to a more concealed location. The dogs were probably smelling the traces of blood left behind."

I sighed and wrapped my arms tightly around me.

Philip reached out to touch my arm in commiseration. "Are you retiring?"

"Yes," I said with a nod. "After I retrieve a book from the library." There was no need to explain how or why that might take some time.

"Then I'll bid you good night." He turned to go, but then stopped and glanced back at me. Worry tightened his features. "Lock your door tonight, Kiera. And every night from here on out until the murderer is caught."

The hairs on the back of my neck stood on end at the implication that he feared for my safety. Perhaps he only worried about the lack-wits like Lord Westlock or the drunken aggression of the guests at dinner, but even those people could do real damage to me if they chose. In any event, after the letter I received last night and the strange shifting shadows today, I had every intention of locking my door, and likely propping a chair beneath the handle as well. I didn't know if it was the killer or an angry guest who was watching me, but if it was the murderer, I doubted they looked kindly on my efforts to assist Gage with the investigation.

I swallowed and nodded.

Satisfied with my acquiescence, Philip returned to the men in the dining room.

The hall seemed open and shadowy now that he had departed, and I stood for a moment gazing into the dark corners where the light from the candles could not reach. I knew my apprehension was due partly to the anxiety Philip's warning had stirred up in me, but I also could not help feeling that someone was watching me. Though from where, I could not tell.

The gloom of the castle had never bothered me before, not even at night. I normally found it more atmospheric than eerie, more melancholy than frightening. But tonight, like last night, was different.

Perhaps the blame for that should fall squarely on the murder, and the knowledge that a killer walked among us, yet for me it also had a great deal to do with Lady Godwin's corpse itself. With Sir Anthony's death, I had escaped the necessity of ever having to deal with another dead body beyond that of a loved one's burial. Or, at least, I thought I had.

But somehow another one had found me. Somehow another corpse had shown up on my doorstep. I knew it was fantastical to think of it in such terms, but surrounded by the darkness and shadows of the old castle, I couldn't help but look over my shoulder to make certain yet another one had not appeared.

Quaking from my ridiculous imaginings, I took a deep breath and exhaled. Then, squaring my shoulders, I marched down the corridor past the grand staircase leading to the bedchambers above, determined not to look either to my left or to my right, lest I see something I did not wish to.

As I passed through the portal leading to the back half of the main hall block, a man stepped into my path from the shadows beneath the stairs. My heart nearly leapt out of my chest.

"Good evening, Lady Darby," Marsdale pronounced with a sly grin and an almost mocking bow.

I skidded to a halt and pressed my hand over my pounding heart to keep it inside my body. "What is the meaning of this?" I gasped, wanting to reach out and smack him like a meddlesome brother. "Did you intend to scare me witless?"

"Ah, well, I could have revealed myself earlier, when you were staring into the shadows as if looking for ghosts, but I assumed that would give you even more of a fright." He sidled closer to me, leaning into my personal space. I could smell the whiskey on his breath. "Besides, I wanted to be close enough to stop you from fleeing if you attempted to do so."

I leaned back, tempted to retreat away from him a step or two, but I knew my withdrawal would only amuse him and give him an excuse to touch me in order to illustrate his point. "If you wanted to speak with me, why didn't you approach me earlier in the drawing room, like a civilized human being instead of skulking about like a . . ." I sucked in a harsh breath at the realization of what I was about to say, and the knowledge that it could be true. I stumbled back a step, studying the emotions that played across Marsdale's face.

"A what?" he prodded, his face lighting with interest. "A murderer?" It was absurd, but he seemed pleased by this prospect. He took a step, closing the distance between us again. "Tell me, Lady Darby," he murmured, lowering his voice as he reached up to flick a wayward curl away from my face. I stiffened. "Do you find me that . . . wicked?" he whispered the last into my ear.

A shiver ran down my spine from the gust of his hot breath against my skin and the thought that he might indeed be an evil man. Leaning away from him, I looked into his face.

It was clear he was enjoying this—toying with me—as if it were some grand game. However, I sensed no real malice behind it, only boredom and selfishness. There was also a weariness, a fatigue, in the faint lines around his mouth and eyes, and a thinly veiled sadness in the droop of his eyelids.

Marsdale was not the murderer. I was at least ninety percent certain of that.

But in the interest of that other ten percent, I still sidled sideways away from him. "Murder is not a game," I told him with a glare. "And neither are my affections."

"Ah, but I'm not playing for your affections, am I?" he replied, allowing his voice to drop to a gravelly timbre.

I supposed many women might have fallen prey to this ploy, including Lady Godwin; however, his deepened voice did nothing except make me want to roll my eyes. "Marsdale," I began with weary patience. "I realize that I present some kind of mystery to you, but I assure you, it's not intentional."

Rather than being miffed, Marsdale seemed entertained by my efforts to gently reject him. "So that's what you and Stratford were talking about at dinner. I wondered how he made you blush so prettily."

I stumbled for a moment, unaware that he had been watching us, and uncertain how to respond. I certainly wasn't well versed in the art of rebuffing men's advances. The few times I received unwanted attention as a young woman, I had simply walked away. I was seriously considering such an option now.

Marsdale chuckled at the evidence of my distress. I frowned, not enjoying being the source of so much amusement, and turned to follow my instinct.

"Oh, come now, Lady Darby," Marsdale called after me. "You can't say you aren't enjoying my attentions. Otherwise you would be discouraging me."

Exasperated, I turned to scowl at him. "I *am* discouraging you."

"No, you're not."

I gritted my teeth to stop myself from cursing. "Yes, I am," I bit out.

He smiled at me as if I were bird-witted. "No, you're not."

"I think I know my own mind."

He shook his head and sighed. "So beautiful, but so naive."

I lifted my eyes to the heavens in search of patience, or perhaps inspiration in how to deal with this vain, infuriating man. "What do I have to do to convince you I'm not interested? What do I have to say to get you to leave me alone?"

A roguish grin spread across his face as he leaned toward me. "Look me in the eye and tell me you don't want me in your bed."

I blushed a fiery red clear to the tips of my ears. Marsdale chuckled, but I was not about to be cowed now. Swallowing my maidenly sensibilities, I leaned into his face and stared directly into his dark brown eyes. "Marsdale."

He widened his smile, flashing his teeth wolfishly.

"I do *not* want you in my bed." I whirled away from him with a rustle of plum silk and resumed my march down the hall.

"Maybe not," he called after me. "But you *do* want in *my* bed."

I shook my head in irritation and hurried down the hall before he could follow me. His laughter rang after me.

Darting around the corner, I dashed into the library, relieved to find it empty. Marsdale had delayed me so long, I was worried Gage and Mr. Fitzpatrick had somehow bypassed us and reached the room first. Knowing how little time there was to waste, I gathered up my skirts and clambered up the spiral staircase tucked into the corner of the chamber to the loft above. As long as Gage did not notice the stairs and decide to investigate, I felt safe that I would not be discovered.

Careful to remain out of sight, I tossed a cushion on the

floor near the southern wall and settled into position. From my vantage point, I would not be able to see their facial expressions, but at least I would hear the inflection of their voices.

They appeared barely two minutes after I was seated, and I roundly cursed Marsdale for stalling me for so long. Several moments longer and they would have passed us in the hall. I wondered what Gage would have thought had he caught me there with the Duke of Norwich's notorious son, and also one of our suspects. Then I wondered why I cared.

Gage gestured for Mr. Fitzpatrick to have a seat in one of the deep brown chairs positioned before the fireplace. I had expected him to conduct their discussion there, where the setting seemed more cozy and intimate than in any of the other seating areas in the expansive library. A fire crackled merrily in the hearth, warding off the chill of the Highland evening. I peered over the edge of the loft at the flames in longing. It was cool up near the eaves, so high above the room's only heat source, and the thin shawl I had worn to dinner was not sufficient enough to warm me. I glanced across the loft at the tartan blanket thrown over the sofa but decided it would be too risky to fetch it now. One creak of the floorboards and I would be found out.

Mr. Fitzpatrick settled into his seat and took a hasty drink from the glass of ruby port cradled in his hand. I wondered whether he was nervous because of the situation or because he felt guilty about something. It seemed safe to assume he knew exactly why Gage had asked for this little tête-à-tête. More than one person had been conscious of Mr. Fitzpatrick's relationship with Lady Godwin.

From this height, I could not see Gage's facial expression, but I could imagine the reassuring smile he had given each of the people he interrogated so far. I somehow didn't imagine him taking a strong-arm approach with Mr. Fitzpatrick. The man was too genial, and clearly already intimidated by

Gage, if the restless bouncing of his knee was any indication.

"Fitzpatrick, I'll get straight to the point," Gage said affably after taking a drink of his own glass of port and setting it aside. "I need to ask you a few questions about Lady Godwin and your relationship with her."

He bobbed his head in response. "I figured as much." He sighed heavily, as if preparing to face an arduous ordeal. "What would you like to know?"

Gage rested his elbows on the chair's arms and clasped his fingers over his stomach, much as he had the previous night in my room. "It is fairly well known that you lately conducted a liaison with the countess."

Mr. Fitzpatrick shifted in his seat. "That is true."

"When did this liaison begin? How long ago?"

Mr. Fitzpatrick leaned his head back, contemplating the matter. "It was just before His Majesty King George's death. So . . . seven, eight weeks?"

In other words, the end of June. Much too recent for him to be the father of her baby.

Gage nodded. "Was everything . . . cozy between you?"

"Of course," he replied much too quickly.

Gage sensed this as well. "Are you sure about that?" He paused a moment, allowing the man time to think before continuing in a silky voice. "Because I would hate to discover later that you lied. It would make you look quite suspicious."

Mr. Fitzpatrick shifted in his seat again. "Well, we haven't shared a bed since the night we arrived at Gairloch, if that's what you're asking," he replied crossly.

Gage's head perked up. "Why's that?"

"Damned if I know."

"Really?" Gage remarked doubtfully. "Nothing happened between you two? No argument?"

He huffed. "Well, how was I to know she would take offense at my mentioning how much I liked her new curves.

Gave her a compliment and what does she do but throw me out of her room. Now, tell me, was that really called for? Women," he muttered, shaking his head. "They don't make any bloody sense."

"Did you try to speak with her about it?"

"I did. I made a right flowery apology, even though I didn't understand what had offended her in the first place. She told me we were finished."

"It sounds like you were upset by this?"

"I was. But then I figured, good riddance. Let some other bloke deal with her tantrums. She wasn't as talented between the sheets as she was rumored to be. And she was starting to get fat."

If Mr. Fitzpatrick's outrage was to be believed, and I found it quite convincing, then he had not been bright enough to connect Lady Godwin's new curves and increasing weight to the fact that she was with child. And in that case, he might have been angry enough to do her harm, but he would never have harmed a baby he didn't know existed.

I assumed Gage deduced the same thing, for he sat quietly contemplating Mr. Fitzpatrick's spent rage. For his part, Mr. Fitzpatrick came to the belated realization that his display of temper could make him a prime suspect in the murder of his former mistress. He leaned forward in his seat to plead his case.

"You don't think I killed her, do you? Because I didn't. I never even contemplated it. I . . . I wouldn't hurt a fly. Well, maybe a fly. But certainly not a woman."

"Hold on, Fitzpatrick." Gage held up his hand to slow the man's panicked monologue. "Take a deep breath."

He took an exaggerated inhale of air before audibly blowing it out.

"Now, tell me where you were when you heard Lady Lydia's scream."

"I . . . I was talking to Mr. Abingdon and Sir David by

the rosebushes that border the lawn near the maze," he said quickly. "We were discussing Mr. Abingdon's new filly."

"And how long were you with them before the scream?" Gage asked, clearly struggling for patience in the face of the man's frightened ramblings.

"Well, I didn't exit the house with them after dinner, if that's what you mean, but I met up with them soon after." Mr. Fitzpatrick brightened, sitting taller in his chair. "So you see, I had no opportunity to kill her."

It did appear that way. Unless Sir David or Mr. Abingdon had assisted him. Still, I had a hard time believing the fidgety Mr. Fitzpatrick had any part in this nasty business.

Gage relaxed back in his seat. He didn't comment on Mr. Fitzpatrick's alibi, although I was beginning to read him well enough to tell that he believed him. It was likely he would confirm Mr. Fitzpatrick's story with at least one of the other men just for the sake of thoroughness, but I felt confident he didn't expect to catch Mr. Fitzpatrick in a lie.

"Are you aware of anyone who might have wished Lady Godwin harm?" Gage asked.

Mr. Fitzpatrick seemed to think this new line of questioning indicated he was no longer a suspect, for he settled deeper into the cushions and took a leisurely sip of his port. "Sure. But I don't think any of them would kill her." He drained his glass and set it aside. "What about Lady Darby? If I thought anyone was capable of such a thing, it would be her."

My stomach dropped and the breath squeezed in my chest. I stared at Gage's head, waiting to hear his reply to this suggestion.

"You are not the first person to suggest such a thing," he said broodingly. "But I have yet to hear a credible reason why she would murder Lady Godwin."

"Surely you heard how she helped her husband with his human dissections." Mr. Fitzpatrick leaned toward Gage. "It's said they hired grave robbers and asked them to commit murder just so they could have more subjects for their experimentations."

"Like Burke and Hare."

"Exactly. It's even rumored that they performed at least one vivisection, slicing open the fellow while he was still alive."

My stomach churned hearing someone speak the now-familiar accusations in a voice filled with such horrified fascination, as if I were a carnival freak show. The scandal over the actions of renowned anatomist Robert Knox at the Royal College of Surgeons of Edinburgh and his relationship with the body snatchers and murderers Burke and Hare had broken only months before Sir Anthony's death. It had not surprised me when questions arose regarding Sir Anthony's methods of procuring bodies. However, I had never known the public possessed such macabre imaginations, or that they would invent even more horrific charges to throw at me.

"But I thought Lady Darby was cleared of all charges?" Gage replied in a leading voice.

Mr. Fitzpatrick nodded. "She was. The authorities placed all blame on her husband, but no one believed she was as ignorant of it all as she protested. I mean, what woman could handle such a gruesome sight if she wasn't already so unnatural."

"Indeed."

Mr. Fitzpatrick missed the dry tone of Gage's voice and continued to level the charges against me. "They say she picked the victims herself by walking the streets of White-chapel and St. Giles looking for handsome young men. I even heard tell that she cut out some of their organs and asked for them to be cooked and served up to her for dinner."

Gage's head jerked backward in disgust. "Mr. Fitzpat-rick!" he admonished.

The other man sat back. "Perhaps the last is a bit sensational," he admitted abashedly. "But I assure you the others have been well documented as truth. Lady Darby is just lucky that her brother and Lord Cromarty are so well respected, or she would have danced the dead man's jig long ago."

I pulled my knees up to my chest, trying to make myself as small as possible. Though I knew that others had been discussing them behind my back, no one had leveled such accusations directly at me since the charges against me were dismissed and I departed London. To hear the words formed again within my hearing made the small amount of food I had consumed at dinner churn in my stomach. I had never understood society's urge to crucify me for the abuses of my husband. I wasn't certain I ever would. And I was so tired of fighting them. Of defending myself at every turn. Of being forced to hide away in the Highlands and conceal my talent.

"I assure you Lady Darby is being closely watched and considered," Gage told Mr. Fitzpatrick. There was a curious twist in his voice I could not decipher. "But I would be foolish not to pursue every possibility. So if you should remember anything suspicious, anything at all, please let me know."

A rock settled in my gut upon hearing Gage so baldly confirm that I was a suspect. Perhaps his prime suspect. I dared not move from my position, for fear that I would hurl something down at him. Instead, I clasped my arms tighter around my legs, heedless of the wrinkles that would form in the skirts of my dress.

"Will you take Lady Darby into custody?" Mr. Fitzpatrick asked eagerly.

"Nothing will be done until either my investigation is complete or the procurator fiscal arrives," he stated carefully. "And I would appreciate it if you would keep everything we have discussed to yourself. I do not want Lady Darby declared the culprit until I uncover proof."

"Of course, of course. No one will hear anything from me."

I could hear the beginnings of a smile forming on Mr.

Fitzpatrick's face, and I dug my fingernails into my arms. The men rose from their seats and exchanged pleasantries, while my fury continued to build.

My worst fears seemed confirmed. The lying snake had used me. Accepting my assistance and all the while building a case against me. He wouldn't have a shred of pertinent evidence if not for me.

I heard the door to the library open and close below me, and then Mr. Gage sighed heavily as he sank back into his chair. Rising from my crouch, I leaned against the banister and glared down at him. He sat in a sprawl, running his hand through his hair as if *he* had had a difficult day.

I swallowed the vile epithets I wanted to yell at him and instead spoke in a calm, clipped voice. "Shall I lead you to where I've buried the baby, then?"

CHAPTER FOURTEEN

If I had been in another state of mind, I might have enjoyed the way Mr. Gage bristled like a cat and leapt out of his chair. As it was, the only thing I could see was the red haze that descended over my vision.

"Or perhaps the real murder weapon? Would you like to know where that is?"

"Damn it, Lady Darby!" Gage exclaimed. "What are you doing here?"

I wandered across the loft, toward the stairs, gliding my hand over the banister. "Even better, shall I come up with a motive for you? I'm certain my unnatural, knife-wielding, cannibalistic tendencies are enough for most people, but perhaps you need a more common explanation for my actions."

"Have you been up there the entire time?" he demanded, and then answered for himself. "But, of course, you have. I thought I specifically told you to stay away while I interviewed Mr. Fitzpatrick."

"No. You only said Mr. Fitzpatrick would not speak freely if I accompanied you. He never knew I was listening. And neither did you." I narrowed my eyes. "I must say I'm rather glad I chose to circumvent your orders. At least now I know what you really think of me." I was amazed by the steadiness of my voice, considering how angry I felt. "I imagine Philip and Alana will be quite unhappy to discover how much you've abused their trust."

"You have to understand, I need to gain these people's confidence," he began impatiently to explain as I slowly descended the spiral staircase. "They all believe you are some ghoul, and if I don't take their concerns about you seriously, they will never trust me enough to speak openly. Besides, if the real murderer believes I'm focusing my attention on you, they might imagine themselves safe and slip up."

He met me at the bottom of the stairs, and I stopped on the next-to-last step so that I was equal to his height. "So you're not intending to name me as a suspect to the procurator fiscal when he arrives?" I raised my eyebrows. "Even if you can't come up with a better person to accuse, you're not going to present me as suspect number one?"

He did not reply immediately, and I took that as the answer it was and narrowed my eyes.

"I have to present all of my findings to the magistrate, regardless of my feelings on the matter."

"Don't you mean *my* findings?" I challenged. "After all, the most damning evidence you have against me are the clues *I* uncovered for you. Without my assistance, you wouldn't have a shred of useful information beyond a bunch of nasty rumors."

"And a corpse, Lady Darby," he snapped, crowding in closer to me and blocking my escape from the stairs. "Don't forget Lady Godwin herself."

"Oh, yes." I sneered. "A dead body, which you would have failed to realize was missing something very precious inside."

"I would have discovered it eventually."

"Of course you would have," I replied sarcastically. "You wouldn't have just assumed someone was trying to disfigure her womanhood."

Gage gritted his teeth as I reminded him of the suppositions he made on the subject of Lady Godwin's abdominal wounds.

"I believe my cooperation with you on the matter is finished. You can continue chasing rumors while I find the real killer." I pushed forward, trying to sweep past Gage, but he would not let me by and, in fact, moved in closer until his nose was nearly touching mine. I refused to step back, even though his proximity made my stomach dip.

"You will not go this alone," he told me, his blue eyes blazing. "You cannot go it alone." I began to protest, but he pushed on. "No one will speak with you about it. They're all too afraid of you and, at the very least, highly suspicious that you are the actual culprit." I frowned, not liking the truth of his words. "Besides, Cromarty will never allow you to continue alone."

"I do not need Philip's permission," I protested.

"In this matter, you do. Otherwise, I can ask him to lock you in your chambers for your own protection."

A bolt of alarm streaked through me. "He wouldn't. *You* wouldn't," I snapped furiously.

He moved his face an inch closer to mine. "I would," he growled.

The air between us crackled with tension, neither of us wanting to be the one to relent. I was so close to Gage that I could pick out the silver flecks dotting his irises near his pupils.

I was furious with him, and myself. Angry that all of the control seemed to be in his hands—my fate yet again relegated to a man, as it had been with my father, Sir Anthony, and even Philip, as I depended on his approval to reside at Gairloch. I could not stand idly by and let Gage decide whether I should be accused before the magistrate. I would be a fool to do so. And I was incensed that I had been inclined to trust him, to share some of myself with him when he so clearly did not trust me in return and, in fact, planned to betray me.

However, irate as I was, I could not seem to shut down my awareness of him. And the longer I glared into his eyes, our bodies inches from touching, the stronger the tingling heat in my chest became, and the fuzzier my anger became. The tension and frustration were still there arcing between us, but they had taken on a blunter edge—one that suddenly seemed to draw me closer rather than push me away.

I sucked in a startled breath, one filled with the sweat and musk of his skin and the spicy scent of his cologne, as I realized what was happening. Gage clearly recognized it, too, for his pupils dilated and flicked down to my mouth. My lips tingled as if his gaze was tangible. For a moment, we hung there in limbo, neither of us moving, nor hardly daring to breathe. I was torn by indecision—and the fact that I was torn at all troubled me.

I watched as Gage swallowed, making the Adam's apple bob up and down in his throat, and then slowly stepped back. I was forced to take a solid grip of the stair rails in order to resist the urge to follow his retreat, as if I were suddenly a lodestone and he was north. I breathed in deeply and exhaled, waiting to hear what he would say.

Only a small tremor in his voice revealed that he was in the least affected by whatever had just passed between us. "Well, it appears you have as much need of my charm and communication skills as I do of your powers of observation and intelligence. It would not be in either of our best interests to split up."

I appreciated his attempt to soften the blow of his earlier declaration, but I did not understand how he thought to make me agree with him. "How can you expect me to continue to assist you when you've just admitted you will be naming me as a suspect to the procurator fiscal?" I demanded, albeit with less heat than before. If he was willing to be calm and reasonable, I could be as well.

His hand lifted from the banister, where it had blocked my path, and he raked it through his hair. "I'm not telling you I would do so in order to hurt you. I don't have a choice, Lady Darby. After one conversation with the other guests, the procurator fiscal is going to name you a suspect himself. *Unless* we can point him toward someone more culpable."

I studied him, reluctant to trust him but aware his words were true.

"For what it's worth," he continued, planting one hand on his hip. "I don't believe you're the murderer." His voice sounded steady enough, but his eyes told me he still held doubts. "Although, it would be helpful if someone would explain to me just what happened during this trial last year everyone keeps alluding to."

I crossed my arms over my chest. "There was never a trial. It never came to that," I replied, but refused to elaborate further. Not after what had just transpired between us.

He searched my face, perhaps looking for any sign of weakness, of willingness to confide, but he quickly discovered I was determined in my silence. A few pretty words would not break through four years of wariness and fear, and a lifetime of circumspection when it came to sharing things about myself.

He moved aside to let me pass down the last step. "We have three days until the procurator fiscal arrives," he told me, as if I didn't already hear the time ticking away. "I would like to question Lord Marsdale and Mr. Calvin, Lady Godwin's other lovers, next. I suspect Mr. Calvin is much like Mr. Fitzpatrick, or worse, and would not speak freely with a woman present, but you may accompany me to question Lord Marsdale if you wish."

I turned to watch Gage closely, wondering if he had witnessed my exchange with Marsdale in the hall earlier.

"I suggest we wait until morning, however," he continued. "Marsdale seemed a little worse for drink this evening." He smirked. "Since he does not normally arise until after noon, I think a morning interview will be just the thing after a night of heavy indulgence. He will be quite grateful to us for waking him so early." He glanced at me, and seeing my expression, his grin widened. "Did you think I hadn't noticed how Marsdale finds you intriguing?" I tensed and he chuckled. "The man can't stand to be turned down, and I suspect you've done it more than once. He's fairly quivering with the need to conquer you before the party is over."

I blushed. "Marsdale is only interested in tormenting me," I protested.

"Which, in your case, indicates interest. You're not like the typical ladies of our acquaintance, where displays of attention and flattery work easily. You're a bit more challenging than all that."

I scowled in indignation. "I should hope so."

Gage smiled as if I had said something humorous. "Marsdale is a rather curious fellow, and I think your presence will actually loosen his lips instead of sealing them."

I didn't want to talk about Marsdale anymore—or contemplate why Gage did not seem bothered by his pursuit. "In the meantime, I wondered if perhaps we should search Lady Godwin's chamber." The thought had occurred to me after we passed by it twice this afternoon when we visited with Lady Stratford.

It was his turn to blush. "I already did."

"When?"

He cleared his throat. "After our interview with Lady Lydia and Mr. Tuthill."

I narrowed my eyes. "*That* was what you needed to do? Why didn't you take me with you?"

He seemed to struggle with answering the question, for he tugged at his coat sleeves. "Well . . . I thought it would be best if you were not caught searching the room with me, just in case someone were to happen by."

I arched an eyebrow in skepticism.

"I didn't find anything of interest, in any case."

"Did you even know what to look for?" I asked, recalling the mental list I'd constructed while I dressed for dinner.

Gage took exception to my criticism. "Madam, this is not my first investigation. I believe I know a bit more than you about what I need to search for."

I ignored his irritation. "Yes, but do you know what to search for in regards to a woman who is with child?"

"How would those items have anything to do with incriminating a murderer?" Gage asked crossly.

"Well, it could tell us how many people knew she was expecting. For example, did her lady's maid know?"

"We can interview her and ask her that."

"Yes, but did Lady Godwin have anything lying around that would imply such a thing to others who might visit her room?" I asked impatiently.

Gage looked upward in thought. "No. It appeared like any lady's bedchamber."

I bit my tongue before I could ask just how many ladies' bedchambers he had been in. I suspected I wouldn't like the answer. "Fine," I replied sharply. "Then I shall wish you a good night." I turned to march out of the library, but he grabbed my arm to stop me.

"Promise me you will not pursue any leads without first informing me."

I scowled.

"Tell me now," he insisted, his pale blue eyes holding my gaze steadily. "Or I *will* ask Philip to lock you away for your own protection."

"I don't need protection," I snapped.

Gage raised a single eyebrow. "Lord Westlock's attack last evening, and the other guests' hostility toward you, say otherwise."

I frowned, hating that he saw as much as I.

He squeezed my arm. "Promise me."

It was clear he was serious. I also knew that as much as Philip believed in me, and as often as he indulged my eccentricities, he would always place the matter of my safety before anything else. He would not hesitate to take Gage's advice.

I stared defiantly at Gage, angry that he would place Philip and me at cross-purposes and win. No matter the futility in the fight, there was no way I was going to give in to his demand without first attempting to extract some assurances of my own. "I will if you will promise me the same," I demanded.

He lowered his brow, clearly not liking the bargain. But after discovering he had searched Lady Godwin's rooms without me, no matter the reasons, I was certainly not going to let him run free while I could not.

"All right," he reluctantly agreed. "But do not think that I will let you control this investigation," he warned, gripping my arm tighter. "You are assisting me. And what I say goes. If I believe for a minute you are in danger, I will pull you from this investigation and have you locked up somewhere safe. Do you understand?"

I had absolutely no intention of complying with such a command, not when I needed to be free in order to catch the murderer and prevent Gage from suggesting me to the magistrate. However, there was no need for Gage to know that. It would be best to carry on with him in blissful ignorance. So I bobbed my head once in agreement before fleeing the room.

I was grateful for the anger fueling my movements as I hurried up the central staircase and through the hallways toward my room, for it distracted me from the gloom and shadows that otherwise might have frightened me. By the time I reached my bedchamber, I was so absorbed in contemplating ways to thwart Gage that I nearly stepped over the piece of paper lying on the floor just inside my door.

I stumbled to a halt and stared down at the folded white foolscap, wondering if I should have been expecting it. I glanced behind me into the corridor, peering in each direction before I closed and locked the door. Only then did I bend and pick up the letter, for I knew that was what it had to be—another note from either the murderer or a guest who was very diligent in their persecution of me. I turned the page around in my fingers, checking it for markings, and then unfolded the paper. It crinkled between my stiff fingers.

PERHAPS YOU SHOULD LEAVE THE INVESTIGATING TO THOSE WHO ARE MORE EXERIENCED BEFORE YOU REGRET IT. ETERNALLY.

I blinked down at the words. Ice formed in my veins, chilling me to the core. If whoever had sent this intended to frighten me, they'd certainly done their job. But there was no way I was going to quit this investigation. There was simply too much at stake for me to heed to threats, especially if they only came from a vindictive guest on a witch hunt.

The idea that the letter might have been written by the killer's hand gave me greater pause, but I was no less determined to defy them and discover why they wanted me off the inquiry so badly. Was there something the murderer worried I would uncover that Gage or Philip might not? Why? Because of my grim experience?

I frowned and refolded the letter, irritated to see that my hands were still shaking. Then I stuffed it into the drawer of my escritoire with the note from the night before. I knew one thing—I certainly wasn't going to show the letter to Gage. After our altercation in the library, I knew he was looking for an excuse to ban me from the inquiry and lock me in my room, and I wasn't about to give it to him. For the time being, I was more scared of what my absence from the investigation could cost me than what the murderer might do, foolish as that might be.

Even so, I tossed and turned long into the night and wondered if I was making a grave mistake.

CHAPTER FIFTEEN

"You'd better have a good reason for pulling me out of bed at such an ungodly hour, Gage," Marsdale drawled as he entered the parlor connected to his bedchamber the next morning.

Under the circumstances, I was inclined to agree with him, having barely pulled *myself* out of bed in time to meet Gage after another long, restless night. I would have been quite happy to allow Marsdale to sleep on, disturbing him closer to his normal rising time at noon. But of course that would have wasted hours of daylight and valuable investigation time. The procurator fiscal would not allow me to make up for lost time, and neither would the murderer.

Marsdale's steps faltered when he saw me, and his eyes lit with a gleeful anticipation I found most unsettling. "Now why didn't you tell me the lovely Lady Darby would be joining us?" he demanded. "I would have hurried along much quicker. And worn much less clothing," he added with a wicked grin before flopping down onto the settee much too close to me.

I knew I should have chosen the chair. I pulled my skirt out from under him and scooted as far away from him as the piece of furniture would allow. My maneuvering only made him grin wider.

"Let Lady Darby be," Gage told Marsdale, his brow lowered in a fierce frown.

The duke's heir slouched deeper into the cushions and stuck out his lower lip in a pout.

As Gage predicted, Marsdale had insisted on being difficult from the moment we appeared at his door that morning. He tried to refuse us when Gage sent Marsdale's valet in to wake him at eight, and then at a quarter after, and half past. Only Gage's threat to send four of Philip's footmen in to drag him out of bed and tie him to a chair seemed sufficient enough to motivate him to move. Even then, he had still taken his time preparing to receive us.

I studied his appearance with some interest, wondering just how terrible he had looked when he rolled out of bed if this was how he appeared after nearly half an hour of primping. His eyes were bloodshot and his hair stood on end, but his jaw had clearly been shaved. I could still smell the soap. In place of a frock coat, he wore a black velvet dressing gown over a pristine white shirt and a pair of buff trousers. The shirt gaped at his throat, providing me a glimpse of the dark whorls of hair sprinkling his chest. I tried not to focus on the sight, lest Marsdale notice my interest. However, it was more difficult than I would have thought. Rarely had a man appeared before me in dishabille. Even Sir Anthony was always punctiliously dressed in my presence, and he came to me at night in the dark wearing his nightshirt. I suppose there were his anatomy subjects to consider, but the body of a living man was quite different from that of a dead one.

"You're becoming quite a bore," Marsdale told Gage, all the while keeping his eyes on me and the neckline of my mauve-and-dove-gray morning dress. "In fact, Mrs. Cline complained to me of it just last evening."

Gage sighed heavily. "We're not here to discuss me. I want to talk about your relationship with Lady Godwin."

"Why would you care about that?" Marsdale replied offhandedly. "She was demanding and dull." His eyes slid over me intently, as if taking inventory. "Lady Darby seems like she would be a much more interesting companion. Did you bring her to share?" I stiffened. "I'm not normally interested in such a thing if it includes another male, but for Lady Darby, I think I might be willing."

"Marsdale!" Gage barked angrily.

A blush heated my face clear to the tips of my ears, and I couldn't stop an image from forming in my head of Gage cradling my face between his hands, and Marsdale . . . My imagination seemed to give out at that point. "But how . . . ?" I began to ask in puzzlement before my brain could stop me from doing so.

Marsdale burst out in delighted laughter while Gage shook his head at me, discouraging me from finishing the question.

"Oh, Lady Darby, you are a treat," Marsdale gasped, cradling his head in his hands. His face was suffused with an interesting combination of pain and amusement. I assumed the ache was caused by last night's overindulgence, and I suddenly wished for him to suffer a great deal more of it. "I could teach you . . ."

"Marsdale," Gage interrupted. "I did not bring Lady Darby with me so that you could torment her. Now, if you will. Let's return to the matter at hand." He glared at the marquess. "You should be taking this seriously. After all, you *are* being considered as a suspect in a murder investigation."

Marsdale turned to give Gage his full attention for the first time since entering the room, and I shifted in my seat, grateful to be released from his gaze.

"I'm a suspect. Truly?" He actually seemed intrigued by the idea. I thought he had only been toying with me last night when he became so interested by such a prospect.

Gage narrowed his eyes. "I was informed that you were involved with Lady Godwin earlier this year."

"Yes. I allowed her to bed me a few times," he replied airily.

Surprised by the way he had chosen to phrase his answer, I couldn't stop myself from asking. "*She* bedded *you?*"

He turned back to me with a smirk. "It was at a house party. I was bored and she was eager, so I let her crawl under my covers. All in all, it was a rather tedious encounter."

I widened my eyes, taken aback by his blasé attitude. I had the distinct feeling Lady Godwin would not have viewed their liaison in such derogatory terms, and that she would have been furious to discover he had.

"Have no worries, Lady Darby," he went on to say, reaching out to drag his finger over the back of my hand. I pulled it away from him, tucking it in my lap. "I'm certain our encounters will be anything but tedious."

I arched an eyebrow haughtily at him. He was certainly in fine form, and I wondered if he was normally this crude in the morning, or if perhaps he was trying to punish me for last night's rejection.

"When was this house party?" Gage interrupted before I could come up with a proper set-down.

Marsdale's eyes laughed at me as he addressed Gage. "Sometime around Saint Valentine's Day. Val Corbett finds it bloody hilarious to host his annual hunting party to correspond with his namesake's holiday."

I glanced at Gage. If that were true, then Marsdale was unlikely to be the father of Lady Godwin's baby.

"You did not bed her again after that?" he pressed, his pale blue eyes washed gray by the bright hue of his bottle-green coat.

Marsdale grimaced and turned to Gage. "God, no. Why are you pressing me so about this? Did someone toss the viscountess's skirts before killing her?" I cringed. "If so, you'd best speak to Fitzpatrick. He's been swiving her for weeks."

"I've already spoken to Fitzpatrick," Gage replied with exaggerated patience.

"And he accused me?"

Gage studiously avoided my eyes. "Well, no."

"Ah, so you're just speaking with all of her former lovers," Marsdale replied, widening his legs so that his left knee almost brushed mine. "That could take a while. The viscountess spread her legs for more men than a twopenny whore. And most of them aren't here at Gairloch."

I screwed up my face in disgust. "Surely not."

"Well, no. Not quite that bad. It's merely an expression." His eyes perused my face lazily. "Perhaps I should be couching my words in more polite terms, but this is hardly a polite conversation. Which makes me wonder why you're here."

I struggled to continue meeting his eyes and not glance at Gage. He was far sharper than either of us had expected him to be at nine o'clock in the morning when he had been foxed the night before. However, I doubted he would run about telling everyone of my presence in his chamber this morning—at least, not in my current capacity. He might try to imply that I had been in his bed.

"Lady Darby is here at my request," Gage pronounced, saving me from coming up with an explanation. "I thought you might cooperate better with a lady present."

"If you really want me to cooperate, you should offer me something in return," Marsdale replied, his words dripping with insinuation.

I frowned at him.

"How about, I won't ask Cromarty to lock you in your chambers without a drop of alcohol or a single woman," Gage threatened, bristling in his chair across the tea table.

Far from being intimidated, Marsdale seemed amused by Gage's irritation. "What else do you want to know? More about Lady Godwin's sexual proclivities?"

"Where were you when Lady Lydia screamed?"

He sighed, as if bored by Gage's question. "Lord Stratford and I retired to the men's parlor for a smoke after dinner. However, Stratford left me shortly after, and I'm afraid no one else joined me until Lord Lewis Effingham stopped in to tell me about the gruesome sight everyone found in the maze. So I have no one to corroborate my alibi." He did not seem particularly worried about this, and even smiled rather smugly.

"Do you have any idea who might have murdered Lady Godwin? Any idea who might have wanted to hurt her?"

Marsdale shrugged. "I haven't the foggiest."

Gage scowled at Marsdale's nonchalant attitude. "Well, if you think of anything, I would appreciate it if you would let me know." He began to rise, and I followed suit.

"I have a question," Marsdale said.

I tensed and braced for whatever lewd jest was about to pop out of his mouth next.

"Lady Darby, do you still paint?"

The query sounded innocent, but I knew that could hardly be the case if Lord Marsdale was asking it. "Yes," I replied cautiously.

"I would like to hire you to paint my portrait," he declared.

My heart jumped at his words. It had been nearly a year and a half since someone other than family had commissioned me to paint for them. All of my recent work had been created from my own whim, in hopes that someone would find the subjects I chose interesting enough to purchase. I longed to paint a real person again, someone beyond the figures in my imagination or the members of my family.

"Truly?" I asked, not certain I could trust Marsdale's words. Not that I doubted he would want a portrait of himself. The aristocracy liked to commission paintings of themselves for posterity, and he was definitely arrogant enough to enjoy such a thing. However, he had teased and tormented me since his arrival, and I wasn't certain how this statement might play out in the private game he seemed to be playing.

"You are certainly talented enough. And I would rather have my image depicted while I am still young, rather than after my father is deceased."

I realized he was speaking of his ducal portrait, and I instantly began imagining how I would dress and pose him to his best advantage. Perhaps at the top of a grand staircase or on a terrace or balcony—something to suit his haughty demeanor. He was handsome enough not to require the softer light of evening, though I still felt the muted shadows of late afternoon would suit him best. No robes or scepters or any of the other silly props so often present in the depictions of lords and royalty. He would look most impressive dressed in his austere evening kit, or perhaps riding attire.

"I would like to pose here, I think," Marsdale said, stretching out on the settee like a large cat.

I stared down at him in confusion, not understanding why he would wish to be depicted so slovenly and lazy.

He smiled up at me, a wicked twinkle in his eyes. "In the nude." He laughed as shock radiated across my face.

I scowled. I should have known better. But the idea of painting a commissioned portrait again had simply been too tempting, too exhilarating, to resist. I wanted to reach down and smack him for raising my hopes so. It would serve him right if I actually accepted the project. I had never painted a living man without clothing before. It might prove to be an interesting experience. Unfortunately, I suspected Marsdale would enjoy it far too much.

"Come, Lady Darby," Gage said, offering me his arm. "I believe Lord Marsdale has had enough fun at your expense this morning." He glared at the marquess, who only continued to chuckle.

I tucked my arm inside Gage's and tried to hide my disappointment at not gaining an actual commission and my growing fascination with the idea of painting a nude. I wondered what it would be like. Would I be embarrassed? Would my subject be? My gaze slid to Gage as he closed the door to Marsdale's parlor. What would it be like to paint Gage? My cheeks heated at the thought.

"I'm sorry Marsdale decided to behave like such a rogue," he told me, marching me down the hall. "Had I known, I'm not sure I would have allowed you to accompany me."

I cleared my throat. "Then I'm glad you didn't know." He glanced at me. "Besides, I've grown quite accustomed to associating with rogues. Aren't you one?"

His arm stiffened beneath mine. "I'm not a rogue, Lady Darby. I'm a rakehell."

I snorted. "What's the difference?"

His voice hardened. "A rogue implies that one is a scoundrel, a villain, taking what he should not and shirking the law and his duty. A rakehell may be debauched in the intimate sense, jumping from skirt to skirt, but never where it is unwanted, and *never* with an innocent."

It sounded as if he had recited this twaddle before, and I wondered if he actually believed it. "I still don't see the difference," I replied.

He paused in the middle of the hall and turned a frosty gaze on me. "I assure you, my lady, that were you closeted with a rogue rather than a rake, you would know the difference. If a rogue decided he wanted you, he would use all of the means at his disposal to persuade you, but ultimately he would debauch you whether you wished it or not. A rake would never dishonor a woman in such a way."

I realized I had insulted him severely. Whether or not I lumped the activities of rakes and rogues together, to Gage there was a clear difference, and I had questioned his honor by implying otherwise. I understood what he was telling me, and I could now see the clear distinction between the two. I had felt safe while alone in Gage's company. However, that was not likely to be the case with a true rogue.

"I apologize," I replied. "You're right. You are not a rogue."

A dull red washed over Gage's cheekbones, and he turned away with a cough. "Thank you."

Pretending not to see his discomfiture, I examined the tapestry hanging against the wall beside me. "Do you really think Marsdale is a rogue?"

"I'm not sure," Gage admitted. "But I wouldn't attempt to find out," he hastened to add, perhaps worried I might do just such a thing.

"I don't think he did it."

He did not pretend to misunderstand me. "Nor do I," he said with a sigh, stepping up beside me to look at the tapestry. "I think he's more enamored with the idea of being considered a suspect, and how wicked that will make him look. Although . . ." Gage paused to take a deep breath. "I have been wrong before, and about less crafty people."

I wanted to ask what he meant, but the sound of hurried footsteps stopped me. One of my brother-in-law's footmen rushed down the hall toward us.

"Lady Darby, Mr. Gage," he exclaimed breathlessly. He paused and tugged nervously at his scarlet-and-black livery. "His lordship says he has urgent need of you in his study."

A heavy feeling settled in my gut. Were Alana and the children safe? Did someone find Lady Godwin's baby or, worse, another body? I glanced at Gage, scared that something terrible had happened.

He pulled my arm through his, squeezing it in reassurance before nodding at the footman. We set off down the corridor at a pace just shy of a run.

CHAPTER SIXTEEN

Philip was seated behind his desk when we entered his study, looking somber and troubled.

"The children?" I gasped.

"They are fine," he assured me, rising from his seat.

"And Alana?"

He smiled at me gently. "Fine as well."

I breathed a heavy sigh of relief before following his gaze to Mrs. MacLean. The housekeeper rose hastily from her perch on one of the red chairs and bobbed a curtsy to Gage and me.

"Mrs. MacLean was kind enough to bring something to my attention."

Her gaze darted between Gage and me, finally settling on him nervously. "One o' my maids found this in Mr. Abingdon's rooms this morn," she replied as she unfolded a towel and showed us the bloodstained rag inside.

"Well done, Mrs. MacLean," he exclaimed, reaching out to take the towel in his hands. "Did your maid mention where in the room she found it?"

Her already ruddy cheeks flushed from his praise. "Beside the washstand, sir. There was also a wee spot or two on the linens. Did ya need to see those as weel?"

"No. But see that they're set aside and not washed until

Lord or Lady Cromarty tell you otherwise. And continue to keep your staff on the lookout for anything usual."

"Aye, sir." She bobbed another swift curtsy and sailed out of the room in her pristine white apron and cap.

Philip and Gage gazed grimly at each other. "I suggest that we ask Mr. Abingdon to join us in his chamber," my brother-in-law said.

Gage nodded before turning to me. I knew the look in his eyes, and I wasn't having any of it.

"Oh, no. I'm coming with you," I told them determinedly. "While you speak with him, I'll search his room for any further evidence. We still need to find that other murder weapon." Philip looked as if he might object. "I'll listen at the door," I threatened. "And how would that look to anyone passing by?"

"Fine," Gage snapped. "But Cromarty and I will do the talking."

I followed the men upstairs to Mr. Abingdon's chamber while a footman was dispatched to find the man himself. My stomach soured at the realization we might have finally found the killer, and that he had been encouraged by Philip's aunt to court Caroline. It sent a shiver down my spine to think of him touching the lovely, sweet-natured girl. I had seen nothing in him to indicate that he might be a cold-blooded murderer, but, of course, that was the problem, wasn't it? No one struck me as being capable of the crime. There were a few who jangled my nerves, but none who plucked a particularly ominous string. And that was what made all of this so difficult. From the outset, there had been no clear suspect, no definitive motive, and no lower masses to blame, even if unjustly, as in the city. It was uncomfortable knowing that whoever had done this likely walked among us unawares. Perhaps that was about to change, but it still did not sit well with me that I had not seen it coming, as it appeared no one had.

Mr. Abingdon's chamber was papered in a fine silk print of sparrows and yarrow branches. It was smaller than both the Stratfords' and Lord Marsdale's rooms and did not adjoin a parlor, but bachelor gentlemen without title were not normally assigned the best rooms. The bedding and drapes were sepia brown trimmed with creamy white, and the sturdy oak furniture was upholstered in goldenrod.

I immediately crossed the room to the escritoire and began rifling through the drawers and cubbyholes while Gage studied the piles of papers on top.

"These are just betting vouchers and correspondence about his horses," Gage informed us. "Have you uncovered anything?"

"Not so far," I answered absently, studying the letter opener for signs of blood or nicks in the sturdy metal frame. I replaced it in the drawer and closed it, crossing the room toward the dresser.

I'd barely had time to rifle through one drawer before Mr. Abingdon entered. I stood with my hands clasped in front of me, waiting for Gage to explain our presence before I continued.

"What . . . what is going on?" Mr. Abingdon asked, taking in the sight of all three of us in his bedchamber.

Philip moved forward to coax him farther into the room. "I'm afraid an unsavory article has come to our attention and we must ask you about it."

His eyes flared wide and he swallowed, dare I say, guiltily. "What article?"

Gage and Philip exchanged a look, and I decided that was my cue to resume searching. I pulled open another drawer and reached in to run my hands under the stack of neatly folded cravats.

"What is she doing?" Abingdon asked in outrage.

"Nothing for you to be concerned with," Gage replied, stopping him from crossing the room toward me. "At least not when there is a more serious matter to discuss. Do you know what this is?" I assumed he was showing our suspect the bloody washcloth.

"I have no idea," Mr. Abingdon lied in a tight voice.

"Really?" Gage queried doubtfully. "Because the maids found this by *your* washstand."

I opened another drawer filled with stockings.

"I . . . I must have cut myself while I was shaving."

"That must have been quite some gash to have bled this much. Do you see any such cuts, Lord Cromarty?"

"*Hmmm.* Looks smooth to me. Not so much as a nick," Philip replied, playing along.

I hesitated at the next drawer, not relishing the idea of digging through Mr. Abingdon's small clothes. I swallowed my distaste and reached in, hoping they were laundered frequently.

"Try again," Gage told Mr. Abingdon in a hard voice.

"I don't see how this is any of your business," he retorted, attempting to put them off with a display of lordly indignation. "Besides, the maid could have lied. You can never trust servants. I bet it was that pert little blonde. She got all uppish when I tried to give her a kiss. How was I to know she wasn't willing? Most chambermaids are quite happy to earn a few extra coins from a quick tumble."

I paused to glance back at the man, shocked to hear him admit he had been propositioning the maids.

Philip's face was tight with anger. "Mr. Abingdon, I will caution you not to touch any of my maids again. I do not condone such behavior with my servants, no matter what other gentlemen may believe is acceptable."

Mr. Abingdon looked displeased by this reprimand.

I turned away to resume searching as my brother-in-law continued. "Regardless, this matter has nothing to do with them. Now, Mr. Gage and I are going to ask you one more time, and you *will* answer truthfully. Otherwise, we shall be forced to assume the worst and have you locked up until the procurator fiscal arrives."

"Lock me up? You can't do that," Mr. Abingdon exclaimed.

"Of course we can. This is my property. And you are now the prime suspect in a murder investigation."

"Hold on. Wait a minute." Mr. Abingdon sounded absurdly alarmed. What had he thought they'd been hinting at? "A murder? You don't think this is Lady Godwin's blood?"

"Who else's blood are we to have assumed it to be?" Gage asked with exaggerated patience.

I moved quietly toward the nightstand.

"It's not Lady Godwin's," Mr. Abingdon stated firmly. He sounded horrified by the idea. "It truly is mine."

"Come, Mr. Abingdon. Do you think us fools? You did not bleed this much by cutting yourself shaving, so *where* did it come from?" When he did not answer, Gage sighed gustily. "Where do you want to hold him?" he asked Philip.

"No, wait!"

"Where?" Gage snapped.

"My nose," he muttered.

I glanced across the counterpane at the three men.

"Your nose?" Gage repeated. "And how did your nose come to be bleeding? And don't feed me any nonsense about frequently having nosebleeds. If that were the case, you wouldn't have lied about it."

"Mr. Darlington punched me," he replied huffily.

I fumbled the book in my hands before catching it and setting it carefully back on the nightstand. From the ringing silence on the other side of the room, I took it that Philip and Gage were just as surprised by Mr. Abingdon's grudging admission.

"Why would Mr. Darlington punch you?" Gage asked carefully, clearly having come to some conclusion I had not yet reached.

Mr. Abingdon's frown turned fiercer. "It was Miss Darlington who came to me. Said she was frightened by all the talk about the murderer at dinner and didn't want to be alone."

"So you . . . protected her?" Gage's tone dripped with sarcasm.

"*She's* the one who followed me out to the terrace and pressed herself against me," he blazed. "She was clinging to me like moss on a stone. A man can't resist that much temptation."

I rolled my eyes.

"And, let me guess, Mr. Darlington happened upon you . . . *embracing* his sister, and he drew your cork."

Mr. Abingdon grunted in confirmation.

"You're lucky he didn't call you out." Philip sounded as if he would like to do so himself.

He glowered up at him. "Darlington was far more concerned with seeing me engaged to his sister."

"And are you?" my brother-in-law pressed, somehow managing to make a man who was half a foot taller and several stones heavier seem smaller than him.

Mr. Abingdon scowled and opened his mouth as if he would like to argue, but Philip's glare cut him off. "Yes," he sulked.

I shook my head and restacked his books on the nightstand before rising to my feet. I felt sorry for Miss Darlington, whether or not she had hoped for just such an outcome when she followed Mr. Abingdon out to the terrace the previous evening or not. Her future bridegroom was clearly a pig, and a brooding one at that. I hoped she had found at least some small amount of comfort in his arms before her brother planted him a facer.

Gage reached for my arm as I rounded the bed. "Come, Lady Darby. I don't think we're needed here anymore. Let's leave Lord Cromarty to sort this out."

Once we were alone in the corridor, he shook his head and added, "Poor Miss Darlington."

"Yes," I murmured sincerely.

His face expressed some surprise at my response.

"What?" I asked.

"Nothing. I just thought your feelings would be less charitable toward Lord Darlington's flighty and naive daughter."

"Well, her decision to follow Mr. Abingdon out to the terrace was certainly foolish, but being a single woman myself, I can sympathize with her distress last evening."

Gage halted us in the middle of the corridor. "Why, Lady Darby, were you frightened?" His tone of voice indicated he was teasing me, but something in his eyes told me he also took my answer seriously.

"It's difficult not to be when you know there is a murderer running loose about the castle." I stared down the gloomy inner corridor stretching before us. Even during the day, it was still shrouded in shadows, with nothing but the flicker of the sconces in the wall to light the way. At night, the passages seemed to take on a life of their own, gripping me in their dark palms and playing with my imagination. They tangibly reminded me of the danger lurking about me, and my solitary existence in facing it.

I had always known that I was a solitary person. Even when wed to Sir Anthony, even while living with my sister and her family, I knew the truth. I was alone. And likely would always be. That normally did not trouble me, but lately I had begun to feel the weight of such a truth, the isolation of such a life, and it upset me more than I would have liked to admit. But I didn't know how to change that. My temperament, my talent, seemed to naturally hold me apart from others. The scandal had only exacerbated the problem.

I glanced at Sebastian Gage, reluctant to confess I was jealous of his ability to charm and allure and fit in wherever he went. I would never be that way, could never be that way. And as proud as I was of my uniqueness, I also despised it.

Gage smiled down at me, and I wondered if he had any inkling as to what my thoughts were. "What next?" I asked, anxious to erase the soft look from his eyes.

"Well, I planned to speak with Mr. Calvin early this afternoon. In his chamber," he added as if to tell me not to attempt to eavesdrop on this conversation. Thankfully, I was just as happy not to. Mr. Calvin was nearing sixty, and fussy and prudish. I had a difficult enough time believing he bedded Lady Godwin, let alone killed her. Appearances could be deceiving, but right now both Mr. and Mrs. Calvin were at the very bottom of my list of possible culprits.

"What about now? Do you have time to interview Lady Godwin's maid?" I asked. "Mrs. MacLean probably knows where she is."

Gage nodded. "You ask the questions this time."

I glanced at him curiously.

"I have a feeling she'll be much more comfortable talking with a woman."

"Should I ask her if she recognizes the embroidery shears?" I had been wondering why he had not yet queried anyone about the potential weapon. I figured he'd been waiting to see if anyone reported them missing.

"I suppose she would be the logical place to start. Just be sure to instruct her not to share our conversation with anyone."

Lady Godwin's maid was a tiny Frenchwoman barely four and a half feet in height. She called to mind a little brown mouse. Her hair was a soft sandy brown, and her eyes a deep shade of coffee, ringed in red from crying. Her mouth was thin and tiny, and her nose narrow and pink at the tip. She was curled into a ball at the top of her small bed, clutching a sodden handkerchief when we entered the room she shared with the maid of another guest. She appeared lost and genuinely distressed, as well as a little alarmed by our presence.

"Are you Faye?" I asked gently, and she nodded hesitantly. "My name is Lady Darby, and this is Mr. Gage." I noticed she tensed when I mentioned my name. Obviously the servants had been gossiping among themselves. "We wanted to ask you a few questions about your employer."

She blinked wide eyes at me and then Gage. "You are zee man who investigates?" she queried in an accent too lilting to be feigned.

"Yes."

She glanced at me again and then reluctantly nodded her agreement to speak with us.

I sat carefully on the end of her bunk, not wanting to threaten or crowd the skittish maid, who sat up and pulled her knees into her chest. Gage leaned against the wall and crossed his arms and ankles, affecting a casual pose.

"First, allow me to offer my condolences." Faye's eyes widened even further as she peered at me over the hills of her knees. "Lady Godwin was your employer and perhaps your friend. I'm sure you feel the loss."

Her eyes saddened once again, drooping at the corners. She nodded.

"How long have you been Lady Godwin's lady's maid?"

"*Mmmm . . .* four years," she hummed.

"Was she your first employer?"

"In England? *Oui*."

I nodded. "Was she fair?"

"Yes," she replied, and then elaborated timidly. "My lady was demanding. She wants to be most beautiful and . . . *très chic*. But she was fair."

"We've been told she took a number of lovers after her husband left for India." I hoped that by leading into my next question the maid would not become hesitant to speak to us, worrying she was betraying her ladyship. "Do you know this to be true?"

She studied me for a moment, clearly debating whether to reply. Her shoulders drooped, and she sighed. "Yes." Then her back stiffened. "Do you zink one of her amours kill her?"

"We don't know," I replied truthfully, exchanging a glance with Gage. "But we think it's a very real possibility."

Faye released her death grip on her knees and leaned her head back against the wall. A fierce frown lowered the corners of her lips. "I tell her such indiscretion not good, but she only laugh at me. A Frenchwoman would never be so careless with her liaisons."

"Faye," I began, trying to decide the most delicate way to phrase what I needed to ask next. "Did Lady Godwin experience an . . . unexpected result from all these encounters?" The maid turned watchful, and I took her silence as encouragement. "Was she enceinte?" I asked bluntly.

She lowered her eyes and nodded.

"Do you know how long?"

"*Mmmm* . . . five months. Physician say to expect *enfant* in early December."

Which meant that if Lord Marsdale had been honest with us, and he had slept with Lady Godwin around mid-February, he could not be the father. We were looking for someone else.

"Did Lady Godwin know who the father was?"

"Yes, but she not tell me. Only say she was pleased."

I looked at Gage. He looked just as puzzled as I was. I would have assumed Lady Godwin would be panicked at the realization she was expecting and that her husband had been hundreds of miles away at the time of conception. There was no way of fooling the man into believing it was his.

"Was she afraid of how her husband would react?"

Faye shrugged. "Not zat I see. His lordship is . . . how do you say, *indulgent*, and generally ignore his wife."

I doubted Lord Godwin would have been so indulgent when it came to his wife having another man's child.

"How many people knew she was expecting?"

The maid tilted her head in thought. "Me, her physician, *mmm* . . . I zink she tell her friend Lady Stratford." She paused. "And maybe her sister. But no one else zat I know."

She must have told someone else. Or Lady Stratford had. I glanced at Faye. Or . . .

"Did you tell anyone? Did the other servants know?"

Faye shook her head as if offended. "I tell no one. The other servants, zay not speak to me, so I not speak to zem."

That must be a lonely existence. No wonder the woman mourned the loss of her employer. But such was the life of ladies' maids and valets—too lowly for their employers, too high for the other servants of the household. I wondered if she'd made friends with any other ladies' maids.

Gage shifted behind me, and I realized I had been gathering wool for too long.

I cleared my throat. "Did Lady Godwin have any enemies that you are aware of?"

"*Oui*," Faye said adamantly. "She tell me all zee other ladies jealous of her beauty and wanting to be her." She shook her head angrily. "Zay not like her."

I exchanged another glance with Gage. Was the maid truly that blind? Surely she'd seen the other ladies, and certainly Lady Stratford, who was a swan to Lady Godwin's, or anyone else's for that matter, duck. I supposed she was only repeating her employer's words, but I had a hard time accepting that she actually believed them.

"One more question," I said. "Did Lady Godwin embroider?"

Faye seemed taken aback by the question. "No," she replied in confusion.

"But did she own any embroidery supplies? Thread, needles, scissors?"

The maid shook her head. "No. She hate stitching." She said it as if Lady Godwin equated it to the plague.

I hid a smile and rose from the end of the bed. "Thank you for answering our questions. For the time being, please keep our conversation to yourself, and if you should remember anything that you think might help us, let Mrs. MacLean know and she will send for one of us."

"Of course," Faye replied. "You will catch him, won't you? Zee person who did zis?" The maid's expression was fierce, and I could see tears gathering at the corners of her eyes again. Whether or not anyone else truly cared about Lady Godwin, this maid had.

I smiled consolingly, thinking of how much I had weighing on the outcome of this as well. "We hope so. We definitely hope so," I added softly. I felt Gage's eyes on me but ignored him. "Faye, what is going to happen to you? Do you have a ride back to London?" I asked, concerned that the maid had been forgotten in all the fervor.

She brushed tears away from the corners of her eyes. "I travel back to London with her ladyship's body and belongings. Lady Stratford say she make sure I taken care of until I find another position."

I thought it spoke well of the countess that she had remembered the maid. Or perhaps it was her lady's maid who had. I recognized the titian-haired girl who entered the room as the same maid who had let us into Lady Stratford's apartments and served us tea.

"Pardon me," she said as Gage held the door for her when we left and allowed her to slip inside. I peered through the crack in the door as it closed and watched the maid approach Faye's bed. The Frenchwoman dissolved into tears again upon seeing the woman, who reached out to hug her as the door latched.

"So her maid knew she was expecting," Gage commented as we descended the tiny set of stairs leading to the servants' quarters at the very top of the castle.

I rubbed my hands up and down my arms to warm them against the chill of the stairwell and sighed. "Which is not really surprising. A lady's maid would often be the first to discover such a thing."

"Even before the husband?" Gage attempted to jest.

I shrugged a shoulder. "Depending on the marriage and the husband. I somehow doubt Lord Godwin was familiar enough with his wife's body that he would have noticed such a thing, even if he were in England."

Gage nodded. "But he eventually would have."

"Yes. And likely soon, if he hadn't already. She would have started putting on weight rapidly at this point." I sighed. "Well, now we know the embroidery scissors aren't Lady Godwin's. So whose are they?"

Gage reached out to open the door at the base of the steps for me. "That's a good question."

"Why didn't you ask Lady Stratford about them?" I asked as we moved down the hall toward the main staircase.

"I was still waiting to hear from Lord Cromarty. Your sister and Mrs. MacLean were asked to check the household inventory to make certain they were not part of it. I also had no reason to suspect Lady Stratford had any part in Lady Godwin's murder."

I paused at the top of the stairs and turned to lean against the banister. "That doesn't mean the killer didn't take the scissors from her or another lady's embroidery basket," I challenged.

"I realize that, but once we bring out those shears and begin asking everyone whether they recognize them, it will be easier for the owner, and possibly the murderer, to hide the fact that they were missing in the first place. Servants can be bribed, replacements made. It would be easier to catch the culprit unaware. Are you coming downstairs?"

I supposed his reasoning made sense. But eventually, suspect or no, he was going to have to reveal the discovery of those scissors.

"No," I replied, pushing away from the railing. "I think I'll visit the children in the nursery."

Gage's smile was teasing. "Hiding again, Lady Darby?"

I lifted my chin to stare down my nose at him. "Just trying to make it more of a challenge for you to find me later," I replied flippantly and strode down the hall so I didn't have to see the look in Gage's eyes that told me he knew I was lying.

CHAPTER SEVENTEEN

I peered through the open doorway of the master suite's private parlor, glad to find my sister alone. We had not spoken privately since the previous morning, and I was curious how she was holding up under the strain of the past few days. She was seated at the end of a settee upholstered in cream-and-oatmeal-striped silk, her arm draped across the back of the seat and her face turned to the sun shining through the window. I paused, smiling at the pretty picture she made. Her hair, which was two shades lighter than my dark chestnut tresses, appeared tipped in a shade of caramel in the afternoon sunlight. She seemed peaceful, as I had not seen her in weeks since preparations for the house party began. I wondered if perhaps I should not interrupt her, and began to back out of the room.

But at that moment she turned and opened her eyes. A soft smile lit her face at the sight of me, and she reached out a hand. Unable to resist the pull of the affection in her gaze, I crossed the room and sat down next to her in front of the window.

"And where have you been all day?" she asked me. "When I went to your room this morning, you were already gone."

"Mr. Gage took me with him to speak with Lord Marsdale."

"Ah," she breathed knowingly. She reached around to the

back of my head to adjust my hair, pulling several pins out and replacing them. "Are you any closer to finding the killer?" she asked in a deceptively casual tone.

"I'm afraid not," I told her. "But we have two and a half days left before the procurator fiscal from Inverness arrives, and I'm going to do everything in my power to catch the culprit before then," I declared, determination ringing in my voice.

Alana smiled in gentle amusement. "That would be nice, dear. Believe me, I would like to know that my children are safe again and send all of these people on their way so that I can have my home back. But even if you haven't caught him by then, I'm sure the procurator fiscal will be grateful for the work you and Mr. Gage have done."

I feigned an interest in the pile of color swatches my sister had laid across the back of the settee. I didn't have the heart to tell her my suspicions about where the blame would fall should we fail to expose the murderer soon. Perhaps tomorrow I would, or the day after, just before the procurator fiscal arrived so that she was prepared, but not now. Not while she was so serene.

"What are these for?" I asked, changing the subject.

She sighed. "The children need new clothes for autumn. But I'm having difficulty choosing colors for Philipa." Her lips quirked wryly. "Especially since she has informed me she now despises pink and yellow."

I smiled. That certainly sounded like my niece. Next year pink and yellow would be her favorite colors. "The cinnamon red and bottle green," I told Alana, tapping the swatches in question.

"Really?" She reached across me for the stack. "I thought perhaps the cinnamon was too dark for her complexion."

It tickled me that Alana was already so concerned with her five-year-old daughter's wardrobe. "No. It will look lovely with her brown eyes."

"All right," she conceded as she tossed the swatches onto

the table. "Well, since that is decided, you can join me for tea." She stood and shook out her skirts. I stared up at her in confusion. "Well, come on then."

"Aren't we taking tea here?"

"Of course not. We shall join the other ladies in the drawing room."

I nearly groaned. I knew that tone of voice. I knew it, and I hated it. It was the voice of the centuries of obstinate, crusading Scotsmen whose blood flowed through our veins. And it had been my great misfortune to be too often the supposed beneficiary of Alana's own brand of stubborn valor.

When I was six, she boosted me onto the back of our father's newest gelding in an effort to convince our sire I was ready to ride a horse like my older siblings instead of a pony. Her plan only succeeded in giving me a sore bottom; first from being thrown from the gelding, and later from the thrashing I received from Father for the stunt.

At fourteen, when I still felt gawky and uncomfortable with the changes to my body, Alana dressed me in one of her gowns and dragged me to the May Day fair in Kelso. She was determined to prove to our neighbors that I was not unattractive or strange. It seemed to work, until a baron's son tried to kiss me and I sneezed in his face. Apparently, no one else thought he smelled too strongly of his cologne, and my protestations that it had tickled my nose fell on deaf ears.

At eighteen, it was a handful of gentlemen mocking my first private art exhibition at our family's London residence. At twenty-one, a debutante who felt she should be allowed to purchase the blue dress I had chosen for my wedding gown because she claimed it made my eyes look possessed. At twenty-four, a mere month after Sir Anthony's death and the accusations that followed, it was the lords and ladies who strolled in front of the shops on Bond Street, whispering about my crimes and unnatural tendencies as Alana and I purchased a few last-minute items in preparation for our journey to Gairloch. None of those situations had worked out well for me when Alana stepped in. The gentlemen had begun wagers in the betting books at the gentlemen's clubs that no one would marry me for three years—they won, just barely. The wedding gown was spitefully ripped by the debutante, and I was still shunned and whispered about by the lords and ladies.

And now Alana wanted us to confront a drawing room filled with gossiping harpies who believed me capable of murder.

As much as I loved my sister and appreciated her righteous indignation on my behalf, there were times when I wished she would simply leave well enough alone.

"I would prefer to have tea here," I told her, prepared to argue my point.

"I'm sure you would. And I can hardly blame you. However . . ." She adopted her lady-of-the-manor voice, the one she had been practicing since the age of seven, somehow knowing she would be a countess someday. "I am not going to let my guests dictate who sits in *my* drawing room and who does not. This is your home, too, Kiera. And if I want to drink tea with you, I can do so anywhere I please."

"Alana," I pleaded.

"No. My mind is firm on this. If Lady Westlock and her fellow harpies are not pleased by your presence, they can eat their biscuits in the dungeons for all I care."

"Please, Alana." I clasped my hands together to beg. "Now is not the time"

"If not now, then when?" My sister perched on the edge of the settee next to me and took hold of my hands. "It will not stop. It never will, unless we do something about it. Now." She raised and lowered our joined hands in emphasis. "I'm tired of watching you fade into the shadows. You were always quiet and reserved around company, but you never ran away and hid. Not until you married Sir Anthony."

I glanced away from her, not wanting to be reminded of

the way I was before corpses became such central figures in my life. It had been so long now that sometimes I wasn't sure if I had ever lived without their specters hanging over my head.

"At the time, it seemed for the best, but sometimes . . ." Alana sighed. "Sometimes I wonder if we did the right thing by allowing you to hide away here at Gairloch."

I looked into Alana's saddened eyes, worrying again that I had caused my sister and her family irreparable harm by staying here.

She smiled sadly. "The reason I haven't mentioned this before was for purely selfish motives. I wanted you here. I had more trouble recovering after Greer was born than I had with the others, and I was floundering a bit." She sucked in a deep breath, blinking her eyes to hold back the wetness shining there. She often got this way when she thought about that difficult time. I had to swallow back my answering emotion. "It was so good to have you here with me. And every time I contemplate your leaving, it feels like someone is cutting out a part of me." She breathed in and exhaled sharply. "However, that time is coming."

I felt a mild stirring of panic pull the air from my lungs.

Alana squeezed my hand. "Please don't mistake me. You will always have a home here. But perhaps it's time you rejoined the world beyond Gairloch's vistas. Perhaps it's time you defied those gossiping windbags instead of trying so hard not to overset the applecart."

I did not reply immediately. I was too disturbed by the idea of leaving here, of facing the angry masses of London or Edinburgh. The ton would cut me dead, and my husband's colleagues would eye me with disgust. I couldn't imagine that my fellow artists would look upon me any more favorably. And then I remembered that none of these worries would matter if I did not find Lady Godwin's murderer and keep Gage from implicating me.

"But those concerns are for another day," Alana declared,

not knowing how dark my thoughts had grown. "For now, you have only to join me for tea in the front parlor."

That stubborn look was back in her eyes, and I suddenly felt every minute of all of the hours of sleep I had missed the last two nights. "Alana," I began, barely summoning the strength to argue.

"No. No protests." She pulled me to my feet with more force than I expected and tucked her arm through mine to drag me toward the door.

A sick feeling settled in my stomach. This could not go well.

It would have been comical how quickly the chatter in the drawing room silenced as soon as we stepped through the door if I hadn't still been so preoccupied with trying to find a way to escape. Alana towed me heedlessly across the room, as if oblivious to the others' reactions, even though there was no way she could have failed to notice the harsh stillness.

"Good afternoon," she announced cheerily.

Several of the ladies murmured polite replies while the others continued to stare at me in disapproving shock. She ignored them, and my dragging heels, and pulled me toward the gold brocade settee at the center of the room, where Lady Stratford sat the previous evening before dinner. The countess sat by the window this afternoon, watching us with the same curiosity as the others, albeit with far more subtlety than the open appraisal of some of the other women.

"Is that the sampler you've been working on?" my sister asked Miss Darlington as we passed behind her chair.

She startled and dropped her gaze from where she had been staring at me. "Yes, my lady."

"It's lovely."

She shifted in her seat. "Thank you."

I wondered if her engagement to Mr. Abingdon had been announced yet. Was she happy with the arrangement? At the moment, she merely looked uncomfortable. Whether that was from worry over her recent conduct in regards to Mr. Abingdon or my presence, I could not tell.

As if on cue, several maids swept into the parlor, bearing heavily laden tea trays, as soon as Alana and I settled onto the settee. They set the tea services strategically throughout the room and then disappeared almost as quickly as they arrived. I knew my brother-in-law's staff was loyal and efficient, but I had expected them to be out of practice after so long a period without guests at Gairloch. I was clearly mistaken. Every meal had been perfection, every room cleaned to a shine, and I had overheard no complaints from the guests, despite the added upheaval the murder had caused. I was impressed and proud of my sister's ability to direct them. I had always known she was a gifted hostess, and this was just added proof.

Alana returned my tight smile with one more genuine, and slid forward to pour for the group of ladies surrounding the tea table before us. Her movements were graceful and her voice genteel as she asked each woman how she preferred her tea, and I wondered at her ability to remain so calm when there was so much tension in the air around us. It settled across my skin like a thousand tiny pinpricks. I had to clasp my hands together in my lap to keep from fidgeting and soothing the tingling sensation across my skin.

"Kiera."

I took the cup of tea Alana poured for me, already prepared as I liked. She had also set a lemon biscuit on the saucer. "Thank you," I replied, even though I wasn't certain I could stomach any of it.

She smiled encouragingly at me and then turned to pour her own cup.

I forced the cup to my lips to take a sip and peered over the rim at the others. Some of them had returned to their conversations, though more quietly than before, and although I sensed that some of their attention was still focused on me, they at least made a good show of pretending it wasn't. Then there were others, like Miss Darlington, who seemed to have great difficulty keeping their eyes off me, even though they knew it was impolite to stare. Miss Darlington's gaze bounced up and down from the sampler in front of her to me so many times I was worried she would give herself a crick in the neck. I tried to smile at her, but she seemed horrified by my notice of her and lifted the sampler to hide her face.

Of course, there were also a few who just couldn't be bothered to hide their disgust of me, namely Lady Westlock and Mrs. Smythe. I ignored their glares and the indignant pitch of their whispers as best as I could.

"The weather is lovely today after last night's rain, is it not?" Alana said politely to the company surrounding us.

There was a moment of uncomfortable silence, which stretched my nerves, and then Philip's cousin, Caroline, spoke into the gap. "Indeed. I forget how refreshing a Highland rain can be." She smiled softly at me.

"Lady Cromarty, I have the most wonderful news," Lady Darlington crowed from across the room. "Mr. Abingdon and my daughter are to be wed."

Well, that answered my earlier question. I wondered if Lady Darlington was aware of the events surrounding her daughter's precipitous engagement or if Miss Darlington and her brother had decided to keep those details to themselves.

I watched Caroline and her mother carefully as my sister offered her congratulations, and was relieved to see that Caroline did not appear the least bit upset by the news and, in fact, seemed pleased as she smiled into her teacup. Clearly, the girl had even more good sense than I'd given her credit for. Her mother, Lady Hollingsworth, on the other hand, looked as if she had just swallowed something very bitter. Her lips pursed and her eyes glared accusingly at her daughter. Perhaps for Caroline's sake, I should encourage Philip to mention something of Mr. Abingdon's unsavory character to his aunt.

"Congratulations," I told Miss Darlington, and tried to sound sincere even though I thought the real congratulations went to Caroline for escaping marriage to the bounder.

Miss Darlington nodded in acknowledgment and shifted once more in her seat.

"When do you plan to have the wedding?" my sister innocently asked. "In the spring?"

Lady Darlington's gaze darted anxiously toward her daughter. "Oh, Sarah has always dreamed of an autumn wedding," she lied smoothly. She evidently knew something of her daughter's conduct. "The colors suit her so well."

I glanced at blonde-haired, blue-eyed Miss Darlington and nearly choked on a bite of biscuit. Anyone with a modicum of sense could see that autumn colors were absolutely the worst match for the girl.

Lady Darlington seemed to realize this and flushed before hurrying on. "So it is rather fortuitous Mr. Abingdon asked for her hand now instead of two months hence. We plan to have the bans called this Sunday, if we are allowed to return home by then."

"So a mid-September wedding. You should have lovely weather, as long as the rain holds," my sister said kindly.

"But they say rain is actually a good omen for a bride," I said and then blushed when everyone turned collectively to look at me. I wasn't entirely certain why I decided to open my mouth.

"That's true," Alana agreed, coming to my rescue. "I had forgotten that old adage." She turned to smile at Miss Darlington. "So perhaps we *should* hope for rain."

"As I recall, it did not rain on your wedding day, Lady Darby," Lady Westlock couldn't seem to resist commenting.

I met her gaze levelly. If she had hoped to disconcert me with such a statement, she was to be sorely disappointed.

And I did not feel enough loyalty toward my deceased husband to even attempt to deny the truth. "No, it did not."

"But it did rain on mine," Alana declared much too cheerily. "What about you, Lady Westlock? Did it rain on your wedding day?"

She narrowed her eyes at my sister and clamped her lips together tightly.

"I remember there wasn't even a cloud in the sky," Lady Darlington supplied helpfully, darting a triumphant look at Lady Westlock. "It did, however, rain for mine." I wondered what had transpired between the two friends to provoke Lady Darlington so.

Lady Westlock ignored her and focused on me again. "I'm curious whether Mr. Gage has had any luck with his investigation yet. Of course, we all know he is just searching for evidence. It's quite clear who the killer is."

I tightened my grip on my teacup.

"Really?" Alana said, brushing an imaginary crumb from her lap. She seemed so calm; I imagined I was the only one who could sense the anger behind her restrained movements. It fairly vibrated down the line of her back. "It is not clear to me. Perhaps you could enlighten me?"

Lady Westlock scowled fiercely.

"No?" My sister's bright blue eyes dared her to say my name. The others leaned forward in their seats, absorbing every nuance of the silent standoff between the two ladies.

My stomach churned. I was so tired of these confrontations. So tired of being accused. And so tired of forcing my sister to defend me. I wanted to scream at them all, and I was afraid if I opened my mouth, I might do exactly that.

Lady Westlock's eyes dropped to her lap, and Alana laid down the gauntlet. "Then I suggest you keep your opinions to yourself. None of us care to hear your nasty assertions."

The air rang with the silence that followed. No one dared speak or move until my sister removed her glare from Lady

Westlock. She swallowed the remnants of her fury and turned toward Lady Hollingsworth.

"Her sister has bewitched her. She can't even see the truth for what it is," Lady Westlock hissed loudly enough for it to carry across the entire room.

"That does it!" Alana slammed her cup down on the table, sloshing the liquid over the sides, and rose to her feet. "Pack your bags! You have fifteen minutes to be off my property before . . ."

"Alana!" I protested, rising to stop her.

"No! I don't care what Philip said. I want . . ."

I gripped her arm and shook her. "Stop!"

She stared at me goggle-eyed.

"Now sit down before you say anything else foolish," I ordered, feeling my blood pumping hard through my veins.

She blinked at me in shock. I couldn't blame her. I was almost in shock myself, unable to believe what I was about to do. All I knew was that I wasn't going to let Alana take the blame for anything I did or upset her husband because her temper got the better of her again. I gentled my hold on her upper arm and tried to look reassuring as I pushed her back down into her seat. Then I marshaled all of my courage and turned to stare down the other guests who were waiting in eager silence.

"See what I mean?" Lady Westlock jeered.

"You, shut your mouth," I ordered.

The others gasped as the baroness's mouth dropped open and she began to splutter.

"I'm not about to let you malign my sister. I've let you and your conspirators," I turned my glare on Mrs. Smythe and Lady Darlington, "pour venom in everyone's ears against me since the day you arrived. But I'm not about to let you speak of my sister in such a way. She is the Countess of Cromarty and your hostess, and above all else, a good woman. A better woman than any of you. And she deserves your respect."

I paused, breathing hard as I struggled to control my own St. Mawr temper. Just because I did not often unleash it, did not mean it did not exist. I could be far worse than either of my siblings when a real rage came over me. Sir Anthony's bedroom in London was proof of that. I left it in shambles after his friends promised to have me arrested for the anatomical sketches my husband forced me to draw.

The other ladies watched me with varying degrees of horror—eyes wide, bodies still, breaths held so as not to miss a single word I uttered. I scowled at the whole foolish lot of them.

"I'm well aware how very little the truth matters to you, but I'm going to speak it anyway." I glanced around the room, pausing to stare into each and every one of their eyes as I continued. "I am not a murderer. Not now, not ever. And when Lady Godwin's killer is caught, a great many of you shall have to eat your words. I shall enjoy every minute of discomfort you feel in my presence when that happens."

Sick of looking at their shocked faces, I turned to my sister to take my leave.

Unfortunately, Lady Westlock had still not learned her lesson. I supposed it could have been her status that drove her to have the last word—after all, she was a baroness, and before that a marquess's daughter. However, I suspected it was more likely a fault of her character.

She sniffed, sticking her nose into the air. "And we shall smile with glee when you are finally carted off to prison or the asylum, as you should have been a year ago."

I clenched my hands into fists, struggling with an urge to march across the room and do her physical harm. I fear the only thing that may have stopped me from doing so was the realization that it would not help my case. Regardless, some of those around me sensed my extreme fury, for they shrank back in their seats.

"You really need to learn to hold your tongue, my lady." My voice was laced with steel. "Your husband is already facing charges of assault. I should hate for you to make it worse for him by adding slander to his bill."

Many of the ladies gasped, swiveling in their seats to look at Lady Westlock, whose eyes now bulged like a fish.

I did not wait to see what else happened, and instead murmured an excuse to my sister before marching out of the room. "Would you please excuse me, sister dear. I fear I've lost my appetite." I could not stand to be in a room with Lady Westlock another moment longer.

"Of course," Alana called after me, but I was already striding through the door.

"She lies," Lady Westlock cried.

I ignored her. In my fit of temper, I'd already revealed more than I was supposed to. I only hoped Lord Westlock was too intimidated by Mr. Gage to expose my part in the events two nights past. If the others knew I was assisting Gage, they might be reluctant to even speak with him, which could jeopardize our entire investigation.

I turned left toward the back of the castle, hoping to make a clean escape, only to plow straight into someone.

CHAPTER EIGHTEEN

"Whoa!" Gage's familiar voice exclaimed as his hands came up to steady me. "Why the rush?"

"I can't stay here another minute," I panted, having trouble controlling my breathing. My anger was still too great, and Gage was much too close. "Please, I need to go." I pushed against his chest, trying to pull away from the grip he had on my arms.

He glanced toward the parlor from where I had come and then back at me. "All right," he said soothingly. "Where to?"

"I don't know," I admitted, disliking the frantic sound of my voice but unable to stop it. "I . . . I need to think, and I can't do it here. Not surrounded by all these people. I need some air," I gasped, seizing on an idea. I pulled against his hold again and broke one arm free and began pulling Gage down the hall after me.

"All right," he replied, falling into step with me. "Let's go for a walk."

I opened my mouth to protest, planning to tell him I wanted to be alone. But I realized I didn't. Alone, my mind would not rest, and I didn't particularly wish to be set adrift in my thoughts at the moment. If it had been Lord Marsdale or Lord Stratford or some other man in attendance, I might have declined the offer, but Gage was different. I didn't want to think too closely about why that was. So instead,

I reminded myself that no one was supposed to go off by themselves, and I pretended that was the reason I allowed him to accompany me.

I grabbed my worn but warm pelisse from the cloakroom and we exited through the rear of the castle. I marched Gage through the gardens with long strides and around the orangery until we hit upon the path I often took that circled the property. As we entered the shaded trail leading us into the woods, I slowed my pace, having burned off enough rage and frustration to cool my blood to a simmer.

I took a deep breath of the forest air, pungent with the scents of rich earth, conifer trees, and wildflowers—bluebells and fuchsias. Birds chirped in the branches above us, serenading us with their woodland song. A squirrel darted across the path and scrambled up an oak tree, pattering up the bark. When we came to a log in the middle of the trail, Gage reached out to help me over it. I allowed it, even though I'd traversed the same log hundreds of times without any assistance.

He glanced at me as he released my hand on the other side. "So what happened in there?" he asked casually, nodding his head back toward the castle.

"Lady Westlock," I replied succinctly.

"*Ahhh.*" His voice was knowing and sympathetic and encouraged me to continue.

"I'm tired enough of her snide comments and bold insinuations. I may be fair game, but my sister is not," my voice rang with finality. "I vow if she says anything else against Alana or Philip or one of the children, I will not be responsible for my actions."

Gage was silent beside me as we passed through a patch of raspberry bushes. I could see the children had already picked the ones closest to the path, but there were plenty more growing in the tiny glen. They looked ripe and lush. I carefully picked one and popped it into my mouth, savoring the burst of sweetness.

Gage reached out to pick a few more that had been beyond the children's reach and then followed me down the trail. "Why are you fair game?" he asked suddenly, harking back to my earlier words.

"Well . . ." I stumbled for words to explain myself. "You know that I am. I'm the one who picked the sorry husband, not Alana."

"But did you choose him?"

I glanced up at Gage as he popped a raspberry into his mouth, and he lifted his eyebrows in query. "No. But I was the one who asked Father to find me a husband of his choosing, so, in a way, I still chose him."

"No. You depended on your father to select an honorable and suitable man. You trusted his judgment, and it happened to be wrong."

I frowned, not liking his excessively reasonable tone, or his disparagement of my father. But I did not refute his words, for I could not. And I knew that was what bothered me most. It felt traitorous to harbor such thoughts against my father, to be angry that he had not selected a better man for me. I had relied on him to see to my future care, and he had failed me. It was somehow easier to blame myself for not taking on the responsibility of finding my own spouse and bemoan my inability to stand up to Sir Anthony than to fault my father, who was not even alive to defend himself.

I shook my head. I didn't want to think about my father and my mixed emotions when it came to him.

"Maybe I'm not fair game," I reluctantly assented. "But Lady Westlock and the others are not going to stop maligning me regardless." Feeling the rising tide of frustration, I clenched my hands into fists. "I don't understand how she can be so cruel."

"She's afraid."

I scoffed. "I know. But a lot of us are afraid. That doesn't give her the right to lash out at me."

"*Are* you afraid, Lady Darby?"

"What kind of question is that?" I said with a scowl. "Of course, I'm afraid. I'm not a fool. Just two days ago someone murdered Lady Godwin, cut her open, and . . ." I swallowed the rest, unwilling to speak the words.

"I only asked because you don't act like you're frightened," he remarked evenly.

I crossed my arms over my chest, protecting the ache I felt there. "Just because someone doesn't show fear, does not mean they don't feel it." I saw him glance at me out of the corner of my eye, but I refused to look at him. "I learned some time ago that displaying fear only makes you weak. Children might be comforted, and young ladies coddled, but no one reassures a grown woman except herself." I pressed harder against the hollow throbbing. "We all must deal with our shadows the best we can. No one can conquer them for us."

Gage did not reply, and in fact seemed lost in thought as the path turned northeast. It angled along a rippling creek, swelled from the summer rains, toward the back of Philip's property. I glanced at the man beside me once or twice, wondering if I had revealed too much about my life with Sir Anthony. Gage seemed content to allow the conversation to lie. I wasn't sure whether or not to be grateful for this. If he was contemplating my past, I thought I might have liked to set him straight rather than have him inferring meaning from my words. But then I would have to explain more about Sir Anthony's death and the accusations and trial, and I did not relish such a turn in the discussion. So I kept silent.

The water in the creek tumbled over rocks and swirled in tiny pools, accompanying the sound of our footsteps with its tinkling music. We passed by the spot where on hot summer days I would lean against an ancient ash and dangle my feet in the stream while I sketched. It was a lovely little nook, large enough for two, but I decided not to share such an intimate setting with Gage. The image of us seated side by side under the tree's boughs made something twist inside me. Besides, he would probably only show Mrs. Cline the location, and the thought of them there together would ruin it for me forever.

"I spoke with Mr. Calvin."

I glanced over my shoulder at him as we slowly wound our way through a narrow part of the path snaking between the trees and the creek. I forgot he had been questioning Lady Godwin's other former lover while my sister was forcing me to brave the inquisition in the parlor. "And?"

"I don't think he did it."

I paused and waited for him to fall in step with me when the trail widened. "He didn't sleep with her?"

"Oh, he admitted to that . . . after a good ten minutes of bluster."

I smiled, imagining the priggish man trying to talk his way out of revealing he'd committed such a sin.

Gage grinned when he saw my humor. "Says it only happened once and he was terribly foxed. I believe he meant to imply that Lady Godwin had taken advantage of him."

"When did this happen?"

He sighed heavily, already telling me what I needed to know. "May or June. He couldn't remember the particulars. Either way, it's too recent for him to be the father of Lady Godwin's child."

"But . . ." I hesitated, still sorting out the ramifications of my thought. "It would give him motive if she threatened to reveal their tryst."

"I can see how he would want to keep it quiet, particularly from his wife and friends, but I do not think he would resort to murder."

I could not argue with him, for I agreed. Mr. Calvin was pompous and annoying when he pontificated, but he seemed otherwise harmless.

We turned east with the stream and approached the edge of the forest where the trees thinned out to reveal a wide moor filled with heather. The land south of the path sloped upward to a little hillock, affording a beautiful view of the land beyond. It was my second-favorite place to sit and sketch. In fact, I had painted several rather mediocre landscapes from that vantage point. I glanced up the small hill, about to suggest to Gage that he might like to see the view, when something caught my eye. I slowed to a stop, staring up the rise.

The earth here was bare, for too much water drained over the hill from the forest to allow plants to take root. Several large rocks were perched haphazardly across the summit. I sat on the largest of the stones when I made my sketches, so I was quite familiar with their landscape.

A chill crept down my spine, raising the hairs on the back of my neck.

"Lady Darby? Is something wrong?"

I swallowed against the lump of dread caught at the back of my throat. "I . . . I think we should get Philip."

"Why?"

I looked up into his puzzled face and gathered my courage. "Because one of those rocks has been moved, and I honestly don't think it was the rain that did it."

An hour later, we were back on the hill with Philip and a pair of Cromarty footmen, along with a few shovels and lanterns. I pulled my pelisse tighter around me as the shadows began to lengthen and watched the four men take turns with the shovels. Neither Philip nor Gage had wanted me to tag along, and I had seriously considered listening to them, but in our rush to gather reinforcements, I had not shown Gage which rock had been moved. I knew the hill best. I knew where each stone should rest and how deep they had each settled into the earth. The others did not, not even Philip. So in the end, there had been no choice except for me to join them.

Perched on my sketching rock, I pulled my knees up to my chest as the men tossed shovelfuls of dirt up out of the three-foot-deep hole they had dug in the earth. The head-sized stone that had covered the spot had been returned to its original position a few feet away so that they could excavate the earth underneath. It was all rather eerie, as if the killer had begun a cairn on the little hillock. That is, if I was correct about what lay underneath.

I dug my fingers into my upper arms and pulled my gaze away from the growing hole. I was sick with dread over what we might find buried there. Fear and revulsion crawled across my skin and underneath my clothing like an insect. Shuddering, I lifted my face to the wind for a breath of fresh air not permeated with the scent of freshly turned earth.

Philip handed his shovel off to Gage and climbed out of the hole. Moving toward me, he swiped the sweat from his brow with the rolled sleeve of his shirt. The men had abandoned their jackets long ago. "This killer is far too intelligent," he declared, propping his hands on his hips. His face screwed up in frustration. "To bury something in a spot where the soil is so often turned by the runoff from the rain, and place a fresh animal carcass nearby. When the dogs dragged me up here, I thought they smelled the raccoon's blood. *All* of this dirt looked as if it had been disturbed recently." He shook his head. "I should have noticed the rock had been moved."

"Stop berating yourself," I told him. "As you said, the murderer was clever. And it looks like he did his best to keep any animals from being able to dig it up."

"Yes, buried deep and placed a rock over it."

None of us spoke of what "it" was, but I could tell Gage and Philip suspected the same thing. Our collective sense of horror weighted the air. The footmen may not have known exactly what we were looking for, but they took their cues from Philip and Gage and dug carefully and quietly.

It looked as if another foot or so of dirt had been cleared

away when Gage halted the footman beside him and bent down to look at something. I shared a look of mutual dread with Philip before he inched toward the hole.

"There's something here," Gage murmured, reaching into the ground.

He slowly lifted the object from the earth, affording me only a brief glimpse of ivory cloth before it was blocked by Philip's kneeling form. My brother-in-law had ordered me to stay out of the way if something was found. A command that had turned out to be wholly unnecessary, for I didn't think my legs would have supported me anyway had I tried to approach. I wrapped my arms tighter around my knees. My heart stuck in my throat as I watched their hunched forms.

"This is no ordinary cloth," Gage murmured. "Look at the pale pink roses embroidered around the edges."

"It seems to be a lady's shawl," Philip said.

Gage's voice tightened. "And here is a second one."

The men fell silent, their bodies so still that all the hairs rose on the back of my neck. I knew without their saying anything what they had found. A fierce surge of emotion burned the back of my eyes at the thought of the tiny, helpless infant. I sunk my teeth into my bottom lip in an effort to withhold the sob building at the back of my throat.

I could barely see through the tears pouring down my cheeks as Gage shifted. "She should be placed in the chapel cellar with her mother," he said quietly.

Philip exchanged some words with him that I did not hear, struggling with my grief as I was. Then he moved to speak with the footmen and searched the hole for anything else.

Gage rose to his feet, his face pale and drawn, and crossed the short distance to me. I swiped at my cheeks and took deep heaving breaths, trying to gain control of myself. All I could think about was how swiftly that baby's life had ended. Had the infant cried? Had she made any sound at all?

I felt sick and disoriented and angry. Angry that someone

could be capable of such savagery. We weren't dealing with a murderer, but a monster. A sick, twisted human being who waltzed through the halls of Gairloch Castle and dined next to us at the table, and then marched outside to disfigure Lady Godwin and her child. Killing the viscountess would have killed the baby, too. But this fiend wasn't satisfied with that. He had to viscerally defile motherhood and terrorize the child by wrenching her away from the only warmth she had ever known and burying her alone in the cold, dark ground.

Gage sat next to me, pulling me toward him. I allowed him to cradle my head against his chest while I sobbed. It was an unexpected comfort, and made me weep all the harder for the security and compassion he gave me when the child had been given none.

When my emotions settled, he and Philip guided me between them back down the path toward the castle. Darkness had begun to fall, so Philip lit one of the lamps to show the way while leaving the other for the footmen, who were re-covering the hole. I clutched both of their arms and allowed them to lead me on, resting my head against Gage's shoulder when it became too heavy for me. At the orangery, he passed the tiny bundle to Philip. Then, with one last troubled glance at me, my brother-in-law set off toward the western hall block and the chapel.

"Come on," Gage said, wrapping his arm securely around me so that I did not stumble. "Let's get you inside. I think maybe a hot bath would make you feel better."

"I don't want a bath," I protested, my voice hoarse from the spent emotion. "I don't want to return to my room." I couldn't lie in the dark and allow images of Lady Godwin and her tiny unborn child to play over and over in my mind. That way lay only madness. "My studio," I insisted before Gage could question me.

"All right," he agreed, although from the tone of his voice I could tell it had been reluctantly.

Revived by his acquiescence, I pointed him toward the servants' entrance, hoping to avoid the other guests. The fewer who knew what had been uncovered tonight the better, particularly if the murderer was watching. One look at my distressed features and the dirt staining Gage's clothing, and the killer would know exactly where we had been and what we had found.

I glanced up at the castle's looming facade, frightened I would see a pair of eyes staring out at me. I trembled, and Gage wrapped his arm more tightly around me.

CHAPTER NINETEEN

When we reached my studio, I realized I did not have my key. I groaned. It looked as if I would have to return to my bedchamber after all.

"What's wrong?" Gage asked.

"It's locked." I reached out to twist the handle in illustration and the door swung open.

My mouth dropped open in shock.

Gage stepped closer to peer into the dim interior. "I take it that should not have happened?"

"I *always* keep it locked. There are volatile chemicals in here. I can't have people wandering in and knocking something over and setting fire to the castle, or opening bottles and inhaling poisonous fumes. Think of the children." I could hear the panic building in my voice.

He squeezed my arm gently. "Stay here."

I watched in trepidation as he inched closer and pushed the door wider. The muted light of gloaming filtered through the large windows, blurring the lines of the furniture, canvases, and easels. He eased one step into the door and reached back under his frock coat to extract a pistol from the waist of his trousers. I wondered if he always carried the weapon. His free hand gestured for me to slide out of view of the door. I considered disobeying, for if I moved, then I wouldn't be able to see what happened inside, but common sense reasserted itself. He wanted me out of the intruder's line of sight, and thus out of firing range should they also have a gun.

Gage crept into the room, and I held my breath, listening for sounds of a struggle. In my mind, I pictured the layout of my studio and imagined him moving quietly around the room, weaving through my mess of easels and canvases, both finished and unfinished. There was a crash and I jumped. I heard his faint curse and strained to hear any other sounds. When there was only silence, I began to worry.

Had Gage been attacked by the intruder? Was he injured? Fear gripped my chest in its tight fist, squeezing the breath from my lungs. I glanced down the corridor, trying to decide what I should do. If something had happened to Gage, his attacker likely knew that I was out here waiting for him. Would he harm me as well? Should I run for help?

My limbs tensed, eager to take flight, but I stopped them from moving. If I ran, the intruder would escape without my identifying him. And then who would be blamed for Gage's injuries or, worse, death?

Me. The only person who was known to have been with him. The person who was already the prime suspect for Lady Godwin's murder in most minds.

If Gage had been harmed, I could not leave him, nor let his attacker get away. I had to stop him.

I reached up and carefully extracted the ivory comb from my hair. As far as weapons went, it was a rather innocuous choice, but it was the sharpest object I had on hand. A few tendrils of hair fell down around my face, and I blew them aside. Then, taking a deep breath, I took one tentative step toward the doorway, sliding along the wall. My palm was sweaty around the comb, so I gripped it tighter, feeling the bone bite into my skin. When I reached the threshold, I closed my eyes and said a prayer for courage. Leaning forward, I peered around the door frame to see into the room and shrieked.

Gage flinched back and reached out to take a hold of my arms. "Kiera. It's just me."

I pressed my hand over my pounding heart and leaned forward to rest my forehead against his chest.

"Are you all right?"

I lifted my head and swatted him. "When I heard the crash, I thought someone had attacked you."

He smiled softly, clearly not injured by my slap. "Sorry. I tripped over something." He glanced behind him. "I hope I didn't damage anything that cannot be replaced."

I saw the dim outline of a twisted canvas and began to push past him, until I remembered why he had been fumbling around in the dark in the first place. I looked up at him.

"There's no one here. If someone broke into your studio, they're long gone now."

I moved to carefully light one of the covered lanterns set on the tables near the door. My hands still shook from my fright. "What do you mean *if?*"

He reached for the lantern on the opposing table and began to light it as well.

"Be careful with that," I snapped.

He looked up at me and nodded. "Are you certain you locked up the last time you were here?"

"Yes," I stated emphatically, angry that he would question me on this. "As I told you, I *always* lock the door when I leave, even if it's only for a moment." I picked up the canvas he had managed to both kick and step through. Fortunately, it was only the background of a portrait I had started months ago and never returned to. I tossed the ruined canvas to the side and knelt to examine the other canvases leaning against the wall near it.

"Who else has a key to this room?"

"Mrs. MacLean."

"No one else?"

"No," I replied testily. "No one else has cause to possess a key."

"Perhaps Mrs. MacLean had the room cleaned and forgot to lock up."

I stood to look back at Gage, who was picking up various jars from the shelves storing my pigments and examining them. "I don't allow anyone to clean this room." He glanced back at me. "If it needs tidying, I do it myself."

He looked back at the jar of deep red madder in his hands and set it carefully back on the shelf. "These pigments are that poisonous?"

"Some of them, yes," I replied, moving toward him. "It's the fumes. They are the most toxic while I am mixing them. That's why I wear gloves and do it outside." I reached out to pick up a bottle. "Once the linseed oil is added in the right increments to make the paint, it stabilizes into something that is much less harmful. However, I still do not want my nieces and nephew stumbling upon it and ingesting it." He nodded his understanding. "I'm much more worried about the maids knocking over a bottle of turpentine and setting the entire castle ablaze."

He grimaced. "Yes. I suppose that would be bad."

I raised my eyebrows at his understatement, and he smiled more genuinely. Uncomfortable with the softness in his eyes and the memory of his arm around me as he guided me into the castle, I turned away to face the rest of the room.

Breathing deeply, I inhaled the familiar, comforting scents of my studio. Fumes that to someone who was not an artist choked and burned the delicate hairs of the nose, welcomed me like a favorite, four-course dinner. For cooks, the smell of herbs and fresh ingredients made their noses tingle and their mouths salivate. For an artist, the scents of linseed oil and turpentine awakened the mind, making it stretch and search for a brush and canvas. After a difficult day, it was like coming home to a loved one. It grounded me like nothing else ever could.

My studio was housed in one of the turret rooms, so the stone walls were rounded. Large windows alternated with stone columns on most of the wall surface because the turret projected out of the corner of the east block of the castle. At my request, Philip had also installed a skylight at a southeast angle on the slanted roof to provide me with more light. It was by far the best art studio I had ever occupied, even with the small amount of Highland sun I contended with in winter. At my childhood homes and Sir Anthony's London town house, I had made do with the conservatory or a small bedroom.

"Can you tell if anything is missing?" Gage asked.

I turned toward my finished canvases first. It seemed likely that if anyone wanted to take something from this room, it would be a painting they could sell, not a raw pigment anyone could purchase in Edinburgh, London, and at least another dozen places in Britain. Apparently, he had the same idea, for he stood over my shoulder, studying each painting as I sorted carefully through the canvases propped against the wall underneath the southern-facing windows out of the reach of the sun's rays. As much as I needed light to create my portraits, so the finished paintings needed to be protected from it to keep the pigments from fading. They all seemed to be accounted for, so I moved to examine the works in progress, currently propped on my three easels, and left Gage to continue studying the finished images.

I sighed in relief as I flipped the canvas cover back over the portrait I had begun of the children and Philip's dogs lying together in a pile. None of the objects worth monetary value were missing. Canvases, linen, pigments, brushes, and other supplies could be replaced. Of course, some of those items were quite expensive—like the set of brushes that had been specifically weighted for my hands—and new canvases took time to treat. I frowned and moved to sort through my equipment, grateful I had taken inventory only the day before.

"Lady Darby."

Gage's voice sounded funny behind me, and I hesitated a second before turning, somehow knowing I was not going to like whatever had tightened his voice.

His face looked pained. "Do you know what this is?" He held up a crumpled white apron that looked as if it had been smeared in carmine paint. If not for the discoveries over the past few days, I might not have recognized it immediately for what it was, but visions of Lady Godwin flashed through my mind and I knew exactly what stained the fabric.

I gasped and clutched the edge of the table behind me. "Where did you find that?"

His Adam's apple bobbed as he swallowed. "Against the wall behind these paintings."

I could feel the blood drain from my face. "That's not mine. I . . . I don't know how it got there." My voice was thin and reedy to my ears. I shook my head in denial. "Please, Gage. You have to believe me," I pleaded. "That's not mine. S-someone must be trying to blame me."

He crossed the room toward me, still holding the apron in front of him. I shrank away from him, my eyes darting back and forth between him and the blood-splattered fabric. His face was controlled and pale. What was he thinking? Did he believe me, or did he think me culpable of such crimes? Was he going to have me locked in my room? If he did, I would be as good as dead. I would never be able to find the actual killer and prove my innocence. The procurator fiscal would pronounce me guilty and see me hanged, or thrown into an asylum where I would wish for death.

I gasped for air, wondering if I could run, if I should run. Or would that be the final nail in the coffin, so to speak, for Gage? Would he see that as an admission of my guilt?

My arms strained against the table to hold me up as my legs threatened to give way.

He stopped a few feet away from me and stared down at me so intently that I felt his gaze to the depths of my soul. I couldn't look away, even if I had wanted to. I just couldn't break eye contact with the man who held my future in his hands. With every ounce of my being, I silently begged for him to understand. Begged for him to trust me.

"Gage, please. It's not mine," I pleaded again.

His pale eyes softened, and the corner of his mouth creased. "All right, Kiera," he murmured, shaking his head almost in bewilderment. "Maybe I'm crazy, but I believe you."

I crumpled to the floor as the breath I had been holding left me in a shuddering sigh. He believed me. I almost couldn't trust it. No one beyond my family ever believed me. I cradled my head against my knees and trembled in relief, smothering the sound of my sobs.

"Hey." Gage placed his hand gently on my shoulder as he sank down beside me.

"Thank you," I gasped between tremulous breaths. "Thank you."

He smiled sadly at me.

I sniffed, swiping at my nose and eyes with the palm of my hand. He handed me his handkerchief and I took it, as mine was already sodden from my tears at Lady Godwin's baby's grave.

"I'm sorry," I said, hearing the husky timbre of my voice. "I don't normally cry so much. In fact, I don't think I've wept so many tears in years."

"Did you cry at your husband's funeral?" he asked evenly. Too evenly.

I hesitated for a moment. "No," I finally confessed. I had often wondered what that said about me. I wondered what Gage would think of my admission. I looked up to find him studying my profile. His gaze was soft, like a caress. My breath fluttered inside my chest and my skin grew warm. I turned away.

"Now will you please tell me what happened to you after your husband died?" he queried gently. I stiffened. "I told you that I believe you are innocent, and I do. But I need to understand, Kiera. I need to know what all these people are accusing you of."

It was the third time he had called me by my given name, but for some reason it affected me differently this time. Perhaps it was because of the warm inflection of his voice or the proximity of his mouth to my ear. Or the fact that he actually believed in me. All I knew was that the sound thrummed through me as if a hand had brushed down my spine.

He was right. He deserved an explanation. Not because I wanted him to keep my name out of the investigation when he spoke to the official from Inverness, not because I wanted to prove my innocence once and for all, but because he trusted me. He believed in my honesty and goodness, and because he was willing to do so, I owed him the truth. And, astoundingly, I realized I wanted him to know.

"Everything is as Philip told you," I began, staring at the mauve skirts of my gown. "Sir Anthony was a renowned anatomist and a friend of my father's, who arranged our marriage. None of us realized why exactly Sir Anthony was interested in me. I suppose my father assumed it was my appearance and normally quiet disposition. At the time, I hadn't cared whom I married so long as he promised to allow me to continue painting." I plucked at the dove-gray piping down my skirt. "Of course, Sir Anthony neglected to tell me until we were wed that there was a provision to his promise."

"He wouldn't let you paint unless you assisted him with his anatomy book?" he guessed.

I nodded. "I . . . I don't know if you can understand, but . . . my artwork is everything to me." I blinked up at him. "If I were not able to paint, well, it would be like perdition. Like . . . losing part of my soul." He did not speak, but the compassion in his eyes told me he grasped what

I was trying to say. I turned back to my skirts as the flush in my cheeks cooled. "I did not want to help my husband with his anatomical sketches, but I didn't want to lose my painting *privileges*," I almost spat the word, "even more."

I took a deep breath and forced myself to remember. "The first dissection was like a living nightmare. The rancid smells, the shush and pop of his instruments slicing into flesh and spreading open the chest cavity, the welling blood and bulging organs. I vomited less than a minute into the procedure. Sir Anthony told me that now that my stomach was empty, it wouldn't happen again, and the next time I would remember not to eat anything beforehand." I couldn't keep the anger out of my voice as I recalled his pompous tone when he talked down to me where I knelt on the floor of his examining room while my body still shook from stomach contractions. "Each time he would slice into the man on his dissection table, I thought I would faint. And the idea that I might collapse on top of the corpse, or that Sir Anthony might reach out to catch me with his blood-smeared hands, made me want to run screaming from the room."

I paused and sucked in a steadying breath, feeling light-headed just from the memories. Gage reached out to rub a hand over my back in comfort. His touch reminded me I was no longer in the past, but grounded firmly in the present. I leaned closer to him, wanting to feel the warmth of his leg against mine.

"I don't know how exactly I made it through that first time. But I will never forget Frederick Oliver." I looked up into Gage's questioning eyes. "That was the name of the man on the dissection table. Sir Anthony did not have names for all of the subjects he examined, or at least he didn't tell them to me, but I did know the name of the first. Frederick Oliver was not particularly attractive or healthy, but seeing him as a man still helped me somehow. I . . . I tried to imagine him as a subject for one of my portraits.

A very odd and . . . disconcerting subject." Gage's eyes crinkled into a smile. "He wasn't the first disconcerting subject
I'd had, after all," I tried to explain. "I had painted a portrait of Lord and Lady Acklen a year before, and Lord Acklen had the most disquieting way of looking at me while I
worked."

His eyes hardened at the mention of Acklen's name. "I
can well imagine," he muttered dryly. "Acklen is a scoundrel
of the highest order."

"Oh," I replied, suddenly seeing that strange experience
in a different light. "I wonder if that explains why he kept
trying to convince me to paint some fellow named John
Thomas." Gage sounded as if he were choking. "I told him
I probably could, but I would have to meet him first."

"I hope you had a male escort with you during those ses-
sions?" He seemed angry for some reason.

"My father always insisted that my brother accompany
me to their house. And Lady Acklen was, of course, present,
since she was also in the portrait."

Gage nodded in satisfaction, and I blinked at him quizzically. "Go on."

I swallowed, thinking back to where I'd stopped.

"How long did you sketch for Sir Anthony?" he asked,
helping me.

"On and off for almost three years. There were weeks
when Sir Anthony insisted on dissecting one part or another
each and every day, and then two months would go by when
we did nothing."

"Did he autopsy a new body every day?" he questioned in
shock.

"No. He used the same body for several days, up to a
week, until the body began to decompose too quickly." I
cringed, remembering how the stench increased with each
passing day the corpse spent on Sir Anthony's table.

"Where did the bodies come from?"

I shook my head sharply. "I honestly do not know. I did

not want to. Perhaps that was wrong of me, but I'm not certain I could have handled knowing. What would I have done with the information anyway? A magistrate would never have listened to me, and if Sir Anthony had discovered I tried to tell someone . . ." I shivered. "It was better to keep quiet." I rubbed my fingers over my amethyst necklace. "I did see two men come to the servants' door one night, but I didn't stay to see what they wanted. I told the magistrate that."

"I thought you didn't go to a magistrate?"

"Not then. Later."

"So you had nothing to do with the requisition of the bodies as Mr. Fitzpatrick claimed."

"Correct. I did not go wandering through the streets at night 'searching for victims.' Nor did I 'seduce men to their early graves,' " I retorted, repeating just a few of the charges leveled at me. "If Sir Anthony performed a human vivisection, I was never present for it," I added, thinking back on Mr. Fitzpatrick's words that day in the library. "I would not have been able to handle that." The blood drained from my face at the thought of someone being forced to endure being dissected alive. I shook my head hard.

"And you don't have to tell me you're not a cannibal." Gage rubbed my back again. "I already know that."

I nodded and swallowed.

"So how did Sir Anthony die? And what happened afterward?"

"An apoplexy," I explained. "At least, that's what his physician said. I was not there when it happened, and I had no reason to doubt the man." I tilted my head to the side. "In light of everything, I'm glad I wasn't there. Otherwise, I'm afraid I might have been blamed for his demise as well." I shook my head. "He was buried, and I prepared to move into my brother's house because I knew Sir Anthony's town house was to go to his cousin. Then, during the reading of his will, his friend Dr. Mayer was given the finished pages of his anatomy textbook and asked to see that the project was finished. My name was not attached to the manuscript, so I assumed I was finally free of it. No one but Sir Anthony and an old assistant of his, who lived in Edinburgh at the time the will was read, knew that I had anything to do with the book." I sighed. "Sadly, I was wrong.

"Of course, I was aware that my husband could not sketch with much skill, but I had no idea that his colleagues often mocked him for it. Dr. Mayer instantly suspected my involvement, but I didn't know that until he and a few more of Sir Anthony's friends stopped by for a not-so-friendly chat a few days later." I pulled my knees up to my chest and hugged them. I felt like I was facing their inquisition once again, having names and epithets hurled my way. "I didn't know that I should have kept my mouth shut. Instead, I tried to make them understand. But they treated me like I was some sort of monstrosity."

I shook my head. "I've always been aware of society's double standard when it comes to women. Ladies are expected to look the other way while gentlemen indulge in affairs and other amoral behavior, but ladies must remain virtuous and above reproach. And, apparently, while a man may take part in a dissection without censure, the thought of a woman doing so is so beyond the pale as to be a criminal atrocity."

Gage's fingers brushed across the skin of my neck as he rubbed my upper back in comfort. "Were Sir Anthony's colleagues the ones who notified the magistrate?"

I nodded. "They sent two Bow Street Runners for me the next day. Fortunately, I had the foresight to move to my brother's house the evening before, and my brother insisted on taking me to the Magistrates' Court in his carriage. He also sent word to Philip, who was in town." I sat up straighter so that I could look at him. "Trevor and Philip were able to convince the magistrate to have my case thrown out on the grounds that I had been following my husband's orders and they had no proof to say otherwise. But the damage was done. Everyone in the courtroom heard the charges leveled against me. By the time we left, the streets had filled with people jeering me and calling me a witch and a murderer. They threw things at the carriage and camped outside my brother's door until I left London."

"They were frightened because of the Burke and Hare case in Edinburgh, afraid that people in London were also being murdered and sold to surgeons and medical schools by enterprising grave robbers."

"I know. But I assure you, understanding the reasoning behind their reactions does not make me feel better about it, especially since I'm innocent of the crimes they charged me with."

He grimaced sympathetically and rubbed the muscles of my neck and up into my hair. His touch made my skin tingle and helped the horrors of the past to fade into the background of my thoughts. I tilted my head so that it rested lightly on his shoulder, wanting to touch and be touched after all the dreadful events of the day.

"What are you going to do?" I had been reluctant to ask it, but the question hovered on my lips and simply would not disappear.

His hand stilled but did not lift from my neck, so I did not move my head. I could smell the dirt and sweat clinging to his clothes and skin.

"Well," he began in a low voice. "We now have several more pieces of evidence besides the scissors—a bloody apron and two shawls."

"What did the second shawl look like?"

He glanced down at me in question.

"I heard you describe the first—the one with the pink roses—but what of the second?"

"It was woven with fine gold thread," he replied, but did not elaborate.

"Then it was likely Lady Godwin's. She wore a gold

shawl to dinner the night she was killed. I wondered about it when it did not turn up near her body. I'd planned to look for it in her rooms."

Gage contemplated this for a moment. "All right, so we have three pieces of evidence. One of which was found near the crime scene, one in the baby's grave, and another that was placed in your studio. I suspect someone is trying to make you look guilty, Lady Darby."

I wished he would call me Kiera again. "Yes, and it's no wonder why. Most of the guests at Gairloch already blame me."

His hand squeezed my neck in commiseration, and I felt the calluses on his palms scrape against my skin. I wondered again why he had such rough hands.

"We need to figure out how someone was able to break in here. Perhaps they picked the lock. Did you notice whether there were any scrapes or scratches on the doorknob?"

"I didn't look." I had been too shocked by it being open in the first place.

"I'll check on my way out."

I lifted my head to gaze up at him in curiosity. "Can *you* pick a lock?"

He smiled and a devilish twinkle entered his eyes. "Well, now. I wouldn't be a very good investigator if I couldn't. But don't go spreading that around about me."

"Is that why you have calluses on your palms?"

He stilled as if I'd surprised him and began to lift his hand away from my neck. Then he stopped himself and rubbed his fingers across my nape. "No. That's from fencing."

He must be quite a serious swordsman to develop such tough skin, and wield his weapon with both hands in order to raise such calluses on each. "Don't you wear gloves?"

He hesitated again, and I glanced up at him in curiosity. "Not often," he finally replied. "I like to feel the sword against my skin. It gives me a better grip."

I tilted my head. "I think I understand." He lifted his eyebrows as if to ask me to elaborate. "It's like with a paintbrush. I need the hold and the angle to be just right, and I can't correctly feel the pressure of the canvas or the texture of the paint already applied if I'm wearing gloves."

He smiled as if I'd said something amusing. "Yes. That's exactly right."

I tried to smile back, but the muscles felt strange after all of the scowling and crying I had done.

"Well." He pushed himself hastily to his feet, and I suddenly got the impression he was eager to change the subject. "I would like to ask Mrs. MacLean about the scissors, shawl, and apron tomorrow." He reached out a hand to help me up. "And see if her staff or any of the guests' servants have reported any items missing. Then maybe we should start questioning the guests again."

I brushed the back of my skirt off. "Why not tonight?"

He waited until I met his eye before answering. "Because people have a tendency to see things that aren't there and give sensational answers when it's dark outside." He pointed up through the skylight. "Especially if there's a full moon."

I stared up at the bright luminescent orb for a moment before turning back to him. "Do you know this from experience or is that superstition talking?"

He twisted his lips. "It is unfortunately a well-known truism among sheriffs, constables, and military men that more trouble breaks out during a full moon than any other time of the month."

I lifted my eyebrows in skepticism but opted not to argue with him. I didn't know that I agreed with his full-moon theory, but it was true in my case, at least, that I tended to be more easily frightened at night. I supposed this fell under the same scope of his explanation.

"Are you retiring?"

"No. I thought I would stay here awhile," I replied, reluctant to return to my room. Sleep would not come easy for me tonight, and I knew I would spend at least half of it pacing up and down the length of my chamber, as I had the previous night.

Gage's expression darkened. "I really don't think that is a good idea."

I frowned. "Why?"

"Have you forgotten that someone recently broke into this room?"

"Well . . ." I paused, trying to come up with an argument. "Did they pick the lock?"

He arched an eyebrow at the irritable tone of my voice and then marched across the room to examine the doorknob. "It appears so. Unless you are particularly bad at sliding your key into the slot?" He glanced up at me in challenge.

"Then they can pick the lock on my bedroom door just as easily."

He glared at me. "Yes. But someone can hear you if you scream in your bedchamber."

"I'll prop a chair underneath the doorknob," I offered weakly, realizing I was not going to win this argument, and uncertain I even wanted to. The prospect of traversing through the darkened corridors of the castle alone made my heart begin to race.

"And then if you accidentally set a fire, you won't be able to get out. No, Lady Darby. I am not leaving you here alone."

I sighed in feigned irritation, not wanting to appear that I had given in easily, and gathered up my sketchbook and the leather container holding my charcoal. If I was to be forced back to my bedchamber, then at least I could take some of my sketching materials with me. My eyes snagged on the bloody apron lying on the floor. "What are we going to do with that?"

"I'll take it," he said, picking it up carefully in a spot that was not stained with red. He held it away from his body and glanced around the room. "Do you have something I might be able to carry it in?"

I emptied out a small box that held old brushes and palette knives and handed it to him. He stuffed the apron inside, closed the lid, and then swiped his hand down his trousers. We each blew out a lamp. Then I waited patiently until the last ember on each wick died before following him through the door.

"Oh, no," I realized. "We still don't have a key, and this door *must* be locked."

Gage looked down at me. "That important?"

"Yes!"

His answering smile told me he was getting far too much enjoyment from exasperating me. "Give me one of your hairpins."

I arched a brow at him curiously and extracted a pin from my hair. A heavy lock of hair tumbled down over my shoulder. He seemed momentarily distracted by the chestnut tresses. "Here," I said, gesturing with the hairpin. He snatched it from my hand and knelt in front of the door.

I tried to watch what he was doing, but the light was too dim and his broad shoulders blocked most of my view.

"There." He stood and tugged soundly on the doorknob several times. "That should hold." He handed me my hairpin, now twisted oddly. "Unless someone has a key or decides to pick it again."

I nodded, impressed by his speed. How often did Gage go about picking locks and locking them again? Of course, I knew nothing about locks. Perhaps it was much easier to bolt a door than unbolt it. I vowed to find out.

"Now," he declared. "If there are no further impediments, let's get you back to your room."

I rolled my eyes at the familiar gleam in his eyes that told me he was pleased to have gotten his way. He clearly believed he had maneuvered me into returning to my bedchamber by overcoming all my faulty objections. I decided it was better not to correct him, and instead clung tighter to his arm as we passed through the dark corridors at the top of the castle where the lit wall sconces were few and far between.

CHAPTER TWENTY

The world was warm and hazy when I floated toward consciousness the next morning, and I lingered there, pulling at the threads of a dream I could not remember, yet I did not want to leave. It was cozy and happy and streamed with sunlight, and it billowed away from me like a kite whose owner has lost hold of its string. It bobbed and drifted, letting the wind carry it far away.

I rolled to my side and instantly regretted it. Muscles in my back and neck wrenched in pain and something clattered to the floor. I blinked open my eyes to find myself staring at the cold hearth. I groaned. I had fallen asleep in my chair again. Which explained the kink in my neck and the numbness in my right arm where it was trapped beneath my body. I shook it, trying to force some blood back into the prickling extremity, and pushed myself up into a seated position with my left hand.

A glance at the clock on the mantel told me it was barely seven. I could still climb into bed for a few more hours of sleep and no one would think it odd, but my sluggish mind was slowly catching up to me. The confrontation with Lady Westlock. The discovery of the baby's grave. The bloody apron in my studio.

I leaned forward to cradle my head in my hands and emitted another groan, though this one was far more despondent. There was still a murderer to be caught—one who was far too devious and clever. I had a sick feeling in my stomach that our investigation was not going to get any easier, or be any less emotionally fraught. There had been no suspicious letter slid under my door the night before, something I was both relieved and curious about. Had the sender decided to stop trying to frighten me, or had they simply lacked the opportunity? I wanted to believe they had ceased to worry about my threat to them, but I understood that to do so would be the height of foolishness. If anything, the lack of a letter made me even more anxious.

I scrubbed my hands over my face and sat up. My sketchbook lay at my feet, and I realized I must have fallen asleep while drawing. Which explained the stripe of charcoal smeared across the mauve skirts of my gown. I sighed and bent to pick up the book. It flipped open to a picture of a woman and child seated in a garden, my imagining of the viscountess and her unborn daughter. Lady Godwin grinned at the child with a far more gentle and maternal smile than I'd ever seen her use in real life. The baby cooed back, lifting her pudgy arms toward her mother. It made me sad to think that this was the only meeting the pair would have, short of heaven.

I sank back into my seat, studying the beautiful woman and her child. What had Lady Godwin planned to do with the baby? It sounded as if she intended to hide away at the home of Lady Stratford's great-aunt until the birth, but what then? I had a hard time believing she intended to keep the little girl. Her husband's return from India would have made that difficult. It seemed more likely the child would be given up for adoption, but to whom? Had the arrangements already been made?

And what of the infant's real father? Did he know about the child? We assumed so, since that was our best lead on a killer with motive to both kill Lady Godwin and destroy any evidence of the baby. But could we be on the wrong track? Perhaps someone else had reason to wish both Lady Godwin and her child dead. I didn't know what that reason could be, but that made it no less a possibility. One that we had overlooked in favor of searching for the father.

Too troubled to continue staring at my rendering of the deceased mother and child, I flipped the page only to gaze into Gage's laughing eyes. I wanted to pretend that I had not spent half the night sketching images of him, but unfortunately I couldn't. The proof rested in my hands. Four pages had been devoted to him—one of him sitting in the chair across the hearth from me, another of him at dinner, dressed in full evening kit, a third of him gazing out the skylight in my art studio, and the last of him shoveling dirt. His muscles seemed to ripple before my eyes under the fine lawn of his shirt as he lifted another heavy load of earth. I felt my cheeks heat at the evidence of the detail I had put into this last picture—the curve of his bottom as he bent, the flex of his upper arms. When had I had time to notice such things while my emotions were so jumbled with fear over what we would find?

I slammed the sketchbook closed and tossed it on the table before rising. My back and ribs ached from too many hours constrained by a corset. I hobbled across the room to tug the bellpull, and then stripped myself of all my clothes except my chemise. My bones and muscles thanked me as I released them. I wrapped a blanket around me, flopped back on the counterpane, and massaged the skin that had been rubbed painfully by the boning of my corset.

Lucy appeared not long after with my normal breakfast fare of chocolate and toast. My stomach growled loudly, reminding me I had forgone dinner the previous evening. I devoured the meal while I waited for my bath to be prepared. When I finally slid into the tub of warm water, it felt so good I thought I might decide to stay there the entire day. I scrubbed the charcoal from my fingers and the splotches I had smeared on my face and settled back in the water to relax.

It was while I was contemplating the stains left behind on the washcloth and that last picture I had drawn of Gage shoveling dirt, which I could not seem to stop thinking about, that I realized I *had* seen something of importance in the maze the night we discovered Lady Godwin's body. I had missed any facial expressions, but I *had* noticed the mud splattering the back of Mr. Fitzpatrick's trousers.

I sat up sharply.

Mr. Fitzpatrick had given Gage an alibi, but was it completely sound? He could have murdered Lady Godwin, ditched the baby in the woods nearby, as we suspected, and *then* joined the men's conversation about horses. Later he could have gone back to retrieve the child and bury her on the hill next to the creek.

But what was his motive in doing such a thing if he was not the father?

I frowned. Maybe Fitzpatrick had lied. Maybe he was the father. Or maybe he was jealous of the father.

I began to scrub my body quickly. I didn't know whether Mr. Fitzpatrick was capable of such a thing or not. But I definitely wanted to hear his explanation for how he managed to splatter mud halfway up the back of his leg in a dry, well-manicured garden.

"I'm not certain that's much to go on, but it is a reason to question him again," Gage told me after I relayed the information I remembered about Mr. Fitzpatrick. "And to actually check his alibi with Sir David and Mr. Abingdon."

I frowned at his unenthusiastic reaction. "Well, I didn't say it was the key to the investigation," I remarked crossly. "Did you speak with Mrs. MacLean?"

He nodded and slouched deeper into the red chair he occupied in my brother-in-law's study. "She's going to ask the staff to see if anyone is missing an apron. Without any adornment, she thought it likely belonged to a servant."

I glanced at Philip where he sat behind his desk. Some pained emotion tightened his features.

"We have another problem," Gage said.

I looked back and forth between the men as my heart-beat sped up. "What?"

Gage nodded toward Philip, telling him to relay the news.

"Alana knows about the baby," he told me in a flat voice.

"How?" I asked.

"She saw me carrying the child to the chapel and demanded to know what was going on."

I pressed a hand to my mouth in thought. I could well imagine my sister demanding such information, but I was surprised he had given it to her. She must have pressured him hard to make him tell her. "Where is she now?"

Philip turned to the side to look out the window. "She won't come out of the nursery."

That seemed a natural response, and, overall, a fairly harmless one. Of course, she would want to be close to her children—to keep them safe. "I'll try to talk to her," I assured him. "But I don't know that it will do much good. At least, not until this murderer is caught."

He nodded and continued to stare out at the courtyard beyond.

My heart ached for his distress. He loved my sister so much. To see her so upset and not be able to do anything about it must be tearing him up inside. I rounded his desk to kneel by his chair.

"She will be all right," I murmured as I grabbed hold of his hand. He gazed back at me blankly. "She's just fright-ened and needs to be with your children now. She knows they are all safe and secure together in the nursery because you made it so." His eyes warmed a bit. "Once the killer is caught . . . And they *will* be caught, Philip. I promised her that, and I promise you. Then she will come out of this. She will." I squeezed his hand determinedly.

He stretched out his other hand to center a page on his desk. "Of course. You're right," he said quietly and then repeated it more confidently. "You're right." He lifted my hand to place a kiss on the back of it, and then helped me to my feet, already looking more like the self-assured man I was used to. He took a deep breath and moved around his desk toward the door. "I'll send a servant to locate Mr. Fitzpatrick and have him meet you here," he told Gage. "It will give you some privacy and a greater image of authority."

"Thank you, Cromarty."

He waved it off with a flick of his wrist and quit the room, closing the door behind him.

Gage turned to look at me, his blue eyes brightened by the midnight hue of his jacket. I spoke before he could say something I did not wish to hear. "You should sit here," I instructed him, touching the back of Philip's large chair. "It will give your appearance more weight."

He arched an eyebrow. "Yes. I'd already planned on that." He crossed behind the desk to the right while I went in the opposite direction. "And just where do you propose to sit?" It was a leading question.

"Why, right here," I proclaimed, settling back into the red wingback chair farthest from the door and straightening the pansy-purple skirts of my morning dress.

He sighed heavily. "I don't suppose I can convince you to sit out on this one?" He sounded so hopeful.

I smiled. "Sorry."

"Somehow, I don't think you are." He gazed at me for a moment, as if trying to decide whether to make any further effort to remove me. "All right," he relented. "But I'll ask the questions."

I nodded, not caring who interrogated the man, so long as I was present.

"You know," he said after a minute longer of staring at me, in which I was beginning to feel quite uncomfortable. "You shouldn't have promised them you would catch the killer."

"Why not? I certainly plan to."

"Not every investigation gets solved, no matter how diligently it is pursued." His words were slow and precise.

"Well," I faltered for words, thrown off by the pity in his eyes. "*This* one is going to be." I crossed my arms over my chest. "So stop trying to discourage me."

"I just wanted to make certain you . . ."

"I understand," I stated firmly. I glared at him, telling him to change the subject.

He sighed and lifted his hands as if to ward off my evil eye. The chair squeaked as he leaned back. "So . . . did you remember anything else you saw in the maze, or just Mr. Fitzpatrick's *trousers?*" The end of his question was heavy with insinuation, as if I'd been intentionally examining the man's lower extremities, and I resented it. The door opened before I could respond.

"Sorry to keep you waiting, Mr. Gage, but I was finishing my breakfast," Mr. Fitzpatrick exclaimed jovially as he entered. "Footman said you wanted to see me."

Gage rose and reached across the desk to shake his hand. "No problem. The Cromartys offer quite a spread, don't they?"

"That they do. The cook must know we men need a hearty break to our fast before we start the day."

"You know Lady Darby." Gage gestured my way, and Mr. Fitzpatrick stiffened.

"Oh. Yes. Yes, of course." He recovered quickly from his shock and offered me a shallow bow. "How do you do, my lady?"

"I am well," I replied, deciding to be cordial. "Thank you for asking. And yourself?"

"Oh, wonderful, wonderful."

I wondered if he planned to keep repeating his words through our entire conversation.

"Have a seat, sir," Gage said, settling back into his own chair. "I just have a few additional questions for you."

Mr. Fitzpatrick glanced at me out of the corner of his eye and shifted uncomfortably. "Of course, of course."

"It has come to my attention that you had mud splattered all over the back of your trousers when you appeared in the maze after the discovery of Lady Godwin's body. Can you explain how it got there?"

"Oh, well," he stammered, flicking his gaze to me once again. He leaned toward Gage and whispered. "Is this really an appropriate conversation to be having while *she* is present?" As if I couldn't hear him.

"*She* is here for a reason," Gage replied with a hard glint in his eye. "Now, ignore her and answer the question."

Mr. Fitzpatrick huffed and fidgeted. "Well, if you really must know . . ." His gaze shifted to me again. "I was . . . chasing Lady Lewis."

I couldn't stop my eyebrows from rising.

"Chasing?" Gage queried, keeping his voice and face carefully neutral.

"Yes," he grumbled. "She promised me a kiss if I could catch her."

A twinkle lit Gage's eyes, and I could tell he was trying not to laugh. "I see. And the mud?"

"I slipped in a flower patch and almost fell. It was damn embarrassing. She saw the whole thing." He glanced at me. "That's when I gave up and joined Sir David and Mr. Abingdon."

"So you didn't traipse into the forest?"

Mr. Fitzpatrick's face crinkled in confusion. "Why would I do that?"

"Oh, there's a great many reasons, but never mind." Gage studied him closely, and I could tell he was trying to make a decision about something. I didn't think it had to do with whether to believe his explanation for the mud, which even I found convincing.

"Mr. Fitzpatrick," he began seriously. "I need your word

that whatever is revealed in this office will not be spoken of to anyone who is not present."

Mr. Fitzpatrick turned to look at me more directly.

"Do I have it?"

He nodded. "Yes. Yes, of course."

I scrutinized Gage and wondered where he was leading this conversation.

"The reason Lady Godwin's figure had begun to change was not because she was getting fat. She was with child."

Mr. Fitzpatrick's eyes opened so wide I thought they might pop out of their sockets. "I . . . well . . . are you sure?" he spluttered.

Gage exchanged a glance with me. "Yes, Mr. Fitzpatrick. Very sure," he replied dryly.

"Well . . ." He pressed his hand to his forehead. "Thank heavens Godwin was in India. If he knew I had been sticking my . . . uh . . ." He flicked a panicked look at me. "Bedding his wife while she was in such a state, he would have chopped my . . . uh . . . hurt me badly."

Gage arched an eyebrow rather eloquently. "Well, Lord Godwin is not here. And he's not the father."

"He's not? Well, I'll be."

I almost sighed aloud at the man's idiocy.

"Then who is?"

"That's what we're trying to find out," Gage replied with much more patience than I could have mustered. "So far we know that Lord Marsdale bedded her in February, about a month before she would have gotten with child, and Mr. Calvin in . . ."

"Mr. Calvin bedded Lady Godwin?" Mr. Fitzpatrick interrupted. "Well, I'll be damned. There's more to the prig than I thought."

Gage ignored him. "And Mr. Calvin in May or June, which is too late. You said you never bedded her until the end of June."

"That's the truth."

"So we're left wondering who lay between her sheets in March. Do you have any idea?"

Mr. Fitzpatrick leaned back in his chair and tapped his chin. "*Hmmm . . . Let me think . . .*"

I couldn't help rolling my eyes at this display of mental acuity, thinking this entire conversation was a waste. Gage's eyes smiled at me.

Mr. Fitzpatrick shrugged. "Don't think I can help you. Lord Stratford was her lover at one point, but I couldn't tell you whether that was in March."

I jerked my gaze back to Gage and sat forward in my chair.

"Did you say Lord Stratford was one of her lovers?" he asked for clarification.

"Well, yes," Mr. Fitzpatrick replied. "But like I said, I don't know if that was in March."

I watched as Gage shifted in his seat, trying to contain his excitement much the way I was. "Anyone else here in attendance who has been linked to Lady Godwin?" he asked the man.

He tapped his chin again and shook his head. "No. Not that I can think of."

Gage nodded and rose from his seat. "Thank you for your assistance, Fitzpatrick." He shook the man's hand. "And remember what I told you about keeping this quiet."

"Of course, of course," he said with a bob of his head.

The door closed behind him with a solid thud, and I leaned toward Gage. "Do you think Lady Stratford didn't know?"

He shook his head sharply from side to side and narrowed his eyes. "Not for a second."

"So she lied to us?"

"A lie of omission is still a lie," he stated.

My muscles tightened in anticipation. "Perhaps we need to have another conversation with her as well."

Gage nodded. "This time unannounced."

CHAPTER TWENTY-ONE

Lady Stratford was not happy to see us when she opened her parlor door. In fact, she made little effort to suppress the scowl furrowing her features. Gage was, of course, charming, and she allowed us in, but she could not be bothered to offer any of the trite pleasantries ladies were taught to. Instead, she settled back on the pale blue settee she occupied the last time we spoke with her and lifted an embroidery hoop and continued to stitch. I noticed the basket at her feet filled with threads, ribbons, and needles, and the distinctive round handles of a pair of dainty shears. Gage perched on the edge of the chocolate-brown chair before Lady Stratford, but I decided to remain standing just over his shoulder.

"Lady Stratford," he began in the voice of a parent scolding his child for a minor infraction. "I was disappointed to discover you lied to us."

She glanced up at him, her brow lowering in irritation. "Do not patronize me, Mr. Gage. I'm not in the mood, nor of the rank, to allow it."

"You neglected to tell us that your husband was one of Lady Godwin's lovers."

"That is just a nasty, uncorroborated rumor," she snapped, stabbing her needle into the fabric.

"Yes, but it also happens to be one I find remarkably credible."

Lady Stratford glared at Gage.

"After all, your husband has never been known for his fidelity or discretion, and neither has Lady Godwin," he continued in an indifferent voice.

Her gray eyes hardened to chips of ice. "Much like yourself."

He nodded once slowly, acknowledging her right to return his rude comment with one of her own. "Can you tell me where you were the evening of Lady Godwin's murder?"

The countess's bosom lifted and lowered as she took a deep breath. "I had a headache after dinner, so I retired to my room." Which explained her absence from the parlor later that evening when Philip addressed everyone, but gave her no real alibi. "My maid attended me. She can confirm my whereabouts."

Except that servants could too easily be bought or threatened if they did not do as their employer wished. Her maid was a witness, but not a very good one. And Lady Stratford seemed aware of this, if the challenge in her gaze, daring us to contradict her, was any indication.

Gage leaned forward and gentled his voice. "You must have been terribly upset when you learned that Lady Godwin was being bedded by your husband."

Lady Stratford's gaze dropped to her needlework. "I *told* you it was only a rumor."

"Yes, but it still must have hurt. It's one thing to be forced to follow convention and sit back and indulge Lord Stratford in his indiscretions, and quite another to discover they involve your closest friend—a woman who should have known better, who should have been loyal." His sympathetic words rattled the countess, for her thread tangled and she flung aside her embroidery with a grunt of frustration. "Lady Godwin must have been aware that you would not approve."

Lady Stratford gazed across the room toward the windows and laughed bitterly. "Since when did she care for anyone's approval?"

Gage hesitated, as if waiting to see if she would elaborate. When she didn't, he goaded her further. "Surely her closest friend's approbation meant something to her."

Her eyes were bleak and wintry when they turned back toward us, as if a blizzard raged behind those icy gray orbs. "You clearly did not know Lady Godwin, Mr. Gage." Her gaze rose to meet mine over his head. "Did you, Lady Darby?" I shook my head, chilled by the loathing in her stare. "No? Well, count yourself lucky."

"Do you know when they . . . ?" Gage began.

"No. I do not. Sometime in the spring, I gather. *If* the rumors are true."

"Is he . . . ?"

Lady Stratford abruptly rose from her seat. "I'm finished. If you want to know anything else, why don't you talk to my husband? I'm sure he'll be happy to swap tales of your conquests," she called over her shoulder, one last parting shot as she exited through the door to her dressing room.

"Well, that went well," I muttered dryly.

"It did, rather," Gage replied as he rose to his feet.

"She just stormed out on us," I reminded him, confused by his satisfied tone.

"Yes." He held the door to the corridor open for me. "And in doing so, proved she is both upset by Lord Stratford and Lady Godwin's relationship and has a temper."

I considered his words, struggling with the idea of Lady Stratford as a murderess. "Do you honestly believe she could have done it?"

He glanced at me. "Why not? She has motive. And a pretty shabby alibi."

"Yes," I replied uncertainly. "But somehow I can't imagine Lady Stratford slicing Lady Godwin's neck just because she bedded her husband, let alone harming that baby. It sounds mad."

"Well, maybe when she discovered their betrayal, she went a little mad. Such things have happened before."

I contemplated this idea and then shook my head. "No. Maybe if she had just found out, but the rumors circulated months ago. People don't focus on old relationships when there are new ones to gossip about, and it sounds as if Lady Godwin has hopped into any number of gentlemen's beds since she was with Lord Stratford."

"True," he conceded, turning down the corridor toward the main hall. "But what if Lady Stratford only recently confirmed the rumors? What if Lady Godwin approached her at this very house party and told her she was expecting her husband's child?" Gage raised his eyebrows. "That would be quite a blow."

I frowned. "I suppose. However, we still have a few other issues to contend with. Such as the amount of strength it took to inflict Lady Godwin's wounds."

"Anger can generate a lot of power, Lady Darby."

That was true, but I still felt Lady Stratford was too dainty to have sliced the viscountess's throat so cleanly. "What about the muscle it would have taken to dig that hole in the forest and bury the baby? Anger is potent, but it also spends itself quickly when exerted."

He was silent for a moment while he thought. "Perhaps she had help."

I looked up to meet his gaze. "Her maid?" I asked, thinking of her alibi.

"She seems the likely choice."

I pressed my hands together, realizing he could be right. I didn't want to believe Lady Stratford could have committed the crime, especially as it involved a child, but I had to at least reconcile myself to the possibility. "All right, then who are we questioning first? Lord Stratford or the maid?"

Before he could reply, my question was answered for us. Mrs. MacLean called our names and came hurrying down the hall toward us. Huffing and puffing with either panic or excitement, she pressed a hand to her side as she tried to catch her breath.

"Oh, Mr. Gage, m'lady," she gasped, the pitch of her voice rising. "I was just comin' to find you."

"What is it, Mrs. MacLean?" Gage asked calmly. "Has something happened?"

"Aye! Faye, Lady Godwin's maid, ya ken. She told me that Celeste, Lady Stratford's lass, borrowed one o' her aprons. Said she couldna find her spare."

His gaze met mine, and his eyes seemed to sharpen like a falcon sighting his prey. "Thank you, Mrs. MacLean. We'll go speak with Faye."

"She's in 'er room. I just came from there." She clucked her tongue. "Wanted to check on the puir dear."

"Let Lord Cromarty know what you've discovered," Gage instructed her. "And send Lady Stratford's maid up. But don't tell her why."

"Course." The housekeeper performed an odd curtsy and hurried off down the hall.

I pulled Gage to a stop just before he entered the servants' stairway. "Aren't you concerned by how all of this suddenly seems to be falling into place?"

"It normally does, once you hit on the right suspect," he replied. I could see the suppressed excitement in his frame as he began to climb. "Perhaps Faye remembers something about Lord or Lady Stratford that can help us?"

"Yes, but will she even speak ill of the countess?" I asked as I followed. "The lady has been so kind to her."

"Maybe."

"What do you mean?" I asked, confused by his ominous tone of voice.

"If Lady Stratford is the murderer, it would certainly shed a different light on her willingness to help the maid."

"Guilt?" I guessed.

"Or something much more nefarious. If Faye knows something, even something she may not realize is important, Lady Stratford might decide she needs to keep her quiet. Permanently."

A chill crept down my spine, and I wrapped my arms around my torso. I just couldn't see Lady Stratford being capable of such evil things, but what if I was wrong? She certainly wouldn't be the first person to fool me. Sir Anthony had seemed harmless enough before we wed. It wasn't until a week after that I discovered how wrong I was. I didn't want to discover the same about Lady Stratford a week too late to help Faye.

"Then I guess we had better help her remember," I said.

He nodded and rapped on the door to Faye and Celeste's room.

"*Entrer*," we heard Faye's heavily accented voice say through the wood.

The little maid stood next to the window, looking out on the garden. When she turned toward us, I was glad to see she was more composed than the last time we visited her. Her eyes were still rimmed in red, but her appearance was neat and tidy.

"*Mon dieu!*" she gasped and pressed a hand to her chest. "*C'était rapide.*"

"Mrs. MacLean met us in the hall," Gage explained. "She said you allowed Lady Stratford's maid to borrow one of your aprons."

"*Oui.* Celeste . . . um . . ." The maid seemed to struggle switching back to English. "She is Lady Stratford's maid. She say her apron missing and borrow mine."

"She also shares this room with you?" I peered around Gage.

"*Oui.*"

"When did she borrow the apron?" Gage queried.

Faye's wide eyes flicked back and forth between us in

growing alarm, and I wondered if her reaction had more to do with her shaky grasp of English or the nervous energy suddenly radiating off of Gage. "*Mmm . . . zee day before zee last day.*"

"Two days ago?"

"*Mmm . . . oui.*" She nodded.

Which would have made it the day after Lady Godwin's murder.

"Did she say how it might have gone missing?"

Her brow furrowed. "No. It just . . . missing." She shrugged.

I stepped back to lean against the wall as he asked Faye if she would like to sit. The maid shook her head no, and clasped her hands in front of her.

I glanced around at the sparseness of the room. As a rule, servants' quarters were normally rather bare and austere, particularly when two visiting servants occupied the room. There were two small beds, barely larger than cots, a small dresser, and a wardrobe. The floor boasted only a worn, thin rug, probably saved from the rubbish bin after it was deemed unusable in the main part of the castle. No curtains or paintings covered the thick stone walls, just a wooden cross hung in the middle of the wall opposite the two beds, so that the maids could reflect on it while they lay in bed, I supposed.

"Was Lord Stratford one of Lady Godwin's lovers?" Gage asked lightly, propping his foot up on the frame of the bed.

Faye seemed to take a long time considering her answer, but I knew she must have understood the question. Gage glanced at me, sharing my curiosity over the maid's hesitation.

Finally the girl sighed and dropped her eyes. "*Oui.*"

"Why didn't you want to tell us?"

"Because Lady Stratford so nice to me. She her ladyship's friend. But my lady say Lady Stratford sleep with my lord, so she sleep with hers," the maid stated and pointed her nose into the air, defending her employer's reprehensible behavior to the last.

"Lady Stratford bedded Lord Godwin?" Gage asked doubtfully.

"*Oui*," Faye nodded her head once decisively.

"All right. Well, do you know when Lady Godwin and Lord Stratford conducted their liaison?"

The maid tipped her head to the side and closed one eye. "*Mmm* . . . Lent."

"Lent?" Gage seemed to contemplate this.

"The six weeks between Ash Wednesday and Maundy Thursday," I reminded him.

He scowled at me. "I know what Lent is."

"It normally falls within March," I added, wondering if this was his issue.

"Thank you," he snapped before turning back toward the maid who was watching our quarrel with great interest. "Could Lord Stratford have been the father of her child?" he asked after taking a calming breath.

Faye shook her head. "No."

This was not the answer either Gage or I expected. "Why not?" he pressed.

"He is . . ." the maid waved her hand in the air as if searching for the word ". . . *stérile*."

"Sterile? You mean he can't have children."

"*Oui*. Many people know zis."

Something nagged at me in the back of my brain, something important. I furrowed my brow, trying to remember.

Gage turned to me and murmured. "I bet you five hundred pounds he's not."

"And how exactly are you going to prove that?" I asked him crossly.

"Why don't you take the bet and wait and see?"

"I don't have five hundred pounds."

He shrugged. "My loss."

We looked up to find Faye scrutinizing us again, and

then her face cleared. "Ah. You are lovers," she stated as if she'd just solved a great mystery.

"No!" We both exclaimed.

I scowled at Gage's reaction. Just because I was horrified by the thought did not mean he should be. I barely restrained myself from asking him what was wrong with the idea of having me for a lover. But such a question would imply that I cared. And I didn't.

I turned away, wanting to escape this awkward situation, when the door opened and in walked Celeste. She seemed fidgety and uncertain, though in all fairness, the expression on our faces was not exactly welcoming.

"Mrs. MacLean said ya wanted ta see me?" she asked, fisting her hands in her skirt.

"Yes." Gage cleared his throat. "Close the door and come in."

She turned around to shut the door softly and then took two short steps into the room before stopping. Her posture was as stiff as a statue, albeit an unstable one. The maid had titian hair and a pink complexion. She looked more like an apple-cheeked dairy maid than a coldhearted killer—a girl who was more likely to be talked into a roll in the hay with a handsome stranger than be convinced to help her employer commit murder.

"How long have you worked for Lady Stratford?" Gage asked gently, trying to put the woman at ease.

"Since a'fore her debut," she replied in a shaky voice. "I were her sister's maid a'fore that, but when Lady Alice married, she decided she wanted a different maid. A'fore that I was but an upstairs maid."

Gage perked up and seemed pleased to discover Celeste was talkative. "You must be grateful her ladyship kept you for her lady's maid when *she* wed?"

"That I am. Lady Alice thought me clumsy, but Lady Charlotte says she's happy to have me. 'Sides, she's much prettier than her older sister. And she's a countess now, and a great lady." Celeste raised her chin in pride, a tight smile stretching her lips.

"We've been told she was a good friend of Lady Godwin's."

Celeste's smile fell, and she looked across the room at Faye. "She was. Took her ladyship's death right hard. 'Specially considerin' . . ." She shrugged, leaving us to wonder what she had not said.

"Especially considering what?" I asked.

The maid chewed her lip and glanced back and forth between me and Gage. "I s'pose ya know by now that Lady Godwin was expectin'." I nodded. "Well, her ladyship didn't want the babe. Least, that's what she told my lady." Her eyes flicked to Faye, who did not dispute this assertion. "My lady convinced her to give the babe to a family near Glasgow so that my lady could visit the babe whenever she stayed with her great-aunt."

Gage folded his arms across his chest and tilted his head. "She did that, even knowing the child's father was Lord Stratford?"

Celeste's eyes widened. "Yes. Even knowin' that." She rocked back on her heels. "Maybe 'specially *'cause* of that."

A frown puckered Faye's brow, as if she was confused by this answer and wasn't certain if she should say something. Gage shifted and squared his body so that he could focus solely on Celeste. I knew the conversation was about to become even more serious.

"Can you tell me where you were the evening of Lady Godwin's murder?"

The maid's body froze, and her hands tightened in her skirt. "I was tendin' my lady. She gets megrims. 'Specially when his lordship is not behavin' himself," she added defiantly. "Her ladyship retired after dinner, and I stayed with her. We didn't even 'ear 'bout the murder 'til the next mornin'."

"Did anyone see you run errands for Lady Stratford that evening? Can anyone vouch for you?" Gage pressed.

"Not after her ladyship called me 'way from the dinner table. I slept in her dressing room case she needed me."

"Do you do this often?"

"Yes. As I says, she gets megrims, and sometimes they be right terrible." The maid sounded frank and confident, but her body language told a different story. Her hands continued to twist in the fabric of her skirt, and she rocked back on her heels several more times. Was she always this fidgety? I wondered whether to trust her verbal or physical cues.

Gage crossed the room to stand over Celeste, intimidating her with his height. She shrank away from him. "Did you borrow an apron from Faye two days ago?"

Celeste's eyes flicked to Faye and back to him again in confusion. "Yes."

"Why?"

"I had to wash mine, and m'spare was missin'," Celeste replied cautiously.

"Did you report this to Mrs. MacLean?" Gage asked, pacing around her.

"No." She watched dazedly as he passed behind her. "I didn't think I needed ta."

"Why?"

"I figured it would turn up. It didn't seem like somethin' somebody would go 'bout stealin'. I got more at her ladyship's house in London."

"I see. Was there anything distinctive about it?"

"Uh . . . no. Just a white apron." By now I was getting dizzy watching Gage circle around the woman, and she looked a bit frantic. "Have you found it then? Is that what this is all 'bout?"

"We have," he admitted.

"Where is it? Did someone have it?"

"*Where* is not as important as *how* we found it, and how it appeared when we did."

Celeste looked positively flummoxed by his clever twist-ing of words. "I don't understand."

"I think you do," he replied, halting in front of her. "Can you tell me whether Lady Stratford embroiders?"

She blinked up at him, clearly thrown by the change of topic. "Y-yes. Yes, she does."

"And what does she embroider?"

"Uh . . . samplers, and blankets, and shawls, and things. Oh, and once she stitched yellow roses onto a pair of gloves. They were right pretty."

My stomach dipped.

"She embroiders shawls?" Gage confirmed, and the maid nodded her head. "Do you know if she stitched pink roses along the border of an ivory silk stole?"

Celeste's eyes widened. "Why, yes. It happens to be one of her favorites. Loves to wear it with her pink satin."

His eyes met mine across the room. "Do you know what her embroidery scissors look like?" he asked.

She looked down and licked her lips, perhaps just real-izing that his questions were not so innocent. "Um. I believe they have vines and flowers and things on 'em."

Gage reached into his pocket. "Like this?" He held up the pair of embroidery scissors we had found in the maze. They had been cleaned and the blood removed.

Celeste seemed to cower from Gage. "Y-yes."

"Are these her ladyship's scissors?"

Her eyes darted down to them and then back to his eyes. She licked her lips again. "Well, they look very like 'em. I . . . I don't know if that's her pair exactly."

I heard Faye gasp behind me and then release a string of curses in French. "You murderer! *Vous le cochon dégoûtant!*" I moved forward to intercept her before she could lunge at Celeste. "*Je découperai votre coeur!*"

"I'm not a murderer," Celeste protested. Her voice rose in panic as if she only now comprehended exactly what all of this questioning was about. "I'm not a murderer. I never touched Lady Godwin. I was with my lady."

"*Meurtrière! Meurtrière!*" Her anger quickly spent, I managed to coax Faye to lie down on her bed, where she curled into herself and began to sob.

I glanced at Gage, who was taking all of this in with a look of careful indifference. I couldn't manage such cold composure. Not while my heart raced and my ears still rang with Faye's cries. *Murderess! Murderess!*

"Lady Darby," Gage said coolly. "Please take Celeste out into the hallway and wait for me there."

"I've done nothin' wrong!" Celeste shouted at him.

"Then you'll have no problem with my searching your things."

"Go right ahead. But I'm not leavin'." She crossed her arms over her chest.

He looked at me. "All right. But stay over by the door with Lady Darby."

Gage began rifling through her belongings, of which, fortunately, there were few. He opened the drawers of the dresser and slammed them shut again when he found nothing. Then he flipped through the garments in the wardrobe and searched the bedding on Celeste's tiny cot.

"See. Nothin'," the maid declared belligerently.

I sighed. Such a cheeky tongue was only going to anger Mr. Gage.

He glared at her. "We've already found more than enough. This was simply a formality to make certain you haven't any more damning evidence."

"A missin' apron and my lady's embroidery scissors don't mean anythin'."

"They do when they're found covered in blood."

Celeste gasped while across the room Faye whimpered. Even I cringed at the bluntness of his words.

"That's not true! It can't be!" Celeste said. "I haven't done anythin'."

"You're coming with us," Gage declared, reaching out to take hold of her arm.

She squirmed against his hold, and he clamped down on her upper arm even harder. "But wait! I . . . I have to fix her ladyship her tonic." Her voice was desperate and her eyes wild. "She needs it. I'm already late."

Something in my memory clicked into place, and I halted Gage before he could drag her out the door. "What tonic?" I questioned her. "What kind?"

"Her . . . her chasteberry tonic. She takes it every afternoon. Please, m'lady," she pleaded. Tears sprang to her eyes, and her lip wobbled. "I . . . I haven't done anythin'."

I looked up at Gage. "Do you know what chasteberry tonic is used for?"

He did not shake his head, but I could tell he was aggravated by the question, believing it to be irrelevant. Like most males, he was clueless as to the tonic's medicinal properties.

"I think you should," I told him gravely.

His gaze sharpened. "Let me place this maid under Mrs. MacLean's supervision. And then we'll talk."

CHAPTER TWENTY-TWO

I rapped twice on the parlor door to the Stratfords' suite, and when no one answered, rapped twice more. There was only silence inside the chamber. Celeste was sequestered in the housekeeper's quarters, and though I wasn't certain where Lord Stratford and his valet were, I strongly suspected Lady Stratford was alone in the suite. At least, I hoped so. It would make all of this easier.

Twisting my hands in my skirts, I glanced up and down the corridor before cautiously opening the door and peering inside. The sun-filled chamber sat empty, save for the furnishings, but still I hesitated at the threshold, troubled by what I might discover within. Afraid I might find that a monster *can* lurk behind even the most fragile facade.

It seemed absurd that I was not relieved by the information Celeste had given us. After all, this was what I had wanted—to catch the murderer and remove suspicion once and for all from myself—but I simply couldn't feel pleased with such a result. Not knowing that a woman like Lady Stratford could be so evil. It sent spiders crawling up and down my spine.

I don't know what I had been expecting. *Someone* murdered Lady Godwin and her child, and though no one at the house party had struck me as a probable suspect, from the beginning, I had been well aware that the likely culprit was a fellow guest. But Lady Stratford? Especially knowing what I did about her health. That was almost beyond my comprehension. It was certainly beyond my understanding.

I shook my head, saddened and confused, and sickened by the knowledge of what I must do. Glancing behind me once more, I stepped into the room and closed it softly behind me. I wished Gage was with me. No matter what he said about Lady Stratford being more comfortable speaking with a woman, *I* would be more comfortable with him by my side. I felt certain he would be better at coaxing her to talk than I, but he insisted that I interrogate her on the matter of the chasteberry tonic while he retrieved the embroidered shawl from the chapel cellar and located Philip and Lord Stratford. I knew the only alternative was for me to revisit the cellar and collect the shawl, and I had absolutely no intention of ever returning to that foul, makeshift crypt. So in the end, my only option was to confront Lady Stratford alone.

I wasn't afraid that the countess would harm me, and, in any case, Gage and the others would be joining us shortly. However, I was still distressed by the task set before me. My hands shook as I tucked a loose strand of hair behind my ear. I surveyed the parlor. Lady Stratford's embroidery hoop lay discarded on the blue settee where she had let it drop when she stormed out earlier. It sat with her work, face up, and I realized, with a jolt, that she was stitching a picture of a rocking horse. For whom? Lady Godwin's baby? Celeste told us Lady Stratford had arranged for the adoption of Lady Godwin's child and planned to visit the little girl. Would a woman do such a thing if she planned to murder the mother and child?

I shook my head and strode across the room. There was no indication that the murder had been premeditated. Perhaps Lady Godwin had changed her mind about the adoption or threatened to take up with Lady Stratford's husband again, upsetting Lady Stratford. Who knew what a person was capable of in a moment of rage or despair?

I knocked once on the dressing-room door before entering, having already expected to find the countess in her bedchamber through the door on the other side. Beautiful gowns lined the walls, and delicate slippers were arranged side by side across the floor. A simple cot stood in one corner. Perhaps Celeste hadn't lied about sleeping in here, or at least she'd done so on one of the subsequent nights following Lady Godwin's murder.

"Lady Stratford," I called, tapping on the bedroom door. No one answered, but I was quite certain the countess was listening. "Lady Stratford, I need to speak with you." There was still no reply. I sighed and leaned my head against the wood, knowing I was going to have to say something far more ruthless to convince her to emerge. "If you do not speak with me now, I'm afraid you will find it far more difficult to do so when Mr. Gage and Lord Cromarty arrive. Such delicate matters really aren't meant for gentlemen's ears."

There was a moment of silence when I began to worry that even those words would not coax her to come out. Then I heard a faint rustling and the whisper of skirts gliding across the floor. Seconds later, the door opened to reveal Lady Stratford's irritated face.

"What do you want?" she snapped, her mouth twisting in anger.

I was so accustomed to seeing her immaculately coiffed that the sight of her wrinkled skirts and crooked fichu momentarily stunned me. I found myself wishing she did not suddenly appear so young and vulnerable. Her harsh perfection would have been much easier to confront, under the circumstances.

The reason for my shock must have been evident, for her scowl deepened and she reached up to re-pin a pale strand of hair that had fallen from her chignon.

Recovering myself, I cleared my throat. "Mr. Gage has a few more questions he would like you to answer. Perhaps we should return to your parlor." Without giving her time to reply, I turned and made my way back across the dressing room, forcing her to either follow me or wait to discuss matters with Mr. Gage. I trusted she knew exactly what "delicate matters" I had been referring to, and their implications, and she would soon join me.

"What if I refuse to answer any further questions?" she challenged, trailing me through the door to the parlor.

I sat on the brocade settee across the tea table from her pale blue one and spread my skirts out. "That is, of course, your choice. However, I believe it is in your best interest that you do. Remaining silent will only make you look more suspicious."

Her frown deepened, and I could see the thoughts flickering across her gray eyes like clouds across the silvery surface of the loch. She seemed nonplussed and uncertain what to do. I wasn't sure whether that was because she genuinely didn't know what was happening or if she had just realized we suspected her of something.

She carefully lowered herself to the cushions and moved her embroidery aside. Her movements were strained and stiff. I could only compare them to the way she behaved two days prior, when she had been agitated by my presence, but not forced in her movements like she was now. I wondered what that meant. Would Lady Stratford turn violent when cornered, as her role as murderess suggested, or would she crumble from within? I perched cautiously on the edge of my seat, not willing to take a chance.

"Have you spoken with my husband?" she surprised me by asking.

"Not yet."

"I told you he could answer these questions far better than I. Why do you continue to pester me in this manner?" She fisted her hands in her lap and lifted her chin. "I can assure you he will be most displeased when he learns how I have been mistreated."

I wasn't entirely certain of that. In fact, Lord Stratford seemed remarkably indifferent to his wife's welfare. I suspected Lady Stratford was keenly aware of this, if her husband's treatment of her at dinner two nights past was any indication of the state of their marriage. I couldn't blame her for wanting to pretend otherwise, particularly in a situation like this. I thought I would have lied as well.

"You know we are only doing our best to uncover Lady Godwin's murderer." I struggled to keep my voice calm, even as my heart pounded in my chest. "Can you blame us for being suspicious when we discovered you lied to us about Lord Stratford being one of Lady Godwin's lovers?"

"I told you, that is a vicious rumor," she snapped.

"One we have confirmed. And one we have confirmed you knew about."

Lady Stratford's mouth tightened into a white line.

"We have also confirmed that you knew your husband was the father of Lady Godwin's baby. And that you convinced Lady Godwin to give the baby to a couple living near your great-aunt, so that you might visit the child from time to time."

She stared back at me boldly, but I could see the edges of her composure beginning to fray. Her chest rose and fell with each agitated breath. "You can't have confirmed it. Not if you haven't spoken to Lord Stratford."

I answered evenly, refusing to rise to her bait. "And when we talk to him? What do you think he's going to tell us?"

She blinked like an animal that realizes it has walked into a trap.

"Let's cease with the denials," I told her more sharply. "They will do you no good. I'm afraid you have much more serious implications to contend with than simply the effect all of this will have on your reputation."

Lady Stratford looked startled by this proclamation. I wondered whether she was one of those ladies who believed reputation was everything or if she truly was naive enough to think that was the only thing at risk in this situation.

"Why did you convince Lady Godwin to give the baby up for adoption to a couple near Glasgow?" I asked.

"Because she didn't want the child," she blurted, as if such a thing was unfathomable to her. "She planned to pass it off to the housekeeper at one of her husband's properties to raise. She didn't care what became of the babe."

I could understand Lady Stratford's distress over such a proclamation. "And this couple actually wanted the child?"

"Yes. They have been desperate for a baby. The wife birthed a stillborn babe not long ago and almost died herself. The midwife told her she would never be able to have another child, so adoption was their only chance to be parents." I heard the fervency in the countess's voice, the desperate need to help this nameless couple from Glasgow. It tugged at my own heart.

"The couple lives close to your great-aunt? Did you plan to assist the child?"

She hesitated, perhaps thinking I might disapprove of her interest in a bastard child that was not even her own. "I thought I might look in on them from time to time, just to make certain the child was well cared for."

I knew she was understating the matter, but I did not press her. I was well aware that a less sympathetic gentle-woman would find her intentions untenable. "You must have been furious with Lady Godwin," I remarked, trying to make the comment sound as if it was not leading. "First for bedding your husband, and then for expecting his child."

Lady Stratford was not completely foiled by my noncha-lance, but she answered me nonetheless, shifting awkwardly in her seat. "Yes. Yes, I was," she answered quietly.

"How unfair it must have seemed for such a lady to be blessed with a baby when there are so many other women who are more worthy."

Lady Stratford stared down at her lap, twirling a diamond-and-ruby ring round and round her finger.

"I'm quite certain that couple who were going to adopt Lady Godwin's little girl would have been much more deserving of . . ."

Lady Stratford's head snapped up. "It was a little girl?" she gasped. Raw longing shimmered in her gaze.

"Yes," I replied, suddenly wary.

Lady Stratford lowered her head, sniffing as tears overflowed her eyes. If she had killed Lady Godwin and taken the child from the womb, then she would know it was a little girl. Was she feigning this emotion, or had she truly not known? Either possibility soured my stomach.

I weighed my next words carefully. It was a terrible thing to know you wielded the power to harm someone just with the knowledge of what rested on your tongue. I did not like it. It gave me new respect for the manner in which Gage conducted his interrogations. The charm he exerted was used as much for personal protection as for softening the blow of his questions. I didn't have that charm. All I had was an innate sensitivity to this subject and the wisdom to cushion the blow.

Leaning toward Lady Stratford, I clutched my hands together and gentled my voice. "You are having difficulty conceiving." I didn't phrase it as a question, but it was in essence one, nonetheless. Lady Stratford glanced up at me, more in confirmation than surprise, as more tears filled her eyes. "The chasteberry tonic, the red-raspberry-leaf tea, even your garnet necklace." I gestured toward the amulet dangling over her décolletage. "They are all supposed to cure barrenness."

The countess pulled out a handkerchief from her sleeve to dab at her eyes but still she did not respond.

"You have been married to the earl for nearly seven years," I pressed, hating the necessity of doing so. "And still you have not given him a child. He must be anxious for an heir."

Her mouth thinned into a line of annoyance. "Is that all anyone ever thinks of? My husband's need of an heir? What about me?" she demanded, pressing her palm to her chest. "All I've ever wanted from this marriage was children. I watch as my sisters and friends fill their homes with babies they don't even want, and yet I remain childless. I have suffered my husband's attentions, and his odd remedies and methods for conception, and still no baby grows in me. I am reminded time and time again of how I have failed in my duties as a wife." She sniffed. "Of all people, Lady Darby, I thought you might understand."

I sat back, realizing what she meant. "I don't know whether I have difficulty conceiving," I admitted. "Sir Anthony visited me so rarely, I don't think it is possible to know." Lady Stratford almost seemed more shocked by this revelation than anything else, and I wondered what that said about both my attractiveness and the earl's sexual proclivities. "But I understood that conceiving an heir would one day become central in his thoughts, and I would be expected to deliver on the implied promise noblemen believe we have made when we agree to marry them."

"All we are is broodmares," she agreed angrily. "And when we can't deliver . . ." Her words trailed away, and she shook her head as more tears filled her eyes. "I *wanted* to deliver. I want a child, Lady Darby."

"And so you promised to care for Lady Godwin's?"

She nodded.

"Even though the baby's father is your husband."

She dropped her eyes and nodded.

Her despair tugged unwillingly at my heart. "You must have been devastated when you discovered Lady Godwin, your friend, was carrying your husband's child. It would have taken away any doubt as to who was to blame for his childless state."

"She threw it in my face," the countess choked out. "She knew how much I wanted to have a child, how much Lord

Stratford and I fought about it, and she waved her conception in front of my face like a prize." Her words were harsh and crisp, strangled with hurt and frustration. "She didn't even want the baby! She slept with my husband, conceived his child, and proved me to be barren, and she didn't even want the baby!" Her shoulders shook, and she pressed a hand to her mouth to withhold her sobs.

"Did you kill her for it, Lady Stratford?" I asked, unable to withhold the question.

The countess shook her head and swallowed audibly. "No. I wanted her dead," she admitted. "I wanted her dead. But I didn't kill her."

I sank back into the cushions, wanting to believe her. Wanting to believe that this woman who so longed for a child of her own would not dare to harm another's. But the evidence said otherwise.

Gage suggested she went mad. That she murdered Lady Godwin, thinking to save the child from her duplicitous, uncaring mother. Was that why the baby had been removed? Someone who is insane might overlook the fact that a baby so young cannot survive outside the womb. A shiver ran down my spine.

I could not withhold a sigh of relief when I heard the knock on the parlor door. Lady Stratford glanced at me curiously as I sat forward.

"That should be Mr. Gage," I told her, crossing the room.

True to form, Gage stood on the other side of the door, gazing at me solemnly in question. I gave him an almost imperceptible nod to let him know Lady Stratford confirmed my suspicions about her infertility. His frown deepened, and the intensity in his eyes sharpened. I stepped back to allow him to enter, nodding quietly to Philip and Lord Stratford as they followed.

Lady Stratford sat up straighter and patted at her eyes with her handkerchief. "What is going on?"

Her dazed expression sought me out, and I suddenly felt

guilty for forcing her to face these men when she was still so vulnerable. I backed up to stand in the shadow of the drapes, wrapping myself in the heat they had collected from the sun.

"I'm afraid we have a few more questions to ask you, Lady Stratford," Gage answered for me. "Questions that we felt it would be best for Lord Stratford to be present for."

Lady Stratford blinked and glanced at her husband. "I don't understand. I've just spoken with Lady Darby. I thought I answered all of her questions." She looked at me again.

"These queries are different, and I'm afraid quite serious." Gage was trying to be gentle with her, but I could hear the repressed anger creeping into his voice.

The countess shifted in her seat. "And I have to answer them?"

"Oh, for heaven's sake!" Lord Stratford barked, marching across the room to stand over his wife. "Just ask the damn questions, Gage." He glared down at her, his hands on his hips. "I'll see to it that my wife cooperates."

I glanced over to where Philip leaned against the wall across the room from me, content to merely observe the proceedings as I was. He looked grim and tired and, at the moment, decidedly displeased with Lord Stratford. If Gage had attempted to interrogate my sister in such a manner, Philip never would have stood for it, no matter what evidence Gage presented him with. Philip was as bloody-minded as one of his wolfhounds with a bone when it came to protecting his wife.

Gage set the box he borrowed from my studio on the back of the leather chair and studied the now-scowling Lady Stratford. She clearly disliked her husband's proclamation. I couldn't blame her. I disliked it as well.

"You told us that on the night of Lady Godwin's murder you immediately went to bed with a megrim after dinner, and that your maid, Celeste, attended you. That you stayed in bed all night and did not hear about the murder until the next morning. Would you like to make any amendments to those statements?"

"No. That is the truth," she replied sharply.

"Did your maid remain with you the entire night?"

Lady Stratford's brow lowered. "She slept on a cot in the dressing room. So, I suppose, I cannot say for certain that she remained there the entire night, but she was there every time I called for her."

"So she conceivably could have slipped from the room sometime that evening after you had fallen asleep to, say, meet a beau?" Gage asked offhandedly.

Lady Stratford shook her head. "Celeste doesn't have a beau. And, besides, she could not have departed before midnight. She stayed with me, alternating hot and cold compresses until I fell asleep."

I held my breath, unable to believe Lady Stratford had just allowed the teeth of Gage's trap to snap down on her. By providing herself with such a seal-tight alibi, placing her in the presence of her maid the entire evening, she had also lost her chance to blame the entire murder on Celeste. The procurator fiscal might have allowed the Stratfords to convince him the maid was responsible, but not now. Not after Lady Stratford had so baldly stated she was with her the entire evening. I glanced at Lord Stratford, wondering if he was just as oblivious to Gage's stratagem.

"So if I accused you of murdering Lady Godwin, you would tell me that was impossible because you were in your bedchamber with your maid the entire time?" Gage asked silkily.

Lady Stratford stiffened, and her eyes widened. Whether in shock or fear, I could not tell.

"Now, just hold on, Gage," her husband suddenly interjected. "What are you hinting at?"

Gage ignored him, keeping his gaze fixed on Lady Stratford. "What if I told you that your maid's apron was found covered in blood?"

The countess's face paled. "I . . . I don't understand," she mumbled in a thready voice, glancing up at her husband in supplication.

Lord Stratford's face darkened. "If that's all the evidence with which you have to threaten my wife, by Jove, Gage, I'll . . ."

"There's more." Gage glared at him to close his mouth.

Lord Stratford huffed a breath and crossed his arms over his chest.

"I've been told you embroider, my lady," Gage said, addressing the countess again, who seemed more bewildered than ever.

"Yes?"

"That you're quite good."

She did not respond to this, just watched him warily, as if waiting for the hatchet to drop.

"Are you, by chance, missing a pair of embroidery scissors?"

She glanced down at the basket at her feet. "I . . . I don't know." She sounded genuinely befuddled and frightened. "When I arrived here at Gairloch, I was missing my normal pair of shears, but I thought I must have left them at home. I always carry a second pair." She leaned over to pick up the scissors sticking up out of the basket to show them to us. "So I never thought much of it."

Her explanation sounded credible; however, even the most foolish of criminals could have concocted such an excuse.

"Are these your scissors?" Gage asked, once again pulling the shears from his pocket.

Lady Stratford leaned forward to take them from Gage, but her husband snatched them out of his grasp before she could reach them. He flipped them over in his hands before handing them to her with a scowl. I could tell the earl wanted to say something, but he held his counsel, waiting to see what else Gage revealed.

"I . . ." Lady Stratford stammered. Her hands shook as she examined the scissors. "They look like mine."

The breath in my chest tightened.

Gage's eyes hardened. "We found them in the maze, near the place where Lady Godwin was butchered." I jerked at his gruesome choice of words. "They were coated with her blood."

Lady Stratford flung the scissors to the ground, cringing away from them. "But . . . but . . . that can't be." Her face was ghastly white. "Someone must have stolen them. I swear to you, I did not . . . could not . . ." She seemed to choke on the words.

Gage reached into the box and extracted the shawl. He unfolded it and held it up for all of us to see. "My lady, is this your shawl?"

Lady Stratford gasped and covered her face with shaking hands. "Yes," she admitted between shallow, quick breaths. "But . . . that . . . I didn't . . . I don't know how that blood got on it."

"We found it wrapped around Lady Godwin's child and buried in a grave by the stream at the far north end of Cromarty's property," Gage said harshly, speaking more to Lord Stratford than his wife.

"Her child?" Lady Stratford gasped. "But Lady Godwin wasn't due for another four months?" Her eyes flew around the room, as if looking for answers from one of us. "I don't understand. Did she begin her labor early?"

"No, Lady Stratford," Gage answered coldly, clearly not taken in by this display. For myself, I was not so sure she was faking. I had seen my fair share of theatrics at the Bow Street Magistrate's Court in London, and the hysteria shining in Lady Stratford's eyes was far too real for my comfort.

The implications of Gage's words must have finally penetrated her mind, for she keeled forward and began to sob uncontrollably. "Oh, no! Oh, that poor child. That poor little girl."

Gage perked up at her words.

"I told her it was a girl," I explained before he could assume otherwise.

He glanced back at me and nodded.

"What will happen to my wife?" Lord Stratford asked in a hard voice, drawing our attention away from the weeping woman.

Gage gestured toward Philip. "Cromarty says there is a set of bachelor quarters at the back of the carriage house. They're being cleaned as we speak. For her own safety and those of the other guests, we think it might be best if she and her maid were removed to there until the procurator fiscal from Inverness arrives."

"She should be perfectly comfortable," Philip added in a tight voice.

Lord Stratford nodded stiffly.

"My God," Lady Stratford gasped. "You all actually believe I did it. You truly believe I . . . *murdered* Helena." Her voice broke, and she pressed her handkerchief to her mouth. "I didn't do it! I swear to you, I . . . I never touched her. I couldn't have."

"Why couldn't you have?" Gage demanded, giving her no leniency, even in her outpouring of emotion.

"Because . . ." Her eyes met mine desperately. "Because of the baby." She shook her head wildly. "I could never have hurt that child. No matter what Helena did."

The men were all silent, and I wondered how they could remain so stoic in the face of her pleas. Emotion burned the back of my eyes and my throat. It took considerable effort not to let the tears fall.

Lady Stratford glanced wildly up at her husband, whose warm chocolate eyes had gone cold. "Please, Derek!" she whispered brokenly. "You must believe me. I did not kill Lady Godwin."

"That will be for the official from Inverness to decide," he replied and turned away from her.

I could almost feel the blow that Lord Stratford's words caused his wife. They ricocheted through her frame like an icy blast from the North Sea. She cowered from him like a whipped dog, seeming to crumple into herself.

I turned away from them, unable to face either of the Stratfords. The earl angered me with his callous treatment and his swift abandonment of his wife, and Lady Stratford's desperate tears and shuddering frame unnerved me. Her emotion seemed all too genuine, and I was suddenly having a very difficult time believing she was the murderer. Either her acting skills were so great that they rivaled even the most celebrated actresses of the stage, or we had just made a serious mistake.

If only I knew for certain which she was—fiend or innocent. For if Lady Stratford was wrongly accused, it placed her in a situation with which I was all too familiar. The thought burned a hole in my stomach.

CHAPTER TWENTY-THREE

Alana was asleep when I slipped into the nursery a short while later. She sat in a Windsor rocking chair, cradling a slumbering Greer on her shoulder.

"Aunt Kiera," Malcolm exclaimed. I shushed him. "Come play with my soldiers," he whispered in the exaggerated way children do. "I'm going to pretend it's the Battle of Waterloo." I crossed the room to peer down at his elaborate setup. "I'll even let you be Napoleon."

I couldn't help but grin at my nephew's magnanimous spirit. The puckish little boy never wanted to play on the side of France, and well I knew it. "Thank you, but . . ."

"No, Aunt Kiera," Philipa cried, racing across the room with one of her dolls. "I wanted you to play with me."

I sighed and glanced at Alana, hoping her older children's voices had not woken her. "Aren't you two supposed to be having lessons?"

"Mother gave our governess the day off," Malcolm replied, smiling happily.

I shook my head at my silly sister. I suspected she dismissed the nursery maids for the day as well. "Your mother and sister are asleep." I leaned down to tell the children as they began to argue. "We need to play quietly."

"We can play soldiers quietly."

I arched an eyebrow. "So none of your cannonballs are

going to explode?" He grinned sheepishly. "And your tea parties are not any quieter," I turned to tell Philipa as she whimpered and tugged on my hand. "Go pick out a book, and I'll read to you until your mother wakes."

They scampered off to the corner where two short bookcases stood, bickering over which story to choose. I only hoped it wasn't "Hansel and Gretel" yet again. I really was in no mood to read about lost children.

Pulling a blanket from one of the children's beds, I laid it over Alana and Greer, careful not to wake them. My sister looked exhausted. Dark circles shadowed her eyes, and her complexion seemed paler than normal. I pressed my wrist to her forehead to feel for a fever and tucked a loose strand of hair behind her ear. Greer's pudgy cheeks were red from rubbing, and her breathing sounded a bit congested, but she was sleeping peacefully. I picked up her twisted teething rag from where it had tumbled to the floor. The knot had begun to slip. I tightened it so that the sugar would not fall out and set it on the table.

Philipa crawled into my lap, and Malcolm squeezed in next to me in a large armchair. "This one." My nephew flipped open the book of the Brothers Grimm's *Children's and Household Tales* to the story of "Rumpelstiltskin" and I breathed a sigh of relief. Philipa snuggled close, and I pressed my cheek against her soft hair as I began to read.

Halfway through the tale, I glanced up to find Alana watching me. A gentle smile curled her lips. She shared my amusement when the children shifted in their seats, squirming with excitement as the queen told the imp his name.

"*Can* you spin straw into gold?" Philipa asked me as I closed the book.

"No, you ninny," Malcolm cried as he hopped off the chair.

"Malcolm, don't call your sister a ninny," Alana scolded.

"How do *you* know?" Philipa dashed after him. "Have you ever tried it?"

"Because it's impossible . . ."

I shook my finger at my sister in mock earnestness as she began to rock her youngest. "You were supposed to stay asleep."

Alana offered me a weary smile and then shifted Greer from one shoulder to the other. The baby grunted and then settled.

"Do you want me to take her?"

She shook her head and tucked the blanket tighter around the child. "Do I have you to thank for this?" she asked, tugging on the quilt.

"I thought you might be cold. Besides, it gave me an excuse to check you for a fever." She looked up at me in surprise. "Alana, are you feeling all right?" I asked in a gentler tone.

She sighed in frustration. "I'm fine." Her eyes narrowed. "Did Philip send you up here?"

"No. But he did tell me that you refuse to leave the nursery."

She brushed her hand over the golden dusting of hair on Greer's head, avoiding my gaze. I glanced at Malcolm and Philipa, who were engaged in some sort of secret conference, presumably about their plans to spin straw into gold.

"Lady Stratford and her maid have been removed to the bachelor quarters in the carriage house." Alana's eyes widened. "Mr. Gage believes they murdered Lady Godwin. And her baby," I added as an afterthought now that my sister knew about the child.

Alana was silent for a moment, watching me as I worried my hands in my lap. "But you don't?"

I started, realizing what I had said. "I don't know," I admitted hesitantly, disturbed by my inability to wholeheartedly accept Lady Stratford's guilt.

"Mr. Gage must have good reason to suspect her," she reasoned. "And I know Philip would not have allowed him to lock Lady Stratford in the carriage house without sufficient proof."

"I know."

"Has Lord Stratford been informed?"

I nodded. "He didn't even put up a fight against it."

Alana's rocking slowed. "Well, then, you must have obtained some pretty convincing evidence."

I leaned against the arm of the chair and cradled my forehead in my hand. "I suppose." I knew I sounded as sulky as a child, and hated myself for it. Alana did not need to deal with me when she already had three little scamps of her own to worry her.

"So what's troubling you?"

I looked up at my sister, seeing the dark shadows under her eyes again. "Do you really want to know?"

She stopped rocking to glare at me. "I wouldn't have asked otherwise."

I glanced at Philipa and Malcolm to be certain they weren't listening, and then leaned toward her. "The evidence is compelling enough, and all linked to the same person, but I can't help but notice that they're also items that could have easily been stolen. They could have been used for the express purpose of throwing blame on Lady Stratford."

Alana arched an eyebrow doubtfully.

"There are also matters of common sense to consider," I hastened to add. "Does Lady Stratford really have the height and strength to inflict those wounds? Could she have crossed the garden, slipped into the maze to kill Lady Godwin, and returned to the house, all without being seen? Could she and her maid have moved that rock and dug the baby's grave?"

"Well?" she asked, knowing me well enough to realize I would have contemplated the answers to these questions before ever bringing them up.

I sighed and sank back in the chair. "Gage believes anger and madness can both give a person more strength than we realize."

"But you don't."

I plucked at the fraying hunter-green upholstery of the chair. "I don't know. And that's the problem. I'm forced to admit that it is possible, if not likely, that she could have done all those things. Just as I'm forced to admit that the murder weapon we found could have made those cuts, even though I have serious doubts. I don't have enough experience with this to assert my opinion strongly." Not even when it came to the remnants of charred cloth Gage had found in Lady Stratford's cold hearth, believing the lady and her servant had burned their bloody clothes from the night of the murder.

The rocking chair creaked as Alana shifted and Greer murmured something in her sleep. "Well, you trust Mr. Gage, don't you?"

I nodded and turned to watch Philipa wrestle one of her dolls out of Malcolm's hands.

"Then if he thinks there is enough evidence to prove Lady Stratford is the murderer, I think we should believe him."

I only wished it was so simple. I did trust Gage, but I also had a deep-seated suspicion of people outside my family, particularly men, and that made it difficult not to continually second-guess my feelings and reactions toward him. The fact that I had found myself in Lady Stratford's position not so very long ago only complicated matters, driving me to find definitive proof rather than trust in the hackneyed legal system that could have so easily failed me.

"So why are you having trouble believing Lady Stratford guilty?" my sister asked, cutting to the heart of the matter. "Is it because she's a noblewoman? Surely you realize the aristocracy are just as capable of committing murder as the lower classes."

"Of course."

"Then what? What is it?"

"I don't know. It's just . . ." I hesitated, trying to put a finger on the reason for my hesitation. "She wants a child *so badly*. Did you know she was having trouble conceiving?"

"I had my suspicions."

I pressed a hand against my stomach. "When I confronted her about it, when I asked her about the child . . ." My breath caught. "Alana, you should have seen the look in her eyes. To struggle for seven years to get with child and then discover that your greatest fears have been realized. That you are, in fact, barren." I shook my head, unable to find the words to express the heartache.

Nevertheless, I could see in my sister's eyes that she understood. She hugged Greer tighter and pressed a kiss to her downy head.

"Despite the fact that Lord Stratford was the father of Lady Godwin's baby . . ."

Alana gasped. "Lord Stratford was the father?"

I nodded. "And despite the fact that Lady Godwin, who was supposed to be Lady Stratford's friend, not only slept with her husband but also proved her to be the one who could not conceive and threw it in her face. I just do not believe Lady Stratford was capable of harming that child. Of removing it from . . ." Remembering my audience, I stopped myself, glancing up to find my sister watching me with horrified eyes. I cleared my throat. "I can imagine her harming Lady Godwin, but not that baby."

She looked toward the hearth, seeming to consider my words. I closed my eyes, trying to shut out the terrible images, the darkness of the last few days. I breathed in deeply the scent of camphor and talcum powder, listening to the soft rocking of Alana's chair against the heavy rug and the merry chatter of my niece's and nephew's voices. The nursery seemed like a cozy little cocoon when compared to the vast echoing corridors of Gairloch Castle. It was no wonder my sister had shut herself up here with her three children.

"Maybe she went mad," she offered.

I blinked open my eyes to stare at the exposed-timber ceiling. "That's what Gage suggested."

"But you don't believe it."

I lowered my gaze to find Alana studying me. I suddenly realized that by expressing all of these doubts, I only gave her more reason to remain closeted in the nursery with her children. Pressing my hand to my forehead, I groaned. "I don't know what I believe, Alana. Mr. Gage is undoubtedly right. I'm probably just jumping at ghosts, remembering when I was accused of those heinous crimes in London."

"Yes, but Kiera, you were innocent," she pointed out.

I nodded, biting back the urge to express my worry that Lady Stratford might also be. "So," I proclaimed, a feeble segue into a different topic. "Are you going to return to sleeping in your own bed tonight? You can't have gotten much rest here. You look exhausted."

Unfortunately, my sister knew me only too well. "Kiera," she scolded gently. "Have you expressed your doubts to Mr. Gage?"

I plucked at the upholstery again. "No."

"Then perhaps you should."

"And if he doesn't listen to me?" I asked, trying to keep my voice light. I already suspected he was not going to accept my doubts easily. To his mind, we had caught the real culprit and proved my innocence. What more could I want?

"Then I think you should do whatever it takes to set your mind at ease." She shook her head at me fondly. "You spend far too much time in your head, dear. And sometimes I worry where it takes you. Especially in this case."

I gave her a grateful smile, thankful that she supported me, even if she didn't understand me. Maybe I was being ridiculous. Maybe I should just let it go. But I couldn't get rid of the terrible feeling in my gut that somehow we got it wrong. I kept seeing Lady Stratford's eyes—the pain and fear and desperation written there—and I worried it wasn't feigned. I wanted to be certain that the real murderer had been caught, not just someone to take my place as the sacrificial lamb. I wanted the truth. And if that truth pointed to Lady Stratford, then so be it. But until I had been convinced, I knew I would never be able to rest.

Greer sniffled and reached up to swipe at her nose, rubbing her already raw cheek. She began to fuss, and Alana tipped her forward to croon to her softly.

"Her teething rag was on the floor," I told her. "Let me clean it off and wet it."

"Thank you," she replied absentmindedly as she tried to clear Greer's nose.

Malcolm and Philipa looked up as their baby sister let out a howl. They were remarkably well behaved today, and I wondered if they sensed their mother's exhaustion.

I tightened the string holding the sugar inside one end of the rag before handing it to my sister. Greer immediately chomped down on it, lapsing into a whimper as she turned into her mother's chest for comfort. Sighing in relief, Alana tipped her head back against the chair and closed her eyes.

"Alana, are you certain you're feeling all right?" I asked, worried by the drawn appearance of her face. The last time I had seen her look so poorly was the morning after she nursed Malcolm through his fever. Her haggard countenance scared me.

She must have sensed this, for her head fell sideways toward her shoulder in defeat. "I'm expecting again," she admitted.

I couldn't stop my eyes from flaring wide in surprise. "Does Philip know?"

"I think so, though I haven't told him."

I nodded, suddenly better understanding the flares of temper between them in the past few days. It had been from anxiety as much as anger. Alana had difficulty during Greer's birth, much more so than with the other two, and the physician had suggested they seriously reconsider having any more children. From my sister's tone of voice, I didn't think they had been trying for another one.

"How far along are you?"

"A month, six weeks. Not long." Greer sobbed, and Alana adjusted her position.

"Do you want me to take her?"

Alana shook her head, stubborn as always.

"How are you feeling?"

"How do you think?" she snapped. She took a deep breath and rested her head back against the seat again. "Sorry. You didn't deserve that."

"It's all right," I told her automatically. Then I broached a topic I knew she was going to dislike even more. "You're exhausted. Why don't you leave the children with me and lie down and take a nap."

"I'm fine," she replied woodenly.

"Alana."

"I promise you I'm fine."

"No you're not."

Her gaze met mine, and I could see the fear holding her in its grip. "I can't leave the children," she replied, knowing what I was really hinting at. "I just can't. Not yet. Maybe when the man from Inverness arrives, but not yet."

I ached for her. The knowledge of what had happened to Lady Godwin's unborn child clearly distressed my sister. Especially now knowing she carried another little one inside her—one she probably had not wished for. Her instinctive reaction was to protect her own babies, and the only way she could do that was by keeping them in her sight.

"Would you lie down on one of the children's beds and take a nap if I took care of the children?" I asked, sensing it would take physical force to pull my sister away from the nursery. Neither Philip nor I wanted to go down that road.

"You have to finish your investigation," she protested. "Besides, I need you to take my place as hostess at dinner this evening."

I balked. "Do they really need a hostess? I mean, surely they could get by without one."

"Kiera, please."

"I should think Philip's aunt, Lady Hollingsworth, would do a much better job."

"Kiera," she begged. "I need you to do this for me. I know it is a lot to ask of you, but I need you to do it, nonetheless."

I groaned, hating the way her tone made me feel guilty. This *wasn't* a lot to ask of me. I was her sister and she had taken me in sixteen months ago without a single hesitation. "Fine. But only if you do something for me in return."

Alana's gaze turned wary.

"I'm going to recall the nursery maid, and when she arrives, I want you to take a nap—right over there on Philipa's bed." I pointed toward the pink-frilled bed in the corner. "Will you do that?"

Sensing my determination to be just as stubborn as she could be, she nodded in defeat. I hopped up to pull the tasseled cord that would ring for Molly before she could change her mind. Planting my hands on my hips, I turned back to find my sister watching me with a small smile playing across her lips.

"It's not often, but once in a while you manage to do something conniving enough to assure me you have our St. Mawr family blood flowing through your veins after all."

I pursed my lips. "Yes, well as conniving as that was, I'm quite certain you got the better end of the bargain."

Her smile brightened, and I whirled around to leave the room.

"Enjoy your dinner, dear," she called after me.

CHAPTER TWENTY-FOUR

Dinner that evening went far better than I expected, though by no means did I actually enjoy it. How could I when no one would stop talking about Lady Stratford's detainment? Many of the guests claimed they had suspected the countess all along, but, of course, none of them found it necessary to apologize for condemning me instead. Only Lord Westlock, who was positioned on my right, now that I sat in Alana's place, had the grace to appear uncomfortable and embarrassed in my presence. And well he should, for I still sported a lump on the back of my head that was tender to the touch.

Gage was lauded and fussed over for uncovering the murderer, while I watched in frustration as glass after glass of wine was lifted to toast his name. More than once, I was forced to bite my tongue, lest I say something inappropriate or, worse, reveal my involvement in the investigation. Perhaps I should merely have been content to have the attention and suspicion removed from me, but I couldn't help feeling dissatisfied and even a little angry.

Philip caught my eye and smiled sympathetically as yet another round of wine was poured for Gage. I nodded in acknowledgment and raised my glass along with everyone else, choking down another sip of the burgundy while most of the others drained their goblets.

"It must be difficult sitting there holding your tongue," Lord Marsdale leaned toward me to drawl, irritating me with the reminder of his presence.

I supposed I shouldn't have been surprised that, as acting hostess, I would be stuck sitting between Marsdale and Westlock, a marquess and baron, respectively. Lord Stratford had declined to join us for dinner; otherwise, he would be seated in Westlock's place. I couldn't say I would have liked that arrangement any better. At least Lord Westlock was quiet. Though, Lord Marsdale more than made up for his silence.

"What?" I asked, having more and more difficulty hiding my annoyance with the man.

He ran his finger around the rim of his glass. "Well, after all, didn't you have a great deal to do with catching Lady Stratford?"

I looked him squarely in the eye for the first time that night. "I don't know what you're talking about."

He chuckled. "Come now, Lady Darby. There's no need to lie to me. Mr. Gage is intelligent and clever, but I'm quite convinced you had more to do with this than anyone is letting on."

I contemplated the surge of pride that welled up inside me and made me want to confirm his statement, to announce to the entire table what I'd done. It seemed unfair that Gage should receive all the credit. I had to remind myself that I hadn't assisted with the investigation for the accolades. I had done it to protect my sister, my nieces and nephew, and to clear my own name. Admitting I had taken part in the autopsy and uncovering the child's grave would only cast more scandal on my name, and that of the family I defended. The guests might be comfortable with Gage in the role of hero, but my participation would only arouse more suspicion. It was better this way, no matter what my pride thought.

"Poor man," Lady Hollingsworth murmured into her empty wineglass from the seat next to Marsdale, distracting me from his bold stare. "Lord Stratford must be beside himself." Her arm wobbled as she raised the glass overhead to signal to the footman passing behind her. How much had Philip's aunt had to drink?

"I would be *horrified*," Lady Bethel bleated from across the table, pressing a hand to her rather substantial bosom. "Why, if Bethel ever did such a thing, I . . . I . . . I don't know *what* I would do."

I hoped she would contact the authorities.

"He must have had some clue as to what kind of woman she was." The marchioness sipped from her refilled glass. "I mean, *I* could see it. Lady Stratford was always so cold. It's no surprise her husband found another woman to warm his bed."

Lady Bethel tittered, and I blushed. Stuffy Lady Hollingsworth had definitely consumed too much wine if she was willing to discuss such intimate matters at the dinner table.

She leaned forward as if to impart some juicy secret; however, her whisper emerged loud enough for half the table to hear. "Or that she was crazy enough to kill his mistress because of it."

I frowned, not liking the woman's suppositions. It was exactly the same kind of cruel speculation that swirled around my reputation after I was dragged before the magistrate. I set my fork aside with an audible clink, unable to palate another bite of the cook's delicious beef tenderloin. The ladies glanced at me distractedly but were too caught up in their conversation to pay me much notice. I stared across the distance of the table, trying to capture Philip's attention. If his aunt was this sotted, I was certain he would want to be warned about it.

"At least now the earl will be able to find a new bride," Lady Hollingsworth declared, her words beginning to slur. "This time, one who can give him an heir." She nodded rather conspicuously toward her daughter Caroline, who smiled at whatever the gentleman next to her was saying, blissfully unaware of her mother's plans. I inwardly cringed. A match between Caroline and the earl would be a disaster—for Caroline. I could not care less how Lord Stratford fared.

"Oh, yes," Lady Bethel nearly cooed. "I hear he's *desperate* for an heir. If he dies now, the title and entailed property goes to some distant *French* cousin." She pronounced the man's nationality as if it carried the plague.

"Oh, how horrid!" Lady Hollingsworth commiserated.

Lady Bethel nodded and then leaned forward over the table. I worried the contents of her bodice would spill out over her plate. "But do you really think they'll *hang* her? A *countess?*" Such a prospect seemed to appall the baroness more than anything else.

Her friend was not similarly afflicted. "But of course. As well they should. She killed another gentlewoman. If Lord Stratford's tart had been some demirep or a servant girl, perhaps it would be a different matter. But one can't simply go around killing gentlewomen, even if you are one yourself."

I opened my mouth to scold the women for their extreme insensitivity when I felt a subtle pressure against my leg under the table. My gaze flicked to Marsdale, whom, in the intensity of my anger, I had forgotten. He shook his head subtly, cautioning me against speaking. Reluctantly, I swallowed the heated words, feeling them scald the back of my throat like a drink of too-hot tea.

"I'm surprised you haven't made any witty rejoinders," I bit out through clenched teeth, wondering at his uncharacteristic silence during the ladies' ridiculous conversation.

He smiled sadly. "Some conversations do not deserve wit." He glanced at the two women still deep in conversation, and when he looked back at me, there was a twinkle in his eyes. "Especially when they lack good taste."

I couldn't stop the small twitch of a smile from curling

my lips at his implied insult to the ladies, who were completely unaware that they had just been reproached, and by one of society's most notorious scoundrels, no less. Marsdale grinned over his wineglass, clearly pleased to have amused me.

Feeling someone's gaze upon me, I glanced up the table to find Gage watching us. Even annoyed as I was by all the praise he was receiving, I couldn't help but be struck by his good looks—made all the more arresting by his black evening kit. I wanted to blame it on my artist's eye, but I knew I would only be lying to myself. Gage was attractive to me as more than just a portrait subject.

Gage nodded, just a slight dip of his head so as not to draw the others' attention. I nodded back, wondering if the gesture was a dismissal. Now that the killer seemed to be caught, did he no longer see a use for me? An ache began to form beneath my breastbone.

"So that's how it is."

I turned distractedly to Marsdale, whose eyes shone with devilry. "That's how what is?"

His head tilted to the side, a sly smile playing over his mouth. "There's no need to play naive with me. All you had to tell me was that you preferred light . . ." he nodded toward Gage ". . . to dark."

A flush of heat raced up my neck and into my cheeks. "I don't know what you're talking about. I don't prefer anything."

He raised his eyebrows.

"I don't," I insisted, reassuring myself that it was the truth. I truly didn't care what color a man's hair was.

"Well, then," he drawled, wagging his eyebrows and adopting his customary lazy grin. I knew it was aimed to disarm me. "There's still hope for me yet."

I sighed and shook my head at the man, but he refused to be deterred, and I unexpectedly welcomed his outrageous flirting and inappropriate commentary, grateful for the distraction it provided from the rest of the table.

After dinner, I accompanied the ladies to the parlor for tea. I anticipated that I would have to endure their gossip and small talk for at least a half an hour before the gentlemen deigned to join us, so when they began to wander in no more than five minutes later, I thought perhaps Philip had taken pity on me. However, it swiftly became clear from the men's excited talk that was not the case. Philip's mare, Freya, was foaling. It was very late in the season for such a thing, but I knew my brother-in-law had been expecting the horse to give birth for days now. He and Mr. Abingdon had rushed directly to the stables from the dinner table, and several of the other men were talking of joining them. Not wishing to remain any longer than necessary, I decided my favor to Alana had been fulfilled and slipped out of the room before anyone could detain me.

The fire in my hearth snapped merrily, casting flickering shadows across the walls. The firelight winked and flashed in the stained glass propped atop the mantel. When I was a little girl, I had taken the two pieces from a broken window being replaced in the village church near my father's estate, loving the way the colors merged and swirled, changing with the light. I brushed my fingers over the cool, smooth glass, watching as the shadows cast by my fingers deepened the colors almost to flat black. In stark comparison, the surface away from my fingers seemed to ripple in the firelight like water, like a living thing.

I turned away, feeling oddly hollow inside. I stared at my bed, the fatigue from so many sleepless nights pulling at my bones, but I knew my head would never rest. Not with this pit growing in my stomach and the fear and doubt coalescing in my mind. I knelt to light a pair of candles from the flames to brighten the room. Then I dragged my tired feet across the carpet and slipped off my shoes to curl up in the window seat. Hugging a pillow to my chest, I parted the curtains and peered out at the carriage house below.

It sat, quiet and unobtrusive, next to the stables, which bustled with activity. Gentlemen milled outside in the carriage yard with the coachmen and stable hands, all waiting for the foal's birth. Even the footman who stood guard at the door to the carriage house was drawn to the excitement, though he was careful to maintain his post. I wondered if Lady Stratford and Celeste could hear the men, and whether they worried they were there for them instead of a horse.

There was a knock on my door, and thinking it was my maid, I called out. "Come in."

"I thought you were locking your door," a deep voice replied.

I looked up to find Gage lounging against the doorjamb, one hand cradling a bottle of champagne, and the other a pair of glasses. My heart tripped in my chest.

"What are you doing here?" Hearing the breathless quality of my voice, I swallowed and added, "I thought you would be joining the other men down in the stables." I nodded toward the window.

"I have seen enough foalings . . ." he closed the door with his foot ". . . to last a lifetime. I have no need to see another."

I had not pegged him for a man who cared much for horseflesh. "How many foalings have you witnessed?"

"Two. One when I was an adolescent still trying to figure out a woman's body, and another years later, while I was deep in my cups. I did not enjoy either experience."

A smile tugged at my lips. "You thought to learn about a woman's body from a horse?"

He grinned wryly. "Silly, I know."

"Do many boys do that?"

He shrugged. "I haven't the foggiest."

I tilted my head to the side. "Well, I suppose it's a good

thing young ladies are not allowed to view such things, or else we might never let any of you gentlemen near us."

He raised his eyebrows. "Better the foaling than the conception."

I threw the pillow at him and turned toward the window to hide my amusement, continuing to watch him out of the corner of my eye.

He dodged and smiled devilishly. "You would have gone to your marriage bed expecting Sir Anthony to bite you on the back of the neck to hold you down."

"Stop!" I gasped, trying my best to stifle my laughter. I was quite sure he could hear it in my voice anyway. "I don't want to imagine that!"

He chuckled. "Well, we certainly don't want that. I don't believe my manly pride could support your thinking of another man while I'm in the room." He began to work the cork out of the bottle. It emerged with a pop.

"What's this for?" I asked.

He poured some of the bubbly liquid into a glass and handed it to me. "I thought we should celebrate." He smiled. "This has been an interesting four days. And they would have been much less enjoyable without your assistance." He poured his own glass and joined me by the window seat. "Shall we make a toast?"

"Haven't you tired of those yet this evening?" I teased.

He grimaced. "Yes. They were all acting a bit ridiculous, weren't they?" When I didn't comment, he laughed. "I'll take that as your agreement. All right, then." He perched on the padded ledge across from me. "This toast is for you, Lady Darby. For I certainly wouldn't have found the murderer without you." Both of our cheeks flushed at the shared realization that he would likely have accused me of the crime. He cleared his throat and raised his glass. "To your future. May it be bright and beautiful."

I drank to that, wanting the embarrassment to stop. The champagne was sweet and peppery and burned as it rolled down my throat. I drained my glass and took a deep breath, feeling a giddy rush to my head.

Gage chuckled. "Shall I top you off?"

I shook my head. "After all the wine at dinner, I think I've had more than enough to drink this evening." Indeed, I felt lethargic and just a tiny bit tipsy.

He polished off his own glass and settled deeper into the window seat. Our bent legs were almost touching. Hidden beneath my skirt, my toes curled into the cushion, tingling with the knowledge that they could stretch out and graze the muscles of his leg. I leaned forward again to see outside, hoping to distract myself from the sensations swirling in my gut. Most of the gentlemen had vanished from the stable yard, and I wondered if they had been run off or had just grown bored.

"What's wrong?"

I glanced up to find him studying me. "What do you mean?"

"I expected to find you relieved, but you seem almost as tense as the evening we made our trip down to the chapel cellar."

I watched my hand smooth back and forth over the velvety fabric of one of the pillows. I couldn't understand why I was so hesitant to explain what was bothering me. Perhaps it was because my doubts seemed insubstantial, even to me. I was worried how he would react, and maybe a bit afraid he would tell me I was being foolish. It had taken considerable effort to convince him to believe in me. I didn't want that to all be ruined by a feeling, a sensation, I couldn't even explain.

"I'm wondering," I began uncertainly. "If we are seeing the big picture. If we really accused the right person."

Gage tapped his champagne flute against his leg twice and leaned over to pick up the bottle. "You don't think Lady Stratford murdered Lady Godwin," he stated evenly as he poured himself another glass.

"I don't know," I admitted, allowing some hint of my distress to creep into my voice. "I just have this feeling that we're missing something."

"What?"

"I don't know." His calm seemed to only exacerbate the turmoil I felt inside me. "There are just a few things that are bothering me."

"Such as?"

"Well, the murder weapon. I still don't believe that a pair of embroidery scissors was used to slice Lady Godwin's neck. The cut was simply too clean, too even."

He took a sip of champagne, watching me steadily over the rim. "So are you saying it is *impossible* that the scissors made that cut?"

"No," I hedged, having already known he would contradict me with such a question. "Just that it is highly unlikely."

"But by that admission you are still saying it is possible."

I frowned at the extreme logic he was using, not liking how silly it made me sound. "Well, anyone could have taken them from her embroidery basket. Just because they were hers does not mean she used them in such a capacity."

"True. But that means they would have also needed to steal her shawl and her maid's apron." The tone of his voice told me just how doubtful he was of such a thing happening. "That would take quite an organized killer—someone with a real vendetta against Lady Stratford."

I dropped my eyes from his gaze, not wanting to see the challenge there. I couldn't argue with his assertions. It did all seem very unlikely, but not impossible. Lady Stratford had as much, if not more, of a capacity to incite enemies as anyone present at Gairloch. Jealousy, be it of her beauty or her position, could do strange things to people, not to mention the hatred a snubbing could cause. And Lady Stratford had snubbed more than her fair share of society.

"Well, what about the amount of strength and stamina it would have taken to dig the baby's grave?" I challenged.

"You can't tell me that you believe Lady Stratford and her maid to be capable of such a thing."

He leaned over to set his glass on the floor. "A footman."

I startled, uncertain I'd heard him correctly. "What?"

"I suspect a footman moved the rock and dug the grave," he replied calmly, as if what he was saying made complete sense.

I glared at him in confusion, irritated by his insouciant demeanor.

"I spoke with the gardener to find out if any shovels have gone missing," he explained. "And he told me that a few mornings ago he noticed one of the spades was not placed in its usual position. As if someone had used it and then returned it." Gage leaned forward. "And the gardener specifically remembers seeing a man lurking about the gardening shed the night before." He nodded his head in emphasis and sat back against the wall. His eyes gleamed with satisfaction at uncovering this last bit of information.

"A man?" I restated.

"Yes."

"Did the gardener get a good look at this . . . *man* . . . or are you just assuming it was a footman?" I snapped in exasperation.

Gage arched an eyebrow at my display of temper. "I didn't *assume* anything. It just so happens that, as of this afternoon, one of Cromarty's footmen has suspiciously gone missing."

I had no reply to that. A footman's disappearance just hours after Lady Stratford's detainment did seem exceedingly suspicious.

"I suspect Lady Stratford convinced this footman to assist her with, if nothing else, at least burying the child."

"How? A bribe?" I had a difficult time imagining one of Philip's loyal staff being coerced into doing something so horrible.

"Money can be a powerful motivator," Gage replied,

correctly reading my thoughts. "And perhaps the footman didn't know exactly what he was being paid to bury. Though, I can't imagine he would be naive enough to believe it was harmless. Perhaps he only realized just how much trouble he could be in after Lady Stratford was detained, and he panicked."

I turned to stare at the log crackling in the hearth. Gage's assumptions seemed logical, I could not dispute that, but how could he know that they were right? "What if the man lurking around the gardening shed wasn't the footman?"

His eyebrows lifted in doubt.

"Well, what if it was someone else?" I persisted. "And what if this footman has disappeared for another reason? What if he's in some kind of trouble?"

"That's a lot of what-ifs," he murmured dryly.

I glared at him. "And your assumptions aren't? You're still jumping to conclusions. Even about Lady Stratford."

Gage closed his eyes and sighed. "Lady Darby, my father has been an inquiry agent for nearly twelve years, and I have been assisting him for a number of those. Rarely, in an incident with no witnesses, do we uncover evidence that is so cut and dry. Lady Stratford cannot convincingly explain away the shawl and the scissors, and neither can I. If I thought I could, I would do everything I could to make certain I had reached the right conclusion. There is simply no other explanation."

"But you should have seen her this afternoon," I pleaded with him to understand. "When I forced her to admit her barren state, she was heartbroken. Her pain and anguish were genuine. She is desperate for a child. I just cannot believe she would have cut into Lady Godwin's womb. Kill Lady Godwin, yes. But she would never have harmed that child."

"The child was not her own. Believe me, my lady, there is a difference. And Lady Stratford would have seen it as such."

"No," I replied, shaking my head. "I can't believe it of her. And you wouldn't either if you had seen the look on her face."

"She was acting," he snapped, as annoyance twisted his features. "You are inexperienced with such things, Lady Darby, but I am not. Being accused of a crime brings out the most brilliant acting you have ever seen. I have seen performances to rival any production on the stage of the Theatre Royal."

"Then how do you know who is telling the truth?"

"You don't. That's why you rely on the evidence. It is the only thing that is certain. Not instincts or strange feelings, which do come in handy from time to time. However, you cannot build a solid case around them."

I understood what he was saying. I even agreed with him—to a certain degree—but I still couldn't escape the horrible sensation pressing down on me that, in this instance, we were very wrong.

"Couldn't we at least follow up on any other leads?"

"What other leads?" He sighed and raked a hand back through his hair. "There is no use in pursuing this further. There is nothing else to even consider. I will find the footman and question him, and then it will be finished."

"Maybe . . ."

"No, Kiera. It's over. I understand you feel some compassion for Lady Stratford, but you cannot change what she has done." His gaze turned brooding, and he seemed to look inward. "There are some people who *are* guilty of the crimes they are accused of."

I turned away, confused by the personal significance he seemed to invest in those words, and hurt by the betrayal I felt because he would not help me with this.

"Now." He rose to his feet. "I think you just need a good night's sleep. You'll feel differently in the morning. The dark has a way of making us see shadows where they are not." The door closed softly behind him.

I pulled my legs up and wrapped my arms around my knees.

Was he right? Was I jumping at shadows, at memories of the time I was dragged before a magistrate and accused of unspeakable acts? I didn't know. All I knew was how hurt and frustrated I was that Gage had not tried harder to understand. It wasn't as if I *wanted* to doubt Lady Stratford's guilt. I *wanted* to feel triumphant and confident we had caught the murderer, just like everyone else. My uncertainties and misgivings certainly weren't welcome sensations. They gnawed at me like an open wound.

I leaned over again to peer out at the darkened carriage house. My sister was right. I couldn't let this go. Not yet. Not until I knew I had done everything I could to uncover the whole truth, whatever it might be. I would try to get a good night's sleep as Gage suggested, and when the doubts did not go away, as I knew they wouldn't, I would start the day with a rested mind and a fresh pair of eyes. I had at least one more day to uncover the truth before the procurator fiscal from Inverness arrived, or else damn my conscience and Lady Stratford to the consequences.

CHAPTER TWENTY-FIVE

The following morning, the weather was damp and dreary. Which was, of course, fitting, considering the mood I awakened in and the course of action I had chosen to take before I finally fell asleep after tossing and turning for half the night. I would be drenched by the time I finished retracing the killer's steps, but perhaps I would be closer to the truth. It appeared I must be made to suffer in my endeavor to acquire proof of Lady Stratford's guilt or innocence.

I dressed in my warm charcoal-gray walking dress and sturdy boots and pulled up the hood of my heavy hunter-green cloak before stepping out into the rain. I picked my way across the muddy carriage yard, careful to avoid the ruts now filled with water. From the outside, the stables appeared lazy and quiet, but inside I found the stable hands bustling about, joking with one another while they completed their morning chores. Old Gaffer, the stable master, pointed me toward the back where Philip leaned over a stall, his arms draped along the top.

He glanced up as I approached and smiled. His eyes drooped with fatigue, and he was badly in need of a shave, but he seemed content. The foaling must have gone well.

"How is she?" I asked.

He waved a hand toward the stall. "Take a look."

I peeked over the wall to see the chestnut-brown foal standing on shaky legs already nursing from her mother. "Is it a she?"

He nodded.

I grinned at the little filly. "She's a beauty."

"Aye."

"Where are Beowulf and Grendel?" I asked, glancing around the floor near his feet. Normally, they followed Philip around like two lovesick swains.

He glanced at me curiously and then whistled. The two wolfhounds trotted around the corner.

I reached out to pet Grendel's shaggy brindle coat. "I'm going to take them for a walk."

Philip's eyebrows rose toward his hairline. "In this weather?"

I diverted my gaze, concentrating on scratching behind the dog's ears. "I want to get out of the castle," I replied, hoping he would think I was just eager to escape the guests. Beowulf bumped into my leg, wanting the same attention as his brother. I laughed.

"Wait your turn, old boy," Philip scolded with a chuckle. His voice was husky from lack of sleep, and his brogue had deepened. "Just be sure they dinna run you ragged," he warned. "They haven't been allowed to run free in days, so they're liable to get a bit carried away."

"Don't worry. I'm well aware of what I'm in for."

The rain fell in a steady shower, drenching my cloak in a matter of minutes. Any sane person would have stayed indoors if they could help it, so I expected to have the grounds completely to myself. I led the two dogs past the carriage house, nodding to the footman guarding its door, and then across the garden toward the path leading into the western woods. I had planned to begin at the maze and retrace the killer's steps around the eastern circuit of the path to the place where we uncovered the baby. However, I was conscious of Philip watching me from the stables' door-yard, and not wanting to arouse his suspicion, I decided instead to work my way around backward.

The rain striking my hood lessened as I stepped beneath the bower of thick pines, sycamores, and yew trees at the edge of the forest, and for a moment I thought it was the loss of this sensation that caused my scalp to tingle and the hairs on the back of my neck to stand on end. I scanned the woods before me, searching the leafy shadows, and then turned back toward the castle. My gaze settled on the deserted western block, carefully studying the windows spanning the facade. The curtain of rain made it difficult to see at such a distance with much clarity, but I could have sworn someone was watching me, observing my progress into the forest. An icy chill ran down my neck like the cold rivulet of a raindrop. I hurried into the shelter of the trees.

The woods were still except for the soft patter of rain against the leaves and the panting of the dogs as they wove to and fro among the vegetation. I tried to reassure myself that the wolfhounds would alert me to any danger long before it reached me, but I could not shake the creeping sensation along my spine. I found myself glancing over my shoulder and easing cautiously around bends in the path.

By the time the wolfhounds and I reached the hill where Lady Godwin's baby had been buried, I was thoroughly sick of my paranoia. There was nothing nefarious about someone watching me from the castle windows, even from the empty west wing. Perhaps it had merely been a bored guest gone exploring or a servant hiding from chores. There was no proof of ill intentions, only my nerves getting the better of me.

I huffed in irritation and directed my attention to the dogs. So far they had found nothing more troubling than a sparrow carcass, which I had to drag them away from. I hoped the eastern loop of the trail, which I had yet to search, would offer up something more pertinent to the investigation.

We set off across the back boundary of Philip's property, strolling through the field of heather that stretched northward, forming a glen between two Highland ridges. The eastern forest swallowed us beneath its branches, thicker than its western cousin, and even more steeped in shadow. With the gloom, the crawling sensation returned, sending my heart tripping in my chest and distracting me from the task at hand. In fact, if not for Beowulf and Grendel, I might have blundered onward unawares.

Their whines raised gooseflesh all over my skin, and I glanced around me before cautiously moving forward to see what the dogs were pawing at. The edge of the forest was not more than fifteen feet away, and I wondered if perhaps this was the spot where Philip and the wolfhounds had found blood three days ago. He had suggested that the killer laid the baby there, just inside the woods, and then rejoined the other guests in the garden, or, in Lady Stratford's case, returned to her bedchamber. Then the murderer returned later to bury the child's body.

I shook my head. Why hadn't the killer left the child with its mother, even after taking it from her body? Why bury it? Had the killer hoped to hide the baby's existence? Had Lady Stratford thought to hide her husband's indiscretion? All of it seemed so extreme, so unnecessary. Returning to the scene to bury the child without being seen, leaving evidence behind in the child's grave—all of those steps left a trail and heightened the risk that they would be caught.

Of course, all of this supposition assumed that the killer had been thinking at all and not just acting mindlessly, whether in anger or fear. Gage certainly believed Lady Stratford had been reacting, and therein lay the crux of my doubt, for I somehow felt that most of this had been carefully thought out, planned for a specific purpose. That did not mesh with the amount of physical evidence we had discovered against Lady Stratford.

Beowulf, who had been circling a tree, suddenly whined

piteously and stood up on his hind legs to paw at the bark above his head. I moved closer and patted his head in reassurance as he dropped down. There was a hole in the trunk of the oak just above the level of my head. I scowled down at Beowulf. "You're supposed to be searching for evidence, not chasing squirrels up trees."

He ignored my scolding and stood up on his hind legs, trying to reach the hole again. Grendel joined him, and the two pinned me between them as they whined and batted at the tree.

I stared up at the hole, unnerved by the dogs' persistence. What if it wasn't a squirrel the wolfhounds were pawing at, but a piece of evidence stashed where no one would ever find it? My mind whirled with possibilities—the real murder weapon, a bloodied piece of clothing, an incriminating letter. I lifted my hand to reach in and then stilled.

What if it wasn't evidence but truly a family of squirrels hiding from the dogs or, worse, some kind of insect or spider's home? I cringed at the thought. I found myself wishing for Gage's solid presence by my side. Certainly, he was self-important and aggravating, but whether it was because of the pistol he carried or the confidence he exuded, at least I felt safe with him. And could rely upon him to conduct some of the more horrifying tasks, such as reaching into a hole in a tree trunk that might be home to an agitated animal. He had been rather a bulwark for me—in the chapel cellar, at the baby's grave, even in my art studio—he had been there when I needed him. I couldn't imagine how I would have made it through the last four days without him, and I badly wished he were there with me now.

Taking a deep breath, I screwed up my courage and shut my eyes. I tentatively probed inside the hole, grateful that at least I was wearing a sturdy pair of kid-leather gloves. When nothing immediately bit me, I leaned forward on tiptoe, trying to reach deeper inside the hollow. My fingers brushed against something soft, and I stilled. When the object did not move, I snagged it with my fingers and began to pull it carefully out of the hole.

My first glimpse of the white fabric made my heart leap into my throat. It was a handkerchief, a rather plain one, covered in streaks of dried crimson blood. The dogs sniffed at it, forcing me to lift it high to keep it out of their reach. The square had clearly belonged to man or a servant, for I had never seen a lady carry such a simple cloth. Customarily, a gentlewoman's handkerchiefs were embroidered and trimmed in lace, and I highly doubted Lady Stratford's were any different. However, the square could be her maid's. Or it could indicate there was a man involved—one we had yet to discover.

I moved toward the edge of the forest, leaning my hip against a sycamore along the path. The air was fresh with rain and summer green and musky from the mud churned up under my feet, but I still fancied I smelled the cloying, metallic scent of blood wafting from the handkerchief. I carefully tucked it inside the pocket of my skirt, shielding it from the rain, and any prying eyes that might still be watching me from the house.

Staring across the expanse of the lawn toward the castle, I searched the facade. It was impossible to tell from such a distance, especially through the rain, but I studied the windows, looking for a twitch of a curtain or a shifting of light to indicate that there was someone there. That someone was spying on me. I couldn't see them, but I felt them there, regardless. Just as I had the morning Gage and I returned from the maze. A trickle of fear caught in my throat.

I was reluctant to leave the shelter of the trees and step out into the wide-open expanse of the lawn. It seemed like such a vulnerable position, even with the dogs in tow. However, there was no alternative route to the stables, unless I planned to slash my way through the thick growth of over a hundred yards of forest to find the little-used path winding through the forest behind the maze, carriage house, and stables. Such an act would be ridiculous.

Scolding myself for my foolishness, I swallowed my nerves and struck out across the lawn. Almost immediately, I felt the unseen pair of eyes tracking my progress, this time from a window in the eastern block. I forced myself to walk, to measure my strides, even though my shoulders inched up around my ears and my heart leapt forward in my chest with each step. Beowulf and Grendel trotted alongside me like two dutiful guards. I suspected their presence was all that kept me from breaking into a run.

Once again, I wished for Gage. This investigation had been much easier to conduct with him by my side. Perhaps I should try talking to him again. He'd said I might view things differently in the light of day, and so might he. Gage was not unreasonable—when he put aside his rather masculine impulse to discount my intuition. With this new piece of evidence, surely he would be forced to take me seriously. I simply had to appeal to his reason.

With bolstered spirits, I hurried across the carriage yard. Philip stood speaking with Old Gaffer just inside the stable door when I shooed Beowulf and Grendel inside. Though he still sported dark circles under his eyes, it appeared Philip had at least found time to bathe, shave, and change clothes at some point during the morning. "Are you just returning?" he asked in surprise. "That was quite a long walk."

I shrugged and quickly changed the subject. "Do you know where I might find Mr. Gage?"

"He rode out with Mr. Fulmer an hour or so ago. They were headed to Drumchork to see if they could locate our errant footman."

I smothered the rather childish impulse to stamp my foot. So that was Gage's chosen course of action—to avoid me. I thought he would at least seek me out this morning, if for no other reason than to make certain I wasn't going to do something foolish, like pursue this investigation further myself. The man could be quite territorial about such things. Instead he'd run off in pursuit of the footman without so much as a by-your-leave, and taken the gardener, whom I desperately wanted to question, with him. Who knew how long it would be before they returned?

"Did you need him for something?" Philip asked me with some concern.

I considered telling him about the handkerchief, about my doubts and suspicions, but he looked so tired—not only from the mare's foaling in the middle of the night but also Alana's continued resistance in leaving the nursery. Telling him about my misgivings would only add to his worries. Besides, he would insist we consult Gage before taking any further steps to remedy the situation, and I had no intention of sitting on my hands waiting for the prodigal son to return while Lady Stratford remained locked in the carriage house and a potential killer ran free. I had a few more ideas how I might uncover information, and Philip would only prevent me from pursuing them.

So I lied. "It's not important." I flashed a reassuring smile. "I'll just speak to him when he returns."

He nodded rather uncertainly but did not question me further.

In an effort to avoid the other guests, I struck out for the side entrance, which fed into the servants' staircase and wound up toward the family hall. As the door swung shut behind me I stumbled to a halt, suddenly realizing how dark and isolated the stairwell was. Dim sunlight filtered through the small windows on each landing, the only sources of light for the entire stairwell. Raindrops pinged against the glass, echoing through the space.

I rubbed my palms down my skirts and ordered myself to stop jumping at ghosts. There was nothing there to get me but the figments of my own imagination. I shook my head at my foolishness and began to climb.

The stairwell was darkest at each kickback, and I found myself hurrying past each one to get closer to the stormy light straining through the windows. One flight below my destination, I heard a shuffle of feet on the landing below me. My heart kicked in my chest. There had been no sound of a door opening or feet stomping up the stairs after me. Was someone intentionally being quiet?

I didn't want to wait and find out. Gripping the banister, I propelled myself upward as fast as I could run.

I couldn't hear much beyond the pounding of my foot-steps and my heart, but it sounded as if someone was pursuing me. Flinging open the door to the family wing, I darted into the hall. I forced my steps to slow to a brisk walk, glancing over my shoulder to see if anyone emerged from the stairwell after me.

When I reached the door to my bedchamber, my hands shook so badly I had difficulty turning the doorknob. I slipped inside, slammed the door, and locked it. I pressed my back against the solid oak, listening for steps outside in the hall.

Half a minute later, when nothing happened, the panic began to drain out of me. My gasping breaths began to slow. Another minute later, I began to feel ridiculous.

I stumbled away from the door and flung my cloak over a chair in front of the hearth to dry. I stared into the low flames crackling in the fireplace.

Had I just made up that entire pursuit in my head? I sank into the chair and scraped a hand through my hair. I tried to think back to the moment in the stairwell when I thought I heard someone on the landing below me, but all I could see were the darkened corners, and feel the surge of terror pumping through my heart.

I shook my head. I needed to stop this nonsense. There was nothing to indicate that anyone had actually been fol-lowing me. If there had been a shuffle, it had doubtless been a mouse. If there were feet pounding up the stairs behind me, it had probably been a servant hurrying to an upper floor. I really had to stop letting my morbid imagina-tion run away with me. Just because I was afraid that the killer was still running free did not mean they were running after me.

I pulled off my sodden half boots and tossed them across the room, angry at my foolishness. Then, rising in a swirl of skirts, I yanked the cord to summon my maid, Lucy. The bottom drawer to my escritoire stuck, as it often did when the weather was damp, and I slammed my fist against its front panel below the handle, prying it loose. My jewelry box lay tucked inside, between an old sketchbook and a journal I hadn't written in since I was twelve. Why I still kept it, I didn't know. I carefully extracted the bloody handkerchief from my pocket and opened the jewelry box to lay the cloth on top. Locking the box, I slid the drawer shut, making certain the swollen wood stuck as before.

After tucking the key inside the loose backing of the landscape painting hanging above my desk, I settled in front of my dressing table and began to pull pins from my wilted hair. Lucy exclaimed in horror when she saw my bedraggled appearance, and began to fuss over me in the same way I suspected she fussed over her numerous siblings. Normally, I found her scolding tiresome, but today it felt familiar and soothing. She helped me to change into a plum afternoon dress with an overlay of black embroidered flowers. It was trimmed with black lace along the wide, low neckline and long sleeves. She pulled a brush through my thick hair and braided it into a tight coronet, which I knew, regardless, would be falling down around my ears by nightfall. Then I devoured the luncheon she brought me on a tray and set out to my next destination, determined not to see danger around every corner.

Striding into the hall where many of the guests were housed, I passed Lady Bethel and Mrs. Calvin. I returned their polite greetings and ignored the curiosity shining in their gazes. I felt their eyes on my back and measured my steps so that the ladies would turn the corridor long before I reached my destination. Pausing at a door near the far end of the hall, I glanced around me to be certain no one was watching before I slipped inside.

The room Lady Godwin had been given was decorated in shades of lavender and pearl gray. The furnishings were dainty and the bedding and draperies covered in ribbons and frills. It was clearly a lady's boudoir. I could just imagine how insulted a man like Mr. Gage or Lord Marsdale would feel if they were assigned such a chamber. They would probably expect a willing lady to come with it.

I locked the door, so as not to be surprised in the middle of my search, and then crossed the room to open the drapes and let in a little light and air. The chamber smelled heavily of Lady Godwin's cloying perfume. I noticed that much of the lady's luggage had been brought to the room so that Faye could perform the tedious task of repacking all of the viscountess's belongings for the journey back to London. I wondered how the maid was faring. If her employer's death hadn't been enough of a shock, to have the lady who so kindly offered to escort her back to England turn up as the suspected murderer must have overwhelmed her completely.

I sorted carefully through the trunk filled with petticoats and other undergarments, including a pair of stays that extended down over the hips. Lady Godwin must have worn it to hide the growing swell at her waistline. Shoes, hats, gloves, and other accessories filled another trunk; however, a thorough search revealed nothing of interest. Her gowns still hung in the wardrobe in a rainbow of exotic colors. I had noticed the viscountess liked color, and the more striking the shade the better.

The surface of her dressing table was covered with potions and unctions, some of which smelled quite horrid. They all claimed to make a woman look younger, slimmer, or more beautiful, and I was curious as to whether any of them actually worked. I found an ornate box in one drawer and thought it might contain jewelry; however, it proved to be filled with a rather lovely collection of delicate paper figurines. A swan, a butterfly, a crane, and a rose—each one lovingly crafted. There was no evidence that Lady Godwin had not created the figures herself, but I somehow knew they were gifts. From whom, I could not begin to guess. I was intensely curious as to why the viscountess would keep such funny little creatures and treasure them enough to carry them with her on her travels. She had not seemed the least sentimental, but this collection proved otherwise. I shook my head and crossed to the desk.

The surface was covered in correspondence. I thumbed through the letters, most of which were from her husband's solicitor or her sister in Shropshire. There were a few bills and one short message from Lady Stratford about the arrangements at her great-aunt's cottage near Glasgow. Nothing to incriminate anyone. Nothing to even hint at an illicit relationship. Just evidence of a woman who was constantly spending money and asking for more. A woman who had a much younger sister who asked eagerly about London and spoke of a gentleman suitor who had recently called upon her. In fact, the single interesting bit of information the correspondence yielded was the creator of Lady Godwin's paper figurines—this selfsame sister, who claimed to miss Lady Godwin so very much, and longed to see her little nephews.

I sank down on the edge of the bed with a sigh. The only thing this search had achieved was to prove how human Lady Godwin had been. She had been more than a woman who took far too many lovers, including her closest friend's husband. Lady Godwin had an existence outside of those bedrooms, a life before she met Lord Godwin, and more depth than many of us had suspected. I almost wished she had remained that vain, unfeeling caricature of my imagination. It made accepting her murder much easier.

I smoothed a hand over my hair and glanced down at my shoes. A piece of paper had fallen to the floor and slid so far under the desk that only a corner peeked out. I picked it up to set it with the rest of the correspondence, skimming it as I did so. The words written there made me stop.

It was a letter begun by Lady Godwin and never finished. It was not addressed, but the information it contained made it easy to guess whom the intended recipient had been. The words jogged something in my memory, something I had read very recently, and I began rifling through the correspondence on the desk looking for one of the letters from Lady Godwin's younger sister. A quick second scan of the note yielded the connection I had been looking for.

I reeled, feeling as if all of the wind had been knocked from my lungs. It seemed almost impossible, the events that I could suddenly see unfurling in my brain. Such actions would require the mind of a heartless, malicious individual. I shivered. I had conversed with just such a person, had perhaps even laughed with them, and I had never suspected what truly lay beneath the jaded exterior.

I stared down at the two missives again. They appeared so innocuous, yet they pieced together a tale so twisted I could scarce believe it. It was no wonder Gage had overlooked their importance, especially when he had yet to uncover the facts that would make sense of the words. Lady Godwin had spoken in such vague terms, I'm not certain I would have seen any more than Gage if I had read them but two short days ago.

I thought of the letter Lady Godwin had been so eager to post to her sister—the one Alana had so casually mentioned when she was trying to give Philip the direction of Lady Godwin's family. I would have given a great deal to read that missive, even though I was quite certain I already knew what it said.

I folded the letters I did have and tucked them securely into my pocket. I swallowed, trying to remove the revulsion that coated my throat. It filled my stomach, making me feel tainted by the evil that continued to lurk among us. If only Gage had not ridden to Drumchork. One glance toward the windows told me that the rain had not abated, but increased, racing down the windows in crooked streaks. The wind stirred up white caps on the gray waves of the loch. Gage would not be returning anytime soon.

I took a deep breath and rose unsteadily to my feet. Perhaps I should speak with Philip. Even if he insisted on waiting for Gage's return, at least someone else would share this burden of knowing.

I scolded myself. That was no reason to explain my suspicions to my brother-in-law. If I told him, it should be out of concern for him and his family's safety. Alana and the children still remained in the nursery, under guard, and as far as I could tell, no one else was in danger from our murderer. Further violence would not be in the killer's best interest, seeing as they had gone to so much trouble to cast the blame on Lady Stratford. It would not be right to share what I had uncovered with Philip. He was already consumed with worry over Alana's condition, and exhausted from dealing with the guests, as well as Freya's foaling. Why should he be made to suffer any more anxiety than he already did just to ease my troubled mind? I could wait a few more hours for Gage's return.

Unlocking the door, I glanced back into the shadowed chamber briefly to make certain I had not overlooked anything, and then slipped out into the hallway. When I turned to make my way back down the corridor toward the stairs, my heart leapt into my throat.

"Faye," I gasped, pressing a hand over my pounding heart as I leaned back weakly against the door. "My goodness, you startled me."

The maid blinked back at me with wide eyes. "*Pardon, Madame.*"

"No, no. It's all right." I laughed a bit breathlessly. "I'm just a bit jumpy today."

The maid nodded hesitantly.

Pushing away from the door, I brushed a hand down the front of my dress. "How are you?" I asked, remembering the girl's predicament.

She swallowed and lifted her chin. "I will survive."

I nodded in appreciation of her bravery. I hoped she would find a worthy new employer upon her return to London, and quickly.

Faye's eyes slid past me to the door.

"How is the packing coming along?" I asked, thinking quickly. The maid must be wondering what I had been doing in Lady Godwin's former bedchamber. "Lady Cromarty asked me to see if you needed anything."

The wariness did not leave her eyes. "I believe I have everything."

I pressed my hands to my skirts, making certain the letters I had tucked inside were still well concealed. "Well, if you think of anything, please let me know."

She nodded.

I pasted a smile across my face, hoping it looked reassuring, and stepped away from the door. Moving swiftly down the hall, I refused to let myself look back to see whether Faye was watching me. It was clear she didn't trust me or my reasons for being in Lady Godwin's chamber. In any case, by tomorrow the truth would be out, and any strange actions on my part would be well justified. However, I didn't want to give her any reason to spread word of my visit to Lady Godwin's chamber before Gage returned from Drumchork. The last thing I needed was for the murderer to catch wind of my actions and begin to wonder whether I suspected anything.

Pausing in my descent of the staircase, I looked up toward the ceiling high above as the drumming rain became deafening, echoing through the space. Its furious pounding was like anvil strikes to my nerves. Closing my eyes, I said a silent prayer for the storms to abate and for Gage to return safely. Then I lifted the skirts of my gown and hurried back to my room to pass the time.

Once Gage returned, this would all be over. The wait would be the worst part.

If only I'd been right.

CHAPTER TWENTY-SIX

I waited all afternoon and into the evening. I wrote letters. I sketched. I stretched new canvas across several empty frames, though, because of the rain, I could not prop open the windows and finish preparing them by brushing them with gesso. I paced the floors and tried, rather unsuccessfully, not to glance at the clock every five minutes. But when darkness fell, transforming the cloud-strewn twilight into murky night, I could wait no more.

Sebastian Gage had not returned to Gairloch. I didn't know why. The rain had stopped two hours earlier, so the weather could not be blamed for his failure to make the thirty-minute journey back from Drumchork. Perhaps he'd been detained. Perhaps the missing footman had put up a fight when Gage confronted him and accused him of assisting a murderer. I hoped Gage wasn't being too hard on the fellow. In light of the evidence I now held, I sincerely doubted the man had anything to do with Lady Godwin's murder or her baby's burial. In any case, Gage should be bringing the footman back to Gairloch, which left me to wonder, once again, why he hadn't appeared.

Maybe Mr. Renshaw had invited him to dinner in the village. Gage would have introduced himself to the squire upon his arrival in Drumchork, and a dinner invitation would likely have been forthcoming. Such a request would only be considered polite, especially when the storms rolled through earlier. However, I couldn't help thinking of the squire's two pretty daughters. I gritted my teeth. They were likely fawning over the handsome Mr. Gage like royalty, and he was probably eating it up, relaxing and enjoying himself while I stewed.

I squeezed my fist around the puzzle piece in my hand, feeling the wooden edges bite into my palm. I was tired of waiting at Gage's leisure. If he couldn't be bothered to present himself, then I saw no need to delay further. I would simply have to take matters into my own hands.

I tossed the puzzle piece down on the table and marched across the room to yank the bellpull. I wanted the truth—I *needed* it—and I was determined to have this matter resolved before I laid my head down on the pillow. Before my loved ones spent another night under the same roof as a murderer.

I locked the letters I had taken from Lady Godwin's room inside my jewelry box with the bloody handkerchief for safekeeping. Then I picked up a page of foolscap and jotted off a quick message to Gage explaining my findings and my intention to speak with Lady Stratford. No matter how much I wished to do otherwise, I knew better than to run off without leaving word of my whereabouts in case Gage returned to the castle and asked for me. Lucy looked at me oddly when I instructed her to slip the note under Gage's door but, upon seeing my seething countenance, wisely held her tongue.

The evening air was cool for late summer, even by the Highlands' standards. I pulled my deep green cloak tighter around me, bowed my head to keep the gusting wind from blowing the hood back, and struck out across the stable yard. It was littered with black puddles, and I was forced to slow my pace to carefully pick my way around them. I jerked my toe back as it slid into one of the inky depths, sending ripples across the water. In the gloom, they appeared bottomless, like cavernous holes an unsuspecting person might tumble into. I shivered and stood still as the moon slipped through a gap in the scuttling clouds overhead and rose in the reflection of one of the pools like a slumbering creature opening its eye. It blinked, making the air seize in my lungs, and then was gone, disappearing behind the smoky gray clouds above that blocked out the stars.

My heart thudded in my throat, and I considered turning back—to wait for Gage or to ask Philip to accompany me. Surely, this could not be a good omen. But then I saw the lantern swaying in the breeze above the door to the carriage house. Its light beckoned me onward.

Abandoning propriety, I lifted my skirts and dashed across the yard, hurdling over the puddles in my path. The guard watched my approach with unabashed interest. I was certain I was giving him quite a good look at my legs, but I didn't care. Let the servant gawk. The creatures lurking in the shadows were far more troubling.

I lurched to a stop before the guard and tried to smile up at him disarmingly.

"Lady Darby, how can I help ye?" the footman asked. He searched the stable yard over my shoulder, as if hoping to see someone had accompanied me.

"I wish to speak with Lady Stratford," I informed him, still huffing from my mad dash.

The guard opened his mouth but seemed at a loss for what to say. "But . . . I'm sure . . ."

"I will speak with her," I added before he could protest. "If you need to lock me in with Lady Stratford or observe us while we speak, so be it. But I *will* speak with her."

The guard frowned and looked like he still might try to object. But then he released a long sigh. He shook his head as if in resignation. "Who'm I to complain?" he grumbled, fumbling with the key in the lock. "His lordship won't be takin' it oot o' *my* hide if yer no' supposed to be here."

I felt a moment's unease, knowing he spoke the truth.

Philip would not be happy with my actions—coming here alone and bullying the guard—but I comforted myself that the end would justify the means. Once we had the real murderer behind lock and key, it wouldn't matter that I'd left the castle alone at night in order to secure the proof we needed. Besides, I was with the guard now, so technically I was not alone.

The lock snicked open, and the footman pulled the lantern from the peg above and pushed open the door. We passed through a short, musty hallway with several doors leading off it. I glanced through a door that stood open to the right into a room cluttered with spare carriage parts and tools. Wheels leaned against the walls and leather tacking hung from the exposed timbers of the ceiling. An old carriage seat was shoved into one corner, its leather cushion covered with ragged holes.

The guard stomped past a door on the left, which I suspected led into the larger part of the building where the carriages were stored, and marched straight toward a heavy oak door in the back. He knocked once. "Visitor," he called before twisting a key in the lock. "I'll leave this'n open, but the outer door'll have to stay locked," he told me apologetically.

"I understand."

"Just knock when ye want let oot."

I thanked him and waited for him to retreat to his post outside before approaching the door he unlocked. Light spilled from beneath it, and I could hear hushed voices within.

Uncertain how I would be received, I reached out and knocked hesitantly. The voices quieted and a pair of feet shuffled toward the door. It creaked open, and Celeste's frightened eyes peered out through the crack.

"Lady Darby!" she gasped.

"Good evening, Celeste," I said gently. "I was hoping I

might speak with Lady Stratford." I tried to look past Celeste into the room, but the door blocked my view.

The maid glanced behind her, presumably to gain permission from her employer, and I hovered for an uncomfortable beat of time while Lady Stratford exercised her prerogative to make me wait. My nerves stretched and tautened, and I was on the verge of saying something to force my way in when Celeste finally stepped aside and allowed me to enter.

The bachelor quarters were smaller than I anticipated but cozy and well maintained, albeit dark. I imagined that even during the brightest day, the room would remain quite gloomy, for a single tiny window high up near the ceiling on the outer wall was the only source of sunlight. As many of the bachelors I knew preferred to carouse all night and sleep during the daylight hours, I could understand how the dearth of windows would be preferable. It also gave Lady Stratford few options for escape.

A large bed, covered in black-and-mahogany-striped fabric, dominated the interior wall of the room, while the opposite side of the chamber boasted a writing desk, wardrobe, and a small breakfast table with two chairs. A sideboard rested against the wall beyond the table. It was covered with assorted bottles of liquor, and I wondered if the countess had given in to the urge to drink herself into oblivion. If our situations were reversed, I certainly would have considered it. I was considering it even now, just standing in this space.

A pair of tan leather chairs was situated before the hearth, which held prime place in the middle of the back wall. This was where Lady Stratford sat glaring at me as I finished my inspection of her prison.

"I hope you haven't come here hoping to coax a confession out of me, for you won't get one," she announced crisply.

I took a deep breath to settle my nerves and swallowed

my impatience. The countess had every right to be angry with me. I would have to be gentle with her. "That's not why I've come. But I do have some questions for you."

"And why should I answer them? So far, your questions have brought me nothing but grief." Her voice rang with bitterness.

Ignoring the stab of guilt her words caused me, I inched closer. "Because I think *these* answers might help prove your innocence."

Lady Stratford stared at me blankly.

"I don't think you killed Lady Godwin," I continued, taking the opportunity her silence presented me. "But I think I know who did." I moved a step closer. "However, I need your help to prove it."

"You . . . you don't think I'm guilty?" she asked uncertainly.

I shook my head. "I don't."

Lady Stratford's rigid posture began to crumple, and she cupped a hand over her mouth. Her eyes were shadowed with fatigue and her complexion was pale, but even racked with grief and detained for a crime she didn't commit, the countess was still impeccably coiffed, with nary a wrinkle in her gown or a hair out of place. It made me feel quite shabby in my own crumpled plum muslin and unruly braided coronet.

I perched on the edge of the other chair. "Will you help me?"

She nodded, allowing me a glimpse of the timid hope blossoming inside her, as yet scared to fully bloom. I wanted nothing more than to promise her that she was safe, that everything would be all right, except I knew it never would be again. Not when she learned what I suspected to be true.

"Do you need a moment," I asked, pressing my hands into my lap to keep them from fidgeting. I had waited half the day with this weight hanging over my head; I could wait a little longer for her to gather herself.

The countess sniffed and pulled a lacy handkerchief from her sleeve to dab at her eyes. "No. No. I want this nightmare to be over with. Go ahead. Ask."

I shifted in my seat. "First of all, do you know if Lord Stratford has visited Shropshire recently?"

Lady Stratford blinked in confusion, clearly not having expected such a question. "Why, yes. He went there to view some property he was considering purchasing."

I suppressed the urge to snort. It was obvious from the countess's expression that when Lord Stratford spoke of property, she believed he was talking about land. Unfortunately, I suspected this property was of a much more human variety. "When did he journey there?"

She tilted her head in thought. "A month ago, maybe two."

I nodded. That fit with my suspicions. "Whose idea was it to accept my sister's invitation to Gairloch? Yours or the earl's?"

Her brow furrowed. "Well, I thought it was mine. But now that you mention it, Derek did seem particularly eager to attend. After I discovered Lady Godwin was going to be present, I thought maybe that was the reason why, even though he had broken off his affair with her in May. Am I . . ." Her eyes widened as the direction of my inquiries became clear. "You don't think . . ."

I held up my hand to forestall her query. "Just a few more questions. Has Lord Stratford visited you in your rooms?" She colored. "I know it seems an indelicate question, but I assure you it *is* relevant."

She looked down at her hands where they were clasped in her lap. Her knuckles were white. "Yes. He has." Her eyes lifted to meet mine, and I could see the hurt and disillusionment shining in their depths. "At the time, I found it odd.

I even remarked upon it to my maid." She gestured toward Celeste, who confirmed her words with a nod. "Derek stopped coming to me months ago—around the time Lady Godwin must have discovered she was expecting. I . . . I had tried to convince him we should try again, but he seemed . . . disinterested." I could hear how much it pained her to discuss these things, but I could not spare her feelings in this. "When he came to me several nights before Lady Godwin's death, I thought he'd changed his mind. Are . . . are you trying to tell me it was for another reason entirely?"

"Maybe," I hedged. My nerves tightened with dread. "Did you ever find him in either your bedchamber or your dressing room at odd times? Times when he had no reason to be there?"

Lady Stratford shook her head. "No. Not that I can recall. And Celeste never mentioned . . ."

"I did." The maid's soft voice rang through the room like a shout. She still stood next to the door, as if uncertain where else to position herself.

"What?" The countess sounded genuinely shocked. "What do you mean? Why didn't you tell me?"

Celeste shrugged awkwardly, wringing her hands. "I didn't know if I should," she stammered before turning to me. "I found his lordship in her ladyship's bedchamber the night of Lady Godwin's murder. He told me he was checkin' on her. I thought it odd, but when I heard 'bout Lady Godwin bein' murdered and how her body was found in the garden that night, it seemed to make more sense. That's why I didn't say nothin'."

The countess seemed momentarily nonplussed by the idea that her husband had looked in on her while she was sleeping. Then she shook herself sharply and tossed her handkerchief into her lap. "Enough questions! I want to know what you are implying." Her eyes were heavy with shadows. "Do you believe that Derek . . ." Her remaining words were swallowed by a choked sound, as if she couldn't bear to say them aloud. "That he . . . stood back and allowed me to take the blame?"

"Oh, I don't think he stood back. I think he deliberately set about blaming you."

Lady Stratford looked as if she might be sick.

"How else do you explain your scissors being found near the body and your shawl wrapped around the baby?" I pressed, wanting to break through any illusions she might still hold about her husband's goodness.

She pressed a fist to her mouth, and I wondered whether it was to hold back a protest or a sob. My gut churned with fury and disgust, and the man wasn't even *my* husband.

Lady Stratford swallowed and lowered her shaking hand to her lap. "What do we do now?"

I leaned toward her. "I left a note for Mr. Gage. As soon as he returns from . . ."

A loud crash reverberated through the walls. We all jumped.

My gaze flew to the door. "What was that?" I gasped, pressing a hand to my racing heart.

Lady Stratford shook her head in bewilderment and opened her mouth to speak when a series of softer thuds and smacks filtered to us through the wood. Celeste backed away from the door, bumping into the small dining table behind her.

I slowly rose to my feet, trying to push back the dread rising inside me like a tidal surge. "It's probably just Mr. Gage," I said, knowing I was trying to reassure myself as much as them. "As I was saying, I left him a note." Another thud shook the walls. "He's probably just upset I came to question you without him," I added with a breathless laugh. "He can be like that." Though, why his arrival would necessitate such violent sounds, I had no idea. "I . . . I was expecting him to join us as soon as he returned to Gairloch. Surely this is him now." I realized I was babbling and clamped my mouth shut, curling up the corners of my lips in some semblance of a smile. I hoped it looked more encouraging than it felt.

A key jiggled unnecessarily in the lock. Had the guard forgotten he left it open for me? I pressed my sweaty palms against my thighs, praying that all I would see was Gage's angry face when the door opened. If a sharp reprimand were in order, I would gladly take it and thank him for it later. If only it was him, and not who I feared it was.

My heart dropped to my knees as Lord Stratford strode through the door.

CHAPTER TWENTY-SEVEN

"Good evening, my dear," Lord Stratford drawled to his wife. There was a harsh gleam in his eyes that belied the insouciance of his words. "I simply had to see if the accommodations they provided you were as lacking as I suspected." His gaze slid over the contents of the room, like a snake slithering through the brush, before landing on me. "Why, Lady Darby. How *kind* of you to keep my wife company." Something about the way he said "kind" made a chill run down my spine. "I'm sure she's enjoyed your visit. It's only too bad it shall be so short-lived."

Lady Stratford and I looked at each other.

"You wished to speak with your wife alone, of course," I gasped, thinking quickly. The countess looked panicked at the prospect, but I knew the best way I could assist her was to get away, to find help. "It was lovely chatting with you," I told her, trying to hide the quaver in my voice as I took several steps toward the door.

The door slammed, making the blood surge sharply in my veins.

Lord Stratford clucked his tongue. "Come now, Lady Darby. You don't really think I'm going to just let you waltz out of here, do you?" A frightening glitter entered his eyes. "I'm afraid it's too late for that."

I swallowed the fear coating my throat and made myself

continue moving forward. "Don't be ridiculous," I replied with forced lightness. "Even in the dark, I'll be quite safe walking from the carriage house to the castle. Besides, there is a guard just outside the door who will be able to observe my progress the entire way."

"Not anymore." Lord Stratford pulled a pepperbox pistol from his pocket.

I stopped short and stared wide-eyed at the weapon. All my concentration seemed to narrow to the two barrels of the gun now trained at my chest. My heartbeat pounded in my ears, making me acutely aware of that weapon's ability to stop it.

Stratford heaved a sigh and shook his head in mock regret. "It's your own fault, my dear. If you'd left well enough alone, you wouldn't be in this predicament."

"So it *was* you!" his wife gasped, momentarily drawing his attention away from me, though not his gun. "You killed Helena! And arranged to have *me* blamed for it." Her voice shook with horror and outrage.

"Very good, Charlotte." He gave her a mocking bow while still somehow managing to keep the pistol leveled on me. "However, I assume Lady Darby helped you to that conclusion. You're not clever enough to have figured it out on your own."

"How could you?" she shrieked, rising to her feet.

"Sit down," the earl ordered as he swung the gun toward his wife.

Air rushed into my lungs, making me feel almost light-headed. I glanced back at Lady Stratford, who stood frozen. She seemed to only just realize how perilous a situation she was in. "You wouldn't shoot me," she declared with far more bravado than I had expected from the china-shepherdess-countess. It jarred me out of my immobility.

Unfortunately, Lord Stratford was not as distracted by his wife as he looked. "Tut-tut," he scolded as I shifted my foot to take a step forward. His eyes were startlingly sharp, like a hawk sighting its prey. "Be a good girl and stand over there by my wife." He waved his gun at me in such a careless manner that I flinched, certain it would go off. He chuckled. "Don't worry, Lady Darby. It won't fire until I'm ready for it to do so."

A shiver ran down my spine. Following his instructions, I backed slowly toward the countess, all the while keeping one eye trained on Lord Stratford's gun while the other frantically searched the room for some kind of weapon. "So you admit it? You admit you killed Lady Godwin and her child?" I accused, trying to keep him talking. There had to be a weapon here of some kind, something sharp or heavy. It appeared that all such objects had been removed, likely to keep them out of the hands of our supposed murderer, Lady Stratford. Even the hearth tools had been confiscated from their usual position next to the fireplace. I prayed they had forgotten something.

Lord Stratford smiled back at me smugly, as if he knew exactly what I was doing. "You there. Maid," he called to Celeste, who stood quivering in the corner behind the dining table. "Come here."

She whimpered and shrank back farther into the corner.

He spared her a glance, narrowing his eyes. "If you do not wish to be shot, I suggest you obey."

With tears streaming down her cheeks, and quaking with fear, she inched toward him. Her hands pleated the fabric of her apron.

"Now!"

Her body jerked forward, propelling her across the room to come to an awkward standstill two feet from the earl. Her breath sawed in and out of her chest at such a rapid rate that I was afraid she might pass out at any moment. Then again, perhaps such an outcome would not be such a bad thing. Especially if she collapsed straight into Lord Stratford. I stared at the maid's mouth, where she sucked in air between parted lips, urging her to breathe even faster.

Stratford reached into the pocket of his greatcoat and pulled out a length of rope. "Hold this," he ordered the girl, who clasped the hemp between her hands as if it were a reptile. Stratford leaned over to extract a wicked-looking blade from a sheath inside his boot. "Now measure out the cord into two equal parts."

The maid blinked up at him in terrified confusion.

"Find the middle," he barked, giving her detailed instructions and then forcing her to hold the rope while he sliced it into two relatively even sections.

I watched in dread, knowing what was about to happen. If only I'd thought to bring a weapon with me—a knife, a letter opener, a bottle of turpentine and a match, *something*. I scolded myself for not taking such a precaution. I thought of the ever-present pistol tucked into the waistband of Gage's trousers with desperation. Why hadn't I done something similar? Even a tiny weapon strapped to my thigh would make me feel better than I did now, whether I was able to get to it without alerting Stratford or not.

I glanced up at the single window, the only exit from the room other than the door blocked by Stratford. The window was positioned too high on the wall for me to boost myself through without assistance, and by the time I reached it, Stratford would put a bullet in my back. Maybe a distraction would work. I turned to Lady Stratford and then the fire, trying to think of some way to stop what was about to happen next.

"Bind Lady Darby's hands," he instructed Celeste, bringing my head back around. "And make certain it's good and tight. I'll be checking your knots, and I will not hesitate to shoot you should they be inadequate."

The maid looked up at me with large, frightened eyes. I knew she had no choice. I knew he would shoot her if she did not do as she was told. But I couldn't comply. I couldn't hold my hands out for her to bind. Not knowing that escape, that self-defense, would be all but impossible with my hands immobilized.

"Lady Darby," Lord Stratford warned.

The click of the gun cocking ricocheted through the room. I flinched, bracing for impact. When it did not come, I blinked up at Stratford.

His lips curled into an evil smile. "Let's cooperate, shall we."

I locked my knees and lifted my chin, refusing to cower. Fear and panic might be choking me, but I was not going to give him the satisfaction of seeing it. At least, not any more than he already had.

Forcing breath into my constricted lungs, I pressed my wrists together and presented them to Celeste. Her hands shook as she wound the rope around my hands. I tried to jostle the cord to keep some slack in the line, but she would not allow it, following Lord Stratford's instructions to the letter. My skin burned from the rub of the rough cord, and my fingers protested the blood loss. I could not stifle a hiss of pain as Celeste tightened the last knot.

Lord Stratford's eyes gleamed with delight. "Very good," he crooned as the maid stepped back to show she was finished. He released the hammer on the pistol. My heart gave a jolt before settling into a steadier rhythm. "Now, my lovely wife."

Celeste flicked a glance filled with terror and shame at me before moving toward Lady Stratford.

"Lady Darby." He gestured for me to move toward him.

I glared at him in disgust, which only seemed to amuse him further, but followed his command, not eager to hear the gun cock again.

"Hold out your hands." He gave the cord such a vicious tug I had to grit my teeth to keep from crying out in pain. "All right, now step back."

I gladly complied.

While Stratford's attention was mostly focused on Celeste tying his wife's hands, I scanned the room again for any potential weapons, any means of escape. I was desperate to knock the gun from Lord Stratford's grasp. If I could disarm him and stun him, perhaps I could make a run for it. Unfortunately, the heaviest object I could see was a book lying on a table on the opposite side of the room. There was no way I could get to it without alerting Stratford to my intentions.

Where was Gage? And for that matter, where was the footman who was supposed to be guarding the carriage house? Had Stratford really killed him like he had implied? We'd heard no gunshots, but a stab from the knife tucked in Stratford's boot or a blow to the head could be just as fatal. Hadn't anyone heard or seen anything? The stables stood next door, filled with horses and stable hands, not to mention Philip's wolfhounds. Surely one of them had witnessed Stratford approaching the carriage house.

I stifled a grunt of frustration. Stratford had clearly planned his actions before coming here, whether my presence was a happy coincidence or not, so there was no reason to believe he would not have made certain his appearance went unnoticed. After all, the man had murdered his mistress and unborn child and managed to place the blame on his wife, all while evading suspicion. Until I decided the evidence provided wasn't enough.

I couldn't be sorry I had been determined to seek the truth, but I wanted to kick myself now for not confiding in Philip. Maybe if I had told him what I had discovered and where I was going, I would not be facing the barrel of a loaded pistol with my hands tied. Or maybe Stratford would have found it necessary to shoot Philip, had he accompanied me. Or Philip might have forced me to wait for Gage, and Stratford could have abducted Lady Stratford and Celeste right from under our noses.

It was clear that Lord Stratford did not intend to murder

us—at least, not immediately. Otherwise, why would he bind our hands? But where was he taking us?

Celeste stepped back from Lady Stratford, and he beckoned her forward to check her knots much the same way he had done mine. I had to admire the countess's bravery, lifting her chin and staring down her nose at her husband as if he were an insect. Only the flicker of her eyelashes told me that his tug on her bindings had been as painful as mine.

"You truly are lovely, my darling," Stratford murmured, running a finger down her pale cheek.

Her face tightened in revulsion, but she did not look away.

"It's too bad. Such beauty should never hide something so barren and useless." The last word hissed through his teeth as he pushed her back.

She flinched and staggered. Celeste steadied her.

"Now," he declared, turning away from his wife as if she no longer mattered and focusing on me. "We're going to take a little walk."

My heartbeat accelerated again.

"My lady wife is going to lead." He smiled, a vicious twist of his lips, and leveled the pistol at me. "And, Lady Darby, you shall have the privilege of walking just before me." He flicked a glance at his wife and her maid. "Should any of you choose to scream or run, I will not hesitate to shoot you. So remember that before you attempt anything heroic . . ." he leaned toward me with coldhearted delight ". . . Lady Darby."

I stiffened in frustration. If he had let me lead, I might have been able to dart into the forest. By standing directly in front of him, the gun would be trained right at my back. I had no hope of escape.

Fear crawled up inside me and squeezed my chest in its icy grip, threatening to block out rational thought. I fought to slow my breath, to stop the fog of panic from taking over.

I had to stay alert. I had to watch for my opportunity. I had to stay alive.

"Move!" Stratford barked, urging his wife through the door.

Celeste fell into step behind her, weeping uncontrollably into her still-unbound hands. If the maid would just pull herself together, she would have the best chance of escape. I glared at her back in frustration.

Stratford prodded me with his gun. "Let's go, Lady Darby."

I shivered as we inched forward through the corridor toward the outer door. Lady Stratford wrangled it open, and I offered up a swift prayer that someone would see us leaving. The words died on my lips as the soft wash of shrouded moonlight illuminated the crumpled form of the guard lying in the storage-room doorway next to the extinguished lantern. I gasped and leaned closer, searching for signs of life, but Stratford propelled me forward, digging the pistol into the skin between my shoulder blades.

"Move."

I stumbled, barely stopping myself from taking a hard tumble onto the broken cobblestones of the path in front of the carriage house. Righting myself, I followed Celeste around the corner of the building, into the woods.

"Right," he ordered his wife, directing us toward the little-used path that ran through the forest behind the carriage house and stables down toward the loch.

The heavy overgrowth of summer whacked against my legs, dampening my skirts with moisture from the earlier rains and dragging down my steps. Whether by Lady Stratford's conscious choice or because she was having difficulty following such an unknown trail in the dark, our progress slowed to a crawl, allowing me to catch my breath. Stratford hissed for them to move faster, jabbing me in the back with his gun, but after a dozen steps, their pace faltered once again.

I tried to ignore the throbbing between my shoulder blades and the pistol aimed at me, and focus on my surroundings. There was no sound beyond the rustle of the wind through the trees and the shuffle of our footsteps against the musky earth. The snap in the breeze and the brine on my tongue told me we were nearing the sea loch. My surroundings were not completely foreign, but I had not traveled this path many times in the last sixteen months, so I could not say whether we had already passed the tiny side trail that looped back toward the front drive or not. Everything looked so different in the dark, and if I darted off into the woods anywhere but that trail, I wasn't certain I would be able to navigate without tripping over a root or becoming entangled in a bramble bush.

Stratford prodded me in the back and snarled at his wife again, who picked up speed as we crested a hill. My stomach sank as the thick bramble of trees and scrub around us parted, allowing me to see the dark, steely waves of the loch glimmer faintly in the light of a stray moonbeam breaking through the clouds. I had missed the side trail, and soon enough we would arrive at the shore.

The trail twisted, and we were out of the forest, descending down a grassy hill toward the beach. A small rowboat was pulled up on the shore. I faltered, and Lord Stratford's hand shot out to squeeze my upper arm in a punishing grip.

"Yes, Lady Darby. We're taking the boat," he hummed into my hair. "Does that bother you?"

Of course, it bothered me. My hands were bound, and he was planning to take me out onto the open waters of the loch. If I fell overboard, I would never be able to swim. The thought terrified me. But I wasn't going to tell him that. "Where are you taking us?" I demanded.

"Oh, I don't think you want to know that yet, love."

The icy bands around my chest tightened. "Then why?" I gasped, suddenly desperate to keep him talking. "You went to so much trouble to place the blame on your wife and her maid . . ."

"And you."

I stilled, remembering the bloody apron in my studio.

"I don't know whether you lied about where you found the apron or Gage finally realized how foolish he was to consider you a suspect, but I was rather impressed you managed to avoid being implicated."

Anger cleaved through my fear. "You knew the others were blaming me."

"And I would have been a fool not to use that hysteria to my advantage," he stated matter-of-factly. "Just in case Gage never found the scissors or the shawls so that he could accuse my wife of the murder."

"You were going to kill her," I spat. "You were going to kill your wife and then marry Lady Godwin's sister." I was furious he had been playing us all against each other. "Except Lady Godwin found out. She sent a letter to her sister, you know. And then she confronted you about it in the maze."

"The bitch threatened to tell my wife," he snarled, squeezing my arm even tighter. "Like she told her about our affair and the bastard growing in her belly." He sighed heavily, as if his display of anger had disappointed him. "I never intended to kill Lady Godwin or her child, but she simply had to be stopped."

The extreme changes in his tone unsettled me. He said the last so lightly, as if he were telling me he had to stop the viscountess from painting her parlor pink, not warning her friend of his treachery. I worried what a man with such quicksilver alterations in mood could be capable of. He was thoroughly unpredictable.

"So you decided to implicate your wife," I asked, leading him on, needing to understand as much as I needed to keep him talking.

"Yes. The murder of both my former mistress and my wife would have thrown too much suspicion on me."

Lady Stratford stumbled ahead of us as she stepped onto the loose sand of the beach and righted herself.

"Careful, darling," her husband called up to her. "We wouldn't want you to hurt yourself. Not yet," he hissed under his breath.

Shaken by his comment, I tried to pull from his grasp, but he yanked me closer. I knew if he took us out in that boat, things could not end well. There would be nowhere to run, no way to escape. As we drew nearer, I realized this might be my last chance. I couldn't climb into that boat. Not without knowing I had done everything in my power, short of dying, to avoid it.

I waited until we reached the point where the ground leveled to give myself the best footing and then whirled around to drive my knee into Stratford's groin. My brother had told me, once upon a time, that it was the most vulnerable spot on a man's body, and should I ever get into trouble, that was the place to aim.

Regrettably, my aim seemed to be off. That, or Stratford was quicker than I gave him credit for. My knee collided with his thigh, and though he dropped his grip on my arm when he flinched, he did not go down as I'd anticipated. He snarled and grabbed me around the waist before I took two steps. Spinning me around, he struck me across the face.

I landed hard on my side in the sand, and it knocked the wind out of me. I gasped for air, and my eyes filled with tears from the sting of the blow. My left cheek throbbed, and I was having difficulty focusing on what was going on around me.

Before I could right myself, Stratford yanked me to my feet and lifted me into the boat. I plopped down on the bench with all the grace of a falling rock and would have tumbled over backward into the bottom of the boat if Celeste had not reached out to steady me. The boat swayed beneath me. Then Stratford hoisted himself over the side and finished maneuvering the tiny vessel out into the water with an oar. Before I could understand what was happening, we were too far away from the shallows to risk jumping out of the boat.

"Now," Stratford declared, standing over me. "I would like you to row, Lady Darby."

He held an oar out to me with one hand while pointing the gun at my chest with the other. I glanced down at my bound hands and he *tsked*. "It doesn't take free hands to row. Though I'm sure Celeste will have a much easier time of it." He glared pointedly at the other oar, and the maid immediately picked it up. He forced the oar between my hands. "No sudden movements," he told us as he backed up to sit down in the stern of the boat. His eyes settled on his wife at the prow of the vessel behind me. "And you, my dear, need only look pretty. As that is all you seem capable of."

I tried to ignore the sting of my cheek and the panic surging through my blood, but the distance growing between the shoreline and me was not helping. The wind whipped across the water, stirring up foamy whitecaps on the waves below my oar. The sky had steadily begun to clear, offering lengthier gaps between cloud banks so that the moon could shine bright and nearly full upon the choppy waters of the sea loch. To the north I could see the hills of the Isle of Ewe rising up out of the middle of the loch. I knew the waters were shallower near its southern tip. I pulled hard on my oar, trying to turn us toward the isle, but Stratford was ever conscious of our direction.

"Straighten out," he ordered, almost shouting to be heard above the wind. "We're heading west, Lady Darby."

Into the deepest part of the loch.

Fear and frustration bubbled up inside me, threatening to overcome my thin veneer of composure. I wanted to cry, and I wanted to scream, and I knew none of this was going to stop Stratford from killing us.

"I don't understand any of this," I exclaimed. "You decided to kill your wife simply because she has not been able to conceive a child?"

"I need an heir, Lady Darby." He spoke slowly and carefully, as if I were stupid. "It's the only reason I wed in the first place. But my wife has been unable to provide me with one." He glared over my shoulder at the countess. "When I discovered Lady Godwin was carrying my child, I finally knew for certain just who was at fault for my wife's lack of conception. She neglected to tell me how worthless she was before we married. She tricked me."

I glanced back at Lady Stratford. Her eyes were icy in the moonlight. "I never knew I was barren. How could I? I was a virgin when I married you."

"You knew." His voice was laced with contempt. "You had to. It was no wonder your family was so eager to see you wed to me."

"You're an earl! That's why they wanted me to marry you."

My hands cramped from trying to hold the oar in such an awkward manner, and my muscles ached from the exertion. Even with her hands free, Celeste seemed to be having just as much difficulty. While Stratford argued with his wife, our progress across the lake had slowed considerably, and I consciously allowed our speed to drop even more. I hoped that by doing so, there would be time for someone to notice we'd gone missing and come searching for us.

"It doesn't matter!" Stratford slammed his fist down on the bench below him, making the boat sway and all of us jump. "You were useless to me. I should have recognized that sooner. I needed an heir, and you couldn't provide one. So you needed to die so that I could remarry."

"And how did you intend to do that?" Lady Stratford replied with an amazing amount of daring. I feared her emotions were making her reckless. "Were you planning to slit my throat like you did Lady Godwin's?"

Stratford's eyes gleamed with relish. "Of course not, my sweet. *Your* death needed to look like a suicide."

His wife stiffened.

"A little bit of laudanum and two slits to the wrists seemed more ladylike."

"With my embroidery shears? You never would have gotten away with it." Her voice was still clipped, but it was fading.

"Ah, but if everyone discovered that Lady Godwin was expecting my child and that you knew about it, it would be all too easy to understand how you could be so distraught." The feigned sorrow in his voice was far more chilling than his anger. "Especially when I told them how I blamed myself for not being more sensitive to your distress over your barrenness."

"You never loved me at all," she accused, heartbreak and disillusionment stretching her voice. "Not even on our wedding trip. When we . . ." She broke off, unable to complete the sentence.

Stratford's jaw hardened as he watched his wife struggle with her emotions.

"All I was to you was a . . . a broodmare," she spat accusingly. The boat shifted as if she intended to rise from her seat.

He swung the pistol around to point it at his wife. "Ah, ah!" he warned her in mockery. "Let's not be too hasty."

Lady Stratford *thunked* back into her seat.

"It matters not to me now how soon you die, so long as your body washes up on shore. But I assume you would rather prolong the matter."

"You said you needed an heir, but why?" I blurted, trying to distract him before his wife provoked him into firing his gun. I still didn't understand his obsession with having a boy child. "Why does it matter who inherits the title after you die?"

"Because the earldom would go to a bloody Frenchman,"

he snarled, leaning toward me. His dark eyes glittered almost feverishly in the moonlight, sending a chill down my spine. "I spent five years fighting the sons of bitches in Spain and Portugal and then at Waterloo. I took a bullet in the shoulder and another one grazed my scalp. I nearly died at the Battle of Salamanca. I'll be damned if I'm going to let one of those frogs hold the title to one of the most ancient and venerable earldoms in all of England."

The man was crazy. He was willing to murder four women and a child just so he could remarry and father an heir. I could understand his continued animosity toward the French, but not his willingness to go to such extreme measures to keep his title out of their hands. Perhaps the bullet that grazed his scalp had damaged his brain somehow, for I could not believe that a man who was right in the head would do such a thing.

My body went cold at the realization that we were in a boat in the middle of a storm-tossed loch with a madman. A murderer was dangerous enough, but as long as he was sane, there was at least some chance of rationalizing with him. A madman was unreasonable and unpredictable. We had no hope. He was going to kill us and dump us over the side.

A whimper caught in my throat, and I felt tears of despair begin to flood my eyes. I blinked them back, determined not to show my panic to this lunatic. I would not give him the satisfaction of watching me fall apart.

I allowed the wind that had picked up almost to a howl to whip the loose strands of my hair across my face, shielding my struggle as I turned to stare out over the loch. The glint of something on the water caught my eye. At first, I thought it might be the way the moonlight was striking the waves, or a seal venturing into the shelter of the loch from the sea, but then I realized that it was a ship. My heart leapt in my chest. *Please let them be searching for us*, I prayed. *Please let it be Gage.*

I studied Stratford through the tendrils of my hair, knowing I had to distract him. I had to give that boat enough time to slip as close to us as possible without the earl noticing. Otherwise, he might panic and shove us all overboard before the others were near enough to help us.

"But why kill the baby?" I asked, drawing Stratford from whatever dark thoughts he was contemplating. He glared at me. "I understand why you killed Lady Godwin. You had to keep her quiet so that she wouldn't warn your wife."

Lady Stratford gasped, having not been privy to our earlier conversation on the beach.

"But I don't understand why you took the child from her womb. Why would you do such a thing? What purpose did it serve?"

Celeste made a gagging sound. I glanced at her out of the corner of my eye, wondering if she was going to be sick.

"It didn't serve a purpose," Lord Stratford replied. "Other than to tell me whether the bitch was telling the truth."

I gaped at him in horror.

"I needed to know whether she really carried my child. And I was curious whether it was a boy."

Lady Stratford choked on a sob behind me.

"Besides . . ." Stratford's mouth curled into a chilling smile. "It all worked out rather well for me in the end. Ripping that bastard from the womb made Mr. Gage believe that the motive was the child. It helped to convince him that my wife was to blame, since she wanted a child so badly and she couldn't have one herself." His tone mocked her.

His eyes returned to me, narrowed in anger. "Everything was working out so well, until *you* decided to go searching for more evidence. You couldn't leave well enough alone." I shrank beneath his glare. "What was it that made you doubt my lady wife's guilt? Couldn't believe a delicate, well-bred creature would be capable of such a thing?" he sneered.

I flicked a glance at the approaching boat, gauging its progress. It still seemed so far away.

"No," I replied, keeping my voice even. "It was, in fact, the very same reason you believed we would suspect her in the first place—her desperate longing for a child."

He scowled, clearly not liking my answer, and began to turn his head back toward Gairloch.

"You were the one watching me today," I accused, frantic to keep his gaze away from the approaching vessel. The snap of the wind and the slap of the waves against our hull drowned out the sounds of the other boat's pursuit, but I knew it was only a matter of time before Lord Stratford heard them.

His stare slid back to mine. "I've been *watching* you for quite some time. Since the night I returned to the castle to find Mr. Gage leading you and Lord Westlock back from the chapel. I knew then that you had been asked to assist him, and your actions since then have only confirmed my suspicions." He shook his head as if in scolding. "You should have listened to my letters."

I tensed. So *he* had written them. But of course he had. That seemed rather obvious now. "Was it you in the servants' stairwell?" I couldn't resist asking. I wanted to know just how many of today's ominous occurrences had been real and how many figments of my imagination.

I could hear the satisfaction in his voice. "What do you think?"

I scowled. "What were you planning to do? Hit me over the head?"

"Perhaps. You're far too resourceful, Lady Darby. First you took the dogs with you on your little walk and made it impossible for me to get close to you without raising an alarm. Then you eluded me on the stairs." My muscles tightened as he gestured with his gun, reminding me just how quickly he could end my life. "When Faye mentioned that you had been in Lady Godwin's chamber today, I knew you were looking for something, and I couldn't risk having you find evidence to implicate me. So when I saw you cross the stable yard toward the carriage house, I knew it was my chance to finish you both." His gaze slid over each occupant of the boat, and he grinned. "It has worked out amazingly well. Perhaps I should thank Cromarty's mare for dropping her foal last night. At the time, I cursed it for preventing me from getting to my lovely wife and her maid, but since waiting has dropped *you* into my lap, Lady Darby, and provided me with a wonderful scapegoat, I cannot be cross."

I gasped. "You intend to blame me."

His smile turned smug. "Whom do you think they will blame when you and Celeste have disappeared and my wife's body washes up on shore with a bullet through her heart?"

My hands tightened around the oar.

"Tut-tut," Stratford scolded me, aiming the pistol directly at the center of my chest. "No sudden movements with that, Lady Darby. My gun is liable to go off."

I gritted my teeth, wanting to snarl at the man. How dare he threaten my life and plot to ruin my reputation, and that of my family, once and for all. What would Philip and Alana, and my nieces and nephews, have thought if he had succeeded? What would Gage? Would they have continued to believe in my innocence? Or be forever shamed by my memory?

I felt an absurd surge of relief that his plans were not to come to fruition. It was obvious now that the other boat was pursuing us, and whether or not I survived this ordeal, they would know I had not orchestrated it. Neither I, nor my family, would be blamed.

I was so absorbed by my conflicting emotions that I failed to act quickly enough when Celeste gasped, obviously having caught sight of the boat. Stratford turned his head to see it. By this point, I could clearly see the prow of the ship slicing through the water toward us, closing the distance fast. My heart surged in my chest. I wanted to reach out and smack the foolish maid.

Stratford growled and leaned forward to yank the oar

from my grasp. "Damn you!" He grabbed hold of the bind-ings around my wrists and pulled me toward him.

Crying out in pain, I tumbled to the floor, purposely trying to evade his grasp. A man shouted from the other boat.

"You saw them coming, didn't you?" Stratford released the rope to tug on my arm. "Get up!"

I struggled against him, even though it wrenched my shoulder terribly, for I knew that if he managed to pull me to my feet, he would use me as a shield. Stratford had no more than two bullets in his double-barreled pistol, and without me for leverage, they would be nearly useless against the four or five men in the other boat. He might shoot two of them, but he would never get away. I cringed at the image of Gage or Philip taking those bullets.

"Get up," Stratford snarled.

And then I saw it. Poking up out of his right Hessian boot was the knife—the blade he had used to cut the rope. The weapon I suspected had actually been used to slice Lady Godwin's throat and abdomen. I glanced up to find Strat-ford's gaze focused on the men in the boat, and reached out to grip the knife handle clumsily between my bound hands. As he jerked me upward, making the muscles in my shoul-der scream in protest, the blade slid cleanly from its sheath.

Stratford whirled me around in front of him, wrapping his arm across my shoulders and pressing the cool muzzle of the gun against my temple. "Stop right there. You, too, darling."

I closed my eyes, terrified for a moment that the pistol would go off. When my pounding heart did not stop beat-ing, I cautiously opened my eyes to see Lady Stratford stand-ing in the back of the boat gripping Celeste's oar. Her icy eyes glimmered with fury. Her gaze met mine and briefly dipped to the knife between my palms, letting me know she had seen it. She did not give me away.

"Drop it," Stratford ordered.

She tossed the oar into the bottom of the boat with a clatter.

Stratford whirled me around to face the water and the other vessel now inching toward us. "I said stop right there. Or I'll put a bullet through her skull."

I sucked in a breath and forced it out again. The world around me seemed suddenly fuzzy, and I knew I had to stay conscious if I was going to survive this ordeal. Passing out was not an option. I had to calm my rampaging heart. The bite of the chain of my mother's pendant against my skin from where it snagged between Stratford's arm and my body helped to sharpen my senses.

"Let her go," I heard Gage order harshly. I blinked open my eyes to find him aiming a pistol toward me. I knew that it was meant to be pointed at Stratford, as was the gun held by another man standing in the boat, but I could not help feeling unnerved to have three weapons pointed at me.

"I think not," Stratford answered calmly—too calmly, for my taste. "Not unless you want her brains splattered all over this boat's stern."

My stomach pitched violently at the threat.

Gage's face tightened, and his gaze dipped to meet mine. I almost wished he hadn't, for I could see genuine fear shining in the depths of his eyes, and I had a terrible suspicion it was for me. It was not the least reassuring. "What do you want, Stratford?" he asked the earl.

"That's a dangerous question," Stratford replied, his words gusting past my ear as the boat rocked beneath our feet. "How about instead I settle for telling you what is going to happen next." Against my hair, the muscles of his cheek pulled upward in a nasty smile. "You, Lord Cromarty, and the others are going to head back to Gairloch Castle while the ladies and I continue on our way."

Celeste sobbed.

"And if we don't?" Gage challenged.

"Then Lady Darby dies, here and now."

I stiffened, knowing his threat to be real.

Philip murmured something behind Gage, who shushed him. "How do we know you won't harm Lady Darby if we do what you say?"

"You don't." Stratford sounded amused with himself. "My way, there's a chance she might survive. Your way, there isn't."

I closed my eyes, swallowing the bitter lump of fear in the back of my throat. There was no way out of this without using the knife. It was ironic to think that only four days ago, I had assured myself that even though I had never held a knife, I would be able to wield one if the need ever arose. Well, that need was now.

If they let him go, Stratford intended to kill us no matter what he told Gage. I was certain of it. And if they refused, he would shoot me and at least one more person before likely being shot in turn. Either way, I would die. And I didn't want to. Not yet. Not like this. Not when I had wasted so much time hiding. I finally felt brave enough to live again, but if I did nothing now, I might never have the chance.

I blinked open my eyes to look into Gage's beautiful pale blue ones. He looked so frightened, so uncertain of what his next course of action should be. And I could lift that burden from him. I only hoped that if something went wrong, he knew how much he meant to me, how much I cared. How much more than a shallow golden lothario I now saw when I looked at him.

"What will it be?" Stratford demanded, tightening his arm across my chest.

I knew what I had to do.

The knife felt awkward and slippery between my hands. I struggled to rotate it without dropping it, cutting myself, or tipping off Stratford to its presence. Gage's eyes dipped, catching the movement, and widened with a look of absolute horror. He shook his head slightly, telling me to stop. But I would not heed. I could not heed.

Offering up a silent prayer, I shifted my arms to the side. "There *is* one other way, you know?" I felt Stratford shift so that he could look down at me, but I only had eyes for Gage. "My way!" The last emerged as more of a grunt as I drove my hands backward with all my might, sinking the blade deep into Stratford's abdomen. Warm blood coated my fingers, and the sickening squelch of torn flesh rent the night air.

Stratford howled and knocked me off balance as he reached down to grip the knife. A gun fired, and another answered. I tumbled forward, and unable to catch myself, I plummeted over the side of the boat into the icy water.

The bitter cold drove the air from my lungs, and a stabbing pain in my side momentarily made the world go dark. When I opened my eyes, I could no longer see the faint light of the moon or tell which way was up or down. The sodden weight of my skirts wrapped around my legs. I panicked, kicking wildly, trying desperately to propel myself in the direction I thought was up. My lungs burned and my eyes stung from the salt water. I tugged and thrashed, trying to loosen my bindings, but they would not come undone. I could not break free.

CHAPTER TWENTY-EIGHT

The world around me went quiet, and a tingling sensation washed up over my skin. I couldn't kick anymore. Then something warm touched my shoulder and wound its way under my arm. I couldn't tell whether it was friend or foe, but it was pulling me along behind it, I hoped toward the surface. My mind began to darken, blurring at the edges, and I struggled to remain conscious.

When my head broke the surface, I gasped, pulling in as much of the cool air as my lungs could hold. It sawed in and out of me, sharp and sweet, ambrosia on my tongue. The haze around my vision began to fade, and my hearing returned with a ringing in my ears accompanied by the sound of slapping waves. Too weak to do anything myself, I leaned into the warmth behind me and just breathed. My chest burned, and my side ached terribly, but I was breathing. I was alive.

I blinked open my eyes, trying to understand, and peered up into Gage's face. "Kiera," he panted, his chest heaving from the exertion it must have taken to pull me to the surface. "Were you hit? Are you bleeding?" One arm held me tightly to the solid heat of his chest while his other hand moved quickly over my limbs and torso.

"I don't think so," I mumbled, having difficulty feeling anything at the moment beyond the warmth of his body and the tingling cold of the water. Even the throbbing in my side, and on my cheekbone where Stratford had struck me, seemed muted. My eyes drifted shut, too tired to stay open. "W-what about y-you?" I stammered.

His fingers combed through my hair, probing my scalp for lacerations. "I'm fine. But we've got to get you out of this water." I could hear the worry in his voice. "Over here," he called. "I've got her."

I heard the rumble of voices and the slap of oars in the water and opened my eyes to see one of the boats moving toward us. Gage's hand cupped my jaw, and I flinched when his thumb brushed across the bruise on my cheekbone from where Stratford had struck me. His eyes hardened, and a muscle twitched in his jaw as he turned my face toward him so that he could view the contusion better.

"Is S-Stratford . . . ?"

"Dead?" he finished for me. "Yes. And if he wasn't, I would wrap my fist around his throat and choke the life out of him."

A stronger wave rolled into us, splashing into my face. I blinked and blew the water from my mouth, tasting the salt on my lips. "And L-Lady Stratford and her m-maid?"

"They're safe."

"And Philip?"

Gage's eyes warmed. "Cromarty," he yelled, never taking his eyes from me.

"Yes?"

At the sound of Philip's voice, I relaxed even deeper into Gage's arms. I wished my arms were unbound. I wanted to wrap them around his neck.

Gage lifted me higher against his shoulder, as if reading my mind. "Kiera wants to know whether you're alive?"

If I'd had the energy, I would have narrowed my eyes at the inappropriateness of his humor.

"Kiera, I'm still breathing," Philip hollered back, his voice tinted with relief.

I turned into Gage's shoulder and pressed my forehead

against his cheek. He was so warm, so nice. I inhaled deeply. And he smelled so good—musky and briny, albeit a bit fishy. But I didn't care about that as long as he held me close like this.

Gage's fingers wrapped gently around my nape and pulled my head back. I resisted at first, not wanting to leave the cozy nook in his shoulder, but I didn't have the will or the energy to fight him.

"Kiera," he murmured. "Kiera, I need you to open your eyes."

I sighed and forced them open, knowing that the concerned tone of his voice should mean something. I just didn't know what.

"Kiera, I need you to stay with me."

I tried to nod, but I couldn't seem to make the muscles in my neck work.

"Kiera." His callused thumb brushed over the pulse at the side of my throat, making it flutter. "Can you stay with me?"

I smiled, and his eyes softened with a tenderness that made me feel pleasantly fuzzy inside.

His warm mouth pressed to my forehead and then my nose. And then, with a sweetness of sincerity, to my lips. My heart stuttered in my chest, and a shiver worked through my frame. When he pulled back, my teeth began to chatter. I wished he would put his warm lips back on mine.

Light suddenly pierced the darkness around us, and I blinked and shied away, blinded by the source.

"There they are," I heard Philip call out. "A little farther to the right."

My eyes adjusted enough to see Philip leaning over the prow of the dinghy, holding a lantern. The small craft pulled up alongside us, and he handed the light to someone behind him and reached out to pull me aboard. With help from another man and Gage, he was able to hoist me up onto the boat.

Philip helped me sit on one of the benches and settled a blanket around my shoulders while Gage pulled himself back onto the boat. "Kiera, are you hurt?" Philip asked, leaning down to look in my eyes.

"I don't know," I mumbled. Now that I was seated, my side throbbed. I twisted, trying to gesture to it. Philip's gaze dropped, and I knew that something was wrong. But I couldn't seem to care. I just wanted to lie down, to close my eyes. It took too much effort to stay upright.

I heard him call Gage over, and the two men studied my side, all the while forcing me to stay seated.

"Kiera, we need you to keep your eyes open," Gage told me.

I shook my head.

"Kiera, you *have* to keep your eyes open."

I shook my head again, confused why he was asking this of me.

He shook me and called my name, but it seemed so very far away. I couldn't understand. I didn't want to understand. And then there was nothing.

I woke to the sensation of fingers brushing through my hair, and for a moment I thought I merely dozed. That I was still floating in the water with Gage's strong hands probing my head for wounds. But the ground below me was far too steady, and my body was much too dry and warm. Oh, how toasty and warm I was. I breathed deeply. The scents of lavender and chamomile were so much lovelier than the briny loch water. I blinked open my eyes to find my sister staring down at me.

"Hello, dearest," she murmured softly. Tiny teardrops flecked her lashes.

I glanced around me, trying to absorb the fact that I truly was lying in my bed in my room and not being tossed about in the choppy loch. Sun streamed in through the windows behind Alana, and birds chirped outside.

"What happened?" I asked, pushing up on my elbows. I sucked in a sharp breath through my teeth as pain shot up my left side.

She leaned forward to push me back down. "Stratford's bullet grazed your side," she replied, answering the most apparent interpretation of my question.

"He shot me?" I gasped in confusion.

She nodded. "You lost a great deal of blood, but the bullet did not lodge in your side or cause any injury to your tissues or organs. The physician assured us you wouldn't suffer any permanent damage."

I wrinkled my brow, trying to remember when Stratford had fired at me. "It must have happened when I fell into the water," I decided.

Alana fussed with my pillows. "That's what Mr. Gage said."

I stilled her hand and forced her to look me in the eye. Her mouth tightened with emotion, and I pulled her head down next to mine, wanting her close. She wept tears I could not yet summon but knew would come later—tears of relief and loss and frustration. For now, I could but hold my sister close and share what comfort I could, soaking it in as well.

Her tears quickly spent, she sniffled and lifted her head, searching the nightstand for a handkerchief. She sank back in her chair and dabbed at her eyes. "Forgive me," she mumbled through her stuffy nose.

I squeezed her hand. "There is nothing to forgive," I replied, and rushed on before she could protest. "Now tell me what happened? How did I get back to the castle?"

"Mr. Gage carried you." Her eyes darkened with remembered fear. "You were unconscious and so very cold." She swallowed. "We all feared the worst."

I recalled hazily the moments in the water before they pulled me into the boat—the extreme fatigue, the warmth of Gage's body, the kiss—but my memory faded to almost nothing after Philip settled the blanket over my shoulders. To be honest, I wasn't even certain whether any of the events I recollected after falling into the water actually happened. I stared up at the deep cobalt blue of my canopy. I wondered if I would ever know whether Gage had actually kissed me.

"So they brought me back to the castle and you summoned the physician?"

She nodded. "I sent for him as soon as I heard Philip and Mr. Gage had gone looking for you. I know you don't like Dr. Gunn, dear, but I didn't know what else to do."

"It's all right," I tried to interject.

"We wouldn't let him bleed you. I know how archaic you believe that procedure."

I squeezed her hand, cutting her off. "Alana, it's all right. I understand. Whatever he did could not have been so bad. I'm still alive, am I not?" I tried to joke.

She frowned. "Yes, well, it was a near thing. If Gage and Lucy and I had not gotten you warm so very quickly it might have been too late."

My chest tightened hearing the distress in her voice. "I'm sure. I'm sorry. I suppose I shouldn't jest about such a thing."

"No. You shouldn't." She turned away to fuss with the items littering the top of my nightstand. She handed me a glass of water and ordered me to drink, which I did gladly.

I peered over the rim of the glass at her. "You've emerged from the nursery," I said, remembering her self-imposed exile. I'd promised Philip I would coax her down from the fourth floor, but I hadn't exactly intended to do so in such a drastic manner.

"Yes, well, somebody has to look after you. I had a terrible premonition all day yesterday that something bad was going to happen to you."

"Alana," I scolded gently.

She waved her hand at me. "I know, I know. There's no way I could have known it would come true. But I shouldn't have locked myself away like that just because I was afraid. Especially when I knew you needed me."

"Your children needed you, too." I couldn't stand for her to take any of the blame upon herself for what had happened to me. "Besides, I should have at least told Philip where I was going," I reluctantly admitted. "Even if I thought he might try to stop me."

"Well . . ." she folded her arms across her chest ". . . don't admit that to Philip."

I stared at her in shock, and her face creased into a reluctant smile. I started to laugh, but the movement pulled at the wound in my side too much.

Alana reached over to help settle me more comfortably. "The man can be insufferable. And you're right, he would have stopped you, and then where would we be? Or perhaps a more pertinent question: Where would Lady Stratford and her maid be? At the bottom of the loch, I'd wager, instead of Lord Stratford."

"Is he really?"

She nodded her head once sharply in satisfaction. "Sir Graham shot him straight through the head. He toppled out of the boat, and the search parties have yet to find his body." She shrugged. "We might never find it."

"Who is Sir Graham?"

"Sir Graham Fraser." She took the glass from my hand and poured me another drink of water. "He's the procurator fiscal from Inverness. He met up with Mr. Gage on the road from Drumchork yesterday evening." She handed me the cup. "They must have arrived not long after Lord Stratford kidnapped you. If they had ridden into Gairloch but a few minutes earlier, they might have encountered Lord Stratford leading you three ladies from the carriage house."

I dismissed the comment, knowing it would do no good to dwell on what-ifs.

"They found poor Beowulf and Grendel drugged near the door to the stables."

"Oh, no! Are they all right?"

"Never fear. The brutes are already recovered. Though I suspect they'll be a bit more cautious of taking food from a stranger in the future."

I wasn't so certain of that. The two wolfhounds were rather fond of filling their bellies. "How are Lady Stratford and Celeste?"

"Resting. Both relatively unharmed, just a bit shaken."

That seemed a huge understatement, especially in Lady Stratford's case. It wasn't every day that your husband framed you for murder and then tried to kill you. But I didn't argue the point.

"And the guard?" I asked more hesitantly, remembering the odd positioning of his body in the doorway to the storage room.

Alana's eyes dropped. "Dead."

My chest tightened in sorrow. "Did he have any family?"

"A mother and sister in the village. Philip has offered to pay for the funeral and provide the mother with a pension. He also promised the sister a position here at the castle when she's old enough."

"That's kind of him."

Alana shrugged. "It was the least he could do."

I nodded and sipped my water.

We sat silently for a moment, both contemplating the deceased footman and his family, I presumed. He was heavy in my thoughts, as was the realization that I had stabbed Lord Stratford. I knew that in the end it was the bullet that killed him, but it still troubled me to know I had harmed another human being, no matter how necessary it had been or how much he had deserved it. I flexed my fingers. How strange it had been to feel the blade sink into human flesh after watching Sir Anthony do it so many times. No matter what I had claimed only four short days ago, the experience had not been even remotely the same, and I had not been prepared for it.

Misunderstanding the alarm and uncertainty tightening my features, Alana leaned closer to squeeze my hand. "Oh, dearest, it's over," she assured me. Her brilliant blue eyes softened with affection. "Stratford is dead, and we're all safe. Because of you." She smiled, and I tried to grin back, but I knew the effort had not been very successful.

"Are you hungry?" she asked, rising to her feet to pull the cord to summon Lucy. "I'm sure they must have some soup left over from luncheon, and there is always some sort of cold meat and cheese lying around."

"Luncheon?" I gasped, turning to stare at the sunlight pouring in through the window. For the first time since waking, I noted the slant of the sunbeams across the floor.

"Why yes, dearest. It's already late afternoon. Your body was exhausted from last night's ordeal."

And the numerous sleepless nights before that, I suspected.

There was a knock at the door and Alana called for my visitor to come in.

"Is she awake?" Philip murmured, poking his head around the door frame. His face broke into a brilliant smile when he saw me looking back at him. "Well, good afternoon. It's nice to see you've returned to the land of the living."

I grinned broadly at him, relieved to see him looking so well.

"Now don't start making her feel guilty," Alana scolded, planting her hands on her hips. "She's already shocked she slept so long. She needed the rest."

"I'm sorry." He raised a hand in defense. "I didn't mean to imply such a thing. I'm just glad to see she's awake." He smiled gently down at me. "How do you feel?"

I shifted so that I could see him better. "Sore, but otherwise fine." I knew he was only asking about my state physically.

"Do you feel up to speaking with Sir Graham?"

"No, she does not," Alana snapped before I could open my mouth. "She was kidnapped, shot, and nearly drowned, for heaven's sake. She needs her rest, not to rehash last night's events."

I appreciated my sister's protectiveness, but I did not want to be shielded. I wanted it to be over. I wanted this entire terrifying experience to be finished. And I knew the only thing I could do to hasten its end was to answer Sir Graham's questions. A part of me, borne from the injustices of my life with Sir Anthony, still feared the procurator fiscal might believe I orchestrated the whole thing, that he would arrest me for murder. No matter how I tried to stifle it, I couldn't shake that fear. It would remain overshadowing my every thought and action until this investigation ended and Sir Graham returned to Inverness.

"Yes," I said over Alana's voice. She glanced back at me in shock. "Yes, Philip, I'll speak with him."

"Kiera," my sister protested, alarm tightening her voice.

"I need to do this," I told her firmly. "*Now*, and not later, after I've stirred myself up with anxiety." I softened my voice, pleading with her to understand. "I need this to be over."

"All right," she agreed begrudgingly. "But you'll conduct the interview here, in your bedchamber, and I'll hear no complaints about it. We can have the chaise longue moved from my parlor for you to recline on so that you don't have to remain in bed."

I hid a smile at her continued effort to control the situation.

"But if he puts too much strain on her, I'm holding you accountable," she threatened her husband, stabbing a finger in his direction.

Philip nodded and looked to me. "I'll be with you the entire time," he promised me, his eyes shining with sincerity and devotion.

"And me as well," Alana added.

A lump formed in my throat, and I had to blink several times to hold back the wetness stinging my eyes. "Thank you," I told them.

Philip nodded.

"Give us an hour," Alana told him.

CHAPTER TWENTY-NINE

As promised, exactly one hour later I found myself reclining on Alana's oatmeal silk chaise longue, primped and presented like a Christmas goose.

Lucy and Alana had fluttered and fussed over my appearance for nearly the entire hour, giving me little time even to ingest a bowl of cock-a-leekie soup. My hair was to be styled neatly but effortlessly, my complexion glowing but not flushed with health, my clothes flattering but not overtly so. When I asked my sister why on earth they had gone to so much trouble just to wrap me in an emerald-green silk dressing gown and pull a quilt over my legs, she only shook her head and muttered something about our mother rolling over in her grave.

After that, I suspected it had something to do with the finer feminine arts I had never bothered to master, since they all seemed to take such a ridiculous amount of effort only to receive indefinite results. Case in point, it would have taken me five minutes to pull half my hair back from my face and don my current attire, even with the gunshot wound in my side. Granted, I might be slightly more winded and perspiring from the exertion. My hair might not have lain so perfectly smooth, my gown so creaseless. But nevertheless, my appearance did not require such detailed planning.

The only benefit I could see to such fussing and primping was that I had been allowed little time to fret over the pending interview with Sir Graham Fraser. So much so that when Alana opened the door to his knock, I was so annoyed with her that I had to remind myself that I was supposed to be worrying. And perhaps that had been Alana's intention all along.

I smothered the irritation still trickling through my veins and pasted on a bland smile to receive the procurator fiscal.

"Lady Darby," Sir Graham proclaimed as he bowed over my hand in greeting. "Allow me to say how glad I am to hear you will recover from your wounds."

The man's eyes twinkled with kindness beneath two bushy white eyebrows. They looked like two scraggly tufts of cotton blossom stuck to his face. His tall forehead was etched deeply with wrinkles, as were the corners of his eyes and the sides of his mouth, making me believe he smiled brightly and often.

"Thank you," I replied, genuinely charmed by the older man. I offered him a small smile. "I'm glad as well."

He chuckled. "Yes. Yes. I'm certain you are. Well then . . ." he looked up to include everyone in the room ". . . let's get this over with as quickly and painlessly as possible, shall we?" His voice was good-natured but brisk—a man accustomed to doing things efficiently.

I appreciated his good wishes, but I valued his willingness to hurry matters along even more. I nodded firmly, feeling the first flutter of nerves in my stomach in the past hour.

Alana directed him to one of the navy-blue chairs before the hearth while Philip claimed the chair opposite. Tea was offered and declined, and then Alana was leaning close to me, uselessly fluffing my pillows. "What about you, dear? Would you like some tea?"

I could tell from my sister's raised eyebrows that she was

asking me far more than whether I was thirsty. "No, thank you," I replied, addressing her concern. "I'm fine."

She searched my eyes anxiously for a moment, as if to ascertain I was telling her the truth, and then nodded. Stepping back, she pulled a ladder-back chair closer to my chaise to sit by my side, hovering over me like a sentry.

Sir Graham, who had waited patiently through our exchange, now folded his hands over his stomach. "Lady Darby, if you're ready to begin?" I dipped my head for him to continue. "I've already spoken with Lady Stratford and her maid, Lord Cromarty," he nodded to Philip, "and Mr. Gage. Which leaves . . ."

"Did someone mention my name?"

My chest tightened at the sound of Gage's voice. I had not seen him since they pulled me from the water, since our kiss, and I had to stop myself from turning toward him where he stood in the doorway over my shoulder. Such a movement would wrench the wound in my side. And make me look far more eager to see him than I wanted to admit, even to myself.

"Am I late?" he asked with what sounded like forced joviality. His confident footsteps crossed the room. "I thought you said half past five, Cromarty?"

"I did. But you don't have to be here, Gage."

I looked up, catching Gage's eyes as he came abreast of Alana's chair. A charming smile was pasted across his mouth, but I could see the lines of worry crisscrossing his forehead.

"I know," he replied. "But I thought perhaps I should be. I'm eager to hear how Lady Darby uncovered the information we missed."

I wanted to take offense at his declaration of interest, particularly since the man had displayed no such curiosity two days prior, when I expressed my concerns regarding Lady Stratford's guilt. But I couldn't maintain my indignation, not when I could so easily read the concern reflected in his eyes. Concern that I suspected was for me.

"Yes, well, it's up to Kiera whether she wants you to stay or not," Alana interjected brusquely, still playing the part of overprotective sister. She turned to me expectantly, awaiting my decision.

I looked to Gage again, noting the tightness around his eyes. He was genuinely worried I would send him away, and for some reason, such a possibility pained him. I felt the tenuous strands of my lingering anger begin to loosen inside me. It seemed small and petty to maintain my irritation when the man had saved my life. He had dived into the freezing waters of the loch, with no small risk to his own safety, and cradled me in his arms as he pulled me to the surface. No matter the fault of his actions beforehand, he had been there when I needed him most, and I would be eternally grateful.

"Kiera?" Alana pressed, interrupting my thoughts. She frowned at me in confusion, making me wonder how long I had been staring at Gage.

Fighting a blush climbing its way up my neck, I cleared my throat. "Of course, he can stay."

The tightness around Gage's eyes eased and the brittleness of his smile softened to something more genuine. I turned away, unsettled by my reaction to him. In the past, my annoyance had always kept any softer feelings I might be contemplating for the man buried, but without that aggravation, that drive to prove him wrong, I suddenly had no armor to block the other confusing emotions. They floated to the surface, pulling and twisting my insides with unfamiliar sensations. They were at once invigorating and frightening, and I was as yet unprepared to deal with them.

I plucked at the stitching on my quilt, watching out of the corner of my eye as Gage moved to stand next to the fireplace. He propped his elbow on the edge of the mantel and leaned his hip into the stone. The man seemed incapable of standing up straight if there was a wall or mantel or doorway to lean on.

Sir Graham cleared his throat, recalling us all to the purpose of this gathering. "As I was saying." He glanced quickly around the room, as if to verify there were to be no more interruptions. "I've already questioned most of the witnesses and, as you already know, I was present for most of the events that transpired last night on the loch. Lord Cromarty and Mr. Gage have already filled me in on the rather . . . unorthodox . . . level of your assistance with the investigation."

My throat tightened at the censure in his voice, even though most of it seemed to be leveled at Philip and Gage.

"But that is not the issue at hand." He turned to study me with a calm demeanor. "What I need from you, Lady Darby, is for you to . . . fill in a few holes, if you will. There are a few matters the gentlemen and I have been unable to piece together ourselves."

I traced an embroidered flower on the quilt over my lap, trying to hide my internal agitation. They must be rather curious how I'd figured out Lord Stratford was the murderer before he admitted as much after kidnapping us from the carriage house.

"Lady Stratford told us that her husband's original plan was to murder her so that he could remarry, and when Lady Godwin found out about it and confronted him, he killed her to keep her quiet."

"That is true," I replied calmly. "He admitted as much in the boat last night."

"But you already knew Lord Stratford was Lady Godwin's murderer, even before he told you so?"

My nerves took to wing inside my stomach. "I suspected it."

"May I ask how, Lady Darby?" Sir Graham asked, gently prodding me. "Was it just a simple hunch? All Lady Stratford could tell us was that you had inquired about a recent trip her husband made to Shropshire to view some property."

"Yes. Except it's not the kind of property you are all thinking of." They glanced at each other quizzically as I turned toward my sister. "I need you to get something for me."

She sat forward in surprise. "Of course."

"It's in the bottom drawer of my desk. The jewelry box." She stood and moved toward the escritoire while I explained to the others. "When I went walking yesterday morning, I found a man's handkerchief stained with blood stuffed inside the hole of a tree. Well, actually, Beowulf and Grendel found it," I amended, "I just retrieved it."

"My wolfhounds," Philip explained to Sir Graham.

"I assume it was near the spot where you found blood several days ago and speculated that the murderer had laid the child there and come back to bury it later."

Philip's eyes looked troubled. "You found this handkerchief *before* you returned to the stable with the dogs?"

I flushed and nodded.

"And you didn't tell me about it," his voice was flat.

"I was waiting for Mr. Gage. You'll remember I asked after him."

He nodded dully, hurt by my apparent unwillingness to confide in him.

"There was nothing we could do about it until he returned," I hastened to add. "And I . . . I didn't want to worry you any more than you already were." My gaze flicked to Alana, who was now standing next to me holding the small wooden box.

Her brow furrowed, clearly realizing I had been referring to his worry over her and her barricading herself in the children's nursery. She held the box out to me. "Is this it?"

"Yes." My gut churned at the hurt gleaming in both Philip's and Alana's eyes. I wanted to explain further, but what could I say? Neither of them had been in a state to help me, and that had not been my fault. "I just . . ." I began to explain before cutting myself off. I shook my head. Now was not the time to discuss family dramatics. "I need the key. It's tucked inside the backing on the frame above the desk, there." Alana moved away solemnly, and I tried to forget the pained expression I had seen on her face.

I turned back to address the men. "At the time, I couldn't be certain it was a man's handkerchief, but unadorned as it was, I knew it wasn't a lady's. Which only increased my suspicion that Lady Stratford was not the murderer. So I decided to search Lady Godwin's chambers. Thank you," I told my sister, taking the key from her hands.

"But I searched her chamber four days ago," Gage said.

"Yes, I know. And had I searched it then, I also would have missed what I'm about to show you." I carefully extracted the handkerchief from the box and handed it to Philip, who rose to transfer it to Sir Graham. "These are two letters I found on Lady Godwin's escritoire," I said, passing them to Philip as well. "The first is not addressed or signed, but it is clear, once you read the contents, that the intended recipient was Lord Stratford. Notice she mentions how they were lovers with a great deal between them. Then she tells him she knows what he is about to do and that he won't get away with it. 'My family is not for sale,'" I quoted.

Gage moved around to read over Sir Graham's shoulder. "I never saw this letter," he replied almost defensively.

"It had fallen to the floor and slid under the writing desk. Perhaps you missed it. In any case, the information it contained was useless until we uncovered Lord Stratford had been her lover and was the father of her child. And without the next letter, there would have been no connection." Sir Graham flipped to the next page. "This note is from Lady Godwin's younger sister, a Miss Carina Herbert, who resides in Diddlebury, Shropshire."

Gage looked up at me, his eyes bright as he quickly realized the implication.

I nodded at him in confirmation. "Miss Carina tells her sister of a Lord S who arrived to pay her court, promising to return as soon as he could to ask her a most important question." I thought of the young lady who had obviously fallen head over heels for the fiend's charms and was about to be given a very harsh and cruel awakening. "I'm sure you can guess that her Lord S is actually Lord Stratford," I said solemnly.

Sir Graham stared at the letter for some time, as if having difficulty digesting the cunning and malice of Lord Stratford's actions. "The man was courting his wife's replacement while plotting to kill her. Despicable," he spat, shaking his head.

"Yes, the man has proven several times over how black his heart was," Philip pronounced in anger as he settled back into his chair.

"You might also remember Alana told us that, on the day she was murdered, Lady Godwin asked her to have a footman meet the mail coach in Drumchork to post a letter to her sister, this Miss Herbert," I told them. "I can only guess that Lady Godwin was so urgent to have the letter posted because she wished to warn her sister."

Alana shook her head. "Poor girl. But why Miss Herbert? Wouldn't Lord Stratford have been wiser to choose someone that none of his acquaintances knew?"

"Yes, but Lady Godwin had already borne two boys to her husband," I pointed out. "And, more important, Lord Stratford himself had been able to impregnate her. I assume that Stratford believed her sister would easily do the same."

"So his only motive for killing his wife was because she had not borne him an heir?" Sir Graham's voice rang with disgusted incredulity.

"I'm afraid so."

"Well, who is the earl's current heir?" he huffed. "A brother? A cousin? Was there some animosity between them?"

"A distant cousin," Philip answered. "A Frenchman, I believe."

I nodded, thinking back on Stratford's angry words the night before. "He seemed to harbor a deep hatred of the French, something he developed during his service in the war."

"The man served under Wellington," Gage confirmed, having returned to his position next to the hearth. He rubbed his chin in thought. "He suffered several gunshot wounds, if I recall."

"One in his shoulder and one that grazed his scalp," I confirmed.

Philip's fingers drummed the arm of his chair in agitation. "What *I* would like to know is whether Stratford deliberately set about blaming his wife." His gaze flicked to his own wife. "I mean, how did Lady Stratford's scissors and shawl end up covered in blood? Did he just happen to have them in his pocket when he went to meet Lady Godwin that night?"

I wrapped my arms around my swirling stomach and stared at my knees. "Make no mistake, Philip. Every move Lord Stratford made from the moment he murdered Lady Godwin—with the knife he carried in his boot, incidentally, not the embroidery shears—was deliberately intended to direct the blame toward his wife." Or me, I added silently. "He smeared the scissors with blood and placed them in the maze. Then he swiped the very shawl his wife had been wearing at dinner that night from her room and wrapped the child in it." My voice hardened with anger. "Even his decision to remove the baby was influenced at least partly by his desire to point the finger at Lady Stratford."

"All of our evidence wasn't actually evidence at all. Even the apron," Gage explained. His voice was clipped, his eyes hard. "He manipulated us from the very beginning."

"Wait." Philip leaned forward in his chair. "Wasn't he one of the first people to appear after Lady Lydia screamed?"

I nodded and sighed. "And if I'd thought deeper about it at the time, I might have realized how odd his appearance was." The others stared at me in confusion. I reached up to fiddle with the lapels of my dressing gown. "The buttons of his frock coat were all off by one, as if they'd been buttoned up very quickly." I shook my head. "I noted it, but I was so distressed that I didn't understand the significance."

"Well, don't scold yourself, Kiera." Philip grimaced. "Stratford helped Gage and me move the body to the cellar, and we never noticed anything suspicious." His brow furrowed. "The man must have had ice in his veins to be able to do such a thing and not give himself away."

"Likely learned from his time fighting France," Sir Graham said grimly. "If he served for any length of time on the peninsula, he would have had to train himself to block off his emotions just to be able to survive." He sighed and shook his head, as if dismissing some troubling memory of his own. I wondered if he had spent time fighting abroad as well. "Though killing an enemy on the battlefield is a far cry from killing one's own mistress and child." He shook his head in disgust. "Did Stratford make up an alibi?"

I thought back, trying to remember whether we had ever questioned him about it.

Gage gave a short bark of laughter. "He thought he had." We all turned toward him curiously. "Unfortunately, he was foolish enough to assume Lord Marsdale would cover for him."

"What do you mean?" I asked.

His eyes crinkled with humor. "Remember when we asked Marsdale where he was during the time of Lady Godwin's murder? He told us he and Lord Stratford retired to the men's parlor for a smoke immediately after dinner."

"Oh, yes," I gasped in remembrance. "He told us Lord Stratford left soon after, leaving him with no one to corroborate his alibi until Lord Lewis Effingham arrived to tell him about the murder."

Sir Graham appeared baffled. "Why would Lord Marsdale do such a thing?"

"Marsdale is the Duke of Norwich's heir," Gage muttered wryly, as if that explained it.

And apparently Marsdale's reputation preceded him, for Sir Graham heaved a sigh in understanding and shook his head. "Well, in this instance, at least, it seems the marquess's devilry has done more good than harm, foiling Lord Stratford's hoped-for alibi." A spark of amusement lit his eyes. "Perhaps I should inform the duke just how helpful his son has been to this investigation."

Philip's mouth twitched. "Yes, I'm sure his grace would be happy to hear that his wastrel heir is finally taking on some responsibility. It might tempt him to give his son more."

Gage laughed. "Marsdale would be so grateful to us."

I shook my head at the men's jesting, but I couldn't stop the smile that curled my own lips. Poor Marsdale. He had merely been attempting to further blacken his reputation, and here he'd gone and done something worthwhile by being so honest. I doubted he would find the realization so humorous.

"There's one thing I just don't understand," Alana huffed in vexation. Her brow was furrowed in serious contemplation. "If Lord Stratford went to all that trouble to blame his wife, then why did he change his mind and decide to murder her? Wasn't he taking a big risk?"

The men's good humor swiftly died, leaving a heavy silence in the room.

"Well," I replied hesitantly, looking away from Alana's earnest face. "I think partly it was because he had begun to worry that he might have missed something—that something or someone could unwittingly connect him to the crime. After all, Celeste had seen him in his wife's chamber the night of the murder, presumably to check in on her. What if Celeste or Lady Stratford remembered something suspicious enough to shift the inquiry his way?" I didn't mention that the earl had also been worried I knew too much, deciding Gage and my sister did not need to be privy to that information—not if it would only worry them and earn me a scolding.

"But, mostly," I continued, "I think it was because he needed his wife to actually be dead before he could remarry."

Alana's hand lifted to cover her mouth.

"He started to realize how lengthy the trial process could be, and that there was no guarantee his wife would be found guilty of the crime or executed for it. A guilty verdict was likely, yes, but not certain. And here in Scotland, the jury could always find the case simply 'not proven,' rather than guilty or not guilty." I glanced at Sir Graham for confirmation, and he nodded. "As for hanging her, well, I'm certain you all realize that the upper classes are not particularly fond of killing their own, particularly when the accused is titled and a female. After all, it sets a dangerous precedent." Justice was often skewed when it came to social class, and the upper echelons preferred for it to stay that way. "Lord Stratford knew that while his wife still drew breath he could not take another bride, and he understood that if he waited for a trial, too many things could go wrong."

Alana's voice was sickened. "So he thought to guarantee her death himself by making it appear as if she'd escaped and then drowned in the loch?"

"Yes."

Her face screwed up in puzzlement. "But what if her body was never found? Wouldn't dumping her in the loch potentially cause him an even bigger problem?"

I shook my head. "He always intended for Lady Stratford's body to conveniently wash ashore. He hoped to make it look like Celeste had killed her and then escaped. He even admitted that he planned to abduct them the night before, but there were too many potential witnesses hanging about when Freya dropped her foal."

"So he was forced to wait until last night," Alana concluded. "And you got in his way."

"Well, yes." I hesitated to elaborate, not wanting to upset my sister further by expounding on Stratford's altered plans.

"Stratford thought to make it look like you kidnapped Lady Stratford and Celeste, didn't he?" Gage crossed his arms over his chest and glared at me, forcing the point.

Alana gasped in outrage.

I scowled at him.

"He was going to make it look like you murdered Lady Stratford and Celeste and then disappeared," he continued doggedly, his voice tight with anger. "He was going to leave us all wondering who the real criminal was."

I felt no need to confirm what he said. I was still too twisted up inside by how very close Lord Stratford had come to making that happen.

Alana pounded her fist on the back of the settee behind my head. "Why, the cad! How dare he!"

"Calm yourself, Alana." Philip murmured. "We've already seen what a manipulative monster the man could be. I suppose we shouldn't be surprised he thought to use Kiera's undeserved reputation against her."

My sister huffed. "Yes, well, the man still deserves to be stuck between the ribs for such vile behavior."

I flinched, wondering if Alana realized Stratford had already been stabbed, and by none other than her baby sister.

Philip glanced at me in concern. "That seems a bit pointless now, Alana, seeing as how the man is already dead."

"Are we certain?" she persisted, glancing from one man to another. "Could he have swum to shore?"

The men all exchanged glances with each other and then me.

"He's dead," Philip told her certainly. "Definitely dead."

Alana opened her mouth as if to protest, but then seemed

to think better of it. She released a heavy breath and nodded her head, staring down at her lap.

Philip rose from his chair and came around to kneel before her. He gripped her hands and leaned forward to peer up into her eyes. They were bright with fear and uncertainty. A lump formed in my throat at the evidence of her distress.

"He truly is dead," he assured her in a soft voice. "We can all vouch for that. Lord Stratford will never be able to hurt anyone again—not Kiera, not the children, not anyone."

She sniffed and nodded, her face contorted by the effort to hold back her tears. Philip gathered her close and turned her face into his shoulder to shield her from our view.

I turned away, feeling like an intruder on this intimate moment. I was, however, relieved to see them getting along again. I'd grown tired of watching them bicker and fight over the past few days.

Sir Graham stared patiently down at his lap, allowing them their privacy. I wondered if he was accustomed to seeing such displays of emotion. In his line of work, it seemed very likely.

Gage had probably witnessed his fair share of tears as well. I glanced up to find him watching me, a strange look in his eyes. It made the blood pump hard through my veins. I didn't understand it, and by the tightness around his eyes, I wasn't certain he did, either. But I knew it signaled that something had changed between us—something that we couldn't reverse. And I wasn't sure how to feel about that.

Gage had come to mean a great deal more to me than I could have ever expected. I cared for him—I couldn't deny that, or the fact that I'd initially misjudged him—but I wasn't easy with the feelings developing between us. Not after his dismissal of my concerns over Lady Stratford's guilt. My anger and frustration at what I viewed as his abandonment might have faded, but the pain and disillusionment had not. I could tell that Gage regretted his actions toward me, though whether that was because of the consequences or a twinge in his own conscience, I could not tell. Either way, I couldn't be certain he wouldn't react the same way again, and I didn't think I could be with a man who doubted me. I might trust Gage with my life, but I did not trust him with my happiness or my heart.

CHAPTER THIRTY

The carriage yard and lower levels of the castle were a madhouse the following morning as the guests jockeyed for position, trying to persuade the Cromarty servants to move their carriages to the front of the line to be loaded next. It seemed everyone was eager to escape Gairloch after the long confinement in the wake of Lady Godwin's murder, and I could only say that the residents of Gairloch were just as happy to see them go. Some more than others.

Though Alana insisted I stay in bed, I simply had too much restless energy. The flesh wound in my side still pained me, and I could not move quickly, but as long as I left off my corset and moved with care, I did not see why I should be confined to my room. My sister scolded when I joined her and Philip for breakfast in the family salon, avoiding the pandemonium downstairs, but I ignored her. When Alana was in the family way, her emotions always swung in great arcs, and I knew that soon enough they would have to take an upward turn.

I largely stayed away from the main areas of the castle, wanting to avoid contact with the guests who gathered in the great hall and front drawing room as they waited to board their carriages for their long journeys home. In the interest of my sanity, and the preservation of even tempers, it seemed best to confine myself to the family wing and the nursery. But late in the morning, when Philipa began to complain of a stomachache, I made the mistake of volunteering to search out Alana. I found her easily enough and coaxed her out into the great hall to explain about her daughter's fussing. She immediately turned her steps toward the stairs, with me trailing alongside her, and we had all but exited through the doorway on the far side of the room, when Lady Westlock's strident voice echoed off the stone walls of the chamber.

Later, I would realize how fitting it was that the confrontation happened in the great hall of the old keep, where weapons and armor decorated the walls from floor to ceiling. The ancestors of the Earls of Cromarty had been warriors and then the lairds of the Matheson clan long before the crown bestowed a title upon them, and they took great pride in displaying these reminders of their former occupation. More than once, I had caught Philip staring up at the emblem on a shield or the battered pommel of a sword in grinning revelry, and his son, Malcolm, showed every sign of following him in this absurd masculine regard for the trophies of war.

"You know, I simply don't believe it," Lady Westlock hissed. I glanced over my shoulder to see that she stood beneath a flanged mace, gossiping with Mrs. Smythe. Her eyes locked with mine, lit with vicious glee. "They say Lady Darby is the one who discovered that Lord Stratford murdered Lady Godwin, but I think her family bribed Mr. Gage into saying so."

I stiffened, both shocked by her derisive words and surprised to hear that Gage had informed the others of my involvement. Part of me was pleased to be acknowledged in such a manner, but another part of me was anxious about how society would react, and what new tales they would invent about me.

"They actually think we'll be foolish enough to fall for

such a blatant ploy to repair her character," Lady Westlock sneered, echoing my fears.

Alana halted in her tracks beside me. Her gaze swung toward Lady Westlock and narrowed with a fury that raised the hairs along my arms. Sensing the impending altercation, I reached out to try to urge her along. But, foolishly, Lady Westlock would not be denied her chance to deride me.

"If she assisted with the investigation, it was only because she wanted an opportunity to view Lady Godwin's corpse," she declared, raising her voice even louder to be heard across the hall. She seemed completely oblivious to her hostess's towering rage, even though Mrs. Smythe was shaking her head at her in warning. Several ladies and gentlemen on the other side of the room had even turned to stare at her, but Lady Westlock would not be deterred. I decided right then and there that the woman was not only cruel but stupid. "She's sick, I tell you. Sick."

"Lady Westlock," Alana snapped, marching across the hall in long strides.

Still oblivious to her peril, the baroness smirked.

"Are your bags being packed?"

Lady Westlock seemed startled by the question. "Why, yes. Yes, they are. My husband and I are eager to be away."

"I'm glad to hear it," Alana announced in clipped tones, her eyes narrowed as if on an insect. "Because you have exactly a quarter of an hour to get off my husband's property or I will have you thrown out."

Lady Westlock's mouth dropped open comically, her chin bobbing as she attempted to form a response. Mrs. Smythe gasped while the others gathered across the hall began to whisper to one another excitedly. I pressed my fingers to my lips, having difficulty suppressing my amusement at seeing Lady Westlock in such a state. My sister ignored all but the baroness, keeping her dark gaze fixed upon her.

"Well . . . well, I never," Lady Westlock spluttered. "How dare you! I will *not* be treated in such a manner."

"You are a guest in *my* home, Lady Westlock," Alana retorted firmly. "A guest who has belittled and berated members of my family, and circulated nasty rumors about them. I am completely in my rights to throw you out." She had steadily shifted forward until she was biting off each word inches from the baroness's face. "Especially in light of the fact that your husband attacked my sister."

Lady Westlock's face flushed as bright as a beet. "He didn't attack her. He thought she was the murderer."

"And bashed her over the head."

The whispers across the hall grew feverish with speculation.

"Figgins," Alana called to her butler without taking her eyes from Lady Westlock. "Note the time. I want you to make certain Lord and Lady Westlock have departed Gairloch in exactly fifteen minutes. If they fail to make that deadline, I give you permission to expel them by force."

Lady Westlock's jowls quivered with indignation.

"As you wish, my lady," Figgins replied without even batting an eyelash at the absurd command.

"You'll regret this," Lady Westlock threatened.

Alana answered swiftly and decidedly. "No, I won't. I would have tossed you out four days ago had we known for certain that neither you nor your husband was the murderer."

Lady Westlock gasped.

"Be glad I didn't set you upon the road in the middle of the night." With a swish of her lavender skirts, my sister turned to stride off.

I remained behind a moment to gloat, wanting the countess to know that although I allowed my sister to defend me, I did not hide behind her skirts. Lady Westlock's jaw was locked in anger.

"Have a safe journey." I glanced at the long clock. "Best

hurry. You only have fourteen minutes." Then with a twirl of my own skirts, I followed my sister through the door.

Had Lady Westlock been able to pull the mace down from the wall, I was quite certain she would have followed her husband's example and bashed me over the head as well.

Much to my sister's disappointment, the Westlocks departed before their quarter hour passed. And though their luggage and servants straggled behind a half an hour later, Alana decided it would not be fair to penalize them for their employers' rudeness. She believed it likely the maids and footmen were punished enough in working for the baron and his harridan of a wife.

The Smythes, as well as the other guests, swiftly followed, one by one, until the great hall and drawing room were blessedly empty. I was surprised when many of them went out of their way to speak with me before they departed, thanking me for my part in the investigation and inquiring after my health. I understood that most of them were only trying to maintain appearances, or prevent themselves from being thrown out on their ear like the Westlocks, but I could tell that some of them were genuinely trying to make amends for their earlier suspicions of me, even if they never actually uttered an apology. I knew better than to expect one. The nobility was notoriously poor at admitting they were wrong. I only hoped my example would encourage them to be more skeptical of gossip, even as I was aware that these very same people would be racing southward to spread the tale about what had happened here. They would be dining out for weeks on such juicy morsels of information.

By noon, the only two guests remaining at Gairloch were Mr. Gage and Lady Stratford, who had not left her chamber since retiring to it after the ordeal on the boat. I knew Alana was looking after the countess and her maid, so I felt no need to bother them. In fact, I suspected Lady Stratford might rather I stayed away. So when *she* sought *me* out just before luncheon, I was shocked, to say the least.

I had settled onto a settee in the sunny family parlor with my sketchbook when the swish of skirts across the floor alerted me to someone's presence. I glanced up with a smile, expecting to see Alana, only to find Lady Stratford hovering in the doorway. She wore a lovely black crepe traveling costume trimmed in braid. I recognized the gown. It had been borrowed from my sister, though it had clearly been altered, and rather swiftly, to fit the petite countess.

I set down my book, waiting for her to advance into the room. She seemed nervous, her hands wringing the kid leather of the gloves encasing them. I pressed my hand against the arm of the settee to help me rise, and that little movement seemed to jostle her out of her stupor, for she met me halfway across the room. Her eyes searched mine frantically, and I realized she was at a loss for words—something I had never expected to witness from the poised Lady Stratford.

Taking pity on her, I offered her my wishes for a safe journey. "Must you leave so soon?"

"Thank you," she replied with trembling breath. "But, yes. I need to go. I . . . I need to get away from here. I think I'll do better at my great-aunt's."

I nodded, understanding her need to escape the place where so many dark and terrible things had happened.

"Faye is coming with me, and . . . Lady Godwin."

I knew Philip had arranged for a wagon to transport Lady Godwin and her child's coffin, as well as her belongings. With the full coterie of Stratford and Godwin servants accompanying her, I was certain Lady Stratford would make it to her great-aunt's home near Glasgow safely, and I told her so.

Her gaze dropped to her hands. "I . . . I wanted to express my gratitude for what you did for me," she added softly, her words stilted with emotion. Her head lifted, and she seemed determined to look me in the eye as she said what came next. "And . . . I wanted to apologize for . . . what my husband . . . did to you . . ."

I reached out to take her hand. "No," I said gently, shaking my head.

Her eyes flared wide with panic. "But . . ."

I squeezed her fingers to stop her. "Your husband's actions are not yours to atone for."

She blinked quickly over her suddenly bright eyes.

"Whatever evil your husband wrought, it was not your doing." Those words twisted inside me, and I smiled sadly. "Believe me, I know."

It had taken me sixteen and a half months after Sir Anthony's death to finally realize that. I didn't want Lady Stratford to take that long to figure it out. We, none of us, should have to live in the shadow of others' misdeeds.

She looked at first as if she might like to argue, but then I could see her come to the realization that, by doing so, she would also be condemning me for my husband's actions. The light in her soft gray eyes shifted, and she seemed to study me with a new understanding. Her head bobbed once in acceptance, and then she pulled her hand from mine to search for a handkerchief in her reticule. She dabbed at her eyes and gave me a watery smile.

"Well." She took a deep breath, regaining her composure. "My carriage awaits."

I nodded.

She looked as if she wished to say more, but instead she merely acknowledged my nod with one of her own and turned to go. I watched her leave, hoping she would be able to make peace with all her husband had done.

At the door, she hesitated and then looked back over her shoulder at me. "When you're in London next, I hope you'll call on me," she declared, sounding more like her old self.

My eyes widened in astonishment, and she smiled. Then

with a swish of her skirts she was gone before I could form a response.

Alana appeared in the doorway only moments later. She glanced after Lady Stratford's retreating form with a satisfied smirk, clearly having heard her closing remark. "Close your mouth, dear," she told me. "It's terribly unbecoming."

CHAPTER THIRTY-ONE

At a quarter of an hour before dawn, the upper corridors were cold and deserted by all but the mice. Not even the chambermaids had yet ventured into the family rooms to stoke up the fires, or at least they hadn't in my chamber, but I didn't normally rise at such an ungodly hour. I shouldn't have had to do so this morning.

Closing my door softly, I wrapped my shawl tighter around my shoulders and set off down the long, shadowed hall. The hush of night rang in my ears, as yet unwilling to give over to the day. Two short days ago, I would have been frightened to travel down this corridor alone at night, fearful of what might lay in wait for me in the darkness. With Lord Stratford's death, the castle's solemn passageways had lost their terror. Their stones seemed to cast off the gloom as they had cast off the guests, and returned to their melancholy sentry of ages. I trailed my fingers over the cold granite, grateful to have my atmospheric sanctuary back.

Turning the corner at the grand staircase, I could see through the windowpanes the pink and yellow streaks of light on the horizon presaging the sun. I blew out my candle and set it on the ledge, worried that the shaking of my hands would be too noticeable if I carried it with me. Turning toward the stairs, I made to descend the first step, but then hesitated with my foot at the edge of the riser.

For a moment, I considered turning back, returning to the warmth and comfort of my bed, and allowing Gage to skulk off into the misty light of daybreak as he wished. It wasn't as if I couldn't use the rest. I had tossed and turned most of the night, sore and uncomfortable because, as Alana predicted, I had overexerted myself the day before. Not that I would admit such a thing to her, even on pain of dismemberment. There were some things I just did not confess to my sister, and acknowledging that she was right in such a dispute was one of them.

Besides, my wound's tenderness had really only been a small part of my unease. More disturbing had been the loss and hurt I felt upon hearing that Gage was leaving in the morning, summoned to Edinburgh by his father on some matter of business. According to the gossip Lucy relayed, he intended to set off at dawn. And as the hours of the evening crept slowly by without a knock at my door, it had become distressingly apparent that Gage intended to set off on his journey without addressing the issues between us, without even saying good-bye.

I had been wrestling with my feelings for Gage since the day Sir Graham interviewed me, uncertain what they meant and whether I welcomed them. There were simply too many unresolved questions between us, too many things left unsaid. And though I was no closer to knowing what, exactly, I wanted to say to him when we did speak, I had always believed that there would be a time when we did, whether or not I was prepared for it. Apparently, Gage was more of the inclination that it was better to leave things left unsaid.

It depressed and bewildered me. It tied my stomach up in knots. And it made the blood boil in my veins.

What right did *he* have to decide for the both of us that we would not speak? *He* was the one who had belittled and dismissed my concerns over Lady Stratford's guilt. I didn't care whether he was embarrassed by that now, or chagrined by his shortsightedness. Whether he'd saved my life or not, he owed me an apology and an explanation, because I did not believe for one second that he was normally so obtuse when it came to his investigations. He was too intelligent, too skilled, to make such an amateur mistake. Maybe it was painful for him to contemplate his error, maybe he regretted it deeply, but for him to skulk off into the dawn without so much as a by-your-leave was cowardly. And of all the faults I could lay at Gage's feet, I had never thought cowardice would be one of them.

But now that I stood poised at the moment of confrontation, I felt my own daring slipping through my clenched fingers. What if I was wrong? What if Gage didn't care one whit for me and his leaving did not pain him in the least? What if it was not cowardice that kept him from coming to me, but indifference?

I was not familiar with the workings of the heart, especially when it came to romantic entanglements. I had no experience with them, and had never thought to, until Gage disrupted my world with his dashing good looks and charming smile. With his arrogant manners and obstinate determination to have his way. With his willingness to believe in my innocence despite the discovery of the bloody apron in my studio and the words of all my naysayers. Until Gage had held me while I cried and rejoiced to see me smile, I had never known any of the tender emotions swirling about my chest, or experienced the hollow ache his leaving left behind. I wasn't certain I could handle it if I saw only apathy in his eyes as he quit Gairloch, and me.

Breathing past the sharp pain in my chest, I forced my foot over the rasping carpet runner and down onto the first step. There was only one way I was going to find the answers to my questions, and that was by confronting Gage. I just didn't understand why this impending confrontation seemed to cause me so much more dread than the interrogations I had faced with the suspects during our murder investigation.

The stairs creaked under my weight and the banister felt icy cold under the tight grip of my fingers. I shivered as I neared the great hall, the cold morning air tickling over my skin and creeping under my skirts as it spilled through the corridors. When I crossed the threshold to the entry hall, I could see Gage standing before the outer door, deep in conference with Philip. The sight of Gage's golden hair limned by the predawn light made the breath catch in my chest and my pulse pound hard. I had not forgotten he was attractive, but somehow the knowledge that I might never see him again made his face seem all the more beautiful.

I knew I was being fanciful. I would see him again. Likely across a crowded ballroom, as he danced and flirted with other women more suited to his standing, scarcely noting my existence. After all, he was a charming, lovable rakehell with a budding career, whose attendance was sought after at all the most exclusive events, and I was a quiet, eccentric artist on the fringe of society, often feared and berated, and barely tolerated. We were two completely different people living two completely separate lives. That our paths had ever crossed in such a meaningful way at all was the true mystery.

Arms crossed over his chest, Gage shifted to allow a servant to pass carrying one of his belongings out to the waiting carriage. His gaze lifted to me and he stiffened. Such a reaction in no way comforted me, though it did a great deal to convince me that he was far from indifferent. Whether his apparent concern meant something good or bad, I could not tell.

I hovered back as Philip finished whatever he was saying to Gage and then shook his hand. Philip paused to lay a hand on my shoulder as he passed by, offering me a cryptic smile. I couldn't tell whether he was trying to encourage me or offer his sympathy. I gritted my teeth against the surge of embarrassment that it might be the latter. Then, before I could say anything, he slipped away, leaving me alone with Gage.

His posture stiff and unwelcoming, Gage stared out at the mist-shrouded courtyard, watching as his carriage was readied for his departure. If not for the sudden tightening of his coat across his shoulders, I would have believed he was ignoring me, but I knew he was aware of each and every step I took in his direction. Nerves tightened my stomach, and for once I was grateful for his stubborn pride, for I wasn't certain I could have crossed the space between us if he had turned to watch. I was using the anger and hurt I felt at his displeasure in seeing me to spur me onward.

The sound of my skirts whispering over the flagstone floor was broken only by the jangling of the horses' harnesses as the beasts stamped and pawed at the muddy drive outside, clearly as eager to be away as their passenger was. As I neared, I could see that the luggage was loaded, the driver in place, all that was left was for Gage to climb inside and be whisked away, gone from my life, perhaps forever. The realization twisted like a knife in my chest.

My steps faltered and I stumbled to a stop behind him. The chill of the dawn air seemed to seep through my bones, and I wrapped my shawl and my arms tighter around me, suddenly certain that the thin material and the grip of my hands around my upper arms was all that was holding me together. A ragged breath escaped through my lips, and I willed my limbs to move, to take me forward or backward, anything but to stand here and stare at Gage's back knowing I was as much a silly fool for this man as all those women I had berated.

I knew not what expression was on my face, but I feared that everything was written there, every hidden emotion shining in my eyes. And when Gage turned to me, I could not wipe them clean. All I could do was stand there dumbly, staring at the contradiction he posed. His deportment remained aloof, but the regret and uncertainty shimmering in his eyes, and the warmth of his gaze as it trailed over my features, told me he was not as unaffected as he wished me to believe. His entire bearing was tightly restrained, even the rasp of his voice as he spoke, as if he was afraid of what he might do if he did not maintain control over himself.

"I'm leaving for Edinburgh."

"I know."

He shifted uncomfortably. "My father asked me to look into a dispute there."

I swallowed and whispered, "I know."

Silence fell between us, charged with the words neither of us seemed to be able to say. I knew I should admonish him, that I should demand answers, but none of it seemed to matter anymore. Not if he was going to walk away without looking back.

He inhaled sharply and opened his mouth to speak, then closed it tightly with a frown. However, either the silence or my muteness seemed to be too much for him, for he forced the words out. "I'm sorry I doubted you."

I raised my eyebrows, surprised by his words.

"I know it may be difficult to believe, but I did not do so lightly." He scowled, and I could tell the displeasure was directed at himself not me. "I do not normally ignore legitimate concerns."

"Why did you?" I asked, more interested in hearing his reasoning behind dismissing my uncertainties over Lady Stratford's guilt than hearing his apology for doing so.

His lips compressed and he stared down at his polished Hessians. "I assure you, my motivation for doing so was not out of pride or malice."

Now it was my turn to frown. "But you won't tell me what it was?"

His gaze lifted to meet mine, and a shadow seemed to pass over his eyes. "No."

I wanted to argue with him, to flay him with guilt, utilize whatever tactic might force him to talk. But I could tell by his troubled gaze and his locked jaw that nothing would induce him to do so. Whatever his motivation had been, it had clearly been personal, and he was not ready to part with it, no matter the method employed.

"Well, can you at least explain to me what you were doing three days ago?" I snapped. "You rode off with Mr. Fulmer before I had a chance to question him, which I assume was your intention in asking him to accompany you in the first place." His eyes shifted guiltily. "And whatever happened to the footman you were pursuing? Did you find him?"

He nodded. "Holed up in a farmer's barn at the edge of the village with his sweetheart." His brow lowered. "It took nearly the entire day to find the scoundrel."

I arched an eyebrow in irritation. "And?"

"Our errant footman got the lass with child."

I blinked in surprise.

"Apparently, when he heard from the other servants how Lady Godwin's killer took the baby from her body and buried it in the woods, he panicked. Somehow, he decided the killer was after all expectant mothers and might attack his lover and child next."

"Oh, my," I murmured, imagining the footman having to tell Gage all of this while under duress. The poor man had already been terrified, and I couldn't imagine Gage had gone easy on him during questioning. "Is he all right?"

"I should say so," he replied indignantly, clearly reading the bent of my thoughts. "Cromarty is going to let him keep his position, even though the man behaved dishonorably and abandoned his post without warning. Provided, of course, that he marries this girl from the village. Rather a light punishment."

"So you didn't eat dinner at Squire Renshaw's?" I asked, and immediately wished I could recall the words. A flush rose in my cheeks.

"No." He studied me closely. "Is that where you thought I was?"

"Well," I hedged, not wanting him to realize the real

motivation behind my question. "When you took so long to return, I just assumed that you had taken shelter somewhere from the rain. Mr. Renshaw's home seemed the obvious choice."

Gage shifted a step closer to me, a smile lurking at the corners of this mouth. "I see. And Squire Renshaw's daughters had nothing to do with your concern over such a thing?"

I lifted my chin, fighting the fiery blush burning its way up into my cheeks. "Of course not."

His eyes sparkled. "Well, regardless, I will tell you that when we were introduced, I found them to be flighty and without charm."

I tried not to feel pleased by such a pronouncement, but I could not stop the surge of satisfaction warming my chest. "Really? Most of the gentlemen in the region seem to find them quite appealing."

He took another step closer to me, forcing me to look up to continue meeting his gaze. "Then most of the gentlemen in this region must be dunces."

He was close enough now that I could see the silver flecks in his pale blue eyes, and watch as the widening of his pupils swallowed them. I inhaled sharply, trying to clear the swirling in my head, but the spicy scent of his now-familiar cologne only made it worse. My gaze dropped to his lips and I swallowed, wanting him to kiss me, wanting to know if my memory of his warm mouth caressing mine as we floated in the icy water of the loch was really true.

The jangle of a harness broke the silence around us, and I blinked. The coachman called out to the horses, scolding their impatience. I glanced to the open door and then back to Gage, who was still watching me with an expression that was as unreadable as it was intense.

"I have to go."

My chest tightened, and the world around me seemed to darken. "I know."

I wanted to tell him to stay, to beg him not to leave. But I couldn't. Not when I knew he would go anyway. That, no matter what I protested, he would choose to climb aboard that coach and journey to Edinburgh. And I would be left standing there watching the distance grow farther and farther between us. My pride couldn't handle it.

So I swallowed the words, though they stuck in my throat like a prayer left unsaid.

"Well, then," he murmured, and my stomach dipped. "I guess this is good-bye."

"Yes," I whispered.

His eyes searched mine, asking for something I did not understand, for something I could not give. Then he leaned forward to kiss my cheek. The sensation was at once sweet and bitterly painful. I closed my eyes and leaned into the warmth of his body, pressing my cheek against the softness of his freshly shaven face. His hands reached out to grip my upper arms, steadying me, holding me in place so that I could not retreat. We lingered there in that loose embrace for a timeless moment, cheek to cheek, and I breathed in deeply the scent of him, trying to capture the memory of his husky voice, the musky mix of his sweat and cologne, the tickle of his breath in my ear. It swelled my heart until I thought it must burst. His callused fingers pressed into the skin of my arms, and then it was over.

He stepped back and I opened my eyes to find his pale blue ones brilliant with longing. He lifted his hands from my body, leaving a chill in their wake and turned to go. The hollowness in my chest grew with each step he took away from me, until I feared there might be nothing left inside me but this sense of loss. He climbed into his carriage, and the door slammed behind him. The curtains twitched once as the coach made the turn and slowly rolled down the drive, picking up speed as it curved past the loch and around the bend toward the main road.

A shaky breath shivered through me. He was gone.

Blindly, I closed the door and retreated into the depths of the castle.

In that moment, I think I honestly believed whatever had been between us was at an end. That whatever twist of fate that had brought us together had played itself out. And someday I would be able to look back on this and smile, and appreciate it for the turning point it had been in my life, the chance to redeem my reputation and break through the shell of fear I had wrapped myself in. To lay my shadows to rest. But, although nearly all of this would prove true, I was mistaken to think that fate was finished with us yet.

For as it happened, trouble was brewing near Edinburgh, and it would once again bring Gage and me together, far sooner than either of us could have predicted, and with unexpected consequences.

HISTORICAL NOTE

The Anatomist's Wife was crafted using many interesting historical facts and tidbits. I would like to share just a few of the most fascinating.

Prior to the Anatomy Act of 1832, British medical schools had difficulty procuring cadavers for their anatomy classes, because only the bodies of executed criminals could be used for this purpose, which amounted to only about two to three bodies annually per school. This led to the practice of body-snatching, where recently buried bodies were stolen from their graves and sold to medical schools. It was a lucrative trade, and Burke and Hare, two laborers in Edinburgh, sought to take advantage of the practice. Rather than risk being caught while performing the difficult labor of disinterring bodies from the local cemeteries, they began inviting victims to their lodging house, plying them with alcohol, and smothering them to death. They then sold the bodies to the Surgeons' Hall at the Royal College of Surgeons of Edinburgh, namely to well-known anatomist and lecturer Dr. Robert Knox.

Burke and Hare were caught in November of 1828, but not before they murdered sixteen people. The case lacked sufficient evidence, so Hare was convinced to testify against his partner, and escaped prosecution. Burke was hanged on January 28, 1829, and afterward his body was transported to the University of Edinburgh to be publicly dissected. His death mask, skeleton, and several articles made from his tanned skin, including a book cover, are on display at the university's Surgeons' Hall Museum. Dr. Knox escaped prosecution, but public opinion turned sharply against him for his part in providing incentive for the murders.

Body snatchers, or resurrectionists, worked all over Great Britain. When security in cemeteries near the medical schools in London and Edinburgh became too tight, bodies robbed from other parts of Britain, and as far away as Ireland, were transported to the schools for use. After the trial of Burke and Hare, citizens in London and Edinburgh were panicked by the idea that similar enterprising criminals might be at work, murdering hapless citizens and selling their bodies to anatomists and medical schools. Medical schools were forced to pay closer attention to where their bodies were procured, and legislation reform became a necessity.

Prior to 1858, there was no inexpensive, definitive anatomy textbook widely available to medical students. British anatomist Henry Gray and his colleague, surgeon and anatomical artist Henry Vandyke Carter, changed that with their now-famous book, *Anatomy: Descriptive and Surgical*, or as it is more commonly known, *Gray's Anatomy*.

Procurator fiscals are public prosecutors in Scotland, similar to a coroner, who investigate all sudden or suspicious deaths. The position originated as a legal office with financial (fiscal) responsibilities, namely collecting fines. Their duties evolved over time, so that by 1701, when the Criminal Procedure (Scotland) Act was passed, they were prosecutors on the Crown's behalf. Since 1728, there have also been three types of verdicts for criminal trials in Scotland—proven, not proven, and not guilty. The "not proven" verdict has sometimes been referred to as the Scottish verdict or, colloquially in Scotland itself, as the "bastard verdict," a term fashioned by Sir Walter Scott.

Chasteberry, red raspberry leaf, and the garnet gemstone are, indeed, all supposed cures for barrenness, and are still utilized in some holistic and alternative-medicine remedies.

Oil painting was an often dangerous undertaking, and more than one artist over the centuries accidentally poisoned themselves to death. Prior to the late nineteenth century, artists were forced to mix their pigments themselves, often from highly toxic raw ingredients made from assorted plants, gemstones, and minerals, and even the ground-up remains of dead humans. It was absolutely necessary for the mixing process to be done with a mortar and pestle while wearing gloves and with proper ventilation. Artists also had to be careful not to chew on their fingernails or brush handles to avoid unintentionally ingesting the remnants of the pigments. Some poisonous pigments include king's yellow and red orpiment, which contain arsenic, and Naples yellow, which contains lead and antimony.

John Spilsbury, a London engraver and mapmaker, created the first jigsaw puzzle in 1750 by affixing one of his maps to a sheet of hardwood and then cutting around the borders of the countries. This production resulted in an educational tool used to teach British children their geography, and until about 1820, jigsaw puzzles were used almost exclusively for this purpose. However, jigsaw puzzles were not known as such until the late nineteenth or early twentieth century, when the treadle saw, a type of jigsaw, began to be used to cut out the pieces. Until that time, jigsaw puzzles were known ironically, at least for Lady Darby, as dissections. I stumbled across this absurd bit of knowledge after I decided to give my heroine this hobby, and elected not to call the jigsaw puzzle by its early nineteenth century title to avoid confusion.